HOUSEKEEPER

By

Geoffrey Mandragora

Rosswyvern Press

This is a work of fiction. Names, characters, businesses, places, events and incidents are either the products of the author's imagination or historical persons and events used in a fictitious manner. Any resemblance to actual persons, living or dead, or actual events is purely coincidental.

ISBN:
978-0-9970569-2-1

In memory of
Dixie Walker,
Talented Fantasy Artist, Vampire Aficionado, Devoted Mother, Best Friend

Acknowledgments

I would like to thank my editor Megan Mcintosh who challenges me to be a better writer by picking at plot holes until they bleed. Every action scene is crisper due to her unrelenting destruction of passive voice and redundancy. I would also like to thank my beta readers, Erin Robbins-Parker and DeAnn Hopewell.

Once again, they deserve all the credit for the things that work right. I, however, am solely responsible for inaccuracies, mistakes and errors.

Prologue

She watched the man stand like a deer caught in headlights, a baby in a harness carrier strapped to his chest as he studied the display of diapers. The outlet store had a bewildering multitude of choices and he was obviously overwhelmed.

Angela rolled her eyes. It never failed. Any night she could close early and no one would notice, a helplessly lost dad would meander in. Might as well text Jill and Taylor to let tell them know it could be a while. After hitting send, she tucked her thick blonde hair behind her ear as she checked the time again. It was only fifteen minutes before she could leave. She was tempted to ignore him, but he looked like he really needed help.

The man caught sight of her, grinned sheepishly and cradled the infant. He was maybe a *few* years older than her, thin, kinda cute with chiseled features and a cleft chin. He was tall, but not so tall he'd make a petite girl look short, and he had sandy brown hair that would look good in the sunlight. *Okay*, Angela thought, *one quick sale for the cutie dad and close*. She smiled back and approached. "May I help you?"

"I hope so," the man spoke just above a whisper. He placed his hand on the baby's knitted cap. "She's asleep."

The girl nodded with a knowing smile.

"Her mother is in the hospital. She gave me a list of supplies, but she just said diapers. I thought there was just one kind."

The girl looked at her phone and quirked her lips, then smiled again. "I can help you. When my cousin was born, I got a crash course in diapers."

Exactly fifteen minutes later she'd racked up a pretty good sale. The man was wary of taking the wrong thing, so he selected several styles. Hypoallergenic, treated with lotion. And a variety of sizes. The store was technically an outlet but Angela would make healthy commission on this kind of sale. Money was tight since her mother's death, at least until the lawyers released the trust fund her holy-roller grandpa set up, so Angela was happy to humor his caution.

Angela locked the door, cleared the cash register and dropped the night receipts in the floor safe before she got her coat and stepped out of the back door into the crisp air. Not really cold. The day had been overcast but unseasonably warm for late September. At six forty-five it was full dark, the parking lot an archipelago of dim light.

She rounded the corner to find her final customer seated on a bench, gently bouncing the baby making shushing noises.

"She woke up?" she whispered.

The baby wiggled and made a snuffling sound.

The man gave an exasperated nod of his head. "I think I got her back." He nodded to the four huge bags of diapers. "I guess I jostled her trying to carry all that." He stood up and bent to pick up one of the bags.

"Here," the girl said quietly and grabbed the bag. "Let me get these, you take care of her."

"I don't want to be any bother."

"No bother." She picked up the remaining bags. "Lead on."

The man had the sheepish grin back. "Thank you. Is there a manager, or someone I can tell about you going the extra mile?"

"That's all right."

He led her through a few aisles of cars. "You like working at the baby store?" His voice sounded awkward, like he was forcing polite conversation.

"It's okay. Better than some retail." They were still walking. "Where's your car?"

He nodded to a dark van parked further out. Even in the dark it looked expensive.

"Sorry. It's brand new, just got it for the baby. I'm afraid to park it any place crowded."

The girl felt a little apprehensive as they moved further, approaching the back of the vehicle, but as they drew closer, she suppressed a smile. There was a set of stickers on the driver's side, male and female stick figures, a wrapped-up baby, and a dancing puppy. On the other side was a cartoon mouse.

"Let me get that." He dug into a pocket and pulled out a remote. He tapped it, the car lights blinked and the rear hatchback opened automatically.

The interior was fitted with a massive metal dog crate that took up the entire back of the van. A squeaky toy shaped like a bone lay on a blanket. "What kind of dog—"

Pain lanced through her body. The man scooped her up and shoved her into the back and hit her with the electric stun gun again. His hands groped at her until he located her cell phone.

"Stay quiet, Angela, or I will do worse to you." He shoved the bags of boxes into the back and slammed the hatch.

~

The man dropped his self-deprecating manner as he casually looked around. No one in sight, no sign of alarm. He dropped the cell phone and kicked it behind the rear tire to back over it. He opened the driver's side rear door. The broad rear bench did not have a car seat, just a large plastic case with an open lid revealing foam packing.

The baby wiggled.

The man reached under the baby blanket and turned off the hyper-realistic doll. With swift, practiced hands he unfastened it, tucked it into the black case and shut the lid.

Chapter One

"Hey, you! Yeah, you, sweet thing, you need a ride?"

Jenny Taylor, wrapped in a wool pea-coat against the early morning chill, mentally gritted her teeth but set her face with the polite, but distant, smile she adopted to deal with jerks. "I'm fine," she replied to the *brotastic* specimen hanging out of the passenger side door of a skeevy white van. No back windows and copious amounts of rust, it just needed "free candy" spray painted on the side.

"Don't be like that, I'm being a nice guy here," the man retorted as he flipped his unfashionably long hair back. The vehicle slowed to keep pace with her.

Jenny liked living in the Highlands of Louisville, and she liked being able to walk to work so she could avoid the expense of a car, but there was one overriding irritation. She had to walk to the coffee shop around four o'clock in the morning, the same time the bars closed. That sometimes led to this kind of awkward encounter on Saturday mornings.

"Thank you, but I like the morning air." She tried to pitch her voice in just the right tone to avoid offense, but just unfriendly enough for the guy to leave her alone. She much preferred the walk in summer with the sun cracking the sky. In November, it was still pitch black with a slight fog clinging to the ground.

"Hey bitch, our van not good enough for you?" The man's scraggly blond mustache bristled.

"I'm just going to the end of the block," she lied. A half-truth, her destination was about a quarter mile beyond that.

The van suddenly halted, rocking back on its anemic suspension. "So, how about I walk with you? Keep you safe, you know?" The man said as he opened the passenger door.

Jenny ran, her coffee stained cross-trainers carrying her quick. At the end of the street she darted into the broad alley behind the closed Starbucks. She ran past the back door of the ice-cream shop and the shoe repair place. The drugstore at the end used to be twenty-four hour, but it had cut its time last year.

She risked a hurried glance over her shoulder and saw no sign of pursuit. The cold air burned in her chest as she stopped to listen for the van's dodgy motor. Crisp silence filled the air around her. She fought to get her breath under control. There was a time not so long ago a sudden sprint would barely have her breathing hard.

She edged out enough to look all the way down the alley. No one coming, no van.

She rubbed her forehead, frustrated by her over-reaction. The guy was a jerk, but likely harmless. But instead of keeping her cool, she panicked and fled, pumping her body with so much adrenalin that she shook.

Normally during the winter walk she would stay on the main street, away from the dark alleys and byways where the homeless lurked. When she felt comfortable she would pass through, occasionally handing out a few dollars, but not in the all-consuming dark. Today it was the street that seemed dangerous and she continued skulking through the backways.

The building was old, separated from its neighbor by a walkway just over a yard wide. She maneuvered from the back alley down the narrow passage to the side staff entrance of the Highland Grindhouse coffee shop. She pulled the key ring from her pocket and sorted through the keys in the dark, looking for the silver skinny one that undid the first deadbolt. She fit the key into the lock and turned it open. The second lock needed the fat brass key and she fumbled for it.

She heard running feet and turned toward the sound just a body hit her in a rough tackle and they tumbled to the ground. The man violently twisted her onto her back and straddled her chest. She tried to scream but he slapped her so hard she heard ringing.

"Why you want to do that? Why you being like this?" The blond man berated her. "You, you... We just wanted to be nice, but you treated us like trash, why do you have to be such a bitch? We coulda been friends, you know, party a little bit. But you have to be a bitch about everything!"

Jenny tried to tell him he had the wrong woman.

Another man entered the narrow passage. For a second she thought he would help her, but then she recognized the Hollywood handsome features, framed by thick black hair. She used to think he was the most attractive man she'd ever seen.

"Move aside Tommy," the man said amused. "You'll get your turn."

Her attacker moved away.

Jenny lay shivering on the cold asphalt. "Thad," she moaned. He found her.

"Hey, Jen. I see you haven't changed, still all stuck up. I'm a nice guy, but you treated me like trash, just like you been treating my bud here. Now you are going to apologize." He bent over and seized her by the hair and dragged her to a sitting position. He tugged harder. "Kneel bitch, you were always best on your knees."

"I've already called 911," a female voice spoke up. "You should leave."

At the end of the passageway, backlit by a streetlight Jenny made out a petite dark woman, the glow of a cell phone in her hand.

The long-haired stranger rushed at the newcomer but kept his distance as he darted to go around, intent only on escape.

Thad slapped at Jenny one more time, but her hands were up and she fended it off. The man climbed up and looked at the petite woman.

"Look bitch. You don't know what you got yourself into. Be smart and walk away before I fuck you up." The look in his eye indicated he meant to do her harm.

The dark woman took a photograph, the cell phone camera light blinking in the dark. "I am recording this."

The man shoved Jenny and charged at the woman. She did not flinch but took one more picture.

Just before he reached her, a man in a grey cashmere coat, open to reveal a well-tailored suit stepped into the passage. There was no subtlety in movement, he simply stopped the charging man by seizing his throat.

For a second, she thought the man in the elegant coat was going to do a Darth Vader on Thad, but he just held the man as if studying him. "Leave," he said and tossed Thad aside.

Jenny's assailant scampered away.

The dark lady moved with brisk, hasty steps to Jenny's side and offered her hand.

"Thank you," Jenny said.

Her rescuer was athletic, with a petite frame that still exhibited curves. She was mixed race, with dark skin, almond eyes and thick black hair that hung straight. She wore an evening dress covered by a wool trench coat. "Are you all right? Is there someone we can call?"

"You said the police were on the way?" Jenny sounded wary.

The dark woman bit her lips. "That was not actually true. My boss," she waved at the well-dressed man, "prefers to avoid anything that might lead to publicity."

"Good, the last time Thad found me the police just messed it all up." She regarded the silent man. "Your boss? The way he stepped in, I thought he worked for you."

The woman chuckled. "Sometimes I think so too. My name is Marquessa King, please call me Marq. And this is my employer." She nodded at the man but did not offer a name.

"We must be going," the man said quietly.

Marq looked Jenny up and down. "You going to be all right?"

"Damn it, I don't know." Jenny shook her head and set her features into a stubborn frown. "He knows where I live. But he's lost the element of surprise. I can deal with that." *Until I can get moved,* she thought.

Marq quirked an eyebrow, the tall man looked impatient.

"I did a stupid. That's my ex-husband, Mister Thaddeus Callun, of the Atlanta Calluns." She nearly snarled the name. "I'm sorry." She held up her key. "I don't have much to thank you. Could I at least make you some coffee?" Jenny fiddled with her key ring again. Her face was numb from the violent slap, but had that throbbing feeling that let you know it was going to hurt.

"Thank you," the man said absently. "Another time perhaps." He tapped his foot.

Jenny pocketed the keys and turned back to Marq, stepping close. She made eye contact. "Thank you, both of you."

Marq responded by talking a nervous step back.

Jenny felt embarrassed, as if she inadvertently invaded the petite woman's space, but Marq changed her manner and extended her hand.

"You are quite welcome. You should also thank my boss, Christopher Stefanov."

He frowned as if he disapproved of his name being used but stepped a little closer.

Jenny extended her hand. "Thank you."

The man reluctantly extended his right hand and took her's as she stepped even closer. His eyes briefly widened in surprise. He shook her hand, now paying attention to her. "You work at this establishment?"

"No, not exactly, I mean, I do work here, but I'm a partner. I co-own this with a friend of mine."

The man bowed his head. "I am Christopher Stefanov." He released her hand and exchanged a glance with Marq. "Actually, a cup of coffee would be nice."

Jenny glanced back at the dark lady. If she was surprised by her boss's abrupt change in attitude, she did not show it.

"Well," Jenny got the keys back and unlocked the door. "Come on in." She snapped on the lights and led the pair through small storeroom, barely bigger than a walk-in closet. They emerged in a cramped space behind the bar of a hole-in-the-wall coffee shop with a dozen small tables scattered throughout the small room. Poster sized photographs and original artwork, some in acrylic, and some in ink, covered the walls in a mixed arrangement.

Jenny guided them out from behind the counter.

Christopher went straight to the art.

Jenny pulled a bandana from her coat pocket and wrapped it around the back of her head, gathering up her dark brown curls in the front like "Rosie the Riveter." She stepped up to the espresso machine. One glance at herself in the shiny chrome and she saw a red, inflamed area on her cheek and around her eye that would be purple soon. "What would you like?" she asked.

"One plain shot of espresso is good for me," Christopher said.

"I'll have a latte, if that is okay."

Jenny nodded. "Coming right up."

"You are the artist?" Christopher asked in a distracted voice.

"Yes," she answered as her practiced hand scooped up the grounds.

"Interesting." Christopher nodded and moved to the next painting.

"No, it's just the crap I couldn't get to work. No one gives a damn about art in a coffee shop."

"Are you a barista that paints, or an artist that that pours coffee to buy art supplies?" Marq asked.

In the cold light of the coffee shop Jenny could see the muscular curves on the *Black? African American?* woman. Her lighter skin tone and eyes suggested some mixed heritage. Her face could be any age from eighteen to forty. Her lips were colored burgundy and very plump.

Jenny turned her attention back to the coffee. The last time she paid that much attention to another woman's lips, things got awkward quickly. "Actually," she continued, not looking at her guest, "I'm on a ten-year plan, or at least I was. I was going to open a gallery about three blocks south of here, but I'll need to find another location."

"That's funny," Marq murmured. "We just came from a gallery opening, or l at least the after party."

"Well, thanks for stopping. I didn't expect anyone to see what was happening."

"We saw your initial encounter," Marq said. "There was something that tripped my creep radar. We followed; just in case."

"She followed, I was a passenger." Christopher wandered away, studying the artwork.

Conversation was impossible as Jenny steamed the milk. As the rushing sound subsided Jenny started trying to make small talk. "So what does your boss do, anyway?"

"Business," Marq replied. "Very diversified. Mostly real-estate, with some venture capital investment."

Jenny's face begged a question.

"I am his personal assistant," Marq answered. "I cover a variety of meetings and contracts for him. He works out of his home so I maintain that as well. It is a small part of my duties, but he likes to refer to me as his housekeeper," she said with a playful smile.

Jenny pressed her lips together and jerked her head from side to side as if getting a thought into the right spot. "I would have taken you for his lawyer."

"No interest in law. I am actually entering medical school next August."

Jenny placed the drinks on the counter. Marq took the espresso over to Christopher. He accepted it absently while he studied the art. Jenny felt nervous with her work under his critical glare.

Marq returned and sipped at her latte without adding sugar. "Tasty."

"Thank you."

"No," Christopher called. "Thank you." He consulted his Rolex. "We do have to get going." He walked to the bar and placed the empty demitasse on the counter.

"Until we meet again." He turned to the main door.

Jenny hustled from behind the bar. "Yes, just let me get the," her speech faltered, "please." She hurried to the customer door and unlocked it as she flipped the switch announcing the shop was open.

Christopher silently ushered Marq out the door.

Once out on the street, Marq spoke up. "I think I know that look in your eye. She *is* one of us, isn't she?"

"Yes."

"What is that, like three? In the last five years?"

"Something like that."

Marq glanced over her shoulder. "What are we going to do about her?"

"That will depend on who she is."

They walked in silence back toward the car parked in an alley. Christopher excused himself and vomited up the coffee by a dumpster. He took out a handkerchief and wiped his lips.

Marq waited for him to rejoin her before going back to the car. She slid into the driver's seat while Christopher settled next to her.

"You drank the coffee? I thought you poured it out?"

Christopher shrugged.

"Do we have to pick up something for you?" Marq asked.

Christopher's face settled into a content smile. "No I had a bite at the party."

Marq turned to him and arched an eyebrow. "Really? That was subtle. Anyone I know?"

Chapter Two

"How are you holding up?" Janet Quin asked her brother. "You seem to be keeping it together pretty well."

Patrick Quin shook his head at his sister's question, and his eyes darted to the coffin at the other end of the viewing room. "I don't know. I think I just don't know what to feel. It's not real, not yet. I feel like there has been a mistake, those weren't Angela's remains the police found."

"I know it's hard Pat but the police are sure. They even went through DNA testing."

"I know, I just—" He stopped talking as a shudder passed through him. "Maybe I'm too numb for grief. First Marti died and that was bad enough, but to lose my daughter like this?" he sighed.

Janet put her hand on her brother's shoulder and gave it a firm squeeze. "At least *you* are keeping it dignified." Her eyes rolled and settled on an older man in a black suit kneeling before the coffin. He'd been in that position for an hour crying.

"He'll get tired of that soon." Patrick scowled. "Then he'll be at me again about how I'm responsible for all his tragedies because I tricked his daughter into marrying a Catholic."

"He's not that bad."

"You don't know. You've only known him since Angela was born.

He toned down the rhetoric. I guess granddaughters can make old men behave better."

The kneeling man staggered to his feet, his face red with the effort of rising. He made his way through the smattering of friends and relatives to the siblings. He kept his left hand in his suitcoat pocket. No one noticed the way he worked to avoid dragging his left foot.

Patrick steeled himself for a verbal onslaught.

The man stopped just out of intimate range, placed his right hand over his paunch, and bowed his head. "I am so sorry," he said.

The siblings blinked. They waited for the man's tone to change into the practiced cadence of an Evangelical pastor preaching condemnation.

Instead he blinked back tears. "I am sorry. It's all my fault."

Now Patrick felt awkward. "It's not the fault of any one but the man who took her."

The old man gave a leaden shake of his head. "I bear the spiritual guilt."

Now Patrick knew where the man was going. "No, you're not going to make it all about you." Grief masquerading as anger poured out. "I know you think your feelings and opinions are the only things that matter. I am not in the mood. You should go." Part of him was hoping that the man would do something stupid; it would give Patrick an excuse to have the police officers escort the old man out.

Again, the old man surprised him. "Yes, you are right. I forfeited the right to be here long ago." He wiped tears from his eyes. "I am sorry that you lost your daughter to this evil. I know losing a child is hard."

Patrick tried to remember his wife's funeral two months ago. Her father had been brusque, touchy, and full of anger at Patrick. Not this restrained person in front of him.

"Mr. Leiter," he addressed the man, unable to bring himself to use man's celebrity title name, The Right Reverend Bobby Leiter. He remembered when Marti, she hated the name Martha, revealed who her father was. At first he'd been impressed. Anyone growing up in Chicago had at least heard of his revivals, or seen him on TV. Of course, that was before Patrick met him. "I really think you should go."

Bobby Leiter nodded carelessly, then raised his head. "Do you know what evil is?"

Janet took in an alarmed breath. Patrick squared his shoulders.

12

"That." He pointed to the coffin. "That, what he did to her, that was evil, do you understand?"

Patrick shook his head.

"I made it my life's work to know evil, to vanquish evil, but I was wasting my time. God help me, it took this for me to understand what evil really is."

Patrick had no idea how to reply.

"I will leave, and I won't bother you again."

There was something in the retired pastor's tone that alarmed Patrick. Now, not only did he not know what to say, he didn't know what to do.

Bobby Leiter turned and walked away.

The reverend made it to the door, nodded to the policeman there, retrieved his black fedora and overcoat from the rack, and prepared himself to deal with the horde of reporters outside. He used to find this exciting. To be at the scene of tragedy, vehemently denouncing what he perceived as the root cause of evil. He always found a way to blame liberals, homosexuals, Catholics, and the occult. But know he knew that But now he knew that blame was misplaced.

His entire life he'd had a clarity of thought. He instinctively knew he was righteous.

He railed against child molesting priests, even as he excused allegations of sexual abuse within his own church. Even when doing wrong, he *knew* with a burning certainty that God would judge him to be right.

He stepped out into the cold November air, still hiding the results of his minor stroke from the dozens of TV cameras. He learned long ago not to show weakness in front of the media. The artificial light formed the world into sharp contrasts and strange shadows.

A black woman in a smart wool coat shoved a microphone at him. "Reverend Leiter, do you have a comment about the murder of your granddaughter?"

He took a deep breath, his face transformed into his "wise" look. Not as easy to manifest as his righteously angry look. "This is a bad time for my family, for the entire city."

A grey Mercedes pulled up.

Leiter tipped his hat to the reporter and walked to the car. Good ole Manuel, always knew when to take him away.

He got in the car without a greeting. "Home."

He settled down with his thoughts. It was a very difficult thing to lose faith in God. So many people he cared about had died, others driven away from him by his judgmental rebukes. He used to take solace in the book of Job. God must love him, that is why he tests him so hard. He read Job again when he saw on the news that Angela's remains were found. It was as if he'd never really read it before. Instead of a God testing a good man, he saw only a sadistic God, in cahoots with Satan himself, torturing a man he professed to love. Leiter searched his heart, and found he hated that God.

The car pulled up to a high rise apartment building. Leiter let himself out. There was another reporter in the lobby.

"I have no comment." As he strode by, oblivious to the mish-mash of questions tumbling from the man, he had enough questions in his own mind. If God was a sadist, what did that make Satan? Is there an afterlife? He didn't believe in it anymore. He would not see his daughter or granddaughter in shining robes in paradise. Even if there was a paradise, he did not deserve it.

The keyed elevator got him to his level. He leased the entire floor.

He sent his staff away before attending the viewing. Alone, he removed his coat and hat, and dropped them on the floor. There didn't seem to be a point to hanging up the clothing.

Where should he do it? In the bathroom, to make it an easier clean up? Or right here by the elevator to make a statement?

He was tired of statements.

He limped to the library, not bothering to hide his dragging left foot. He paused at the gun safe in the corner, then unlocked it and studied his collection. He needed something powerful enough to do the job. He considered a .50 cal Desert Eagle but settled on the .357 Colt Cobra revolver. He checked it was loaded and flicked the safety off.

The bathroom was about twenty feet down the hall, but it took him several minutes of halting footsteps to reach it.

To hate God was to hate himself, he thought as he stood in the shower. An EMT at the scene of a botched suicide pointed out what the person had done wrong. Now he followed the paramedic's advice and placed the gun in his mouth, recoiling at the taste of steel and gun oil.

His finger tensed on the trigger, there was no doubt in his mind that this was the only solution. But he did not actually pull the trigger.

A thought needled him. What if God wasn't evil? What if the Reverend Mr. Bobby Leiter was wrong? Had always been wrong? He told his son-in-law he now knew what evil was, but did he?

He took the gun out of his mouth and reengaged the safety. He was still going to do this, probably, but first he wanted to make some notes.

He spent the rest of the night writing what he now saw as true evil. The epitome of evil started with sadistic glee in killing your fellow man. As he wrote the words he found them a sickening echo of the glee he used to feel condemning someone for how they worshiped, or did not worship. All the vitriol he used to attack "perverted" homosexuality and the "confused" view of gender seemed so petty, now. By the end of the exercise he saw that it was not God who was evil, but rather the hypocrites who preached in his name.

He picked up the Bible again, but this time, he went to the New Testament, and read the Sermon on the Mount.

Twenty years ago, he thought he'd discovered true evil. A blood sucking fiend from hell itself. He gathered people and to destroy it, but only succeeded in driving it away.

But compared to the human monster that did such unspeakable things to his Angela, how much evil was there in the creature he persecuted? The thing did not leave bodies, no evidence of murder Leiter ever found. The demon had supporters, friends even. Families were not torn apart by his actions. But he was a creature of Satan. He preyed on the righteous, didn't he? Just because there were no bodies didn't mean there were no murders. Supposedly the creature only needed to drink blood, but might he have also eaten the bodies? The realization of how stupid that thought was indicated he was in need of rest. Then another part of his mind realized that for the first time, he humanized that creature. Thinking of the being as "him," rather than "it."

He picked up the .357 magnum and hobbled back to the bathroom. He stood and stared at the open shower door, sighed and went to put the gun away.

He lay in his bed without bothering to undress. His mind was suddenly on fire as thoughts cascaded through it. He was going to atone for his evil. He was going to fight real evil, and use the tools of the devil to do it.

Chapter Three

Saturday continued to be a very long day for Jenny. The erratic flow of customers was not enough to keep her distracted, but too many to allow her to rest. The girl for the next shift never turned up and it was the second Saturday she ditched without notice.

Luckily, Clio stopped by.

The tall, African-American woman walked in about three o'clock during an ebb in business, so they were the only people in the shop. She looked Jenny up and down, then quirked her pierced eyebrow at Jenny's black eye. "Girl, what is up with you?"

Jenny meant to blow it off, but before she realized it, she led her friend into the tiny back room and words were tumbling out of her mouth.

Clio held up her hand. "Wait a minute, wait just a minute. You're telling me that bastard ex-husband of yours is in Louisville? After what, three years? And what's he doing with some skeevy looking van? I thought he was like some bigshot?"

"I don't know. He knows where I live." Jenny tapped on the sides of her skull. "I don't know what to do."

"Stop." Clio grasped Jenny's hands. "First, you are going to move back in with me." She squeezed Jenny's hands tighter to prevent her friend

17

from protesting. "I know you like your own place. But I still have the spare room and you will need a few days to get things together. Should we go and get a protective order?"

Jenny bowed her head. "Yeah, that did so much good last time."

"Last time, it was in Georgia, Where Taddy-boy's family is among the privileged. Here in Kentucky the Callun name means nothing. He won't have his daddy telling the judge to let him go." She studied her friend again. "You're moving funny. How bad did he hurt you?"

Jenny knew her injuries were real, but the attack itself seemed like something that happened to someone else. Clio's words triggered the numb spot in her memory and she started trembling. That embarrassed her so much she wanted to cry, and that sensation embarrassed her even more. Then the tears started.

Clio hugged her. "Girl. You go sit down."

The bell over the door announced a customer.

Clio gently pushed Jenny away. "I can handle this, in fact I'll stay. Didn't have any plans." She guided Jenny toward a metal folding chair. "Sit. Take a minute."

The day stretched on. Roger, the majority owner, came it at four. He frowned at Clio behind the counter with Jenny cleaning up the espresso machine. "I thought you quit?" His frown eased into a tight, ironic smirk.

"New girl didn't show, and Jenny's not feeling well. In fact, she should go home." She turned to Jenny. "And by home, I mean my place."

"I'm all right," Jenny protested. "I would rather work than sit somewhere right now."

Roger looked at both the women. "What's the problem?"

"Stomach bug," Jenny blurted before Clio could speak.

There was an awkward silence as Roger stared at Jenny's face. "Odd kind of bug to give you a black eye."

Jenny's hand went to her cheek.

"I'm not going to meddle. You don't want to tell me, that's fine, as long it has nothing to do with the café."

"Nothing."

He looked back and forth between the two of them. "All right. I will pay Clio cash to work to six. Todd is coming in around five. I will help him close. Jenny, you good?"

She nodded.

18

"And you are scheduled off tomorrow, so I don't want to see you, right?"

When the workday finally ended, the pair headed out. They walked toJenny's place first, a well-preserved Victorian home painted in dark red and gold, the formerly spacious home now converted into cramped apartments. Hers was on the second floor' one-bedroom unit with a view of the cherry trees lining the road. One bedroom was a generous description; it was more of one room with a walk-in closet just big enough for a twin bed and nightstand. She climbed the steps on stiff, sore legs and the stabbing pain in her side did not react well to the effort.

"I don't like being chased out of my home." Jenny protested as she pulled an overnight bag out of her Ikea armoire.

"You are not being chased out. You are making a strategic retreat."

There was a knock on the door. Both girls froze.

"How did he get past the front door?" Clio asked.

"Anyone could have buzzed him in. He wouldn't do anything with you here."

"Wouldn't he?" Clio fished in her pocket and produced some pepper spray. "You said there was two of them." She snapped off the protective cap. "Had this for over three years, I hope it's still good."

Jenny crept up to the door and reached to secure the deadbolts as she looked out the peephole. She jerked her head back.

"Is it them?"

Jenny shook her head in confusion. "No. Someone else." She thought to engage the chain bolt, but that felt silly. It would be hard to forget the combination of dark café au lait skin and smoky almond eyes, not to mention those lips. The striking woman was dressed much more casually, this time in a canvas trench coat. Jenny opened the door. "Hi."

"Hi," Marq said. "Just checking up on you. Everything okay?"

Jenny stared in confusion. "How did you find me? Why?"

"How, took two minutes on the internet. You may want to look at some websites to remove your address. I know somebody good at that. Why? I was worried about you and just wanted to see that you are okay." Marq looked past Jenny and waved to Clio. "Hi, I'm Marquesa."

"Clio." She held her hand up and offered a tentative wave that managed to mock Marq's gesture.

Jenny shrugged. "I'd invite you in but we were just leaving. I'm

19

going to stay with Clio for a bit."

Marq smiled. "I have the car parked right out front. I would be happy to give you a lift."

"We can walk it," Clio said, her tone dry, wary.

"Of course you can. But what if the man from this morning is watching? What if he follows you?" Now it was Marq's turn to shrug. "If you drive off with me, I can make sure we are not followed, then double back to Clio's house."

Jenny looked over her shoulder at Clio, who took her turn to shrug. She turned back to Marq. "I don't want to impose…"

"No imposition. Seriously."

Jenny looked again at her friend, who waved to let the woman in.

"Then you may as well come in." Jenny opened the door wider. "Sorry the place is a mess."

"Thank you." Marq stepped into the little apartment. "This is not a mess." The entrance gave way to one room, with a kitchenette along the far side. The one large table was covered with sketchpads and photographs. Bundled art supply lay scattered around the room. It was cluttered, but clean and organized. One canvas sat on an easel, while another dozen or so leaned in a rack along the wall.

"Would you like to sit down?" Jenny cleared a spot at the table. "I'd offer you coffee, but I don't keep any here, beside I make it much better at the shop."

Marq cocked her head too one side, then nodded. "That would be nice." She undid the belt of her trench coat revealing a UofL sweatshirt and a pair of designer jeans. She moved across the room with measured steps. In fact, she moved with an air of repressed power, like a ballerina, until she perched on the edge of the indicated chair. "I'm here to check up on you, but Christopher wants me to invite you to a small cocktail party he is hosting next Friday night."

"That's not creepy at all," Clio muttered.

Jenny was taken aback. "I don't know, I usually have to juggle the work schedule for an evening out." Then she paused. "Why is he inviting me, anyway?"

"Did I mention that my employer was interested in your artwork?"

"He said polite things about it."

"He was actually quite impressed, although it took a few hours for him to make up his mind. He asked me to acquire a piece from the coffee shop." Marq rose and stepped toward an easel with a cloth covering it. "Unless, of course, you are working on something more interesting."

"Not that painting," Jenny objected. "That is something personal. An exercise, if you will."

Marq frowned and nodded, conveying both disappointment and acceptance. "There was the one with the ravens he liked."

Marq stalked around the room. Her movements were at once totally random and completely precise.

Not a ballerina, Jenny thought. She remembered meeting an NFL cheerleader. She moved like that. Well muscled, with an air of scrupulous control.

Marq stopped in front of Jenny's bookshelves, which represented a small portion of Jenny's collection, with most stored in boxes in the bedroom. She studied the assortment of hardback and paperbacks with care.

"The painting with the ravens, you said," Jenny spoke hastily, trying to draw Marq's attention away from the shelf. She cringed when Marq selected one book.

"Dracula?" Marq asked with a quirked eyebrow.

Jenny nodded.

Marq continued. "I see the Ann Rice books, Charlaine Harris's southern vampires— Ooh, you have most of the Chelsea Quinn Yarbro books." Marq smiled mischievously. "I am sensing a pattern."

"I like fantasy," Jenny replied defensively.

"Nothing wrong with that. I love fantasy stories. Vampires, werewolves, all that 'children of the night' stuff." Marq lowered her voice conspiratorially. "We won't mention this to Christopher, though. He sees these books; his eyes will roll so hard you will hear them." Marq gave a tight smile. "Not big on imagination, he prefers non-fiction. Tell you what, you come to the party and I'll show you my books. I think I have some good vampire stories you may have missed."

"Look," Clio spoke up. "I appreciate that you are concerned, but—"

"I'm sorry, how remiss of me. Clio, isn't it? You are also invited, of course."

"It sounds great but…" Jenny said. "I don't think we would fit in at a cocktail party."

"It'll be casual. If you have any friends that you would like to have around, feel free to bring them. At these parties Christopher prefers to meet new people. He rarely knows half the guests."

The two friends looked at each other. Clio shrugged.

"Okay, then." Marq took their reaction for acceptance. "Party will start around eight. I'll send a car for you."

"That's not—"

"It's no bother. We generally hire a few cars for these events, to ensure that every one gets home safe." She surveyed the room. "Now, what supplies are we taking with us?"

The three women gathered everything necessary from the apartment and bundled it out to Marq's dark grey sedan.

Marq drove them well away to ensure that no one was following, then followed Clio's directions back to her place, an older Georgian style brick house, divided into a duplex. By the time they got everything situated, it was well past dark.

"If everything is settled, then I'll be going. I can show myself out." Marq gave a good-natured wave and headed out the door.

The door clicked shut. "I'll show myself out," Clio mocked other woman's tone. "I like the part where they hire cars for a 'casual' event."

"Be nice," Jenny remonstrated. "She's trying to be helpful."

"Yeah, I don't know. I mean, she's very courteous, but I just get as weird vibe. My creep alarm is active, big time. And her employer? That just seems bizarre. They want something from you and they are not going to tell you straight up what it is."

"Well, I sort of like her. Her boss is a little distant. I can see why she says he lacks imagination."

Marq drove away in the stop-and-go Bardstown Road traffic. A smile played across her lips as she considered the conversation with the two women. *Don't tell Christopher about the vampire books*, she thought. But she would have to tell him he was having a party.

Chapter Four

Manuel brought the car around the next morning, dressed to accompany Leiter to Sunday services. When the reverend saw him park, he waved Manuel to get out of the car.

"Is there a problem, sir?"

"I won't be needing you today, Manuel, I'll be driving myself."

The driver blinked, and the reverend knew the poor driver was confused because he greeted the man by properly pronouncing his name, which he intentionally anglicized for the last ten years so the name sounded like "manual," as in labor.

Purposely mispronouncing foreign names, using inappropriate diminutives; power plays.

"To service?" Manuel sounded concerned.

"Not today. I have something I need to attend to."

Hours later he gripped the wheel too tight as he steered his elegant charcoal grey town car down a rutted gravel road. The drive should have been about two hours, but he misremembered landmarks and made multiple wrong turns.

Each mistake enraged him. He was used to rage, he spent many years summoning it, channeling it. He could make the most innocuous action by

23

one of his targets a cause for screaming outrage. And there were so many targets. Now that anger focused inward, frustrated at his lapses of memory. He took some solace in the peculiar feeling he was thinking clearly for the first time.

Leiter wished Manuel could have come along to navigate the rough country roads. The place he was going was not on any map, no GPS could plot a course. Hell, he didn't even know if they were still there. What had it been, ten years? Time slipped away from him. He exchanged one single email with the leader less than a year ago to test if the militia was still out there, but even using the encryption his old compatriot insisted on, this conversation was too personal for the internet.

It was four hours later when he eventually reached a gate blocking a rutted gravel road. A dilapidated chain-link fence surrounded a field that contained a few mature trees, sprouting saplings, and piles of brush. At the far end sat the remains of an abandoned farmhouse, collapsing on itself. Leiter opened the door and got his stiff legs moving, using his arms to lever himself to standing. He struggled to keep his left foot from dragging, he could not afford to look weak, especially here. You never knew who was watching.

The gate swung open with a screech of neglected steel. Leiter didn't care about the noise; the man who lived here could already see him on his security system.

He got back into the car to pull it through, then reclosed the gate. He drove off-road across the field with deliberate care toward the ruined dwelling. He parked about fifty feet away at a nondescript pile of rocks and trash. He got out of the car, studied the pile, then removed a particular stone to reveal a military surplus TA 312 field telephone. There was a hand crank on the side and he squatted down to give it a few hard winds to send a signal to the other end of the secure point-to-point communication system.

There was a long pause, and he signaled again. Still no reply.

Leiter stood up and looked around the field. He held up his hands and turned slowly.

The telephone signaled. He picked it up.

A familiar voice, thickly graveled from decades of cigarettes, growled, "What do you want?"

"Information," Leiter replied, incensed by the rude greeting.

"You alone?" the voice demanded. "Did you tell anyone where you were going?"

"I am alone and no. Against my better judgement, no one knows where I am."

There was a long pause. "Your car, GPS? Phone?"

Leiter sighed. "Left the phone at home. GPS on the car turned off. I took the precautions."

There was another extended pause. "You may proceed."

Leiter hung up the phone and walked toward the house. He circled around back to a pair of rotted cellar doors. He pulled them open, revealing steel plates behind the ruined wood. The electromagnetic lock clicked open as he trudged down the stairs to another steel door. He stood before it, frowned and waited.

The door swung open on well-maintained hinges, revealing a man who looked far older than he should. He was shorter than Leiter remembered, but that might be due to his hunched posture. His hair was unkempt, long. He wore wrinkled military fatigues that were at least fifty years old. Incongruously, he was clean shaven.

"To what do I owe this honor?" the man grumbled.

Leiter started to speak, but the other man waved him quiet. "Come on in, best make yourself comfortable."

"Nice to see you too, Grant. Still getting ready for the end of the world? How is the militia?"

Grant led him down a narrow passage made of concrete block to a small spartan room equipped with a folding table, a few shelves of tools and miscellaneous hardware.

Grant indicated a steel chair by the table and the men sat. "Have you been following the news? You might think Armageddon is a long way off, but it's already started."

"And you intend to stay here and ride it out?"

Grant rose from the table, fetched two glasses and a dusty bottle of bourbon from behind a huge tin can of weed killer. He poured two stingy servings and passed one to Leiter. "At one time I had a plan."

"I remember. You were hoarding seeds and enough preserved food to feed twenty men for one hundred days; or was it one hundred men for twenty days? How many of your recruits are still active?"

"About a dozen dues paying members. No one wants to live out here,

25

but everyone wants the option when the end comes. It takes a lot of faith and discipline to stay prepared. The fall will not come over night. You have to watch the news, search corners of the internet to see it coming."

"Internet, out here?"

"I can't discuss that, but what I can tell you is that we will have a nuclear exchange with Russia, or China within a decade. When the dust settles, there won't be nothing left but cockroaches and *them*."

Leiter sipped at the whiskey. "You think they will survive?"

"Yes, and they will hunt us down. They'll be starving, too."

"How many do you think are out there?" Leiter mused.

"Hundreds? Thousands? I don't know. They have too many people covering their tracks. I have only confirmed four. There was the one we killed, two in California, and then Christophe."

"That is why I am here."

Grant took a deep breath. "We should have killed it when we had the chance. It's coming for us, isn't it?"

"We were in no position to kill him. He let us go."

"You made a bargain with it, and when it let us go, we could have—" Grant accused.

"He agreed to leave us alone, to leave Chicago. Now, I want to find him."

Grant pondered that statement. "We haven't got enough men."

Leiter grimaced. "I don't want to kill him; I want to talk to him. You've been keeping track of these creatures. Do you know where he is?"

"No," Grant said the word in a measured tone. "But if you want to talk to him, I do have his email address."

Leiter's eyes opened wide, then shook his head. "Of course he has an email address."

"The account belongs to a fake person. Allegedly, the email belongs to a farmer in rural Kentucky, but he used it to reply to one of his old girlfriends and we managed to intercept it."

Grant got up from the table and rummaged in a set of drawers along his workbench. He produced a grubby notebook and a pencil. He wrote down the email address and passed it over to Leiter.

Leiter looked at it and furrowed his brow. The devil had a gmail account.

"May I use your internet to send him a message?" His tone was sarcastic.

"No," Grant laughed. "We're behind multiple proxies, but I still would not want the bastard to get any whiff of an IP address. If I were you, I'd create an anonymous email account, go into hotel with a business center and send the message from there."

Leiter shook his head. "I'll send it from my home computer, my private account. I want him to find me."

"Suit yourself."

Leiter looked about. "Jasper around anywhere?"

"Naw, he's got a woman in town. He's in touch but he lit out nigh on about four years ago."

Leiter rose, brushed the front of his pants and extended a hand.

Grant eyed it with suspicion.

Leiter kept his hand out. "We have had our differences. I know you resented that I didn't want to move into the bunker, but I always respected your dedication and integrity."

Grant remained seated and shook Leiter's hand. "If it sees you, it'll kill you. I will not be in a position to avenge you."

"That's fine," Leiter answered. "I don't think it will come to that. I can show myself out."

The box sat on a low sturdy table in a small room, barely eight-foot square. The container was rectangular, flat, sort of a fancy matte black packing crate.

The top opened silently on pneumatic lifters. As the cover opened, the side panel lowered, which fell supported by its own pneumatic cylinders. A dim ceiling light turned on, activated by the rising lid.

Christopher Stefanov swung his legs out and sat on the edge. He did not think of the case he rested in as a coffin, but rather like a custom bed.

He could see in the dark, but only in shades of grey and he liked a touch of light for color once his eyes adjusted. He brushed the loose dirt from his khaki cotton trousers.

"Don't dump it on the floor like that," Marq grumbled from just inside the basement room door. "It will get ruined. How much do you have left?"

Christopher made no move at the sound of her voice. "Eight more fifty-pound bags."

Marq put her fists on her hips. "You do know how hard it is to traffic dirt in from Europe? The European Union regulations…"

Christopher nodded. "Produce is harder to smuggle than diamonds." He frowned. "I wish I could find a local source."

"Ah, speaking with your Bulgarian accent? You must be lazy today." Normally her boss worked to sound completely American. "Where were you last night?"

"Here."

"You didn't even bother to get up?"

He shrugged. "I didn't need to feed. Just felt like…" He looked at his hands, the nails were long and ragged. He picked at a thumbnail. Like his hair, they grew far faster than a normal human's.

"Stop," Marq sighed. "I'll give you a manicure. And a shave."

Christopher felt his face and the hair that was well beyond the stubble phase. He sighed and resumed picking at the nail. "I'll get it."

"No, it'll look odd. You need to be groomed. We are having a party on Friday night."

"A party? Didn't we just have one?" He did not sound enthusiastic.

"Two years ago," Marq snapped. "We're due. I'll take care of everything, as usual, but you will need to be there."

Christopher frowned. "What's the occasion?"

"The girl from the coffee shop. We need to get to know her better and introduce her to potential patrons."

"Patrons?"

"For her artwork. By the way, you're purchasing one of her paintings."

Christopher snorted. "You realize she is not very good."

"No," Marq corrected her boss. "She is not very experienced. She needs some teaching, but there is talent there. Also, I am certain her best work is not hanging in a coffee shop."

Christopher sighed. "Why do we want to get involved?"

"Because she is like us."

Christopher waved Marq away.

"Two reasons. First, I am going back to school soon. You will need an assistant, she's the first viable candidate we've seen in a while."

"I can get by."

Marq rolled her eyes. "You think you can, but the second reason is more to the point. You need a project. You're getting mopey, and I mean more mopey than normal. You have your face set in that brooding mode." She waved a finger at him. "Not the sexy brooding either. Anyway, Magda told me you used to love throwing huge parties."

"Magda talked too much. And that was before you were part of the household." He paused and glanced up to his left. "Technically you were born about that time."

"She told me that while you were in Chicago, you competed with Hugh Hefner for outrageous gatherings."

"We were not competing, I didn't know the man." He shrugged. "It was a strange time."

"Want to tell me about it?" Marq gave a smile of eager anticipation. "No."

"Oh, come on." Marq wheedled. She'd learned to read her boss's tone over the years. That was not a final "no," but rather a negotiation "no." "Tell me about your wild times. You rarely talk about anything that happened before you hired my mother."

Christopher shook his head. "No, I am not going into details. But to try to explain the excesses; I was born and raised in a very rigid culture. I was not very experienced when I changed. The sexual revolution caught me off guard."

"But you had fun?"

Christopher sighed. "For a couple of decades, but it gets old. I did it all until it just seemed too much effort."

"But you still enjoy sex?"

Christopher's mouth gave an ambivalent twitch. "Somewhat, you know how complicated that is. I am tired of complications."

"This will be a casual gathering. No naked women serving champagne," Marq teased.

"Magda talked too much."

Marq nodded. "I miss her. All right, let's get you a manicure, and trim your hair. Also, you should spend a couple of hours out in the moonlight, you're really pale." Marq took a deep breath as she dispensed with the pleasantries and prepared to present an annoyance. "Also, you have an email."

"I don't read emails, that is what you're for."

Marq glowered. "Mopey and rude. You definitely need a hobby. Unlike the regular email, this came to your private account."

Christopher cocked an eyebrow.

"It is from the right reverend Mister Bobby Leiter."

Christopher frowned; his brow furrowed. "That's a blast from the past. I—" He shook his head. "I do not think I've been flabbergasted by anything in a long time, but that is a surprise. So that person has my email address? That is going to be annoying."

"Exactly the word I was thinking. He wants to ask you for a favor," Marq said with a hint of a smile.

Christopher's laugh held an ominous ring. "A favor? I let him live. I moved away. If anyone owes a favor it is him."

"Do you want to know what he wants?"

"No."

Marq smiled, that "no" meant "yes." "Oh well, it was sort of interesting. I can just delete it."

"That would be best." Christopher replied through gritted teeth. "Fine," he snapped. "What does he want?"

Marq shrugged. "He didn't say. He wants to meet you, in person, to talk."

Christopher laughed. "Oh yes, let's have him over for tea?"

"It is an interesting missive. He fails to apologize for what he did, but claims he has had a new insight into good and evil."

Christopher sighed, a respiratory gesture strictly for Marq's benefit. "Sure he has."

"Did some research," Marq said. "He's been having a bad year. His wife died, complications of Alzheimer's. Four months ago his daughter died of cancer. Then, just a few days ago the police found his granddaughter murdered."

"Sorry to hear that. So, everything has gone wrong and I am sure he blames me. Please, someone save me from fearless vampire killers."

"You liked Buffy. Hell, you binge-watched the entire series."

Christopher shook his head. "That was fun and Buffy is a lot cuter than Leiter. I can't be bothered with his problems." He squared his shoulders. "And as for the girl…"

"Jenny. She calls herself Jenny Taylor, but that's part of hiding from her ex. Not sure what her real name is."

Chapter Five

Jenny startled awake and fumbled at the nightstand to shut off the alarm clock's obscene incessant beep. She grimaced as sharp pain stabbed her shoulder and traveled down her left side. The attack was two days ago, but she swore it hurt more now. She blinked at her surroundings, both familiar and strange.

The air was frigid, and she did not want to move. After soaking a few minutes in the warmth of her electric blanket, she pushed it off and gently pulled up her long t-shirt. Her ribs were decorated by a dark purple bruise the size of a dinner plate. That contusion hurt more than the pulled muscle in her back, the scrapes on her hands and her black eye combined. She probed it again with cautious fingers to confirm nothing was actually broken, not that she could do anything about a broken rib. She had health insurance, but it was cheap with a two-thousand-dollar deductible. She hadn't been to a doctor all year and she would have to pay for an immediate care visit out of pocket. *Not an option.*

She dragged herself to the bathroom to discover her face was much worse. Overnight her simple black eye exploded into blues, greens and a sickly, sallow shade of yellow with red streaks in her eye. She managed to dress but started trembling when it was time to go.

Clio was waiting for her as she exited the bedroom. "Time for work, sunshine."

Jenny didn't hate Clio's chipper morning banter, not really. Okay, a little…

"I figure I need a morning walk," Clio said with a smile. "I'll just keep you company."

"That's not necessary."

"I called my boss to tell him I'd be working from home today. I got my laptop." Clio held up her hand as her friend tried to protest then hefted an ancient navy-blue canvas Verdi suitcase. "Look, let me hang out for a bit, just in case."

"Okay," Jenny finally assented. She couldn't bring herself to admit that Clio's company was the only thing making her shakes abate. Even without the admission, Jenny suspected her friend knew.

When they got there, Clio set up at a table while Jenny got ready for her first wave of early morning customers, which included making her and Clio breakfast.

Jenny tied her hair up in the bandana just as the panini press dinged. "Breakfast is ready!" Jenny called to her friend as she placed a latte on the counter along with the warm panini sandwich.

Clio got up to get her food but paused by the wall, looking at a piece of artwork. "Is this the painting that woman was talking about?" She gestured at a two by three-foot monochrome of ravens on a stone wall. "Not your best work."

"No, but if that man wants to buy it there are two likely reasons, and one remotely possible intention."

Clio picked up her coffee. "I'm listening."

"Either he doesn't know much about art, or he has an ulterior motive."

"I'll bet money on the latter," Clio muttered.

"Yeah, I tend to agree."

"What is the remote possibility?"

Jenny shrugged. "That he knows art very well. 'The Ravens' is actually a very good painting."

"I don't know much about art, but that painting has always bothered me. Sorry buddy. Hell I can't even tell ya why."

"It doesn't work, but I am very proud of it." Jenny smiled.

"If you say so."

"You know why it looks weird?"

"Because," Clio said slowly, "you made it look weird?"

Jenny moved to the painting and traced a grid pattern with her finger. "Look closely. There are sixteen different sections, each done in a variety of techniques and mediums. The fact that it looks mostly coherent alone is impressive."

"I see where the edges look more like water color…"

"Exactly, and the background is done in ink. Pointillism for the piece of tree. The stone wall and the mass of the birds are oil. See the luster of the feathers? The fine detail is done with acrylic, which I textured by using a needle to scratch in the fine lines. I wasn't able to make the transitions as seamless as I wanted, but I think I really stretched my abilities to paint that. But yeah, it is not pretty. It looks odd." A timer dinged. "I got to open the door."

Clio's 'just in case' walked in around ten a.m.

Thaddeus surveyed the scattering of customers and sauntered over to the counter. A second later his helpful blond friend loitered in the doorway.

Clio started to rise, but Jenny gestured her to stay put as she glared at the unwelcome customer. "What do you want?"

"Jesus, calm down. You're always so freaking edgy. I'm just here for one of them, things, you know, one of your *lattes*." He made the drink sound indecent.

"All right, one latte." She turned away.

Thad reached across the narrow counter and grabbed her arm.

Jenny shrugged free. Her face grew hot as she realized customers were looking. She leaned across the counter and hissed. "Please, just stop!"

"*Please,*" he mocked her in a voice just above a whisper. "You stupid cunt. Before I'm done, you'll have a lot more to deal with than that cigarette burn I put on your arm."

"You're threatening me?" Jenny said in her best calm voice.

"No, I am promising you that you will get what your lying ass deserves. You ruined my life."

Jenny rocked back. "I ruined *your* life? Forget it. I'm not making you a latte, I ain't making anything but a call to the police."

He smirked. "Your word against mine. We know how that goes."

Jenny pulled a smart phone from under the counter and brandished it. "I have your threats recorded so—"

Thad snatched the phone with his left hand and punched Jenny with his right fist.

Jenny staggered back, blood dripping from her nose.

There was the sound of chairs scraping as several people stood up, including Clio.

"Stop!" Jenny yelled in a weird nasal voice as she covered her bloody face. "All of you, please." She glared at Thad. "Just go."

He flourished the smart phone at her and tucked it in his pocket.

Two men moved up on him.

"Eric, right? I don't want a fight in here." She waved her arms. "Everybody! Just let him go."

There was an awkward silence and the patron's indecisive eyes darted around the room.

Thad joined his friend at the door and the pair walked out as if they didn't have a care in the world.

Clio ran to the counter. "Call the cops."

"No," Jenny shot back in a wretched voice. "We can't! I can't go through that again. I hoped that recording him would intimidate him a little, make him back off."

"You're not going to the cops?"

"I can't."

Clio leaned back and studied her friend. "What are you not telling me?"

The bell rang over the door and both women jumped. Jenny looked past Clio to see Roger step in. He stared at the pair.

"The stomach bug is now causing a bloody nose?" He looked at the patrons. "This *is* affecting the café."

Clio interrupted. "Can we talk about this later? I need to tend to Jenny's face."

"Okay, go get cleaned up. I'll take over out here."

Jenny came around the counter and Clio took her by the arm and led her to one of the unisex bathrooms. Once they locked the door, Clio pulled a handful of paper towels while Jenny bent over the sink, gently pinching her nose.

"Why no cops?"

Jenny deflated. "He will see that as a reason to escalate—"

"Stealing your phone is a reason to escalate."

Also…" She gritted her teeth. "They might arrest me."

Clio crossed her arms and nodded. "I'm listening."

"After I got the restraining order he came to 'talk some sense' into me. I called the cops. While we were waiting for the hearing, he did something. Something online, and got people to tell stories."

"Stories?"

"That I was a prostitute and a thief. He put up a website offering my services with pictures."

"Nudes?"

"Lewd nudes. When we were newly married, he said he just wanted to take some 'fun' photos. I really slutted it up for him. He got some really strange men to write reviews of my services. One of them implied that I offered him my little sister."

"You never said anything about a sister," Clio said as she ran warm water over the paper towels.

"I don't have one. My family is all dead or might as well be. But you see, I ran from Georgia after the police warned me to not leave town. They take any hint of child prostitution very seriously."

Clio gently patted at the drying blood under Jenny's nose. "If it's a white kid."

"What?"

"Never mind."

"I don't know if there is a warrant or not. But when he published my actual phone number and address, I had to go. Some drunk showed up at my doorstep pounding and screaming that he'd already paid for my services and was there to collect."

"Asshole."

"Yeah. I packed a bag and I went. I left artwork, supplies, everything. I was never a prostitute."

Clio quirked her eyebrow. "That sentence sounded like it should end in 'but.'"

"There was a woman who introduced me to some old men when I first got to Atlanta, they bought me gifts in exchange for my company. But it's not like that. They were over seventy and there isn't enough Viagra in the world to help them, but I did let them take a few liberties. I know, don't hate me."

"Hey, bills are due when the bills are due. I've paid them," Clio murmured with an imperiously raised eyebrow.

"Clio?"

"Not directly. But I won't turn my back on my friends who have had to do what they did to get by. Hold still." Clio continued cleaning her face.

Jenny suddenly pulled away from her friend. "The lease."

"What lease?"

"The one I'm going to have to skip out on. For the apartment. I had to use my real name."

"Real name?"

"Torres. Jennifer Torres."

"I always thought you looked Latina." Clio moved back and dabbed at the wounds. "There are laws."

"Which his family can twist." Unable to breathe through her nose, Jenny took a bushel of air through her mouth. "I'm going to have talk to Roger. I have to go." Her shoulders slumped. "Most of my money is tied up in this place."

"No talking to Roger." Clio gripped Jenny's shoulder to keep her from objecting. "First, we are going to get you home. Next, we get a lawyer."

"I can't afford that!"

"We can find—"

Jenny shrugged from Clio's hand. "No, we can't. You don't think I've tried? The system doesn't work if you don't have the money. I don't have the money. Thad has the money."

"Really. He's looking about one step away from homeless."

Jenny sniffed. "He only takes care of hygiene when he wants something."

Clio shook her head. "Why in hell did you marry him?"

"Stupid, desperate, broke. Barely earned enough to keep an apartment. He is very charming when he wants something, and he wanted me. I was too stupid to see the red flags."

Clio tugged at the bandana that held Jenny's hair back. "Fix your hair. I'm calling an Uber and we're going home. No arguments. It is like that lady said the other day. If we walk, he may follow us."

It was just after noon. Jenny sat on the couch in front of the TV. She took in the images but wasn't making any effort to comprehend them. Fear, anger, anxiety, and deep loneliness fought for supremacy, leaving her emotionally paralyzed.

She watched Clio working on her laptop at the kitchen table. She already missed her.

There was a knock on the door.

Jenny sighed.

"I'll get it." Clio strode to the door and looked out the peephole. "It's that lady again." She opened the door and stood aside for the visitor.

Marq was dressed much the same as before, but a knit top replaced the sweatshirt. "You going to ask me in?"

Clio squinted at Marq. "Please, come in." Clio turned away and rolled her eyes.

Marq stepped in and focused on Jenny. "You okay? You made the local news."

"Christ."

"The police want to talk to you." Marq sounded concerned. "They want you to make a statement."

Jenny shook her head with agitated, abrupt jerks; then regretted it as her nose throbbed. "I can't. I'm leaving in the morning."

"Where?" Clio demanded.

Jenny ignored the question. "I'll call Roger. We can make some arrangement. He might be able to buy me out if I make the price low enough."

"Why the urgency?" Marq asked.

"The police," Clio answered for her friend. "She's afraid of them."

"General fear, or a specific reason?"

Jenny hesitated. When it was clear both the other women were going to wait, she mumbled, "Reason."

"Okay, we'll take care of that first." Marq held up her hand. "I'll have Christopher make some calls. Your life is your business, but it would help if I knew the circumstance."

Clio started to speak, thought better of it and looked to Jenny.

Jenny shook her head. She meant to be vague, but once she looked into Marq's dark eyes, she felt herself babbling. Words spilled out detailing her marriage, divorce, the smear campaign and her escape to Louisville.

Marq listened impassively, only her eyes grew colder at the story.

Soon Jenny ran out of details and faltered to an awkward silence.

"Well," Marq spoke up. "That will not do."

"What?"

"You will not run. You have a party to go to Friday night, and you have a life to live."

"I can't go to your stupid party."

"It is more than just a party."

Clio arced an eyebrow. "Ulterior motive."

"Yes," Marq admitted. "I have a certain ability. I can sense a lot about some people, and I sense some exceptionally unique qualities in you. The party is actually an informal job interview."

"What kind of job?"

Marq smiled. "Mine. I am going to be focusing on schoolwork for a few years. This is not a cookie-cutter position, it demands a very specific type of person. Someone like you."

"You don't know me."

"Told you, I have a sense. But getting to know you is the purpose of the party. Christopher wants to see how you interact with his business associates."

"And friends?"

Marq shook her head. "He has friends, but most are introverts and do not like parties. The job pays well. It put me through college, and I have saved an awkward amount of money."

"Awkward?" Clio asked.

"Enough money to do whatever I want with my life, but not enough to do nothing."

Jenny felt a prickle of temptation but shook her head.

"What have you got to lose? You are not going to work while you recover. Take a few days to heal. Attend the party. If nothing comes of it, you can bugout Saturday morning."

Clio spoke in the ensuing silence. "It would give you a few days to work something out with Roger." Clio kept her eyes on Marq as she spoke.

"In fact, I think Roger and I should accompany her to this party."

Two hours later it was dark and Marq sat in the car on her way home when the phone rang. She checked the heads-up display. Christopher calling. She used the blue tooth switch on the steering wheel to answer. "You're up early."

"Still in bed, but I am not resting. I've been considering a plan to meet with Reverend Leiter."

"That worries me." Marq gave a sad smile. "You are too trusting. When I get home, I listen to your plan, but only if you agree to any safety measures I add to it."

"It was your idea to see what he wants."

"No reason to be careless."

Chapter Six

Bobby Leiter did not like to be driven by strangers. His past interactions with Chicago cabbies were more than enough to convince him to hire a personal driver. He never cared for the word "chauffeur," it seemed effete. But with his new way of thinking, it didn't matter.

The car swerved to avoid a pothole and brought him back to the present. Against his expectations he had to admit the car from the internet service was clean, smelled good and the driver was friendly and competent.

It was a long ride. The email instructed him to take a hotel room in the college town of Lafayette, Indiana. The car picked him up at his hotel Thursday and drove him out into the country for well over an hour. The late afternoon sun was bright and clear but would be gone soon.

The car came to a gentle stop, edging into the shallow depression on the side of the road. "This is it. Would you like another bottle of water?" The young, brown-haired man smiled, showing teeth that probably cost his parents a fortune in braces.

"No, thank you." Leiter glared out over the cornfields. He didn't bother to ask where they were; he had strict instruction not to ask questions. He opened the car door.

"Look," the driver said. "This is where I was paid to take you, but is it the right place? I mean, all I have is GPS coordinates. I'm only asking 'cause there is nothin' out here."

"No, I am sure this is where I am meant to be."

"Yeah, but it's cold out there, you don't even have a coat." The driver sounded genuinely concerned.

"I won't be out here long." Leiter got out of the car. He knocked on the driver's window and pulled out his wallet as it glided open.

"No sir, I can't take your money. I've already been paid, and even a good tip. I'm under strict instructions to not take anything from you. But if you give me an email address, I will send you a survey."

The reverend handed the young man a business card.

"You're *the* Bobby Leiter? I can't wait to tell my granddad." He paused. "Unless this is, like, some sort of confidential thing." He flushed.

"No secret. You can tell your granddad." Leiter looked down at the earnest young man. "Well, have good trip back." There was a time when he would have struck up more of a conversation. Ask the young man about his faith and pretend to be interested. Now, when anyone recognized him the conversation turned awkward.

He waved as the car pulled away. It faded from view and he felt the first real bite of the cold as a gust of wind made him shiver. It would not be good to be out here after dark with no warmth, no phone, and no one who even knew where he'd gone. He wondered if that was the plan.

Barely a minute passed before he heard a car engine and a subcompact grey hatchback drove out from the yellow, dried out corn rows. A local rental company sticker decorated its front bumper.

The car pulled to a stop before Leiter.

Leiter approached the driver-side window and saw the mixed-race woman wearing dark glasses. Years before he called her a "mongrel," among other slurs.

The window rolled down.

"Miss Koenig. You haven't changed a bit?"

As an answer to the awkward question, the lady removed her sunglasses and held her arm out of the window into the direct rays of the sun. "Satisfied?"

Leiter frowned. "Didn't matter either way."

The lady quirked a curious eyebrow at him and climbed out of the car. "Let's get the preliminaries over with. Step to the back of the car,

41

stand about three feet away, put your hands on the roof of the car."

Leiter complied.

"Now step back, one more foot. Do not move your hands," she ordered as she delivered a swift pat-down.

"Stay there." She rummaged in the front of the vehicle and produced a wand, some sort of electrical device. She waved it around him. "Be warned. You will be scanned again. If any sort of location device is discovered on your person, this meeting is over, and all previous agreements are suspended. Understand?"

"Yes, Miss Koenig. I'm sorry, I never got your first name?"

"That is correct," she snapped. "Stand up. Open the hatchback."

Leiter fumbled with the switch but got it to open revealing a compact space, just big enough for him by folding down the rear seat.

The woman stood behind him. "I am putting a hood over your head, with a drawstring that I will tie loosely around your neck."

He stood as she fastened the hood.

"I am not going to tie your hands. I have been instructed not to, against my better judgment. Get in the back."

He felt his way into the cramped compartment and settled in a curled position, his face right up to the driver's seat. He heard rustling and assumed she was putting in a screen or barrier to hide his presence.

The hatchback closed and the car swayed slightly as the woman regained the driver's seat. The engine started and he felt the car move.

"Miss Koenig, I want you to know that I never bore any animosity toward you."

"Really?" There was an angry edge in her voice.

"I thought I was doing the Lord's work. It was never directed at you."

"Right. Just my friends." There was a long pause. "You tried to kill one of them."

"I don't know what to say. I regret things went the way they did. In my mind, at least, I thought I was protecting you."

"Then why did you leave me alone with that pervert?"

"What?"

"Daryl Grant. The only reason he still has certain appendages is because he put his dick back in his pants when you called for him. That and Christophe asked me not to."

"And you do what Christophe says?"

"Sometimes," the woman replied. The anger was still there, but he heard a touch of humor. "If he asks politely." The humor was gone. "It is his nature to abide by the letter of an agreement. It is his character to abide by the spirit as well."

Leiter mulled that over. "He is a man of his word? And you?"

He could hear a grim smile in her voice. "I will lie to your face. I owe you nothing."

"I cannot believe what you are accusing Grant of. That doesn't sound like him." The reverend felt compelled to defend his associate.

"He just needed the right opportunity. Some men cannot resist a tied-up woman, especially if you think she is less than human."

"We never considered you less than human."

She did not answer. After twenty minutes the woman put on some music; something loud with a Latin beat and variety of voices rapping in Spanish. He wondered if that was the driver's actual musical taste, or a convenient noise so he could not determine their whereabouts by sound.

It was well after dark before the car came to a stop. The hatchback opened and the woman helped him out into the frigid cold with a surprisingly gentle touch.

She tucked his right hand into the inside of her elbow. "Walk with me. In front of us are five stairs up. Grab the handrail on your left."

They marched up the stairs and walked along uneven flagstones until the woman stepped away and he heard a door open. Ms. Koenig led him on. He expected some deserted location but could hear party noises and music playing in the distance.

"Directly in front are fifteen stairs up, too narrow for me to guide you. There are handrails on both sides. Stop at the top."

Once he reached the landing the woman was back directing him. "Stand here."

He heard a door close behind him.

A different, all but forgotten voice spoke. "You may remove the blindfold. I apologize, my associate insisted on these precautions."

Leiter removed the hood and blinked in the softly lit room. The voice belonged to a man attired in black slacks and burgundy dress shirt. No coat. His hair was different, but the face and piercing eyes, were the same. Not aged at all in twenty years. The man sat in a faux-leather and chrome chair that looked more gaudy than comfortable.

"Have a seat."

Leiter sat in a matching chair across the table. *I was correct*, he thought, *not comfortable.*

The room was plain and in need of maintenance. The walls were dingy and there were no windows. The room contained a queen bed that sagged in the middle, two chairs, a small table. The air smelled of disinfectant sprayed over the subtler scent of sex.

"What do you want from me?"

"Christophe," Leiter addressed the man, then paused.

The man Leiter knew as Christophe nodded. "I haven't got all night. You asked for a meeting."

Leiter clasped his hands and set them on the table. "First, may I ask you a question?"

The man drummed his fingers on the table. "You may ask."

"How many people have you killed?"

The man cocked his head to one side and regarded the reverend.

"I suppose it is possible that you don't remember, but a rough estimate—"

"Sixty-three living people. Three Nosferatu."

"Nosferatu, that's another type of vampire, right? And you are?"

"I am Vampyr."

"Vam peer?"

"Nosferatu are creatures that did not change successfully. Imagine them equivalent to rabid dogs. They have to be put down for everyone's safety."

"Those must be the ones Grant goes on about. And the humans? Are those dead the ones you feed on?"

"No. I wouldn't touch their blood. Fifty-eight were Nazi officers and camp guards. I was a partisan in the Balkans during the war." He frowned and there was a certain air of regret in his voice. "I put the fear of the night into the Germans. The rest were self-defense or defense of my friends."

"Do you enjoy killing?"

Christophe's lip twitched, then he frowned. "You are not here for a lesson on the undead, but I will say it is not in the nature of the vampyr to enjoy the pain of others. To inflict pain, hurts us in turn."

"And yet—"

"What do you want?" Christophe's voice had an unsettling edge of impatience.

"My granddaughter was murdered."

"I am sorry for your loss." He sounded as if he meant it.

"Her body was drained of blood."

"It wasn't one of us, it would take over two dozen vampyr to drain a body."

Leiter held up a hand. "Of course. It was just the detail about the blood made me think of you. She was drained postmortem, part of the killer's disposal method. The man is evil." The reverend took a deep breath. "I thought you were evil because of your nature, but there were never any bodies. No victims came forward. This person, yes this *human*, revels in torture. He keeps his victims for weeks. The bodies have evidence of bruising, tearing, trauma that is truly sadistic." He paused. Christophe did not speak, so he continued. "She died by suffocation. Slow, deliberate, denial of air. I am told it probably took hours."

Christophe leaned back. "How does this concern me?"

Leiter raised his clasped hands his chin. He closed his eyes and bowed his head as if in prayer. He lowered his hands and took in a deep breath. "You have connections, you know how to find out things. You can achieve things no one else can. I want you to find this man, and kill him, slowly, visiting all the horrors of hell on him."

Christophe shook his head with exaggerated slowness. "I can't do that. I could find him, but I would not kill him and I cannot torture him."

"Then have Miss Koenig do it, or one of your other minions." Leiter snapped.

Christophe rose. "This conversation is over. Do not seek me again."

Leiter's hands trembled; he brought them to his face while wracking sobs shook him. "She was good, you see? The best of all of us. Please, help me."

"This is none of my business."

"Do you not have a shred of your soul left?" The reverend sniffed but his voice was calmer. "You help me, and I will give you anything you want. Money? Power? Influence?"

"You are asking me for a favor. I don't owe you anything. If there is debt, it is on you."

"Please. I am begging you."

The vampyr scratched his head. "If I were to do you this favor, you would owe me a service."

Leiter's eyes shone with tears held back.

The vampyr sighed for Leiter's benefit. "Okay, pull yourself together. I will think on it."

The reverend produced a handkerchief and held it to his face. "Think on it, please."

"Once I make a decision I will email you. Miss Koenig!"

The dark-skinned woman opened the door

Leiter wiped his nose; he felt his face was blotched and he blinked back more tears. He looked away from her, embarrassed to be seen in this state.

She ignored him. "Yes?" she addressed her employer.

"If you would please take him to his hotel. Once you are out of town, you can move him to the front seat and dispose of the blindfold." He addressed Leiter. "I assume you have more information about the killer?"

"I didn't bring it because of your instruction, but I have a file on my computer."

"Email it to me." Christophe stood and strode out the door.

"Miss Koenig?" Leiter asked.

"Shut up. Turn around." She replaced the blindfold and led him back downstairs out into the cold night.

As they passed through the door, he heard an impassioned shriek and a titter of laughter. "What is this place, a brothel?"

"No, but you are on the right track. A private club that takes no notice of a blindfolded man being brought in. Thursday is bondage night." She chuckled, "does that make you uncomfortable, reverend?"

"Honestly? No. They are just seeking their version of happiness, they're not hurting anyone."

Miss Koenig was silent, as if startled. "Come." She led him across the uneven flagstones, down the steps. The woman opened the hatchback and guided the man in.

The music turned back on and he actually found himself enjoying the rhythm. He never really listened to music until the stroke. Miss Koenig drove for about forty-five minutes before the car pulled over and Leiter was allowed into the front seat.

Miss Koenig moved out onto a deserted road but within half a mile they were at the onramp for I-65 North.

"Thank you for letting me out. I am staying—"

"I know where you are staying. I know your room number. I know every place you've been."

"I see."

"Give your man Grant a message from me. He can leave his bunker. It isn't any protection, anyway. You both are alive because—" She caught herself before she could say something wrong. "Because *Christophe* insists."

Chapter Seven

"You're up early." Marq checked her watch. "Won't be dark for another hour or so."

Overstuffed bookshelves dominated the windowless walls of the cramped study, and three wingback chairs formed a conversation pit in the center of the room. Christopher sat at an ornate roll top desk, studying a computer screen. "I couldn't rest. Did you look at this material?"

"Yes, then I took a bath," Marq answered as if she'd touched something slimy.

"I may have to do some cleansing as well. This man is sick. I have seen sadism, wanton murder, old women mowed down by machine guns, children bayoneted, but this…"

Marq nodded. "So, what are we going to do about it?"

"Nothing. It is none of our business. There is no upside."

Marq chose her words and tone carefully. "So, are you going to do something?"

"No."

Marq kept her lip from twitching. That was a negotiation "no."

Christopher regarded her. "Why should I do anything for that man?"

Marq threw up her hands "What have you done in the last decade? You've been hiding out, mostly staying home and reading medical books. You are bored." She said each word with a deliberate pause.

48

"The girl—"

"Evaluating Jenny's potential is a start." Marq drew in a breath. "You like to do good, for all your misanthropic moping."

"It will take too much time."

Marq laughed sardonically. "What else are you doing? You don't want to do it for Leiter, do it for me."

Christopher leaned back in his chair and eyed Marq. "For you? You dislike the reverend even more than I do."

"That was before I read what that murdering bastard did to his granddaughter."

Christopher drummed his fingers on the desk. "I will take it under advisement."

Now Marq let herself smile. She won.

"Last time I tied to find a serial killer; it didn't go very well."

"You've hunted a serial killer?"

He shrugged. "Technically twice. I was in London in 1888. Everyone who was out late at night was looking for him."

"No way, you're talking about Jack the Ripper? Who was he?"

"Don't know; didn't catch him. I know who did, a pimp. He didn't ask for the guy's name, just caught him slitting the throat of one of his girls. He beat the ripper with a hammer and threw him in the Thames."

"And the murders stopped?"

Christopher nodded.

"The other time?"

"That gets more complicated. What is the plan for tonight?" Christopher changed the subject.

Marq snorted impatience. "The caterers will be here at six. The invitations have the party starting at eight. I invited the Norvilles, so some guests will be here right on time."

"Did you invite anyone I actually like?"

"You don't like anybody. But I figured you'd be a bit peckish after so I called Lilith to be your escort this evening. She will be here by seven."

Christopher perked up a bit. "Lilith?"

"I have also set up a sort of test for Miss Jennifer Torres."

"I thought her name was Taylor?"

"Did you read the notes I left you?"

He held up placating hands. "I will."

Jenny paced.

"Stop it you are making me tired," Clio said from behind her laptop.

"You gonna work all night?"

"Just let me finish these emails. Got to keep the boss happy so he will stay flexible with my hours."

Jenny stopped. "Flexible?" She shook her head. "I suppose he lets you choose which eighty hours a week to work. Am I under dressed?"

Clio looked at her friend. Jenny wore a pair of black dress slacks with a pink button-down shirt and a navy blue bolero style jacket. For herself, Clio was in the ubiquitous little black dress. "Yes, but you look great."

"She said casual."

Clio grinned at her. "Rich people casual. Not the same."

Jenny stomped to a mirror and checked her face. Aggressive icing and expensive eye cream reduced the swelling, but she was dependent on bold makeup to cover the bruising. "I look like a clown."

"Your makeup is fine."

There was a knock on the door.

"Too late to change now," Clio said.

"Maybe we shouldn't go. I don't have the right clothes and I would feel better if Roger came with us."

"He's busy."

There was another knock.

Clio closed her laptop, stood up and grabbed a heavy coat from the back of the chair. "I'm going. Not gonna miss out on rich people food."

"All right." Jenny walked to the door and checked the peephole. Marquessa stood in place of the hired driver.

"Hi, ready?" Marq said with a smile.

"Yeah, let me get a coat." She hastily donned her wool pea coat and added a striped scarf to ward off the chill of the night.

As they walked down the stairs to the car, Marq spoke up. "We did some checking. There are no longer any legal issues with you in Georgia."

"Really?"

"A lawyer friend had to produce some paperwork, but it is all behind you. How do you want me to introduce you, as Jenny Taylor, or Torres?"

Jenny paused; her eyes darted around the narrow staircase. "Torres will be fine."

The three women climbed into the warm car. Once they settled, Jenny said, "I'm surprised you came yourself."

"It was close." Marq answered as she started the car

"Close?" Clio asked. "I thought Christopher would live out in the East End."

"Nope, just three miles away." Marq pulled onto Highland Avenue, crossed to Third Street and went south. Six minutes later she turned right onto Magnolia and left toward the fountain.

"No way!" Clio exclaimed. "No one actually *lives* on Saint James Court. I thought they were all touristy mansions, B&Bs and hipster condos."

"Went to the big art show last year," Jenny muttered. "What a circus." She didn't mention how much she envied the exhibitors.

The car parked in front of a well-lit three-story building with brownstone façade, 1454 St. James Court. Gentle light shone through the curtains over the picture window, but the upper floors were unlit and blended into the dark. She could just make out the Victorian turret on the left side of the house.

"Home sweet home," Marq said as they got out.

Jenny paused to examine a tin sign by the front porch with a fanciful drawing of a mechanical bat.

"Come on," Marq said as she ushered the two women up the steps. A woman from the caterers opened the door and greeted them. "Please, come in."

Marq stepped through the door and moved aside so that the caterer could take their coats.

Jenny avoided looking at the crowd, focusing instead on the room itself. Deep red leather furniture sat neatly arranged on a polished hardwood floor covered by islands of thick Turkish rugs. The walls were an understated rose tinted white and were populated by a multitude of paintings in various styles. When she realized the lovely Pollard print she was admiring was actually an original, Jenny's head spun.

Above the mantle hung an oil painting of an intense looking man with black hair tucked under a red cap thickly trimmed in white fur. His eyes dominated a face covered with a long black beard. Although he held a scimitar, he did not seem warlike. Somehow the artist managed to make

51

him look simultaneously calm and passionate. It took her a minute to notice the man held a rust brown bat in his other hand, the wings draped over his wrist.

"That would be Boyar Christophe." Marq said. "Christopher's great, great—several greats actually— grandfather."

"Bats?" Jenny asked.

"Yeah, Christophe was a naturalist. He was very interested in bats, even accompanied the William Chandless expedition to the Amazon, eighteen sixties, specifically to study bats."

"Oh," was the only response Jenny could manage. She tore her eyes from the art and considered the crowd, about forty people, mostly congregating around side tables heaped with hors d'œuvres. Everyone bore that well-groomed rich people look, although there was an intermingling of a few artsy types. By the bar where a woman was serving drinks Jenny caught sight of jazz musician she sort of knew. He looked like a guest though, not as if he were working. He waved at her.

Her apprehension about her clothes returned as she noticed she was the only woman in the room wearing slacks. Dark fall colors on mid length dresses was the norm, though she spotted one guest in a white dress with a flower print. Her artist eye took over; the dress was hand-painted silk.

"Miss Torres."

Jenny started. She did not hear Christopher approach.

Her eyes darted between the man and his ancestor, definitely a family resemblance. His eyes were deep brown, nearly black, startling against his pale complexion. His hair was dark brown with a hint of grey at the temples. He stared back at her. She remembered her manners and offered her hand. "Thank you for inviting me."

He took her hand in both of his; cold hands with a warm gesture. "Thank you for coming." He indicated a woman behind Jenny. "This is Lilith; Lilith, Jenny." The woman nodded at Jenny. Lilith looked to be a few years older that her host. She was slender, dressed in a simple skirt with a linen shirt and laugh lines surrounded her eyes. Her hair was natural iron gray cut short, but well-shaped to frame her face.

Christopher waved at the tables. "Jenny, help yourself to some snacks." He took Lilith by the elbow to guide her away. "We'll talk later."

Jenny realized Marq and Clio had also headed for the food. Rationally, she knew she was not underdressed but still felt out of place.

She took a deep breath and put on a polite smile.

"Miss Torres?" A new voice addressed her.

She turned, and froze. Her stomach dropped as fear and panic threatened to engulf her. For a moment she was a terrified battered wife accused of being the villain, again. She fought to keep her composure and not bolt out of the room.

The man was in his early sixties with thinning white hair and liver spots. She knew him very well. She'd written his invitation to the wedding, and later read the accounts, under oath, he made in her police report. He was a retired judge and her ex-husbands uncle.

The look on the man's face was a mixture of astonishment and embarrassment.

"Mister Fields," she greeted him, barely able to maintain her polite smile. She wanted to claw his eyes out. Jenny felt a smoldering anger at this man who, with a pen stroke turned her into someone with legal issues, whether they were relevant or not.

"I didn't expect to see you here," he said with a mixture of mortification and… anxiety?

"I suppose not. Last I heard Thad was telling everyone I was in prison."

The man grimaced. He lowered his eyes and sighed. "I am glad to see you doing well. I am really, truly, sorry about the way things happened."

Anger bubbled over and Jenny concentrated on her breathing to keep her poise. *Sorry, is he?* She remembered very well how he'd enthusiastically joined in the smear operation. He vilified her during his reelection campaign for local magistrate. She was tempted to "sorry" his ass with a punch to his face.

He faltered. "I know what you must think of me. In my defense, I was lied to. I truly believed everything I heard about you."

Jenny leaned forward and glared at Fields. "And that made it all right? Because you were honestly slandering me?"

"In light of recent events, I am ashamed." He stared at the ground before Jenny's feet.

Jenny blinked. "Recent events?"

Fields pursed his lips. "Thad got involved with another woman. A sweet girl, I know her family quite well. The way I understand it, she served him undercooked bacon and he put her in the hospital."

"That's the Thad I knew."

"The doctors called the police. There was enough bruising and damage to show that the beating was not an isolated incident."

Jenny felt a wave of anxiety, a commiseration with the unknown girl.

"So, anyway. Once that made the news, other women came forward. He was arrested but got out on bail and skipped town."

"So, he is a wanted man?" *I let him steal my damn phone, I should have called the police.*

"Not by any of his family, I can tell you that. Not only are they losing the bond money, but he took everything that wasn't nailed down when he left." The judge's shoulders dropped. "I truly am sorry I did not believe you."

"And that police report?"

"I honestly believed that it happened and I…" he took a deep breath and sighed. "I knew that the process would be smoother if there was a witness, so I helped things along. I was trying to look out for family." He said the last like it was a reasonable excuse.

"Family? I got your family values right here. See this?" she hissed and pointed at her right eye. "That asshole is still after me. I can pull up my shirt and show you the rest of the 'family values' right here."

The judges mouth moved, but no sound came out until he said, "If you wish to file perjury charges, I'll understand."

She didn't want to file charges. She wanted to scream. Grab a tray off of the table and pummel him. But she kept her rage in check. "You want to help? Go away." She managed to fake a strained smile. "I never want to see your face again." *Should I bring charges?* No, he was a judge and Jenny never had an encounter with the legal system that worked to her favor.

"I—"

"No." Now Jenny's smile took on a vicious twist. "You don't get to explain anymore. You don't get the privilege of making amends." Her voice dropped to a cold, quiet tenor. "And you sure as hell don't get to ask for forgiveness." She jerked her head toward the door. "But you do get to stay the hell away from me."

Judge Fields nodded and silently made his way to the coat room as Clio returned. "What was all that about?"

"Nothing," Jenny said through clenched teeth. "Everything. I'll tell you later."

Marq approached the pair. "I hope you all are enjoying the party? Jenny, may I steal you away for a minute? Christopher would like a word."

Jenny jerked her head toward Marq. "Well, I don't want to talk to him. How in the hell did Judge Fields happen to be at this party?"

"Please, let Christopher explain." She gestured at the stairs.

Jenny shook her head. "Clio, I think we are out of here."

Clio frowned at her friend. "Okay…"

"Please," Marq gave Jenny an apologetic smile. "Give us a minute."

Clio turned to Jenny. "Girlfriend, go. Tell that man to his face what he did to piss you off. If you're not back in five minutes, I'll come get you." Clio looked at Marq as she spoke.

Jenny sighed and unclenched her jaw. "Five minutes."

Marq led Jenny through the throng to a staircase and climbed to the second floor.

"So, Lilith. Is that his wife?"

"Oh, no. Christopher is not going to get married again. She's a friend, a very close friend. He has a few of those."

Down a short hallway, she opened a door and gestured Jenny in.

The room had a welcoming ambiance, even without windows. Floor to ceiling bookcases and an adorable roll top desk. Three wingback leather armchairs sat gathered in a circle.

Christopher sat in one, rolling a glass of amber liquid in his hands. "Please, have a seat."

She hastily scanned the books. They seemed to be medical books, many obvious antiques. The warm comfort of the room almost made her repress her anger as she settled onto the edge of the leather chair. "What is Judge Fields doing here?"

"Fields? I had him flown up for the party. He is the sponsor of a charity that I am going to support. He thinks he is here for a donation."

"And," Marq interrupted, "he will get a generous one. But—"

"You set me up."

"Exactly," Marq said without apology. "I have a certain sense about people. I needed to see you under sudden, unexpected, stress. To see if you could keep your poise. Your reactions were —"

Jenny stood up. "You can take your mind games and go—"

"I like you," Christopher said.

Jenny blinked.

"Marq told you this was a job interview. Time to make it a job offer." He produced an envelope from his inner jacket pocket. "This is half your first month's pay, in advance."

Jenny waved her hands. "What, exactly, am I supposed to do? You said housekeeper, like cleaning, cooking laundry? Or am I supposed to be one of your 'close friends?'"

Marq shook her head. "We have a service come in three times a week for cleaning. He's rarely home for meals. And he does his own laundry because he's picky. As for the other, believe me, that is not what he is looking for."

"So, what would I do?"

"Everything," Christopher replied. "You are a presence in the house while I am gone all day. There are appointments and meetings you will attend to. Marq will train you. Also, there will be some travel involved. I have a medical condition and need assistance when I am away from home."

"Oh, is it a serious condition?"

"Nothing I will die from, a rare blood disorder. I will provide you a smart phone, which you will need to have on you at all times. Tell Marq what make and model you want and she'll take care of it. One more perk, you will have room on the first floor to use as a studio."

"I don't know. I mean, thank you for letting me know that I'm not in trouble with the police, and that Thad is on the run. Next time he shows up I'll have the police all over him, and I'm still part owner of the café."

Marq took the envelope from her employer and passed it to Jenny. "Look at the check."

Jenny rubbed the envelope between her thumbs and forefingers.

"That is a lot of money." Jenny stood at the top of the stairs, still holding the envelope, regretting she didn't have any pockets except the decorative ones on her slacks.

"It will be a lot of work," Marq explained. "This job, if you stay with it, will take over a huge part of your life."

"But that kind of money. Is Christopher connected?"

"Connected?"

Jenny looked around. "He is vague about his business, something to do with real-estate. He has a connection with Chicago, and he throws money around like a rap star. So, is he like *Chicago* connected?"

"Oh," Marq exclaimed as she understood. "You're asking if he is in organized crime, the mafia, whatever you want to call it." She smiled. "Is that a deal breaker?"

"You're damn right it is."

Marq waved her hand like pushing the idea away. "Don't worry, he's a legitimate businessman."

Jenny glared at the petite woman. "That's what I expect a mobster to say."

"When you get to the point of traveling with him, you might recognize some faces from the news, but his business is not newsworthy." Marq patted Jenny on the shoulder and made eye contact. "I swear he is no mobster."

Jenny really wanted to believe it, but she shook her head. "I'm going to have to think about this."

"If you decide to take the position, deposit the check on Monday and show up here around noon and I will show you what's what."

The night turned clear and the temperature dropped. By the time Marq drove Jenny and Clio home ice formed on the windshield. The pair bundled into the car while Marq scraped at the frozen coating. Jenny shivered watching her.

Marq slid into the driver's seat and started the car. "Heat will be on in a minute. Warning, the seat warmers are aggressive, so be prepared."

Aggressive? Jenny thought, *More like heavenly*. She snuggled deeper into the growing heat.

"Nice party," Clio said from the back seat. "Jenny, you met what? Three gallery owners?"

"They weren't interested."

"I saw that one guy give you his card."

Jenny gave her friend a sidelong glance. "He wasn't interested in my paintings."

Clio settled back. "I'm going to have to get used to you being Miss Torres."

"Well," Jenny replied, "if I'm going to be Torres again, I am going to stop getting my eyebrows waxed."

"Girlfriend, don't stop. I've seen those things go wild. They're scary."

"Clio, you should talk—" She stopped herself and turned to the driver. "Where are we going?" Her baseline paranoia jumped.

"Precaution," Marq said. "There is a white van behind us."

Jenny and Clio craned their necks to see behind.

"Is that your ex?" Clio muttered.

"I can't tell, but it is a white van." Jenny frowned.

Marq made an abrupt right turn without using a turn signal. She drove up one block and turned again. The van didn't follow.

"Okay," Jenny said. "I can't be jumpy every time I see a white van."

Marq nodded. "Odds are, it wasn't him, but if it was, he was behind us long enough to get our license number."

"I'm sorry, I don't want you to get involved," Jenny sighed.

"We're already involved. The security at the house is top grade, I'll call them in the morning and have them check things out. See you on Monday?"

Jenny fought down a sigh. "I'll think about it."

Chapter Eight

Of all the joys in life, for one man there was nothing like Sunday at the mall during the first weeks of a new hunt.

The man cultivated the appearance of average. He was not really tall, but also not short. He had a few extra pounds, but not enough to be called fat. His hair was brown in artificial light but appeared sandy blond in sunlight. He had brown eyes and dressed for each occasion as he calculated the majority of people would be attired.

Today it was khaki cargo pants and light blue polo shirt with a dark blue fleece jacket. And the outfit blended perfectly with the throng of customers window-shopping for the upcoming black Friday sales.

He was also window-shopping, idly walking down the broad aisle close to the shops on his left. He liked this part of the pursuit the best, when everything was still possible. His list already had two really good candidates in Indiana, one in Merrillville and the other in Clarksville. The girl up north liked the waterpark near the highway, and there was something that excited him about taking a girl in a wet swimsuit. But that meant he would need to delay his timetable by about six months.

It amazed him how much he could find out about young girls in public places, he just needed a little bit of information and a picture. He had a special app on his phone that made it look like he was reading email while he snapped a surreptitious photo. With a little facial recognition software, it was on to stalking the little creatures on social media. The vulnerabilities become evident quickly.

He repressed a smile remembering when he accessed little Angela's home computer. Using the camera, he spied on her every night. It was so entertaining he put off taking her for weeks. It also paid off later. Generally, the girls lost hope after the first week, resigned to what he did to them. He found ways to give them hope so they would still struggle. The information he gathered about that girl and her family gave him the ability keep her hopes up for almost the full month.

His attention returned to the current herd. Most predators sought the weak animal at the edge of the group, but he had taste for the prettiest. And suddenly she was in front of him.

He almost staggered when he saw her. Not any girl he'd seen before, he would remember.

She was angelic with blonde hair caught up in a high ponytail and shining eyes of the brightest blue. Petite, waifish with perfect skin and cheekbones models would die for. All in all, a face designed to be painted by a master or carved into the finest marble. Her lips were thin, but with a strong bow set in an unconscious sexy pout. The thought of what he could do to those lips made him breathe a little faster.

Add to that the way she moved. She wore jean style leggings with a short brown fleece jacket and walked with a comfortable wiggle and her face had an expression that was hungry.

She couldn't be over fifteen, but she was ripe.

He kept his expression neutral as he passed her. Out of the corner of his eye he saw her stop and study the display in the window of a well-known lingerie franchise. A few steps beyond was a row of coin operated massage chairs for weary shoppers. He fed in the quarters, sat down, laid back and half closed his eyes while he examined her.

There was a sensuality pouring from her. She pulled out a phone and took a picture of a dress, a slinky low-cut number, not at all suitable for such a young girl. But she wouldn't understand that, she'd think of it like a dress for one of those ridiculous fashion dolls. She turned to walk away and he was mesmerized by the sway of her hips as the leggings revealed every curve.

He had to find out who she was, that one was definitely going on the list. If he could get enough information on her, she might very well be headed to the top of the list. Eyes closed, he took deep breath, there was time to savor that exhilarating "getting to know all about you" phase. She looked comfortable here, familiar. It may take time, but he could find her again.

He was shifting his weight to get up and—not exactly— follow her, but move in the same direction. Before he committed to standing, she turned back and was now walking toward him. He settled back into the chair while she approached. She strolled in leisurely steps, her hips swaying even more.

He meant to turn away but was powerless to take his eyes off of her.

She looked at him, their eyes met, and she smiled. It was the kind of smile that a girl that young shouldn't be able to pull off.

He jerked his head away. Making eye contact was a mistake, one of the disastrous mistakes. She noticed him. She would remember him, which made physically stalking her too dangerous. Now he had to distance himself. He remembered her smile and he wanted her but glowered at the ground as she was swallowed by the flock of shoppers.

He looked down the mall corridor; opposite the way she'd gone. *Take a few cleansing breaths,* he thought, *There will be others. Don't be so eager you act like an idiot.*

"You seem like a nice man. Could I ask a favor?"

The voice was right behind him and it was soft, almost a purr.

He craned his neck to look while the blonde angel came around the row of chairs to sit next to him.

He stuttered, "Excuse me?"

"I'm sorry, I know what you must think of me. Foolish little girl, but I was supposed to meet my friend here to give me a ride. He didn't show." Her words tumbled over each other. "I don't have a car, you see. I noticed you looking at me and you just seemed…" She paused and looked him right in the eyes as she pouted, "Nice."

A physical tremor raced through his body; this was not how it was supposed to work. "I see." He closed his eyes. She was ripe and was just asking for him to pluck her. They were always asking for it, they just didn't know it. She was so ready.

He knew the location of the security cams throughout the mall. He didn't know every single site but was confident he knew most. The only camera that could observe them together was located several yards away. There was series of potted trees that partially blocked the view. Most likely there would be no clear image of him sitting there. But if he stood up and walked out with the girl there would be some very clear pictures.

She touched his forearm. "I just need a ride to downtown Jeff. There is something I need to get. I'd be ever so grateful."

He opened his eyes and shook his head. "I don't think it is a good idea."

The girl's lips puffed out, creating a sultry sad smile. "Please? I really have to get there, it's just a few minutes away."

He wanted her and this was his only opportunity. It would be risky, but if he didn't take her now, she would remember him too well. He would have to avoid this mall for a year or more.

"I have something I need to do first." The man muttered, plans forming in his head. He looked up at the darkening sky thought the mall's plexiglass skylight. "My car is parked out the bookstore entrance, straight down that aisle to the end. It's a full-size red van. Give me fifteen minutes, and I will meet you there."

The clouds left her expression and she smiled that smile. There was no way such a young girl could intentionally give such promises with her eyes. "Thank you." She didn't lick her lips, but sort of exposed the tip of her tongue. The gesture so sensual and so innocent at the same time.

He was sweating.

He got up, left her, and headed for a department store. He was still weighing his options. It might be safest to just give a ride. She would forget his face soon enough. She wouldn't spoil in a year.

He walked outside through a department store entrance and took his time circling the building. He always parked in a place with low chance of surveillance. She wanted a ride so he should be able to keep her quiet until he knew they would be alone.

The plan clicked in his brain. He knew the place and he knew how to get her there.

She was at the car waiting when he approached. He waved and unlocked the passenger door. She stepped in.

He offered a clueless smile. "Where to?"

"Downtown, you know, by the river? Down Market street, you know, just beyond where Jeffboat used to be?" She sounded a little anxious now.

He didn't know but started the car. He *did* know a *place*. "I have to make a stop on the way, is that all right?"

"Sure, sure." Now she didn't sound so much anxious, but impatient. Her eyes were bright with excitement and she shivered a little.

He drove down Lewis and Clark boulevard, under the highway and turned into an industrial park.

"Where we going?" She looked at him quizzically.

"Where I work," he lied. "I need to drop something off. I have it in a box in the back. It's not heavy but it's awkward. I'd appreciate if you could give me a hand?"

"Whatever." The girl shrugged.

~

The girl woke writhing in pain. The right side of her body had burns where he'd used the stun gun on her. The little tart fought back with such unexpected fury that he had to stun her again, and again, and again…

Now he had her on a plywood table, her hands fastened level to her head, secured to a hole in the table with iron manacles. Her feet were bound together with duct tape, but not secured to the table. He liked the movement they made when they kicked bound like that. Like little mermaids.

He removed her jacket already but was waiting for her to wake before cutting off her clothes. He often dreamed about that first wave of humiliation but for now she was decently covered as she lay there in her leggings and a vintage rock t-shirt.

She tried to scream but only managed a whimper.

"You can scream if you want, there is no one to hear you." He stood several feet behind her. She tried to look at him but could not get her head back far enough, even inching back to get her head over the edge of the table.

"Don't move." He loomed over her holding a set of pliers. "Go ahead and scream. In fact, I insist." He used the tool to pinch her, right by the burn marks.

She screamed, he smiled.

It was several minutes before her voice gave out. Her screams were everything he'd imagined while driving her here, and more. Soon all she could muster was a hoarse sobbing. He enjoyed that even more.

"What do you want from me?" the girl shouted in a hoarse roar.

The man tenderly touched her cheek. "Everything." He took his hand away and walked around her, his fingers trailing down her legs. "I am going to use your body."

Her body relaxed as though his words actually calmed her. "You don't have to do this." she said and shifted her voice to sultry.

The man stared at her.

"You look like the daddy type. Does daddy want to use my body?" She licked her lips. "I do it all, everything."

Now the man looked nervous. "What do you mean?"

"I mean," she licked her lips again and said the word slowly. "Everything." She smiled. "I just need a little something from you. A taste."

"A taste?"

"A pick me up." She looked at him in anticipation. "You want to do things to me, and I want to be ready, I just need a little bit."

"A bit of what?" The man was puzzled.

"Crank."

"What?"

She dropped the sultry voice. "Jesus, dude, some meth, you know? Look if you don't have any, I can tell you how to get some." Now she was pleading.

"You sell your body for drugs," he said, dropping the pliers.

"Drugs, money whatever I can get. Look, you got some vodka?"

"How old are you?"

"Eighteen," she said in reflex, he didn't believe her.

"All right," he said his voice resigned. "You give me what I want and I will give you what you need."

The girl nodded.

"Let's get this over with. Do like before, see if you can scoot until your head hangs over the edge of the table."

The girl complied.

He left her like that while he looked around the shed. He brought a musky smelling rag and tied it as a blindfold.

The only movement from the girl was to shift her head to make the angle more comfortable. "You want me to open my mouth?" She didn't wait for a reply, she just parted her lips.

It was the most obscene thing he ever saw. From under the table he pulled a small knife, hand forged with a Damascus steel blade. He intended to start slow, but that disgusting open mouth enraged him. He used his left hand to press her head back and slit her throat with the blade. He jumped back from the unexpected spurt of blood from her carotid artery. His most recent victims were dead when he drained the blood, it was some time since he needed to cut a live one. He should have known that would happen, but the rage made him stupid.

The edge was so sharp the girl had no idea what occurred, until she was choking on her own blood.

Her gurgling sound added to his rage. The man threw the knife to the concrete floor. He kicked the table and screamed. "You filthy whore, you goddam slut!" He was screaming more at his own stupidity than at her corpse. He hadn't put the plastic down, that blood was everywhere and it had to infected with every disease imaginable.

He walked over to a pile of female cloths and used a blouse to wipe the blood from his arms. Thank god it didn't spray in his face. He opened up a case of bleach and took out the first bottle. He poured the liquid over his arms to cleanse himself from her disease.

He picked up the knife. He forged it in a special class by a special knife smith in Bloomington, Indiana. He kept it sharp enough to shave with, but in his rage he'd broken substantial chunk from the tip from the blade. He threw it back down in disgust. Even if it wasn't actually broken, the filthy blood from the cock dumpster tramp ruined everything he felt about it.

It didn't matter at the moment that he did not get what he wanted, or how stupid he'd been in killing her, he had to stop and clean up and prepare the body for disposal. Good thing he bought a couple cases of bleach.

He looked at the roles of waxed butcher paper suspended above the table and shook his head. She was no prime bit of meat. He would go buy some trash bags to throw out the garbage.

Chapter Nine

Jenny took and Uber to the brownstone mansion at 1454 St. James Court. Her arrival time was 11:53 am. The house looked romantic when it was lit up for the party, but in the stark autumn sun it was nothing less than intimidating. In addition to the metal rail and columns, daylight revealed a huge wrought iron figure above the door. The figure bore a certain-over-the- top Victorian ornateness that puzzled Jenny until she realized she was looking at another bat.

The grey sedan from last night was not in evidence. She checked the time on the track phone Clio got for her. Marq said noonish. Would 11:59 seem neurotic?

She climbed the front steps, rang the doorbell and shivered as she waited. She winced as the movement aggravated her bruised ribs.

After a few minutes, she rang again. Maybe this was a bad time. *Hell, she thought, maybe this is a bad idea.* Jenny suddenly felt exposed in the clear frigid air. She thumbed her phone to summon a ride home when the door opened.

Marq greeted her dressed in black leggings with a gray zip up hoodie open to show a sports bra. "Hi, glad you came, please come in."

"Thanks." Jenny stepped over the threshold. "I wasn't sure anyone was home; I didn't see the car."

"Oh, I just parked at the curb for convenience the other night. There's a converted carriage house out back. And I really lost track of time for a while. I thought I'd get a workout and listen to an audio book."

"Good for you. I mean to work out. I used to go running a lot, but lately I've been out of time and energy."

"Well, you will have plenty of opportunity; there is a fitness room back beside the kitchen." Marq held up a hand to interrupt herself. "But business first, follow me." She led Jenny up the stairs and into a small office across from the study? Library? Where Christopher had summoned Jenny during the party. This new room barely had space for a larger, more elaborate roll top desk bearing two computer monitors. The rest of the cramped room was filled with file cabinets. Two leather banker's chairs sat on a circular oriental rug covering the hardwood floor.

Marq sat down and opened the center drawer on the desk, exposing a keyboard and mouse. "This is where most of the work is done. Phones are VOIP through the computer, you'll need the headset. When you're not in the office calls will be forwarded to your phone. Unexpected calls are rare as we generally schedule discussions. And the majority of those are video conferences."

"What am I supposed to do with calls or conferences?"

"For now, if necessary, you take notes and write up reports for Christopher. You will also have to keep a close watch on three email accounts. He doesn't like checking email, so you have to bring anything important to his attention, sometimes forcibly. In addition, he has a private email account which I monitor, and I don't know if he's going to give that responsibility to you." Marq opened a Gmail account. "Oh, he's got mail."

Jenny did not mean to read over Marq's shoulder, but the name of the sender surprised her. "Bobby Leiter? The evangelist?"

Marq regarded her. "You're a follower?"

Jenny shook her head. "No, no, no. He did a lot of shows in Atlanta and was associated with people in my ex's family. So, is Christopher a follower?"

"No," Marq's voice betrayed a bitter tone. "He and the reverend go way back. As far as religion, Christopher was raised in an Eastern Orthodox household, but has lapsed."

"Yeah," Jenny nodded understanding. "Lapsed catholic here. You?"

"Buddhist."

Jenny blinked. "I did not see that coming."

"My father was an African-American serviceman. My mother was Thai. She raised me as a Buddhist."

Marq opened the email. The top displayed an old picture of Leiter back in his glory days.

Jenny turned away.

"It's okay. You may as well know about this. You asked if Christopher was 'connected' and he certainly is. Leiter's granddaughter was murdered recently."

"Saw that on the news, terrible."

"So," Marq bit her lip as she concentrated on the message. "Leiter has asked my boss to use some of his connections to get more information."

"Like some kind of investigator?" Jenny said. "Does he do that sort of thing?"

Marq considered for a moment. "I think he did some work like that a long time ago, before I worked for him. But this is special." She shook her head. "And I don't mean in a good way." She sighed and focused on the screen. "Anyway, you will need to know what is going on, but you don't have to be involved." She glowered at the communication. "Leiter wants to meet again Tuesday or Thursday. I'll let Christopher know." Marq checked three more email accounts; there were no other messages. "So, any experience with bookkeeping?"

"Been working with accounting software since I became a partner at the store."

"Cool, well enough of that, for now. I get talking about the minutia of the daily routine, your eyes will glaze over." Marq jumped up from her chair. "I promised to show you my bookshelf." She crooked a finger and led Jenny to a room down the hall. "This is my place."

Jenny walked into the room and felt right at home. The walls were painted a deep purple, with black curtains. The carpet was maroon. It reminded Jenny of her goth years, and her mother's obsession with Prince videos.

The bed was made, also in black. Jenny's attention was caught by a chaise lounge, in Victorian fainting couch style, also deep purple with black wood accents. "I like that."

"Thanks. Here is my private bookshelf." She pulled a book and offered it to Jenny. "Ever heard of her?"

The book boasted a lurid cover of a corseted woman with impressive cleavage in the embrace of a shadowy figure. The title was "His Sanguine Embrace" by Beth Daniels. Jenny took the book and gave the pages a skeptical fan.

"This is the first in the series. It's really much better written than it looks."

"I'll read it," Jenny said, still unconvinced. She looked up at the open bathroom door. "That's one hell of a shower."

"It's a steam shower, it feels really good on a cold day like today. You're free to use it anytime." She smiled as if the invitation was immediate.

Jenny shook her head. "I'll pass for now."

Marq waved. "Unlike Christopher's, my room is always open. Drop in if you want to use the shower or borrow the next in the Sanguine series."

"But I can't go in Christopher's room?"

Marq smiled. "It's not like he keeps it locked or anything, but he is private. Plus, he does business with China." She rolled her eyes. "He will change his sleep routine without telling anyone and you will go in there in the middle of the day and find him asleep."

"Oh."

"The only place you cannot go—" Marq spoke with an exaggerated air of menace. "—is the basement. Never go to the basement."

Jenny pulled back. "Oh, that doesn't sound ominous at all. What's he got down there? Some 'Fifty Shades of Gray' playroom?"

Marq laughed. "No, come on I'll show you." She led Jenny back downstairs to a door in the back of the kitchen. She flipped on the basement light switch. "The basement wasn't finished when he moved in, it still had a dirt floor with a rough limestone foundation. He had a contractor dig it out more and put in a concrete floor and had the rest of the foundation strengthened. Come on." She led the way down to a large room filled with a variety of power tools. There were traces of sawdust all over the room. "Woodwork is one of his hobbies and he doesn't like anyone touching it. Also, he is afraid someone will get hurt."

"Pity, I'd love to have access." Jenny frowned.

"Really?" Marq quirked an appraising eyebrow.

"Oh, really," Jenny nodded enthusiastically. "I know my way around most of these, except the lathe. And I'd like to learn that. So, what's in there?" She pointed to a door at the far end.

"Big closet. Nothing in there but a box of dirt."

"Dirt?"

Marq took on a thoughtful look and tapped a finger on her chin. "And yard tools. How are you with gardening? We have a service that tends to the flowers and shrubs but I like to putter around in the spring, you?"

"No." Jenny waved a negative. "Brown thumb. My mother tried to interest me in gardening, but it didn't take."

Marq brushed her hands together. "All right. Back upstairs. Have you eaten? I'm starved."

Jenny followed the woman back to the kitchen.

Marq took ham, salami, thick cut roast beef and four different cheeses out of the refrigerator.

Jenny watched her host lay out bread for multiple sandwiches. "Thanks, but I did eat."

"Okay. This is for me anyway." She piled on the ingredients to complete three generous sandwiches. "High metabolism," she sighed. "It's a curse, really."

Jenny walked back toward the front room and pulled back a sheer curtain to look outside. "Crap." She said. "I'm sorry, that just came out."

Marq appeared from the kitchen still holding a sandwich and a saucer. "That's okay, what kind of crap are we talking about?"

"There's a skeevy white van parked right outside."

Marq's good humor evaporated. "I'm calling security You think it is him?."

"It might be him. Wait, someone's getting out. Double crap, it *is* him." Jenny's heartbeat sped up and she began to shake. "He's headed to the door. I think he saw the curtain move."

Marq shooed Jenny from the window and handed her the saucer and sandwich. "Go on back to the kitchen. I can handle him."

Jenny looked at Marq's tight form. "I'm sure you can."

The doorbell rang.

Marq waited until Jenny was out of sight. She zipped up her hoodie and opened the door without using the chain bolt. "May I help you?" She stood in the center of the doorway with her arms crossed.

70

Jenny cowered behind the kitchen doorway and peered around the corner. Thad looked cleaner and better dressed than their last encounter.

"Hi," he said, his tone respectful and non-threatening. "I just wanted to apologize for our little dustup the other evening." He opened his hands in an expansive manner, meant to create a sense of sincerity. "It is all a big misunderstanding." His face took on a sad smile. "I came to town to apologize to my ex-wife."

"Most people don't give out black eyes for an apology."

"See! That there is what I mean." He pointed a finger at her. "You don't know the whole story. You don't know what she did to me before you showed up. What you and your boyfriend saw was self-defense." He smiled with what looked like absolute sincerity.

Marq shook her head. "Nice try. We saw your bud catcalling her. We saw her run and while she couldn't see you, we saw you go after her."

He held up his hands. "I didn't want to hurt her, I just wanted to talk."

"Like you talked to her on Monday morning."

He grimaced. "You don't know what she's like." He held his hand apart, fingers toward each other. "She twists things." He twisted the air, fingers clinched. "I try to order a cup of coffee and she turns it into assault."

Marq searched his face but could not detect any malice or deceit.

"I just want for her to hear my apology." He shrugged. "If she understood how much trouble she causes every time she opens her mouth, she'd sew it shut. I just want to ask her to please stop causing me trouble, but I can't find her. She skipped work, and there's no one in her apartment."

Mara spoke deliberately, "You went *into* her apartment?"

He held up his hands. "The door was open. Figured she was home and if the door was open, she'd be expecting company. Look," he continued with a calm sincerity meant to intimidate. "Tell me where she is. I'll say what I need to say. I'll be gone for good."

Marq couldn't decide if he was really imagined he was that smooth, or if he had convinced himself that his version was true. Either way he was dangerous. "Okay, you had your say. Now leave."

He moved toward her, smiling. "Oh, come on, let me see her. I'll behave."

Marq produced a cell phone from her hoodie pocket. "Security is on speed dial. Their response time is three minutes." She pushed a button. "That starts now."

Thad looked at her, then back at the van and lost control of his expression. "Look bitch, this ain't over."

Marq smiled. "Yes, it is. This conversation has been recorded."

Thad's face darkened. "You don't know how much trouble you're buying into." He turned and walked quickly back to his ride. There was some spirited discussion with the other occupant before they drove off.

Marq stood in the freezing cold until they were out of sight. She closed the door.

"That's what he's like," Jenny said from the kitchen doorway. "It's like he's in a different reality, and he's always so sincere."

"All right." Marq closed her eyes and pinched a spot between them. "We need to find a way to get you in and out, unobserved. Tonight, we'll use a classic. One of Christopher's friends…" She paused. "Let me back up. Christopher has several female friends."

"So you said," Jenny commented wryly.

"The thing you need to know is you'll find one here when you get here in the morning. Make conversation if you want or ignore them. Just make sure they have a good breakfast and show them out."

"Breakfast?"

"Christopher has a strong sense of hospitality. A woman spends the night, he owes her certain things, including breakfast."

"You always call him Christopher, it sounds so formal. Anyone ever just call him Chris?"

Marq chuckled. "I wouldn't call him 'Chris,' and I've slept with him."

"Wait, you said this wasn't that kind of a job." Jenny's hand went to her mouth. "I'm sorry, didn't mean…"

"That's okay. I would have to tell you eventually. It was a long time ago. All my idea and I talked him into it." Marq shrugged. "We were a thing, then we drifted apart."

"And you still work for him?"

"Yes, and we are still friends, but without benefits."

"So, he's like some Lothario?" Jenny frowned. "I worked at a place where the boss was always trying to make some less than subtle sexual innuendo. I quit. There is no job worth putting up with an asshole."

Marq laughed. "Don't worry, Christopher doesn't go around seducing women. With his personality and money, he doesn't get the chance. Seriously, he has no designs on you." Marq sighed. "He has a supply of friends—with benefits. Speaking of which, I will get either Lilith or Rhiannon to come over in a bulky coat, hat, and sunglasses."

Jenny looked puzzled.

"Which you will wear as you leave. Are you still interested in the position?"

Jenny nodded, with some misgivings. *But what she could do with the money*.

"Come by tomorrow around nine, and I will get you started on your duties. Same for Wednesday, but we will probably have to go out of town Wednesday night to meet Reverend Leiter on Thursday."

"What kind of clothes should I pack?"

Marq regarded her. "Eventually you will travel with Christopher. There's his medical issues, but I can take care of him for now."

"If I am going to do the job, I might as well jump into the deep end."

Marq looked at her with lowered lids. "All right." Her voice sounded like she made some calculation or evaluation. "You have the option to pay for your own hotel room or share one with me."

Christopher stepped out of his box to find Marq waiting for him, again. "So, how was her first day?"

"Interesting, not in a good way. Her ex showed up. He acted like he knew she was here, so that's how I played it. Had Rhiannon drop by and give Jenny her coat and hat to sneak her out. Jenny wants to go with us to Indianapolis."

Christopher grunted, "Anything else?"

"Yeah, she saw me eat, I think she was concerned by how much."

Christopher looked at her. "How much are you eating?"

"I calculated it to around 6000 calories. A day."

"That doesn't mean anything to me."

Marq smiled. "Enough for three people."

Christopher chuckled. "What about raw meat?"

"Gross."

"Good. Let me know when you start to crave raw meat, or living things. What about counting?"

"No compulsion. Are you sure that's part of the transformation, or just your personal OCD?"

"Yes, I'm sure. I think we can hold off four years for you to complete medical school. You sure you don't want to do residency?"

"No, just finish my MD degree. I can do night work for my Ph.D. I want to get on our research as soon as I can."

Chapter Ten

The man pulled the dark red van up to a split-level home just outside Bloomington, Indiana. He ignored the house and made his way down a barren dirt path to a shed out back. The temperature had dropped down into the twenties by the time he stepped out of the car and frozen dirt crunched under his boots. He was dressed in an army surplus field jacket and a brown fur lined hunters cap. His face sprouted a new beard, at this point not much beyond the stubble stage.

The sign over the shed door announced, "Freya's Forge." Smoke wafted from the smokestack—"Freya" was waiting for him.

He knocked on the shed door and a husky feminine voice yelled, "Come on in."

Hunting is about preparation. He forgot that when tempted by the mall-rat whore, but now he threw himself back into obsessive planning. This forge and its smith were essential to his design. He took a deep breath and entered.

The proprietor gave him a cursory glance as he entered. Rachel Starre was striking by any standard. A six-foot tall, curvy redhead who did not suffer fools gladly. She was very upfront about being a trans woman, and as far as he could tell she was *all* woman, without the weaknesses. But he knew her nature and to his mind that made anything she crafted of fire and steel imbued with mystical properties.

Light came from three bare bulbs hanging above. The only heat emanated from the propane forge in the center of the room making that area too hot, while you could see your breath in the rest of the shack. On one side stood an anvil with a two-pound crosspein hammer accompanied by small pieces of steel to form the Damascus billet.

"Tab, right?" she said. "Is that short for something?"

"Nope," the man replied, "just Tab." That was the name he used four years ago when he forged the first blade. The only "Tab" he knew of was the actor Tab Hunter and the only reason he knew that name was a 2015 documentary.

Rachel straightened up. She wore a wool knit cap holding back her long blonde hair and a down jacket to fight the chill, covered with a leather "green split" apron to protect her from sparks.

The last class had been in the fall, three years prior. At that time Rachel worked with a thin t-shirt under the same apron, her newly devolved breasts jiggling as she hammered.

"You got the money?" Her tone was suspicious as if she expected him to renege on the deal.

He took an envelope from his pocket and handed it over. The man once read an article in a local business magazine highlighting "Ms. Starre." She disclosed how she been forced to get rid of some male customers for trying to cheat her in business. Justifying deceit because of her gender. He did not want to endanger his access to this forge.

In other words, he happily paid in cash, without haggling.

She snatched the envelope with hands encased in leather fingerless gloves. At the sight of four one-hundred-dollar bills, she relaxed. "You have the knife you broke?"

"Yes, but it is ruined." He pulled out the bare blade and handed it to her, tang first.

She frowned in concentration. "You were here what? About three summers ago?" She examined the blade. "Or maybe that fall?"

"Yes." He fidgeted; he hadn't expected her to remember him that well.

"Hmm, that was when I was experimenting with using a core of twisted wrought iron to make a regular pattern. I don't have any right now, but I can order some." Rachel handed the blade back with an air of resignation.

"I'm in a hurry." He smiled.

"Okay," She flexed her shoulders, warming them up for hammer work. "I have some high carbon and nickel steel here. But, you know, you just broke the very tip off. I'll still go through the lesson, but with some stock removal I can get that fixed up in a jiff. In fact, it looks like you've done that before."

"Yeah, I originally broke the tip off hunting. I was field stripping and dug it right into the bone."

Rachel frowned.

"Yeah, I know. I was doing it wrong. That little nick I fixed, but now it's ruined." He spoke, his voice flat, but he couldn't suppress a grimace of disgust. He saw her face flicker distaste at his tone. He smiled again. "I really want to make a new, clean one."

Rachel shrugged. "You will need to sign a waiver, then we'll get you some goggles and an apron. Then we'll assemble the billet, weld a bit of rebar to hold it in the furnace and we'll start. What do you want for grips? I have several different types of wood."

"I'll add them later. I like to use bone."

Jenny peered back at the slumped figure in the rear seat. "Is he sleeping?" She checked her new cellphone. It was nearly 8:30 in the evening

"No," Marq replied. She glanced up at her boss in the rearview mirror. "He doesn't travel well and it makes him lethargic."

"He's so still. He isn't snoring, I mean it looks like he isn't breathing," Jenny whispered.

"I'm breathing," Christopher said without opening his eyes.

Marq gnawed her upper lip and stared at the road ahead. "There are things you need to know for this job. Christopher has some weird issues."

"I can hear you; you know," Christopher grumbled, still not moving.

"Are you familiar with obsessive compulsive disorder?"

"I've heard of it," Jenny answered tentatively.

"Christopher has a rare blood condition that requires medical treatment. There are mental issues associated with it. Christopher has OCD, but is high functioning."

"Meaning?"

"Meaning that he can usually overcome his smaller compulsions like constantly counting things, but he has a hard time driving highways at night because of the reflectors on the road. The amount of concentration necessary to keep from counting them takes away from his focus on driving."

"Like The Count!" Jenny held up a finger and mimicked the Sesame Street character. "Von, Two, Three, ah,ah,ah—"

"I am familiar with the character," Christopher muttered.

Marq gave Jenny a side eye.

The artist blushed. "Sorry. Didn't mean to make fun of a medical condition."

"We're almost there." Marq changed lanes as they approached the exit off I-465 for the upscale Keystone Crossing area, passing three pyramid shaped office buildings that dominated the skyline. It took a few turns and they pulled up at hotel in Indianapolis.

Jenny stared at the building. It was boutique hotel and the kind of place she'd never able to afford. It looked new, and very old at once. She wondered if it might have been converted from a nineteenth century factory or built to look like it.

Jenny self-consciously followed Marq to check in and stayed behind her.

The clerk smiled, "Nice to have your back, Ms. King."

"Thank you. You were able to obtain our regular rooms?"

"Of course." He handed two packets of key cards over. Marq handed Jenny her key card and the trio made their way to their adjoining suites. They passed a few other guests and Jenny felt affluent, judgmental eyes on her ragged suitcase. She sighed with relief when she entered the two-bedroom suite and tucked her bag by the closet. Maybe she didn't have enough refinement for this job. Marq described her salary as "an uncomfortable amount of money," but the skills necessary to integrate with the rich might be beyond her.

Marq placed her elegant chocolate brown leather bag next to Jenny's. "Go ahead and freshen up. I'll go help Christopher get situated."

"What is the plan, exactly?"

"Christopher has a meeting tomorrow evening with Bobby Leiter and a local prosecutor."

"I get that. The way you talked I thought it was much further away, but it's barely a two-hour drive. Look at this place!" She spread her hands out. "Wouldn't it have been more economical to drive up tomorrow afternoon and back after the meeting? We are going to get back around the same time."

Marq chewed her lip. "Yes, if you look at it that way. Christopher has business interests in the city. Since we were making the trip, I arranged a series of meetings to keep him busy until we get to his personal business in the evening."

"So, we're going to be driving him around tomorrow?"

Marq laughed. "No, when he comes to visit, his clients either come to him, or provide transportation." She opened the door. "Get yourself together, and we'll get dinner. I know a great place."

"What about Christopher?"

Marq hesitated. "Tonight? He has a lady friend in town."

An hour later they were seated in a restaurant that oozed refinement. The scents alone clouded Jenny's mind as she felt even more out of place. Her beaded bolero jacket certainly looked great, but she was embarrassed by its thrift store origin. Marq exuded nonchalance in her burgundy silk dress.

The dark woman chose to accentuate her full lips in dark violet tonight. Marq noticed Jenny's attention and smiled.

Jenny took refuge in the menu, then blanched.

Marq's head perked up at Jenny's reaction. "It is a little over-priced."

"I…"

"Don't worry, it's on the expense account. They have a fantastic tomahawk steak."

"I'm not familiar with that." Jenny scanned the menu and found a description. There was no price listed. However, the price for lobster dumplings was listed, and it was the least expensive entrée.

Marq ordered Albert Bichot Cote de Nuits Villages 2012, in a perfect French accent without consulting the wine list.

The waiter raised his eyebrows, but Jenny couldn't tell if he approved or disapproved. Marq clearly did not care.

"And I think we are ready to order?" She smiled wolfishly at Jenny.

"Yes," she replied.

Marq smiled at the waiter. "I'd like the tomahawk steak medium, the large cut please."

The waiter did not change expression. "Very good."

"I'll have the lobster dumplings."

"A very good choice." He gathered the menus and left.

They sat in awkward silence for a minute. "So, Marq…"

The sommelier rolled up a cart interrupting her. After the ritual of opening, tasting and pouring, they were left alone again.

Marq leaned back and eyed Jenny like she was the entrée, large cut. "You had a question?"

Jenny sipped at her wine. "So, you've been his housekeeper how long?"

Marq twisted her lips to one side in consideration. "A long time, but my mother worked for him before I did. She was the cleaning lady that came in three days a week."

"Your mother, you said she was Thai? How did she end up working for him?"

"There's a lot to that story, but the short version is, it was my fault. I was thirteen, and very uncoordinated. My mother ensured I got a good education. She was working at a garment factory."

"Garment factory?"

Marq ran her finger on the rim of the glass. "Yeah, it was brutal. She was paid as a contractor per finished item. Sweatshop conditions." She tapped at the glass. "So, it was January, and my school had arranged a sleepover at The Museum of Science and Industry. We were just getting there at closing time when I ran right into Christopher, I mean physically. Tripped over my own feet and slammed into him. He was with a group of very wealthy patrons and celebrities. My mother was mortified and tried to hustle me away, but Christopher introduced himself and shook my hand and apologized for running into *me*." She tapped herself on the chest. "Then he had Magda come over and talk to us."

"Magda?"

"Magda was the housekeeper at the time," Marq explained, her eyes thoughtful she picked up her purse. "I have a picture. Wonderful woman, face sharp as an axe, not patient with vendors or contractors, but a huge heart for everyone else."

The waiter interrupted with their food. He looked dubious as he placed the three-pound steak in front of Marq. The meat was cut from the rib and had one log bone sticking out of it.

Once they settled in with the food Jenny spoke up, "So Magda…"

Marq grunted and wiped her fingers on the linen napkin. "Anyway, Magda talked to my mother. I thought she was just being polite and didn't pay attention until I heard her spilling things about our life, private things. So, Magda put us in touch with the cleaning agency and mother was better paid and actually enjoyed her work and had time to try and keep me out of trouble."

Jenny picked at her dumplings. They were good, but the serving size was way more than she could eat. "Would you like some of this?"

Marq looked at the remaining steak, pursed her lips. "What were you thinking about for dessert?"

Jenny gaped.

"Okay." Marq chuckled but still looked like she meant it. "No dessert then. If you've had enough, I would like to try one, or two of your dumplings."

Any other time Jenny would have gotten a to-go box, but she felt intimidated by the atmosphere. "So how long did Magda work for him? I mean, he looks around forty…"

"He's a lot older than he looks and he comes from old money. There is some connection to Bulgarian nobility." Marq finished her steak and dabbed at the corners of her mouth with her napkin.

"Right, Boyar Christophe. I looked up Boyar, it means count."

"Actually, it just means Boyar, basically land-owner. Some writers try to create a false equivalency with nobility of different regions, but it is never accurate."

"Oh."

"He emigrated to the U.S. at a young age." Marq drank some water, then took a taste of her wine. She closed her eyes to savor the essence.

Jenny gave her wine a tentative sniff. It just smelled like wine, no different than what came in a box. Delicious but… Jenny wasn't sure she was catching the same experience as Marq. Was she supposed to learn about wine? "The wine satisfactory?"

Marq grinned. "Yes," she purred. "Have to appreciate it now. Probably have to give it up sometime. Family history of hypertension, diabetes." She shrugged.

"And Christopher?"

"He doesn't care for wine, too sweet for him."

The waiter brought the check, stared at Marq's clean plate decorated with the bare rib bone and looked with approval at the petite dark-skinned woman. She responded with a smug raised eyebrow.

Marq studied the bill. "You sure you don't want dessert?" She gave Jenny a hopeful look.

Jenny couldn't keep her eyes from widening at the thought.

"Just being sure."

Jenny waddled out of the restaurant, but Marq showed no sign she'd just consumed such an amount of food.

As they got in the car, Marq spoke. "You want to go do something? There are a lot of little clubs with live entertainment in this area."

Jenny rested her hands on her distended stomach. "I think I really need to go and get a good night's sleep."

"Suit yourself. I'll take you back to the hotel, maybe Christopher and Agatha will want to do something."

"Agatha. His Indianapolis lady friend?"

"Yeah. Don't mean to leave you all alone. I'm a bit of a night owl." Marq's eyes flashed with an electric energy. "Sometimes I don't even feel awake until sunset."

Jenny chuckled ruefully. "I used to be that way, until I invested in a business that opens at five a.m."

Jenny ended up by herself in the hotel room with the TV on, though barely watched. She was consumed with a feeling of inadequacy. This room, and that meal, were the most expensive indulgences she'd ever had. That food alone was more than she made in half a week at the coffee shop.

Obviously, if they were going to spend that kind of money on her, they were going to expect a lot in return. What did she have to offer? Two years of college studying English literature? They couldn't like her artwork that much.

She turned off the television and fell asleep somewhere around eleven.

Jenny woke to a knock on the door. She froze. Marq would not knock like that. Who else knew where she was?

"Room service," a muffled voice announced.

"I got it," Marq called from the sitting room.

Jenny joined her and was treated to a full breakfast and later a sumptuous lunch. In fact, she spent most of the day on the couch in their room reading in a stupor from the huge bulk of food. In the future she'd have to show more restraint.

Marq was fun to be around and they chatted about common interests, growing up goth, and got into politics. But even as she felt they were warming to each other, she felt an apprehensive sensitivity about what was expected of her. Finally, she couldn't handle the stress of the unknown anymore.

"You've given me a few lists of responsibilities," Jenny started out. "but that can't be it. Like tonight, what am I expected to do?"

"Just take notes," Marq replied as if it were the simplest thing. "And be prepared, the man who killed the reverend's granddaughter is vile, sadistic and there will be discussion about what he does. How is your stomach?"

For a second Jenny thought Marq was asking about all the food, then she realized the woman meant how was she at tolerating conversation about torture and murder. Jenny took in a deep breath through her nose and all that good food loaded in her stomach felt like a bad idea. "I'm not sure. I like to think I'm a tough girl, but…" She shrugged. "I guess we'll find out tonight."

Chapter Eleven

Shortly after five PM Marq suddenly raised her head as if she was startled and snapped her laptop shut. "Time to check on Christopher."

Jenny looked up from her book, unaware so much time passed. She'd brought the book Marq loaned her to show she appreciated the gesture and wound up absorbed in the story. "Okay," she answered for lack a better reply.

Marq stood and smoothed her clothing with her hands. "Be right back." She scuttled out of the room.

She must have got a text, Jenny mused.

Marq returned forty-five minutes later with Christopher. He wore a charcoal gray business suit and a strained expression.

Jenny went to get her coat. "Are we ready to go?"

"Yes," Christopher sighed. "I guess we must."

It took a while to get through rush hour traffic to the Marion County Prosecutor's office on Ohio Street. The guard checked them in and directed the trio to an office on the second floor.

Jenny kept her hands in the pockets of her serviceable, but not fashionable, quilted coat; a cheap knockoff of a down jacket. She was trying to asses her feelings about meeting, in person, Reverend Bobby Leiter. She'd seen him on television, and when she married into the Callun family she was commanded to respect him. So much so that at the two family gatherings where he appeared, she avoided him, refusing to even make eye contact.

None of her previous experiences prepared her for meeting the man. Her first reaction at seeing him waiting in the hall was awe at seeing a powerful celebrity, advisor to presidents, and the moral compass for a generation. He was older, but still seemed to project a certain undefinable charisma.

He nodded at their approach and Marq sped up to arrive first. She held out a small tablet computer and turned the screen so the retired pastor could see. "Mr. Stefanov is very busy and is too polite to rush you, so I will be the timekeeper, understand?"

Leiter nodded and studied what was on the screen. Jenny watched his eyes leave the tablet and examine her as if looking for something not easy to see.

Neither Christopher nor Marquessa offered a hand in greeting.

Christopher cocked his head toward Jenny. "This is Miss Torres, my new associate. I expect you to give her the same respect as me or Miss King."

"Miss King?" The reverend's eyes widened at the new name. "Mister Stefanov." He nodded again. "And Miss Torres. Thank you for your assistance."

His words were polite, but Jenny could read uncertainty in his eyes.

Up close, the celebrity awe fell away as Jenny saw Leiter without her preconceived notions. The fine lines around his lips and jowl spoke of a man who spent more effort in frowning and passing judgment than laughing. But those were lines from the past. His face was grey with dark bags under his eyes and the tracks in his face were deep, as if recently plowed. Jenny moved from awe to pity for the broken man standing outside the prosecutor's office glass paneled door.

The reverend tapped at the frame. "He's waiting for us." He opened the door and ushered the others into the cramped office. "This is Edward Zien from the Marion County Prosecutor's Office." During the ensuing flurry of introductions, polite greetings and perfunctory handshakes, Jenny noticed that her associates still did not shake hands with Leiter.

Edward Zien was slight, balding, nearsighted and had skin about the same color as the manila folders on his desk. If Jenny were central casting for a serial killer movie, she'd call this man to play "stereotypical middle manager 2."

"First of all," the prosecutor said as he patted two piles of folders on his desk. On the right the files were plain while each folder on the left had a red and white cover declaring them "confidential." "If anyone other than Reverend Leiter requested this meeting and this information, I would have denied them." He looked at Christopher. "I did some research on you and I am not comfortable with what I could find out. People with a public record as small as yours are always hiding something." He sighed. "But Reverend Leiter vouches for you… and I've dealt with worse. Most importantly, I don't think you have any previous involvement with this case. So, I am going to share what is known, far more than the summary notes I gave the reverend."

"I am much obliged," Leiter said with a nod.

Zien flipped open the top folder on the left. "Angela Quin, the reverend's granddaughter, was the latest victim of a serial killer who has taken victims from as far south as Alabama to all the way up to Illinois. He has six known victims, and we believe the first one was killed in October, four years ago. There was a year between the first and second killing, and the second and third. The next victim was six months later, then five months, then four months. The FBI believes there are more. They feel that his level of confidence and the detailed methods he uses indicates a history culminating in this string of murders."

"The killings are so separated, Why does the FBI they think they're connected?" Christopher asked in a forward tone like the prosecutor was there at his directive.

The prosecutor made a snorting noise. "The way he kills them and disposes of the body is identical. This guy is a right bastard. Sorry, reverend."

"No apology necessary. I agree."

The prosecutor exhaled and shook his head. "He also has a specific age range. The oldest victim was eighteen, the youngest thirteen."

"Children," Christopher murmured with distaste.

"Yes. The victims were abused." He looked toward Christopher to avoid eye contact with the reverend. "Sexually. Brutally. After he gets tired of them, generally about three to four weeks, he kills them. The FBI believes he takes sexual pleasure in their suffering. The coroner estimates he can take hours to suffocate his victims."

"Hours?" Christopher asked, his voice low and calm.

"It's atrocious. He tortures his victims by depriving them of breath. He binds them and wraps duct tape around their head to cover their mouth. Then he used a tool to close off the nose. Eventually he moves to superglue to seal the nostrils, one at a time." The prosecutor spoke without inflection.

Jenny felt claustrophobic as she empathized with the dead girls. She looked at Marquessa and noted her face was set in stone.

"But what really seals the connection is the way he disposes of the bodies. All of the victims are dumped along the southbound lane of Interstate 65. After he kills them, he drains the blood by slitting the throat. Except his first victim, he stabbed her in the throat. It was a vicious strike and penetrated into her spine. A tiny bit of the tip of the weapon's tip broke off."

Christopher held up a hand. "Anything special about the knife?"

The prosecutor nodded. "We will get to that in a minute. After exsanguination, he cleans the body, thoroughly scrubbing it with bleach. When he decides it is clean enough, he ties and tapes the body into a fetal position using duct tape and twine. He then wraps the body in wax-backed butcher's paper. He prepares the body in this manner, exactly, every time. The FBI is working to keep the press from reporting on him as the 'I-65 Butcher.'"

"Why?" Christopher said. "Warning people about the threat would surely do better than harm."

"The FBI disagrees with you. The crimes are so distant from each other that there is no way to make a localized warning. Also, if we try, the man is smart and may very well change his venue. The prevailing theory is that he is a long-range trucker with a sleepover cab to transport the bodies."

Christopher frowned. "And you have no suspects?"

The prosecutor sighed, deflated. "No, not even a person of interest. Do you have any idea how many trucks traverse the I-65 corridor?" The prosecutor put his hand down on the pile of folders. "This is where I need to tread lightly. I told you what is commonly known, now we are moving into the realm of facts the FBI is keeping secret." The balding man licked his lips and looked at each person in turn. "Initially, they thought the killer might have been involved in law enforcement. Records were misplaced, mishandled so it took a year longer to realize there was only one perpetrator."

Christopher scratched the back of his neck. "But they have abandoned that theory?"

"They found no tampering, just incompetence."

"DNA evidence?"

The prosecutor's lips twisted into a self-conscious grimace. "That is the tricky part. There are DNA traces on *all* the disposals. The problem is that there are always at least three different male samples. And not the same three on each body. We believe he is planting DNA samples."

"Just to confuse the matter?"

"That, and we think he is preparing a defense for when he gets caught. He can cast doubt by pointing out the other samples. We were able to track down eight of the people and they all have airtight alibis for the murders their DNA was associated with." The balding man drummed his fingers on the desk. "The FBI thinks that planting DNA is a positive. Preparing a defense means that if cornered he will likely surrender and not go out in blaze of glory. And then there is the knife."

"Back to that." Christopher nodded.

"It is a custom blade of Damascus steel. An expert who studied the sample says the heat treating was not the best, leaving the blade on the brittle side. We believe the killer hand-forged the knife himself."

"That should narrow down the search a little."

The prosecutor shook his head. "It doesn't, really. Between professional blade smiths and hobbyists there are hundreds of people in the five states. Moreover, he may not live anywhere near where he is hunting. The FBI has interviewed hundreds of 'em, but without something more to go on, they really don't have specific questions. None of the recent leads have panned out. We believe once he has his victim, he will be off the grid for a month in some well secluded place. A place where his victims can scream. That doesn't match any lead we got from the blade smithing community."

Christopher frowned. "That is not easy. The place would have to be at least a mile from any road."

The prosecutor patted a stack of folders on the right. "These are copies of all official reports and they contain everything." Christopher leaned forward in his seat, like he was about to stand.

"One more thing." The prosecutor waved him down and paused in consideration. "I have another file. We don't know for sure if it is related to the I-65 killings or not. It may be a copycat. Crime scene analysts are still processing everything."

Christopher inclined his head. "I'm listening."

"The victim is Carol Greene, age fifteen. Went by the name 'Kitty.' Her body was dumped on I-65 just south of Merrillville but, instead of butcher-paper, she was wrapped in garbage bags. No indication of sexual assault, and her throat was cut, no breath play. She was only missing 72 hours."

Marq spoke for the first time. "That would be a massive change."

"Indeed. We disregarded Kitty at first." The prosecutor frowned and rolled his pen in his hands. "There are other, substantial differences. The FBI profile indicates a man who stalks his victims, gets to know them. Plans some method to make them drop their guard. Also, all his previous victims were from good families, good students, no criminal activity." He scratched the back of his ear. "Kitty, on the other hand, was a drug addict. He couldn't have been stalking her because she just got out of six months of rehab. That poor girl never had a chance."

"How so?"

"Before her death Kitty Greene's life was an all too common tragedy. A young woman who fell through the cracks of the system. Her mother was also a drug addict and died when Kitty was fourteen. The girl ended up in the custody of her step-dad—a drug dealer. He started pimping her out before she was fifteen."

Marq stiffened. "White girl?"

"Yes. We picked her up for prostitution twice, but she wouldn't testify against her stepfather. They put her in juvenile detention, rehab—twice—and finally a foster home. People experienced with troubled teens." He shook his head.

Jenny thought the gesture looked more like guilt than empathy.

"She got away. She was at an apartment building down by the river, turning tricks for a new pimp named Sonny Marne. She wouldn't testify against him either, but they did get him on some drug charges." Zein grimaced.

"They put her in rehab the second time, an extended stay. And then gave her to another experienced set of foster parents, good track record of dealing with runaways." He shrugged. "She still managed to get away. Three days later her body was found. Tied and taped into a fetal position, bathed in bleach and with planted DNA."

"Include her folder," Marq said in a voice so cold Jenny shivered. She didn't understand her new friend's reaction, but she knew the feelings were real, and deep.

"Told you they were hiding her," Thad murmured, adjusting the binoculars to observe where his quarry had parked the grey sedan outside the Marion County Prosecutor's Office. He watched from his van a block away, obscured by an advertising display.

"So?" Tommy retorted; his voice thick as he took a draw from his vape pipe. "How we going to separate them? Should have grabbed the bitch last night."

Thad's gut tightened. Taking Jen was not a problem, but he was wary of the black chick.

The two men jumped when someone slapped the side of the door with a vigorous, open-handed blow.

Thad looked out the driver's side window to see a man staring at them. He had long, grey hair pulled back in a ponytail. He wore very old-style army fatigue pants and a new camouflaged field jacket. He made a rolling gesture for Thad to lower the window.

Thad's first instinct was to get out and put a hurt on the asshole with the tire iron under his seat, but he was suspicious of the man's demeanor. The geezer stood with an air of confidence that spoke of unseen back up, or superior firepower.

Security? Thad thought, like the rent-a-cops at the house? He considered driving off, but the man stood a safe distance away and seemed to want to talk, so Thad rolled down the window. "What the hell you want?"

The man frowned in disapproval. "Your technique is clumsy. I saw how intent you are on the car over there, and those that got out of it."

"So, what's it to you?"

The cleanshaven man cocked his head to one side. "Nothing, except if you are hell bent on suicide you should know what you're dealing with."

Thad trotted out his most annoying smirk. "I think I know pretty well."

The older man smirked right back at him. "Suit yourself." The smirk shifted in a glare of condemnation.

Thad felt anger as he saw the man judging him.

The man smiled, a cocky "I know something you don't" grin. "We should talk. I've been after that…" His face contorted with the effort to find a suitable word. "That individual, and his mongrel woman for a long time. What is your interest in them?"

Thad glanced at his partner, then back at the man outside. "None of your fucking business."

"Well," the man drawled. "You can be that way, or you can listen to me and let me help you take what you want."

The way the man said "take" stirred something in Thad's mind. "Those assholes are helping my lying ex-wife. I need to talk to her about some matters that need to be set straight. Those shitheads are in the way."

The man in army dress smiled. "Works for me." His smile tightened and he glanced back and forth. "You can call me Grant. I'm gonna lay my cards on the table. I intend to destroy those two. You help me, and I can ensure that you will have the time and tools necessary to deal with that ex of yours. Any way you want. Now, let me in, we have a lot to discuss."

Chapter Twelve

The phone rang and the man glanced at the screen on the dashboard for a calling number. He tapped his Bluetooth earpiece to take the call. "Yes?"

"Baden," the voice rang in his ear and the man hit the volume down key. "How soon can you be at my office?"

"The Chicago office?" He looked at the interstate traffic moving in the dark. It was not as frantic at night. He was about an hour from the city and figured another hour for Chicago traffic. "Midnight. I assume you have a job?"

"Old school. Details when you get here."

Baden twitched with impatience. He knew better than to press his boss over a cell phone, but he preferred to know some particulars in advance.

He slid through downtown traffic and made much better time than he expected through downtown and arrived before 11:30 pm. He parked in the underground garage off Michigan Street, putting his special pass on the dashboard before taking an elevator up to the 63rd floor. The lights were on in the office of Alexander, Cannon and Associates—Attorneys at Law.

The name was a misnomer. True, the nondescript office housed a legal firm, bit its members were essentially "fixers" hired to keep clients out of court and the public eye. And they had a lot of clients.

Baden pushed through the office without bothering to knock. "You wanted to see me, Mr. Cannon?"

The man waiting for him was the product of an army of specialists paid to keep him healthy, handsome and looking less than his sixty years. He was far too artificial for Baden to ever trust him, but he paid well for services.

"Ah, Baden. Ahead of schedule as always. Good to see you," Cannon greeted Baden. Even at this late hour the lawyer looked freshly shaven, his hair perfectly styled. He wore a custom fit navy-blue suit devoid of a single wrinkle.

Sitting with him was an old man, maybe seventy or eighty. His face was shrunk in on itself and liver spots dotted his thinning white hairline. Like the other man, he was dressed in a suit that cost more that Baden was paid in a week. And Baden was paid a good deal of money.

Baden, still in the rough clothes he wore as "Tab" at the forge, glared at the pair, but he also put on a professional smile. He eyed the white-haired man as he addressed Cannon. "You said 'old school?'"

Mr. Cannon rose. "Yes," he turned to the old man as he spread his arms in an expansive gesture at the new arrival. "This is Scott Baden, the best bonded courier in the business. Bonded for a million, insured up to ten million."

The presumed client turned an unimpressed, rheumy eye at the courier. "How fast can you get to Birmingham?" His voice crackled like an old speaker and carried just a hint of southern accent.

"Alabama?" Baden asked.

"Is there another?" The old man muttered.

"Yes, but Michigan's not part of my customary routes. Just clarifying as I would need to adjust the fee for an unfamiliar run." Baden thought as he ignored the disdain. Inwardly he felt a thrill, the destination was in line with his plans. He had expected it would be months before anyone paid him to go that far south. "What am I carrying?"

The old man glared at him.

Cannon put a placating hand on the man's shoulder. "I told you, he doesn't carry blind. I've used him for a long time, and he is our most reliable."

The old man looked pained. "How fast?"

"Depends on the shipment. But if it doesn't require special handling

93

like refrigeration I can leave now and have it there by noon Central Standard Time."

"Noon is good." The old man admitted. He turned to the lawyer. "You sure you cain't have him fly down with it?"

Cannon shook his head. "While the heyday of civil forfeiture is behind us, there is still a risk. We cannot guarantee discretion passing airport security."

The old man chewed on that, physically moving his jaw left and right. "You will be carrying five million dollars in bearer bonds."

Bearer bonds? Baden thought. *Old school, indeed.* He tried to remember the last time he dealt with bearer bonds. Very popular decades ago, now he only saw them used for untraceable exchanges by paranoid old people who were suspicious of the better options. Baden shrugged.

Cannon produced a worn, black fabric suitcase. Its only distinguishing feature was a bandana tied around the handle.

The old man glowered at it; his face twisted as if it smelled bad. "You sure that container is safe? My man carried them here in a better one."

Cannon glanced at Baden. "He sent us a high-tech aluminum case, with a handcuff to fasten to your wrist. I told him that it was far too conspicuous."

Baden eyed the familiar suitcase. Behind its worn covering were layers of Kevlar, rubber and insulation over a hardened steel mesh making it practically cutproof, waterproof, and fireproof.

Cannon opened the bag and displayed the contents. Baden pulled his phone out and took pictures.

"What are you doing?" The old man asked.

"He's making a record of the shipment. He'll take pictures when it is delivered and send them to you. Once the transaction is approved, we do not keep them."

You don't keep them, Baden thought.

Cannon closed the interlocking pieces to seal and locked the case with a black steel padlock. It was specified as level three security, the shackle integrated into the body to make it nearly impossible to get bolt cutters around it. Not that they'd have much effect. Maybe an angle grinder and an hour of work could undo it. Maybe.

"We already sent the corresponding key to your recipient overnight." Cannon offered a small silver key to the client.

94

The old man nodded and accepted it with grudging approval.

Baden collected the bag, thinking about an opportunity in Athens. He considered how much Dexedrine he had left; it should keep him awake. He calculated how much he should take now to stay awake but not enough to be reckless or draw attention.

"Have your boy get out and open the gate, let us through, then close it behind." The grey-haired man ordered in a slow lazy drawl.

Thad looked over his shoulder at Grant. His firepower assumption was correct, of course. As soon as he'd settled into the back seat, the newcomer drew a .357 Magnum revolver and set it in his lap. The display was not menacing, but did point out who was running the show. Thad grunted and Tommy got out.

"Where the hell are we?" Thad demanded. It was after two am and they were parked just left of nowhere.

"My place." The older man waved for Thad to drive on.

The moonlight was just enough to reveal an old house collapsed in on itself. They parked the car on a slab of concrete that might have been a patio at one time.

"You live in that wreck? I thought you were going to show us something," Tommy muttered.

"Get out and you'll see something." Grant waved the revolver directing them out of the van and toward the house. "Inside." Grant led them away from the front door to the dilapidated cellar stairs and produced a key fob.

There was a sharp click from the door in response. The older man gestured to Tommy to open the rotted-out cellar door.

Thad watched him strain to get the rotted boards clear to divulge hidden steel.

The trio trudged down into the opening. The old man clicked at another high security door and motioned them in. Once the door closed, the man sauntered to a table and set the Magnum pistol down.

Tommy glared at the utilitarian room. "Nice place."

"It serves." Grant lowered into a chair.

"Okay, Grant. What the hell you going to show us?" Thad tried to wrest control of the conversation.

"You might say I am kind of a hunter."

"What do you hunt?" Tommy asked.

"Things that ain't human."

"Like what?" Thad quipped. "Lions and tigers and bears, oh my?" Grant chuckled.

Thad glanced at his partner. "We haven't got all night."

"Yeah, you do. My guys are keeping an eye on the targets, and doin' a better job than you. Honestly, you boys are so sloppy I don't know how you kept up with them."

"Got a GPS tracker on their car," Thad indulged in a little bit of defensive bragging.

The older man nodded and looked impressed. "Not bad."

"So, you got us out here…"

Grant held up his hands. "All right, seeing is believing." He stood up and holstered his weapon.

He walked to a security door equipped with a heavy deadbolt security lock. He unlocked it and led the men through to a barracks furnished with narrow steel framed bunks and lockers. Grant paused to pick up a cage holding the largest rat Thad ever saw. The creature darted about its cage, impotently trying to flee.

Grant opened another door into a short hallway and paused at a door on the left. He opened his mouth to say something but looked as if he thought better of it. Instead he just said, "Here it is." He turned the wheels that engaged the three security locks.

A light came on as he opened the door, Tommy followed Grant then froze, bewildered.

On the left was a table with a pile of clothes, and personal effects laid out as well as random tools and pieces of wood. But the main attraction was a cage, maybe four-foot square in the center of the room. Inside, a naked woman was shackled on her knees. She was concentration camp thin, her skin cast a grayish pallor. Her long black hair was streaked with white and hung limply in a matted tangle. Her hands were claws with ragged curled nails more than two inches long.

Two welded chains held her hands apart allowing only limited motion. The steel manacles draped limply on her emaciated wrists. Old burn scars covered her right arm, and there were similar marks on her shoulders and lower belly. Her legs were free, but the limited confines of the cage kept her from moving them.

She smelled bad but was relatively clean, no evidence of filth around her. She scowled at the intruders, her face distorted by something hidden in her mouth.

"What have we got here?" Tommy spoke up, his interest piqued. He leered at the prisoner. "She's a bit scrawny, and what has she got in her mouth"

Grant snorted. "Let me show you why you don't want to go anywhere near that mouth." He opened the small rodent cage, seized the rat and tossed it through the bars to the chained woman.

The prisoner snatched it in midair and shook the rat, jerking its legs, twisting one until it broke. The horrified animal convulsed, writhed and thrashed.

"It's not enough for it to kill its prey," Grant explained, his speech thick with disgust. "It has to torture first."

The other two men watched in fascination. The rat squealed, trying to squirm free but the woman held firm, still wrenching the appendages. The rat bit at her fingers and the woman's head flew back with a snarl. The rodent shook in her grip as she opened her mouth.

Tommy gasped and Thad gaped as the parted lips revealed sharp curving fangs. Thad felt sick and shivered as the creature sank those wicked looking fangs into the squirming rat and sucked at the neck, draining the desperate creature. It glared back at them; eyes full of malice. Red gore stained its lips and fangs and dribbled down its chin.

"What the fuck is that?" Thad nearly screamed.

The creature glared at him and licked the rat's lifeblood off its lips. He fought to stop shuddering, he had a queasy feeling the thing wanted him to be afraid.

"Don't that beat all." Tommy smacked his hands together in a slow clap. "Do it again."

"That—" Grant said without expression. "—is an honest to god vampire."

Thad shook his head, trying to make sense of the display. "There ain't no such thing as vampires." His bold words were meant to overcome the sinking feeling in his stomach.

Grant jerked a thumb at the cage where the creature was slowly transforming. Not getting healthy, but a little better filled out. "Tell that to the blood slurping maniac that changes when it feeds and can't tolerate the sunlight."

"All right," Thad mumbled through gritted teeth. "It's real. Where did that thing come from?"

Grant didn't answer immediately and Tommy spoke up. "She's still pretty human on the other end? I see there's a door front and back, and her legs are spread nice."

The two remaining men stared at him, Thad with disgust and Grant with a sick grin.

Tommy shrugged. "Just saying."

"If that's your idea of entertainment." Grant snorted. "Some of my boys had a go at it, but that was back when it could still act human."

Tommy licked his lips.

Thad punched Tommy's arm. He was well acquainted with the fact his associate was one sick fuck, *but whatcha you gonna do*? Good help is hard to find. "This thing lives on rats?" he asked, trying to derail the current topic.

"It lives on blood," Grant said, his voice full of loathing. "Has to be right from the source. A rat every other day keeps it…" he wrinkled his nose. "I wouldn't say alive but keeps it not comatose. We didn't feed the thing for a month once and it just lay there, but as soon as a rat got close enough… damn cockroaches are hard to kill."

"How long have you had it?" Thad asked.

"Not quite five years since we seized the thing. Since then it keeps wasting away while becoming more feral. And that, gentlemen, is what the man you're following is."

"Wait, the pathetic rich twit?" Thad pointed at the cage. "The same as that?"

"Oh yeah, at feeding time. Something your ex will know all about soon."

Thad imagined Jen being torn to pieces and her throat ripped out. It would serve her right, but Thad wanted to be the one to do it, after he did everything else she deserved. "Why don't you kill that thing?"

"Recruiting tool. Seeing—"

"I get it," Thad blurted. "But this dude, you going to kill it? Put a stake through its heart?"

Grant nodded. "And cut off its head."

"And that thing? You gonna see how long it can survive on rats?"

Grant frowned. "We've conducted some experiments. Exposed weaknesses. We're getting down to the final phase, then we are going to vivisect it."

"Viva what?" Tommy asked.

Thad snarled at him. "That's dissecting it while it is alive."

"I knew that," Tommy muttered. "Sounds kinda cool."

Thad tore his eyes away from the cage and walked over to the table. "This is what you use for your experiments?" He picked up a crossbow.

"Yep. The other stuff was what it had when we picked it up. We kept it for research purposes."

Thad frowned at the personal effects. It was just the junk a normal person carries. The dusty pile of cloth was the tattered remains of a black dress. The underwear was more intact but stained with something brown and black. A leather purse lay empty, its contents arranged in order beside it. He picked up an aged, laminated card with the picture of an attractive, but sharp faced woman in her thirties. The card was labeled as an international driver's license. Thad turned the I.D. over in his hands. The thing once had an identity, a name. Magda Kovács.

Chapter Thirteen

It was three a.m. somewhere north of Indianapolis in a location that was practically nowhere. Baden took a swig from his water bottle to ease the dry feeling in his mouth. He felt he'd hit the mark with the stimulant; alert but not shaking. But damn, he didn't remember those things making his mouth so dry. He checked the clock; he was making good time. There was an opportune place coming up to take a short stop and piss out all that water he'd been drinking.

He pulled off I-65 to a truck stop, convenience store and fast food conglomeration. He didn't need gas but topped off the tank anyway, legs tingling with pins and needles as he took a few tentative steps. He moved the vehicle by the store opening and parked. His cargo was sealed in the cage protected by a metal plate wired to the battery that would hit any curious idiot with a 20,000 volt surprise. The steering wheel was similarly rigged. The window-dressing magnets that made it look like the property of some doting parent bragging about his honor roll son were protection via deception. Always look harmless.

He pulled a pair of latex gloves and two zip-lock plastic bags from the glove compartment and shoved them into his pocket. He licked his lips and took another mouthful of water. He checked the vanity mirror. His face was flushed and his pupils dilated, but not enough for people to notice. He eased out of the van and into the store.

There were three people milling about; a grizzled old trucker in jeans with a flannel shirt, a wilted looking mother dealing with a cranky kid screaming for candy, and a black guy picking up an energy drink. He ignored them and walked to the empty men's room. It was large, with ten individual stalls and a twelve-foot-long counter housing six sinks.

Baden donned the rubber gloves as he inspected the row of stalls. At the fourth he found something promising; some slob puked and left vomit splattered on the toilet seat. He took a piece of toilet paper, wiped up some of the stinking mess and stuck it in the plastic bag. He checked to ensure no one was coming before he examined the rest of the stalls. The ninth had a wad of toilet paper clinging to the inside rim.

His ears, hyperalert from the Dexedrine, picked up the sound of an approaching voice. He stepped into the stall with the wad of tissue and closed the door. He waited, listening to the urinal flush, water running, the hand dryer, and then silence. He collected the bit of toilet paper. *DNA was DNA*. Two samples were enough, he wouldn't have to risk digging in the trash although used condoms were prized.

With his full plastic bags tucked into one pocket he inverted the latex gloves surgeon style for disposal later, opened the stall and made for the urinal. Though he had samples, he glanced to see if there was any pubic hair left behind—none. He scrupulously washed his hands, went back to the store for a bottle of water, and was on his way.

Thad Callun woke to the sound Tommy Mercer tossing in the narrow berth next to him, mattress springs creaking at the motion. They both slept fully clothed, covered by military wool blankets that smelled of mothballs on thin pads. Actually, everything in the place stank. There was a greasy petroleum smell from the weapons locker, a musty "old-man'" smell that permeated everything, and some other objectionable stench he couldn't quite identify.

Tommy moved again and this time the springs screeched.

"Would you cut that out?" Thad snapped.

"This bed sucks," Tommy groused in much the same tone. "We'd be better off sleeping in the van."

Thad shook his head. He picked up the phone beside the bed and groaned at the time. A dim red light over the door cast a hellish light on everything, creating weird shadows. Thad blinked as he made his way to the light switch by the door. A handful of LED bulbs produced a stark unforgiving white light.

"Dammit,." Tommy groaned and pulled his blanket over his head.

"May as well get up." Thad snapped; his mood not improved by being upright. "Grant said he'd be back around seven. It's six forty-five."

Tommy groaned again.

The door opened and Grant strode in. "You're up already, good." He nodded at Thad and gave a side eye to Tommy. "After we eat the sun should be up, that thing will be, well… not asleep, but inactive during daylight hours. Unless you expose it to the daylight and then it flops around making wild shrieking noises."

"I thought sunlight would turn it to ash, like in the movies," Thad interjected.

Grant grinned. "Yeah. A minute of morning sun damn near killed it, but by midday it just smokes and shrieks. Used to be we could set it out for, oh, five, ten minutes before it got all red and started smoking. Now the damned thing starts wailing and squirming before you can see the burns. We'll get into its other…vulnerabilities, after we eat."

The meal consisted of pouches of scrambled eggs, freeze dried fruit with the consistency of Styrofoam, and dehydrated sausage that Grant ate without following the instructions to soak it in hot water. The pork patty made an annoying snapping sound when he chomped on it. "Hope you boys are good at holdin' yer food down. Let's go."

"Wait a minute," Thad said. "I don't like being held prisoner."

"Wadda you mean?" Grant cocked his head.

"I mean, how do we get out of here? And what exactly is this place?"

"Well let's give you boys the nickel tour." Grant stood. "The front doors are electromagnetic, the other three are mechanical."

Grant led them through the rooms and pointed out how things operated. Soon, the trio was back in the cage with the listless vampire and Grant rolled in a wooden box.

"Daytime, they get like that, but it'll come around when we start. Gonna give you a short primer on how to kill a bloodsucker." He procured a set of safety glasses from the container and donned a pair of heavy rubber gloves. Next, he pulled a wooden cross from the box. He eased around to the back of the cage, reached through the bars and pressed the religious symbol against the thing's haunch. Nothing happened.

"Yeah, crosses don't work." He moved back to the box and took out a glass bottle with a silver cross fixed to its flat surface and a stopper in the form of an angel. "Holy water doesn't work either, unless you use this kind." He opened the flask and flicked the contents at the vamp's currently uninjured arm. Where the liquid touched the skin it bubbled and fizzed. The creature writhed and reared as it hissed.

"What is that shit, the pope's piss?" Tommy asked.

"Sulphuric acid. You better have gloves and glasses if you throw it. We pack it in holy water bottles so the demons think it won't hurt them. The first time we brought it out that damned thing just gave us an arrogant look. You should have seen its face as the acid hit. Took a year for it to fully heal."

Thad grimaced as he caught a whiff of the caustic rotten-egg smell. That was the source of the stink he couldn't identify.

"Bullets," Grant said as he pulled out a .22 revolver, no bigger that a starter pistol. "Something weird about this thing." He stepped close to the cage and raised the weapon.

"You're not going to shoot that in here." Thad knew enough about firearm safety that he winced at the idea of gunshot in the small concrete room.

"Stick your fingers in your ears, if you like." Grant put a bullet through the fleshiest part of the creature's skeletal thigh.

The bullet dug itself into a cinder block wall behind. There was no blood, just a brownish mark where the round punched through. The creature writhed in pain for moment then settled back down. Thad noticed the pock marks from previous impacts.

"Bullet wounds shut themselves right up." He put the pistol back in the box. "If you want to ruin this thing's whole day you will get satisfaction using these." He produced a dagger made of silver, a heavy mallet and a wooden stake.

Jenny blinked in the dark room. The main window faced east but the blackout curtains revealed only a faint reddish glow at the edges. Her first night at her employer's house. She protested at the invitation but Marq pointed out it was late and the only thing she would accomplish would be to disturb her roommate. So, Jenny hauled her suitcase up the stairs to the room next to Marq's. She pulled out her sweatpants and long t-shirt. The bed was amazingly comfortable.

She flipped on the bedside light and checked the time on her phone. She felt a pang of guilt. The last time she slept to almost noon was right after she moved to Kentucky. She sighed and sat up. She might as well take the time to properly bathe. As the shower steam rose, Jenny thought about the sophisticated shower in Marq's room. Another time.

Clean, but still in yesterday's clothes she made her way downstairs to the kitchen.

Marq sat at the table holding one of the confidential files, a huge cup of coffee and a plate of danishes before her as well as four pictures. She sat engrossed, reading the file and ignored Jenny's entrance.

Jenny got coffee and sat eying the pastries.

"Help yourself." Marq said without looking up.

So she did notice me. Jenny snatched a lemon danish. She studied the dark-skinned woman, alarmed at the determination Marq was pouring into the documents. "Which file is that?" Jenny asked around a mouthful of pastry.

"Kitty Greene."

"The pictures?" Jenny turned one around to see it clearly.

"Surveillance photos. Kitty talked to at least four men at the mall. Only two have been identified and questioned."

There was clear picture of Kitty, leaning over a massage chair and talking to a man, but the photo only showed the back of his head.

Jenny shook her head. "Why does this one bother you so much?"

Marq took a deep breath, raised her head, and pinched the bridge of her nose. She let out a breath and maneuvered her head to get the cricks out of her neck. "Do you think we're friends?"

Jenny winced at Marq's expression. "I hope we are becoming friends. Are you telling me to just be an employee?"

Marq looked taken aback. "That's not what I meant." She shook her head. "I mean, I like you, but you don't know anything about me, whereas I know everything about you. Everything in the public record, plus my observations and special sense."

It was Jenny's turn to be taken aback by the way Marq said "everything."

"Well…" Jenny drew out the word to gather her thoughts. "You've been good to me and I like you."

"But you don't know me. Remember what I told you about my parents?"

"Your mother was Thai and she moved to America and worked in a sweatshop. Your father was a soldier."

Marq nodded. "That is the beginning and the end. There is a lot of convoluted crap in the middle."

Jenny finished the pastry and picked up her coffee. "You want to tell me?"

"No." Another deep breath. "There are old wounds I do not want to pick at. But if we are going to be friends, honest friends, I should tell you. Also, while I am striving to be honest there are some things I can't tell you because it is not my place."

"About Mr. Stefanov?"

"Christopher. Yes, and others." Marq gathered her thoughts. "In Thailand my mother worked in what is euphemistically called a massage parlor." She looked at Jenny.

Jenny blinked. "Oh."

"To put a fine point on it, my mother was a prostitute." Her voice held no condemnation. "She started a relationship with one of her regulars. She got careless and I was conceived." Marq paused and shrugged.

Jenny still did not know what to say.

"Her lover was already married. I don't know if he was a good man, but my mother thought he was. He tried to do right by us. Bought her from the parlor manager and got her to the United States. He sent money each month. I was born in New York City and shortly after that, he died. There was no will, no provision made for us. Mother could have sued for support, but that would expose her to the courts, and she was terrified of that."

"I can relate. So, what did she do? Is that when she went to work in the sweatshop?"

"No. At that time she did the same thing she did in Thailand, worked in a massage parlor."

"That must have been awful."

Marq shook her head. "No. At least as far as I knew. She told me how much better it was here than where she worked in Bangkok. She only stayed out late four nights a week, never past two a.m. The rest of her time she spent with me. She was happy and we were together. She was determined that I get an education. I didn't understand at that time exactly how she made her money, but she made enough to live on and have an occasional indulgence." Marq relaxed into a smile at some distant memory. "She did that until I was fourteen, and everything changed."

"What happened?"

Marq frowned at a memory, the most vulnerable expression Jenny had seen from Marq, then she shrugged. "She got older. She didn't look that old but fewer clients requested her. Then the police came."

"They arrested her?"

"No, she wasn't working at the time, but the place was closed down." Marq sighed. "Raids happened before, occasionally. They were an, occupational risk. Mother considered it a vacation. She expected that in a few days her employers would send her to another location, but that didn't happen."

Jenny opened her mouth to say something, but couldn't formulate a thought, *sometimes you shouldn't speak.*

"A Korean woman came to our house. Mother told me to stay in my room. Apparently, the woman knew about me and demanded to see me." Marq sneered. "That was the first time in my life I felt less than human. That bitch inspected me like a horse, even checked my teeth. I should have bitten her. Mother objected when this woman ordered me to undress and they argued something fierce, both of them so angry they started yelling in their respective languages, which of course the other one didn't understand." Marq gave a cold, humorless chuckle at that part of her memory. "Finally, the woman said, 'she looks younger, we can sell her virginity at least three or four times. You are a virgin?'" Marq made a growling sound. "I knew what my mother did but hadn't really grasped the details and I didn't know how to answer. They fought on. The woman swore that my mother would not be able to work again, unless she brought me. She stormed out saying that others would come calling, and they wouldn't be as nice."

Marq drummed her fingers on the table. "We left most of our things behind. Mom kept a hoard of cash and that got us set up in Chicago and then she tried to get a 'massage' job but that Korean woman had a long reach. So, mother found an 'honest' job as a sewing contractor doing piece work, paid only for each item she finished. No steady pay, no benefits. She worked hard twelve to fourteen hours a day. She was never happy and had no energy to spend with me. Funny," Marq took in a deep breath, "how if a woman is a sex worker—she is 'selling her body' but if she ruins her fingers and her health making an 'honest living,' that is moral and righteous."

"Hypocrisy." Jenny scratched her ear. "I never would have thought you had those kind of experiences. You seem so happy all the time, always smiling."

Marq arched her eyebrows, then smiled. "You mean like this?"

Jenny regarded the familiar expression, cheerful, bright and just a bit aloof. "Yes."

"That's the one I taught myself. This is the one my mother taught me." Her expression changed slightly but it made her appear more affable, friendlier. "My mother taught me to smile because pain, grief, and disappointments were far too personal, displaying those emotions make a woman far too vulnerable." Marq's expression changed into a tight wan smile. "There a few others. If we are going to be friends, I have to let you see what is behind the mask."

Marq took in a deep breath. "So, it's not just Kitty cut up and tossed like garbage, it could have been me, or my mother. These others…" She waved at the rest of the folders. "They deserve justice, but they had a good life. Friends and family. This girl, her life was a catastrophe. She deserves justice for her murder, but also for her life."

"That sounds ominous."

"It is."

"What are you going to do?"

"I'm gonna make sure the killings stop. Then, there are a few other names that need attention, Sonny Marne for instance." Marq drew a deep breath and relaxed her shoulders.

Jenny had not realized how tense her own shoulders were.

"So," Marq fixed her with a hard stare. "Still want to be my friend?"

Jenny wanted to hug the other woman but didn't because of the look in those dark eyes. Instead, she touched Marq's hand. "Yes." She let go and grabbed at a file. "Let's get this bastard."

Marq lips twisted in a sardonic smile and said with quiet irony. "Go team!"

Chapter Fourteen

Baden easily met his noon deadline and ensured payment was wired to his account before finding a cheap motel to get some sleep.

When he finally laid down, slumber eluded him—the dose had been too high after all. After four dreary hours of watching television, he finally broke down and decided to use the diazepam.

He did not wake up until Sunday afternoon. His mouth was so dry his tongue stuck to the roof of his mouth. Both felt rough, as if he'd been licking desert sand.

He dragged himself out to a soda machine and guzzled a can in one go. It seemed his girls all woke up drooling after he gave them the sedative and he envied them.

"Fuck it," he said and dragged more money out of his wallet and bought another soda to take back to his room and drink slowly.

He still felt groggy and Sunday afternoon was not the best time for his next move. He sat down on the bed and watched some more TV. He was asleep within the hour and a national geographic special played on.

Bright and early Monday morning he put on a pair of khaki slacks and a dark brown polo shirt and made for a leisurely drive to his favorite neighborhood in Athens, Alabama.

After an hour on the road he pulled off the highway to a busy truck stop for fuel. Too busy for collection. He drove to a secluded side lot and parked close to a gated area where the smell let him know the dumpsters were ready for pick up. He opened the rear passenger door, lifted the back seat and pulled out a locked metal box. It actually had two locks, one with a key and one a combination. Inside, he flipped through a pile of license plates and settled on a local one he'd stolen from a nearby outlet mall on his last visit.

Fricken Georgia peach. Chattahoochee County. He scowled at it.

Stealing plates took time, but it was worth it. He could usually find a red van and that was the plate he kept. Then he stole another to replace it and then switched three more, sort of an automobile musical chairs. The car left without a plate did not match the plate he was going to use. At least twice he'd heard an Amber Alert based on one of his stolen tags.

A swift twist from the tool on his keychain and the quick release screws gave way. The new plate was in place in less than thirty seconds. Then, from the back he pulled out two large magnetic signs that advertised the van as belonging to a dog groomer.

Another half hour found him just north of Athens proper. East of I-65 was the tiny development with the unlikely name of Herawoode. Actually, wood was in short supply since the land was cleared in 2007 and construction began just before the collapse of the housing market in 2008. Real estate speculators erratically changed investments and canceled projects, leaving empty lots. A new contactor set out to build more affordable starter homes, not the McMansions originally planned. Homes where husband and wife had to work to keep financially afloat. No retirees and few school children meant that the tangle of streets with its contrived cul-de-sacs was virtually deserted during the day.

He visited there over a dozen times and only saw someone close enough to greet once. His target was a small brick, ranch style residence with a fenced in back yard.

He parked the van about two houses down from his goal. He walked in measured pace around the house to the chain-link gate at the back. A chubby beagle going grey around the muzzle waddled up to him, his tail wagging.

"Hey Buddy, how you been?" Baden offered the canine peanut butter flavored doggy treats, and just like on his last two visits the dog greedily sucked them down. The beagle looked up with sad eyes and licked its chops silently, begging for more.

Baden waved an electronic wand over the animal. The owner hadn't chipped the beast since his last visit. Good. The only identification was on his collar, the tag simply reading "Buddy."

He opened the unlocked gate, picked up the friendly dog and tucked it safely in the van, confident no one noticed him in the empty streets.

North on I-65 he didn't stop until he reached Indiana where he changed his license plate again to one local to his destination.

Jenny knocked on the door with subdued raps.

"Come on in." Marq's sighed words carried through the door.

Jenny entered her friend's bedroom. Marq sat at her narrow desk, hands on a wireless keyboard and her eyes fixed on several PDF's displayed across the twin thirty-inch monitors. The computer was a shiny black cylinder bearing an apple logo. Jenny got the feeling you couldn't purchase this sleek model at the local mall.

Marq sighed again, pulled her fingers from the keyboard and leaned back in her chair, head lolling back in an effort to ease her neck. "Yes?"

Jenny noticed the piles of spiral bound notebooks scattered across the desk. "Lunch?"

Marq shook her head. "Later," she said through pinched lips. Her tone was indeterminate, listless and her face was a grayish color, deep shadows encased her eyes.

"No," Jenny replied firmly. "You barely ate anything yesterday. Did you even eat breakfast before I got here?"

Marq nodded. "Some eggs, some cheese."

"And?"

Marq shrugged.

"What about that super metabolism of yours? You look like you haven't eaten in a week."

Marq showed her teeth in an awkward grimace. "I've been busy."

"I see, and if you want to keep going, you are going to need your strength." Jenny stepped closer to look at the images on the screens. "What's got you so absorbed?"

Marq took her fingers and wiped the inside corners of her eyes. "Turns out we didn't get the full FBI report, just the part they shared with the local police. An infuriatingly vague profile—I'm sure they know more—and a few notes. One statement says they are certain that the first identified victim wasn't his first victim. His methodology was too precise, his actions confident like he'd done this before. I don't have access to the FBI databases, but I've been searching newspaper accounts all across the country for similar killings." Marq scowled at the screen. "In every damn TV show, the hero has a super hacker who can get the necessary information." She paused. "Don't suppose you know anyone?"

Jenny blinked, and for lack of any relevant reply, said, "Come on. I made you three sandwiches and cottage fried potatoes."

Marq wavered.

"I also bought some chocolate glazed croissants." That didn't have the reaction she hoped for. "Look, come eat and you can catch me up on what you are doing."

Marq slumped in her chair, then stood unsteadily and straightened her back.

"How long have you been sitting there?" Jenny chided.

That earned a side-eye from the dark woman.

Marq started by picking at her food, but was soon shoveling in the calories, making short work of the sandwiches, potatoes, and three of the croissants.

Jenny watched Marq eat until she came up for air. "So, what have you found?"

Marq eyed the remaining croissants. Jenny snagged one and moved it to her own plate.

"His first known victim was found four years ago, and his subsequent killings were about a year apart but he's shorted that time, I concentrated my search in the five-year period before that."

"Find anything?"

Marq looked disgusted. "Too much. There are some sick people out there. I concentrated on newspaper articles, sorting for unsolved murder cases of young girls where the body was bathed in bleach, or tied into a fetal position." An awkward silence fell over the room as Marq's gaze rested on the last croissant.

Jenny grinned, "Marq, I bought them for you. Eat it. That's my job, isn't it? Keep this house and everything in it in top working order?"

Marq took the last croissant and ate it in a more controlled manner. "Found about a hundred that resembles our killer in some nascent phase. I also looked into cases where the victim was never found. There are too many of those. He prefers blondes, so I sorted for that, which narrowed the list down. Then I included violent unsolved sexual assaults where the victim lived."

"Let me guess, hundreds of those, too?"

"Yeah, but I am reviewing what was released about each case again."

"Again?"

"Finished my first assessment and… I told you that I sense things about people?"

Jenny frowned, "Like a psychic or something?"

"Uh, no," Marq snorted, sounding more like her normal self. "But I've lived through some odd experiences and dealt with some shitty people. I dwell on details and my subconscious often pulls me into recognizing patterns. I need to talk to Christopher when he gets, uh, home. His issues make him super good at pattern recognition."

"So how many of the cases twinged your subconscious?"

"Three. But I need for Christopher to look at them. There is a case that I think might have been his first attack. The victim lived. She was assaulted, tortured with something like pliers, then beaten. The assailant probably thought she was dead and he doused her with bleach before dumping her by a public street. That was seven years ago."

"Near I-65?"

"No, in New Jersey."

Jenny moved her mouth in a negative response. "Seems similar, but only in a vague way."

"True enough. The next case is so unrelated I do not know why I'm so fixated on it. That crime occurred ten years ago in Okinawa, Japan. The victim was a twelve-year-old local girl. She was assaulted, killed, bleached and bound with nylon cord. An American sailor was accused, and he seems to have been exonerated. His Facebook page says he lives in Oregon, but I don't have access to any more salient information. Two years after that, a blonde girl, 16, was kidnapped and missing for several weeks before her body showed up, bleached and bound in a fetal position. I think the FBI is paying attention to that one."

"Where was that?"

Marq took in a deep breath. "San Diego, California."

"I think you are stretching the pattern."

"Me too. But a year and half after that, the police found our man's first victim in butcher-paper."

Baden made far better time than he expected driving from Athens, and he reached Noblesville, Indiana too early. Instead of savoring his opening moves, he was eager to get into the heart of the game. It was only eight days since the mall rat whore and every bit of reason told him to lay low. But he couldn't. That bitch polluted him, left a bad taste in his mouth. He *needed* to set things right, get back in the groove. He drove idly around for an hour.

It was a cold overcast evening, just past dark. He cruised by his target. The "open" sign was on, and he saw his new girl through the glass doors, illuminated by the clinic lights. She had a smile that would look beautiful as he physically wiped it right off her face. He checked the time; six forty-five. He was confident in the twilight hours no one inside saw him make his first pass, checking out the parking spaces right by the door.

The animal clinic stayed open to eight when her mother, the veterinarian, would take her home.

This was going to be his most dangerous abduction. There was no question he'd be seen, noticed. He just had to ensure they noticed the wrong things.

He steered away from town. The thing he loved about Indiana was that you could drive a few minutes in any direction and find yourself in a cornfield. Baden found a remote spot and pulled over.

He stepped out of the van and took a baseball bat from the rear seat. Opening the rear hatchback, he fed the beagle a treat and opened the cage. The dog jumped out of the van and landed with a thump, wagging his tail. Baden fed him another treat as he secured a cord to the dog's collar. Once the animal couldn't flee, Baden looked around, then hit the dog squarely on the head with the bat. The dog yelped and tried to bolt, choking itself on the secured collar. His body twisted from momentum, his head snapped back and Buddy collapsed in the dirt.

Damn dog better not be dead. Baden thought just as the dog whimpered and tried to move.

Baden hit the dog three more times. The bat landed with solid, meaty thuds, eliciting a keening wail until the dog lay motionless and whimpering. Baden stood back to admire his handiwork, more satisfying that he thought it would be.

He scooped up the dog and Buddy made a weak attempt to snap at him. In the back of the van he set the panting dog down, removed the collar and wedged it in the bars at the far end of the cage. He rubbed his hands in the dirt beside the road, then regained the driver's seat.

He'd been growing his beard for this and he used white makeup to turn it a dull grey, aging him about fifteen years. A kit from his glove compartment produced a tiny brush and spirit gum and he applied it to the side of his nose, then stuck on a very convincing wart.

Now for the *pièce de résistance*. He reached into his mouth and removed the lower right partial plate where he'd lost four teeth in the barfight that got him thrown out of the navy. This gave his face an asymmetrical appearance. He then detached the front partial plate depriving him of three front teeth lost in the same fight. It might have cost him his naval career but at least that judgmental bastard got what was coming to him.

He pulled a dirty farmer's cap from the glove compartment and pulled it low over his eyes, then donned a pair of leather palm canvas work gloves. He smiled at himself in the driver's vanity mirror and drove back to the animal clinic. He pulled into the empty parking space near the door, but in the shadows away from the clinic's light. As he stopped, he rubbed a slice of onion over each eye and uncontrolled tears streamed down his face. He blinked against the tears. He should have practiced this, it fucking hurt and he could hardly see. He fumbled in the glove compartment for eyedrops and did his best to flush away the burn. It took a few seconds for him to see again. He ran to the back and frantically scooped up the dog before shoving open the glass doors and running through them.

Chapter Fifteen

Marq stood in the dimly lit room staring at the time on her phone, unconsciously tapping her foot on the ground. She gave up on patience, walked up to the sturdy black box and knocked on the lid. Hard.

There was no reply. She knocked harder.

"Okay, okay," an aggravated voice replied.

She gave three more impatient raps.

The lid opened silently, the side dropping away; the quiet automatic motion creating an eerie supernatural effect in the gloom. Christopher swung his legs around. He wasn't fully dressed, wearing just a pair of black silk boxer shorts. This time he careful to conserve the dirt.

Marq cocked an eyebrow. He had a certain glow, almost healthy looking.

"Yes?" Christopher demanded.

"You're way past sunset."

"Your point?"

Something stirred in the box. Marq did not have the night vison of her boss but quickly detected a human form stretched out on the far side. There was only one person who Christopher ever shared his box with. Lilith was not a vampire, nor would she ever have the opportunity but she was Christopher's most devoted lover.

"Good effening, Marquessa." Lilith chuckled as she affected a Dracula impression; she was a big fan of Bela Lugosi. She slipped further out and sat up. Unlike Christopher she was naked, wrapped in a printed cotton sheet, the bright floral pattern a stark contrast to the shadowy box.

"Didn't know you were in town." Marq smiled.

The fifty-three year old woman tied the corners of the sheet at the back of her neck to become a sarong. She sat next to Christopher. "Wasn't planning to come to town, but…" She put her arm across Christopher's shoulder and gave a sideways hug. "I got lonely."

Marq nodded in agreement, momentarily reveling in sharp memories of her experiences with the vampire. "Maybe you should move up to Louisville? We'd both enjoy your company."

"No, though tempting, the great-grand-kiddos are more appealing than this one. They need me." She stood up, the thin sheet revealing her mature shape. Her breasts were perky due to a very talented surgeon, but the rest of her taut body and gravity defying back side was the result of an impressive yoga regimen. She smelled of expensive perfume and sex.

"Did you have something important to say?" Christopher was trying to not sound annoyed.

Marq shrugged. "I would not have bothered you if I knew you were entertaining. Leiter would like you to call him. He sent a phone number in an email."

Christopher clenched his eyes tight, a pained expression momentarily taking command of his face. "What does he want now? If I keep up this relationship I will have to change my Facebook status to 'complicated.'"

Marq blinked. "Since when do you have a Facebook page?"

Christopher opened wide innocent eyes at Marq.

"Oh. Sarcasm," Marq acknowledged. "You haven't made the effort in so long I thought you forgot how." She brandished a generic prepaid cell phone.

Christopher stood and took it from her.

"It's the only contact. Just make the call."

Christopher frowned his resignation and touched the screen. His call was answered on the first ring.

"Christophe?" Bobby Leiter's anxious voice sounded from the handset.

Christopher switched it to speaker phone. "What can I do for you?"

His tone of repressed irritation sounded like a parent appeasing a spoiled child.

"I have a lead on some information." The preacher sounded excited but there was something else in the tone.

"Go on."

"You know those militia men I used to work with?"

"Intimately."

"Sorry." Leiter sounded sincere. "Of course you would remember. One of the guys who left soon after our…eh…" His voice trailed off into an apprehensive silence.

Christopher let that silence hang for a beat. "After you tried to kill me?"

Leiter ignored the remark. "I was asking people who might know anything about knife makers. Did you know Jasper?"

Christopher shook his head.

"he can't see you," Marq hissed.

"Jasper told me about someone who knows just about every custom bladesmith and blacksmith in the region. Show him a piece of blade and he'll have a good idea where it likely came from."

"Has he talked to the FBI?" Christopher did not sound interested.

"No, he hasn't." Leiter exhaled and took an awkward breath. "There are difficulties. This guy, Beauregard Morgan, he lives off the grid. Doesn't trust governmental and considers himself a 'sovereign' citizen."

"What does that mean?" Christopher snapped.

Marq spoke up. "He doesn't pay taxes and thinks the law doesn't apply to him."

"Great, an outlaw," Christopher sighed. Marq knew he meant the 19th century definition, and was not at all sympathetic.

"Beauregard?"

"They just call him Bo."

"Where is he at?" Christopher continued. "I'll send Marq to talk to him."

"See," Leiter sounded disconcerted. "He has agreed to talk to you, but there is no way he will talk to Miss Koenig, or King right?"

"King will do," Marq replied sharply.

"Sorry, Miss King. This guy is sort of a white supremacist. He won't give any information to a mixed-race person."

"Sounds like a real sweetheart," Marq mumbled.

"Does he know about me?" Christopher asked.

"No, I don't think he knows anything about vampires, but he believes in Bigfoot and UFOs."

Christopher rolled his eyes. "Where is he?" he repeated.

"Outside of Palmyra, Tennessee. He has some land there—although I don't know if he owns it or is squatting. Has a cabin and a workshop."

"This sounds better and better." Marq muttered.

Christopher waved her quiet. "Send me directions by email. How do I contact him?"

"No easy way," Leiter said, drawing out the words as if searching for the most discreet way to comment. "He is expecting you, so you can drive to his place. Slowly."

"Send the directions." Christopher disconnected the call.

"Marquessa dear?" Lilith said. "May I use your shower to clean up? Have to get back home."

"Absolutely."

Lilith nodded at Christopher. "Want to wash my back?"

"Another time."

Lilith arched a playful eyebrow at Marquessa who replied with an accommodating smile and a concise shake of her head. Lilith waved as she left the room.

"Miss Torres?" Christopher demanded.

"Gone for the day."

Christopher scratched at the back of his head. "Call her up, see if she is disposed for a quick trip. We'll go to Palmyra tonight and get a hotel. Go see this 'sovereign citizen' tomorrow evening."

Baden could barely see the young woman leap to her feet as he lugged the squealing animal into the clinic. He imagined her all cute in her short veterinary smock with the "No-Kill Shelters Only" button. He's memorized every inch of her from the proud photos her mother posted online. Mostly in reference to her work with animal charities.

"Oh god, you got t' hep me," he bellowed, the words almost incomprehensible without his front teeth but the girl got the gist of what he was saying.

"Mom?" she yelled, her voice urgent but with an affected calm. "We have an emergency."

A petite blonde woman in her thirties wearing a white lab coat over blue scrubs burst out of the next room. She took one look at the situation and grabbed a wheeled tray table. "Put 'im here."

Baden complied, unable to talk as his body shook with unrestricted sobs.

The dog whined and made an effort to bite Baden.

"Dere was dees boys beatin' 'im." He choked up. "He's been wit me forever."

"We will do what we can. Tracey? Get a history." The veterinarian wheeled the tray into the back room.

Baden collapsed into a chair and buried his face in his hands, shoulders shaking, as he took control; the very picture of a brave man overcome by emotion willing himself calm.

The girl took a clipboard from the front desk and approached him, reluctant to intrude in the apparent grief. "Sir? I need some information. Name? Other conditions? Age?"

Baden nodded and acted as if forcing himself to breathe normally. The tears were still flowing. *Too damn much onion*, he thought. "Name's Buddy. He's fourteen. He got one o' dem things…"

"Chip?" the girl asked

"No." He made a vague gesture plugging something in. "One o'dem things ya plug in."

"Like to a computer, a USB?"

Baden nodded. "In his collar." He pushed against the armrests of the chair, his wobbly legs making it difficult to rise. "I go get it."

"Oh, it's not on the dog?"

"Took it off, he were chokin,'"

"Where is it?"

"Van, by de door."

"Is it unlocked?" Her tone sounded like she very much wanted to help.

Baden nodded.

"I'll get it, you just sit here, okay?"

Baden sank back into the chair, his shoulders slumped. "T'ank you. It's in the back, dog crate."

119

"Would you like me to lock it for you?"

Baden shook his head as if were too distracted by the injured animal to think about his van.

"Just a minute." The girl scampered to the door.

Oh Tracey, that was too easy. Baden counted to ten and followed, drawing the stun gun from his pocket.

The girl already had the back end open and was on tiptoe as her stomach rested on the floor of the built-in cage, reaching for the collar. It was purposely wedged tight, and she would have to pull hard.

The struggle made her short white smock and long-sleeve fitted t-shirt ride up from her jeans to display a strip of white flesh.

Tracey tried to scream at the sudden pain, but he kept on zapping her. The crackling weapon raised burned welts on her lower back over her kidneys. She managed to curl up for protection, in agony and whimpering.

He liked the way she whined.

"You stay quiet or I will kill you." He slammed the back door.

It would take half an hour for the Amber alert to go out, by then he'd be well out of town. He'd planned a route were there was no chance for the police to stop him. He drove away at a moderate pace.

He was on I-65 North for just a bit and pulled off at an exit where he knew a deserted gas station lay. He turned his lights off at the base of the exit, relying on his memory to take him the rest of the way to the small abandoned building. The underground tank was gone and only a collage of broken signage and shattered windows remained. He steered into the lot behind the derelict building and rolled down the front windows before he killed the engine. His ears heard nothing, the cold night air almost devoid of any sound, even the traffic on the highway was nothing more than a muted rumble. The moon was in its last quarter phase and would not rise for hours. The only light was the stars, bright so far away from the city and sharp in the chill air.

He flicked the wart out the window.

There was a shifting in the back.

He took a minute to put in his partial plates, grinding his teeth to ensure they were fully settled. The shifting increased, his new girl testing her limits.

"You are going to want to remain very still, or die in pain you cannot imagine." He didn't bother to turn around and look. "Then I will go to that cute mother of yours and beat her worse than the stupid dog." He snorted. "Oh, I'll leave her alive. She'll just wish I killed her."

Tracey sobbed and there was a gulping sound as she tried to suppress the noise. The girls he chose reacted better to threats to their about family.

Baden opened the door of the van and stepped out into the cold, his breath barely visible in the starlit cold. He pulled a bib from a lobster restaurant and a box from under the driver's seat. He donned the bib and opened the box revealing an electric beard trimmer and razor. His whiskers were clipped to nothing in seconds. He took more time with the electric razor, being careful and to use his fingers to probe for stubble to get as even a shave as possible in the dark. The last bit was shorn, revealing the cleft chin that was his most recognizable feature. He brushed off the bib and put it back.

He took an apparently sealed soft drink bottle to the back of the van, opened the door, smiling at the repressed whimpering noise that echoed the uproar from the dog.

"This is sealed bottle of soda. It's going to be a long trip." He tossed it in and stared at the girl. Under her smock she had on a long sleeve t-shirt and jeans; modest jeans without the fashionable distress slashes. He bent over and tugged at her white smock as she tried to squirm away. He pulled off the "No kill Shelters Only" pin and threw it over his shoulder.

He took a minute to secure the cage and slammed the hatchback into place. The girl would not taste the rohypnol and the drug should ensure she stayed quiet. His source only had the new formula that turned blue when dissolved, but she would not detect the tampered bottle in the dark. Once they were further away, he'd use the diazepam, or if he needed her out for a while the horse drug Xyazine.

He changed the license again, tossing the last plate into the brush collecting in the vacant space and removing his gloves.

His new girl should sleep soundly until she woke up in her new reality.

Chapter Sixteen

Jenny sat in the chrome and faux leather chair and worked in her sketch book. Her pencil flew across the sheet in a marvel of controlled inspiration. She couldn't recall the last time she felt so engrossed in her work. *True inspiration is rare but exhilarating.*

She'd started with a small sketch of her new boss, but he was not the subject. As she worked his form gave way to the forest around him. Now his figure served only to give perspective to the trees… and the wolf. She smeared her forefinger over some lines along the animal's side to create a grey sheen over the wolf's fur.

She did not realize the sun had set until Marq returned. The dark woman entered with a bright smile. "We need—"

Jenny held up an imposing finger to hush her. She wanted to hold onto this creative surge for just a moment more. A few more fine lines made the texture of the wolf's pelt pop out of the page. Jenny sighed and sat down the pencil. "Time to see our subject?" Earlier she referred to the man as a Nazi, which earned a cold glare from Christopher.

"Yes, Christopher is already at the car."

"You driving?"

Marq shrugged. "He insists. Right now, he only trusts me and Lilith behind the wheel. I am sure he will eventually include you. Right now,

I've got a strip map with directions. I need you to navigate; this place is not on google. Come on."

"Strip map?"

"Courtesy of Jasper. Directions to get you there, but no information about where 'there' is."

Christopher waited in the parking lot, dressed in a wool jacket over a cable knit sweater. His dark hair waved in the breeze and he didn't even bother to put his hands in his pockets.

Jenny shivered in the cold and wondered how Christopher could be so resistant to the temperature. There was something else that bugged her, but she couldn't put her finger on it. As she dropped into the passenger seat, she realized what it was.

"Excuse me, uh, Christopher? Sir? Are you breathing okay? I noticed your breath doesn't fog like me and Marq." The rational part of her brain dismissed it with ten explanations for the difference before she finished the question.

"Shallow breathing is a side effect of my condition." He explained. "My body temperature is a bit low and the blood circulates cooler, so I take smaller, colder breaths. That was an astute observation, Jennifer." Christopher gave a quick side glance and Marq. "I also tolerate the cold weather better."

Jenny frowned. She thought cold blooded animals needed external heat more, not less.

"Jenny, when do we turn? Is it here?" Marq interrupted.

Jenny squinted at the hand drawn map. "The next turn is two miles up."

The trip was longer than expected. The distance was not great, but the directions led them down rutted roads that barely earned the name 'road'. The women passed the time discussing top forty radio and Jenny admitted to crushing on a boy band as a teenager.

"The entire band?" Marq inquired.

"Couldn't make up my mind." Jenny regarded the barely adequate map. "It looks like you take the next left."

The cabin sat in a clutch of trees built on the side of a knoll, low enough so the roof was deep in the shadow of the hill crest.

Keeping to directions, Marq eased forward slowly. There were no visible lights; the only sign of life was a slender trail of smoke rising from the chimney.

Bright, stark sodium light bathed the car in a yellow-tinged luminosity brighter than the sun. Marq hit the brakes, momentarily blinded.

Jenny gasped and heard Christopher leap out of the back seat, letting the chill air into the warm car. He held his hand up against the beam to shade his eyes, clearly not liking it. "I believe we are expected?" he shouted. "Bo Morgan?"

There was a disquieting pause, then a strong voice with a thick rural southern accent called back. "Who sent you?"

"Reverend Bobby Leiter."

The voice did not respond.

Christopher continued. "But we were referred to you by Jasper Coyle."

Another pause. "How is Jasper?"

"I don't know," Christopher admitted. "Didn't talk to him, he passed us the information through Leiter."

There was a drawn-out pause. "Yeah, I'm Bo Morgan."

The sodium light switched off, replaced by incandescent flood lamps. Jenny blinked, trying to adjust her eyes.

Christopher lowered his hand.

A man stepped from the shadows, casually wielding a shotgun. He sized them up and seemed assured enough to lower the weapon. His face was weathered and unkempt hair fell out of a cap bearing a Gadsden flag patch on the front. He looked hard as he walked toward them with stiff measured steps; relaxed but also ready to bring the weapon to bear. He looked at the car as if it offended him. "Who's the colored woman?"

"My driver," Christopher answered as he waved Jenny out of the vehicle.

The man looked dubious. "I don't cotton to havin' no negro mongrel here on my land, negro lovers are bad enough. She stays in the car."

Jenny figured he had to work to avoid using another word that started with "N."

The man jerked his chin toward Jenny. "And that one?"

Christopher's voice suddenly sounded imperious. "Do you expect me to take my own notes?" He tinged the words with confident, natural arrogance.

The man snorted. "Didn't expect you to take notes at all. Your helpers, do they know their place?"

Christopher gave the women a dismissive wave and continued his condescending tone. "My servants always know their place."

Jenny bristled at being called a servant but decided to play along. She bowed her head submissively, but they were definitely going to have a human resources meeting regarding this later.

Now the man chuckled. "Come on up. I'll make some coffee."

Jenny followed her boss to the cabin door. Christopher halted at the open door and glared at the disorderly room beyond.

Morgan turned back. "Well, come on in, we're letting the heat out. It's cluttered, but its clean."

Christopher seemed comforted by the assertion and strode in. Jenny was dubious but followed.

The sparsely furnished room was littered with hunting equipment, outdoor magazines and reams of xeroxed newsletters that bore the label "Stormfront."

In the kitchenette, their host indicated spindly chairs at a cheap Formica table that was probably manufactured long before Jenny was born. The finish was chipped at the edges, betraying gritty, fake wood. The man busied himself at a marred side table with an old-fashioned coffee percolator. Beside that sat an old-fashioned touch-tone landline. "How do you like your coffee?"

"Black," Christopher answered. "This one will take her coffee black as well."

Jenny did not like that dismissive tone, especially as it had a certain authenticity, as if this was his real self.

Bo Morgan set heavy steaming mugs of coffee on the table.

Christopher took one, raised it to his lips, grimaced at the heat and set it aside.

The man plopped down on the last chair. "Jasper told me what you're doin,' and I think finding that varmint is proper. How can I help?"

"I have three pictures of a piece of blade and a spectrograph of composition." Christopher nodded to Jenny. "Show him the photos."

Jenny took out the pictures and an analysis record from her portfolio.

Morgan frowned as he accepted the documents. He tossed the analysis aside, but his eyes fixed on the pictures. He reached behind himself to a drawer in the side table and pulled out a lighted magnifier. "Huh. Amateur hour. Don't get me wrong, he's experienced, or has a good teacher, but in my judgment, this guy didn't normalize his work enough. He left the tip work hardened and brittle."

"Any idea whose work it might be?"

Morgan scratched his temple. "I know a lot of the students, online, but cain't say I knows 'em all. But the teachers… I know of six that would teach this kind of work, I can get you their names and where they are."

"Just six? No more?"

"Well there's two others, but I know all I need to know about them."

"How so?"

"They're queer. One in Illinois is a damn faggot, and don't get me started on the confused pervert in Indiana." He looked at Jenny. "You think I'd like to see the negro outside in some sort of camp, but I don't. Not her fault her parents were idjits. I hope she has the good sense to get sterilized. You got to feel sorry for the kids, ya know? Just let those mongrel genes die out. Now queers, *they* should be locked up. They reproduce by recruitment, get them out of the population and there won't be any more in a generation." He spread his hands. "It's simple science."

Jenny leaned back from the table; her mouth clamped shut. If she started talking, she didn't think she could control what came out.

Christopher intervened. "Any contact information for those two?"

Jenny looked at her boss and thought. *I can google "gay bladesmith classes" and the states and likely find them.*

"No. I don't hold with them sort. But there is one guy you should talk to."

Jenny sat straighter.

"One o' the six. Lives around Joliet, Indiana. He's a character, but he's found himself a niche market."

Christopher waited for Bo to continue.

"He teaches hunting, survivalism, blacksmithing and uh, , , " He rubbed his jaw.

"Yes?"

"Name's Butch Dunn. He's got a bunch of devotees among the incels. He teaches them how to be 'real men.'"

Jenny groaned.

Christopher blinked, "Excuse me? Incel?"

Jenny spoke up, unable to hold her tongue another moment. "'Involuntary Celibates;' men who can't get laid because they spend all their time whining on the internet about how they can't get laid."

Morgan glared at her contribution but nodded his head. "She ain't wrong."

"Seriously?" Christopher asked. This was the first time Jenny saw her boss surprised.

"Oh yeah, but they lap up the macho shit he sells. Fills them up with how to really get their manhood restored."

"So..." Christopher scratched the edge of his chin with his thumb. "His students would be the type to resent women, make their own knives and praise violence?"

"Yep. I've met some of them. They think the height of humor are jokes about rape. And most of them will go on some complicated story about the time they put some uppity woman in their place." He snorted in disgust. "I respect women." He nodded at Jenny. "As wives and mothers as the good Lord made them to be. But the ones who get all full of 'emselves and think they can go around and act like a man, that there is a problem. That's when a little gentle correction is in order, but I don't take with hurtin' 'em. Not even the disobedient kind."

Jenny bit her tongue. Hard.

Christopher nodded as if he agreed. "The list and contact information?"

The man got up and opened a cabinet to reveal an old computer with a bulky cathode ray monitor that still ran Windows XP.

He fiddled with keys and then opened a drawer where an old dot-matrix printer lurked. He waited for the thing to stop before tearing off two sheets of tractor fed paper.

"Here ya go."

Christopher accepted the list and scoured the directions. "This first guy? Dennis Roiter? It looks like he lives just about twenty miles from here."

"Yeah," Morgan said. "It's about an hour drive. I can draw ya a strip map."

Christopher consulted the time on his phone. "It's only eight o'clock. Do you think he would be available tonight?"

"Prob'ly. He is a night owl. He posts on the internet a lot after

127

midnight. I can call him."

"Please."

The man went back to the side table where the landline phone sat. He punched in a number and spoke in muffled tones into the receiver. "He's up and he'll be waiting for you. He'll also prefer you to leave the black woman in the car."

Jenny followed her boss outside, fuming. She took the passenger seat while Christopher got in the back.

Marq raised her reclined car seat. "Where to?"

"Yes, massa," Jenny exclaimed, no longer able to hide her resentment. "Do tell us servants what do to. What the actual fuck was that all about?"

To her surprise Marq chuckled and Christopher adopted a wry smile.

"Woops," Marq said. "I should have warned her about…the voice."

"The voice?" Jenny turned wide eyes at Marq.

Christopher's current tone was tinged with self-conscious humility. "My family comes from nobility, and they kept servants. They adopted a certain tone of voice to keep from becoming too familiar, and to assert their aristocracy. It's been passed down."

Marq patte4d Jenny on the shoulder. "Christopher has a special talent for it."

"It is an act," Christopher said.

Jenny refused to be mollified. "I found that tone more objectionable than the Nazi."

Christopher manufactured a disgusted sigh. "Calling that racist a Nazi does a disservice to Nazis. That man is a casual bigot, he wouldn't make the effort to send people to concentration camps. He will be the guy who turns a blind eye, or shrugs when someone speaks out. That kind of indifference spreads much quicker than extremism, and it is far more destructive."

Jenny replied. "He's vile, but at least he's polite, I've seen worse."

"Right," Christopher glowered. "His kind is always polite. It is the people who will not put up with his nonsense that tend to be rude about it."

"Turn left after the trees." Jenny pointed as the road suddenly went from dirt to smooth, fresh asphalt. They rolled up toward a large house in a rural community. The closest neighbors were about a half dozen football fields away. Dennis Roiter's home was a brick two story dwelling, well-lit with enormous picture windows.

"Look at all that glass," Marq murmured as she pulled into the long driveway. "Not very secure, or private, but looks expensive."

"Not all of the alt right lives like hermits." Jenny murmured. "Privacy? No worries with no one living within a half mile. Security? Out here that means you have a lot of guns."

As the car approached the house, dim motion sensor lights blinked on. A three-car garage faced the road and Marq parked before it.

Robust, well-trimmed hedges framed a walkway lit by landscape lights in stakes along the path leading to the house. A topiary cut to resemble a bird stood outlined against cheerful brilliance spilling from the front windows. The house rooms were clearly visible though the open curtains—and empty.

Christopher and Jenny stepped out. She was still miffed by the earlier encounter but pulled herself together. If that was what it took to get information, she could hold her tongue. She let Christopher get about three steps in front before she followed in a submissive performance. Her concentration on her role made her a second late to react.

A man burst out of the hedges brandishing a glass bottle with a silver cross glinting in the moonlight.

Jenny recoiled as recognition set in, "Thad! No!"

Christopher looked at the intruder with contempt and took a step toward him.

Thad made a broad sweeping gesture to flick the contents toward her boss. Something must have alarmed Christopher at the last second. He dropped his contemptuous glare and held up a hand to protect his face as the liquid splashed over him.

Time froze and nothing seemed to happen.

Then an anguished groan burst from Christopher as his bare skin bubbled, blistered, and even smoked where the liquid had touched.

Christopher recoiled in pain, his agony expressed in a guttural snarl, words in a language Jenny did not recognize.

Thad smirked and waved as another man in fatigues slipped out of the hedges, brandishing a hunting crossbow, but instead of an arrow it was loaded with a piece of sharpened wood about an inch in diameter with a gleam of metal at its tip.

He fired.

The stake hit Christopher in the lower ribcage. He dropped to his knees and collapsed to the ground.

Jenny screamed.

Chapter Seventeen

The Amber Alert hit his phone about when Baden expected. An hour later he heard Tracey's desperate mother on the news.

"She is so much help to me, so good with the animals. Since her father died, she's been my whole word, my only child. I'm begging anyone listening, help me. Help me find my Tracey. Please bring her back!"

Baden smirked; imaging Dr. Weller's tear-stained face. He loved it when they begged. He'd have to dig up the internet stream of Mommy's little tear fest and play it for Tracey when she was about half gone.

It took hours driving through backroads to get her to their final destination. The log cabin was built sturdy, its squat shape hidden deep in the Indiana woods. The ground was frozen and betrayed no sign of his frequent visits. The air was sharp, bitter, with a slight sent of pine.

A lone coyoted yipped in the distance, destroying Baden's otherwise perfect silence. He considered himself an authentic predator. Those mutts were scavengers, not noble hunters like real wolves. But tonight, he liked the sound of it baying in the cold, clear air. It seemed right, somehow.

Baden hoisted the unconscious girl from the back of the van and carried her like a precious child. He liked them to be unspoiled, no trace of injury when he began to play.

The isolated structure previously belonged to a guy he knew in the navy. Petty Officer Zachery Bryant told Baden all about it, how he built his off-grid retirement home, even showed Baden where it was on a map. No property taxes, no utilities, no outside interference. Only two cramped bedrooms, a sitting area/kitchenette off a diminutive mudroom and a closet bathroom; water provided by a cistern on the roof. No one knew about Bryant's perfect little escape—not even his family.

Zach wouldn't be needing his retirement get away. One well-placed nudge and PO Bryant had a fatal accident.

Baden carried Tracey up the two stairs to the porch, carefully stepping around the tricycle and other "window dressing" designed to make the owner look harmless. Once he opened the door, he carried her to the second inner room. Her room. Her world. His playground.

The smaller room held a tool rack, iron framed bed and plywood table with a fresh plastic tarp; cleansed of the garbage that recently occupied it. Both the bed and table were equipped with leather restraints and iron manacles.

Start her on the table or the bed? The heavy frame did not have a mattress, just supporting springs. He could start with the leather restraints but didn't want her to damage her wrists and bleed on the metal chains. Not yet.

The girl shivered in her sleep.

Once she was secured on the table, he studied her unconscious form as he considered her reaction when she woke up. First, he would calm her and watch the look on her face when he betrayed her. *Or should he get right to playtime?* He liked that idea at the moment, but he had time to consider.

She would scream, of course. They all screamed themselves until the only sound they could make was a raspy wail. He wondered if they would still scream if they knew how much that excited him.

He went to build a fire and stepped out on the front porch to fetch a beer from an insulated box by the railing. A good day's work.

Jenny stood frozen. Someone with her ex-husband just put a stake in her employer. Another man emerged from the bushes brandishing an axe, Thad's friend Tommy. He strolled up to Christopher believing they had the situation completely in their control.

Some inexplicable instinct compelled Jenny forward and she was halfway to Christopher before she realized she was moving. Tommy licked his lips and made a practice swing with the axe, slicing the air as if testing the balance. Jenny's ex stood there grinning like a lunatic while the unknown man with the crossbow reloaded.

These men were going kill Christopher in a very brutal manner. Tommy grinned, hefted the axe and raised it above his head, aiming for Christopher's neck. They were going to cut off her boss's head. *Why?*

Fury welled up inside her and she launched herself at Tommy, raining ineffectual blows at his body. He held her away with the axe handle until she faltered. He clubbed her upside her head and she fell to her knees. Tommy followed that with a vicious kick to her ribs, driving the wind from her lungs.

A shot rang out. The guy with the crossbow jerked and grunted. Another shot and Tommy screamed, although Jenny couldn't see any blood. The trio of assailants turned and ran.

There were two more shots. Jenny sat up and turned to see Marquessa standing in a shooters crouch, a gun in her hand. She put the pistol back into her concealed carry holster and ran toward Christopher. "Help me get him in the car!" she ordered.

"We shouldn't move him," Jenny gasped. "We need an ambulance!"

Marq bent down and wrapped her arms around Christopher's chest. She bodily hefted him up. "This would be easier if you grabbed his legs," she grunted.

Jenny sat frozen. Her ears were ringing and pained lanced through her skull. The situation was so absurdly surreal she couldn't process anything. Her friend was dragging her boss while a crossbow stake jutted out from under his left rib cage. Marq lugged Christopher's body the toward the car.

He must be dead, that's why he's not bleeding. Jenny caught her breath and rose on unsteady feet. She staggered after Marq and made a clumsy effort to grab Christopher's feet. The pair hauled their injured boss along, with Marq bearing most of the weight while Jenny led the way to the car. Once there, she dropped his feet and jerked the back door open.

Marq bundled Christopher into the rear seat and joined him. "Drive."

Jenny flew to the driver's seat, as Marq thumbed the starter fob. She spun the car in a wide U-turn, sweeping through a flowerbed and accelerating across the lawn back to the driveway. As the vehicle hurtled down the blacktop to the road she yelled over her shoulder. "Where is the closest E.R.?"

"No," Marq snapped. "He needs someone experienced with his condition. Get back to the highway."

"Rare blood disease, my ass," Jenny swore, letting all her frustration and confusion pour out and she steeled herself to ask the stupid question. "They threw holy water on him. They staked him and tried to cut his head off. They think he's a goddamn vampire." She kept her eyes on the road as she said the most ridiculous thing she'd ever heard. "I need you to tell me, right now, that my boss is *not* a goddamn vampire. I mean, does this rare disorder require him to drink blood? Cause, if so, he is a goddamn vampire."

The absurdity of the words made her rational mind flinch, even as her emotions already knew the answer.

"He's a goddamned vampire," Marq snapped back.

Jenny smacked the wheel. "Goddammit!"

"And that wasn't holy water," Marq continued, "more like hell water."

Jenny was suddenly aware of an acrid sulphurous smell in car. "Acid?" She shook her head. "Is he alive, or undead, or whatever you call it?"

"It's hard to tell," Marq sighed again. "Pull over at the first chance. We have to get the stake out of him." Marq grasped the wood. "Never mind, just keep going, I can pull it out."

"Don't," Jenny snapped.

Marq ignored her and braced herself to get enough leverage. "The wood is keeping his wound open."

"Don't pull it out!"

Marq hesitated.

"My ex is a sadist. He is fascinated by stories of how to kill people, and I am sure those guys are too. You can bet the tip of the stake is barbed so it'll break if you try to pull it out. There was metal at the tip. Probably steel, but if it is silver and it stays inside him…"

"It would poison him," Marq finished. "That would make it difficult for him to recover."

"The stake needs to be removed surgically."

"Not an option," Marq said. "I think I can drive it through."

Jenny flinched. "Better than pulling it out, I guess. It's not near his heart—or does that matter?"

"Through the heart would kill him, I mean once and for all. Good thing they are superstitious, they would have done more damage with a shotgun blast. Pull over."

Jenny spied a dirt road in the distance and parked in the turn off.

Marq flew out the door as the car rolled to a stop. She scurried to the trunk and returned with a hammer.

Jenny's eye bulged. "Can't you just, like, push it through gently?"

"Gently?" Marq shook her head. "Those old Peter Cushing movies were accurate. It takes a lot of force to get a shaft of wood through a body. This is not going to be gentle."

Christopher lay on his side, legs pushed up toward his chest. Marq pulled his feet out the open door and adjusted his body supine on the back seat. Marq crawled over him and braced herself.

"You're gonna to do that in here?"

"No alternative. I have enough room to swing and drive the stake into the seat cushion." Marq lifted the hammer, took aim and delivered a solid blow.

Christopher twitched and Jenny bit back a sudden rush of bile.

Marq checked his back and tenderly touched his cheek.

She hit him again. And again.

Christopher twitched and jerked with each hit.

"I think it went through." Jenny pointed.

"Damn." Marq rolled him back onto his side. "You were right; the tip broke off in the cushion. There's enough of the end sticking out that I can get ahold of it." She took a deep breath and grabbed the stake with a grip that might break a person's wrist. "Sorry!" Marq practically wailed.

Jenny never heard so much anguish in a voice before, not even her own as Thad took out his troubles on her.

With a loud grunt Marq pulled the stake through him with everything she had.

Christopher's body convulsed. Pale pink froth formed around his lips.

Marq dug into the upholstery and pulled out a blackened barbed arrowhead. "Silver," she muttered. "Bastards." She ran her hand along the wound as it visibly closed. She sprang back out of the car. "Help me, we gotta get him in his travel bag."

Jenny got out of the car as Marq pulled a long black garment bag from the trunk.

"We'll have to make do." Marq manipulated the thick black material and unfolded plastic rods built into it until the object was shaped like a box. She unzipped the lid.

A body bag, Jenny thought. *A mobile coffin. Just the thing for the fashionable vampire on the go.* She was astounded by how easily she was accepting the vampire thing even though the rational part of her brain still refused to process it. "Wait, is that dirt in there?" She touched her hand over her face. "Of course, his native soil."

"Not quite, but dirt from the Carpathian Mountains has restorative effect."

The pair wrangled Christopher into the travel coffin. Marq shoved him in, bending his legs. The case covered the entire back seat and hung out about two feet.

"Crap, do we stick his legs out the window?"

Marq collapsed the excess part and folded it into the car.

"Okay then." Jenny dove into the driver seat.

Marq climbed in beside her. "Drive."

As Jenny backed onto the paved road, Marq fished a phone out of her pocket and activated the voice recognition. "Contact list. Call Lilith."

"From the party?" Jenny asked as she pulled onto the highway.

"She lives in Nashville; her real name is Patricia Kierland."

"Patricia is Lilith? I don't—"

Marq waved her quiet. "Lilith," she cried into the phone. "No time to explain. Christopher is wounded. He needs you now. We are about an hour south of you. Take I-65. We'll get a motel room and I will call you back." She nodded. "Yes, immediately. Really? Yes, yes yes!" Marq continued enthusiastically. "Bring Hecate." She hung up. "Hecate was visiting, they'll both come."

Jenny hit the high beams. "So, He-ca-te," she said the unfamiliar name slowly. "Not her real name?"

"Lilith, Sabrina, Tabitha, Marie, Wanda and the others; they use names associated with witches. There are thirteen of them organized by Lilith. They call themselves Christophe's Coven. When you're guarding a secret, you take precautions." Marq fumbled with her smart phone. "Found a motel, the kind you can park right in front of the door, about twenty miles away." She turned on the GPS navigation.

"They're witches?"

"No. Well, Sabrina practices wicca, but they just call themselves that. They have their own Facebook group."

"Uh, I guess it's marked private?" Surrealism was the new normal.

Jenny handed her license over to the Indian night clerk who was more interested in something on his computer monitor.

"Thank you very much." He didn't actually look at her, just scanned the ID.

Jenny tapped her foot as he programmed the key cards, still without looking at her.

Jenny did not mind. The less he saw of her now, the less he could recall for Thad later.

He handed the key packet over and his eyes flickered on her face, but he seemed unimpressed. "Room 131, around the back. The wifi—" He stopped talking when Jenny ran out.

She flew to the car. "Room 131," she announced.

Marq nodded and texted Lilith.

Jenny drove the car up to their room door and Marq got out. She reassembled the end of the bag and hefted the entire thing by two thick straps. Jenny opened the motel room door as Marq hustled her burden into the room, dropping it beside the far bed. They both unzipped the top, checking to ensure the trip did not harm Christopher.

Jenny grimaced. "Is he, I guess, dead dead?"

"I don't think so." Marq shut the top. "He needs rest and blood."

Jenny plopped down on one bed. "So, what's with the gun?"

"Goodwin's rule."

"Isn't that some internet thing about Nazi's?"

"That's Godwin. Archie Goodwin is the sidekick of the fictional detective, Nero Wolfe. He made himself a rule that as soon as a case became a murder investigation, he carried a gun."

Jenny chewed her lip and nodded. "What happens when Lilith gets here?"

Marq sat down on the other bed and considered her friend. "It's complicated."

Chapter Eighteen

"You didn't say a damn thing about them having guns," Thad snapped from the far back row of the van, hovering over the wounded Grant. "That's kind of a stupid detail to leave out."

Grant lay back in the seat and peeled away the white gauze from the gash. Thad stared at the gory mess covering the militia leader's upper shoulder. The parked van was dark, the only illumination from a streetlight so the blood soaking into the olive drab military shirt looked black in the shadows.

Grant grunted. "They never had guns before. Here." He rummaged through a satchel and dug out a military issue field dressing. "You know how to apply a pressure bandage?"

Thad frowned. "Yeah, my dad's hunting group made me take first aid. Passed the course with a C average."

"Good enough. It's just a graze." He raised his voice and called to the Tommy, "You okay?"

"No!" he bellowed back. "That was too damn close. Jesus! I could hear it go by."

"You think we got it?"

"Not likely," Grant smiled a rictus grin as he tugged off his shirt, the stiff material sticking to his wound. Pulling that material away brought fresh blood oozing down his arm.

"It's gonna come after us, ain't it?" Tommy said.

"It'll try." Grant produced a tube of antibiotic ointment and smeared it in the gash. "We hurt it. We have a while before it'll get around to us, though. Several days, maybe weeks, to get its strength back. You can put the bandage on now."

Thad fumbled the plastic wrapper open. The bandage consisted of a 4"x7" cotton pad, secured by long strips of forest green gauze. He managed to keep the sterile part from falling on the seat and held it up by one of the straps. "Old school. I expected an Israeli bandage. That's what the first aid class used."

"This is simpler for a minor gash."

This shit isn't minor, Thad thought as he arranged the pad into place and wrapped the gauze strip around Grant's arm. "Where I'm from, wounded prey is the most dangerous," he said as Grant sucked in air, gritting his teeth. "We need to finish it while it's weak." He tucked the tied ends into place.

"In good time," Grant muttered.

"You're going to need stitches. What hospital?"

"No hospital, I know a guy. Let's get to the highway."

"Tommy, crank it up. North?"

Grant nodded, scratched his head and lowered his voice. "You know, you seem a mite bit brighter than your friend there. That, and you kept calm when it went to shit."

"Tommy's all right." Thad replied in a quiet voice. "He will wail like a bitch and he's no Einstein, but he's all right."

"Yeah, I need ninety more men like him. But I need *one* like you. Smart, keeps his head," Grant continued in a voice barely audible over the road noise. "What do you think I am trying to accomplish?"

Thad shrugged to indicate he didn't give a damn what Grant wanted to accomplish. "Kill a vampire?"

Grand managed a painful chuckle. "Then what? Killing one bloodsucker doesn't support my overall goals. You see, I need a solid militia. I've been able to recruit members, but they won't stay long unless they feel threatened. You got to keep them scared and believing only you can protect them. We elevate the threat by not killing it, instead we just sort of… draw it out."

"You want them to come after us." Thad raised his voice. "What the hell are you up to?"

"What's up?" Tommy called from the front.

Grant made a lowering motion with his hand. "Let's just keep this between the two of us. I need a second in command, not a second and third, you follow?"

Thad's eyes narrowed. "Think I'm on the trail."

"That one we got locked up will convince people the threat is real, but it's locked up and not even pretending to be human anymore." Grant made a sweeping gesture with his unwounded hand. "Now, the wounded one makes the threat imminent."

Thad shook his head. "That's insane." But even as he said it a hunger started in his mind. He'd never been given any real authority in his life. He'd like to see her face when his militia men took care of her.

Grant tapped Thad's shoulder. "That is how you amass power. I built my little group up over fifty people at one point. Some are still hangers on, but most left because they felt safe. Didn't need the group. This isn't just about killing a vampire, this is about raising an army, a small one that will generate a lot of money and a crew that will do our bidding."

"But they're coming after us," Thad said.

Grant waived the concern aside. "We get back to the compound, they can't touch us. And they aren't around during the day."

"That black girl with the gun walks in the daylight."

"Just one bitch. Hell, I took her before. I ain't afraid of her. Kind of wish she would come at me. Last time we were interrupted before things got real fun."

Thad bit his lip and looked over his shoulder to Tommy, then turned back to Grant with an appraising glare.

"When you got a militia," Grant said with a sly smile. "You can just take what you need, especially women. You want the black bitch with the gun? You want to punish that wife of yours? We'll help you get over her when you get a few others under you."

Thad sneered. He was over that bitch, but she destroyed his life and she would have to pay. Having an army to help…

Jenny lay on the motel bed and contemplated the sliver of light spilling from the half-shut bathroom door. She wasn't asleep and not really awake, either; she was in some sort of dissociative state. *This must be how an out of body experience feels*, she thought, like she was looking at herself from above to see if she could make sense of the situation. Her emotions were numb.

There was a knock at the door.

Jenny sat up as Marq crept to the door and peered through the peephole. She sighed with relief, opened the door and two women hurried in. Patricia Kierland, Lilith, had her gray hair pulled back in a loose ponytail and wore a down vest with jeans. The other, Hecate, was young. She wore a denim jacket over a gray hoodie and had "snakebite" piercings on her lower lip. Her short black hair revealed multiple piercings in her left ear, including a cartilage bar. The three exchanged hugs.

Lilith nodded to Jenny. "So, she knows?"

Marq provided a grim smile. "She's the new me, officially. Needs some catching up."

Marq led them to the body bag.

"How bad is it?" Lilith asked.

"Bad enough. They threw acid at him, he's not pleasant to look at."

"Can he heal from that?" Jenny asked.

Hecate nodded. "Yeah, he heals from burns, with care. But it'll be a while before we see his pretty face again."

Jenny furrowed her brow. She didn't think of Christopher as "pretty." Not bad to look at, but…

Lilith bent down to unzip the container and Marq crouched beside her.

"Wait a minute," Jenny said, still sitting cross-legged on the bed. "What's about to happen?"

The other three women exchanged glances.

Marq stood back up. "You know Jenny, I'm sort of hungry."

Jenny bit back several angry retorts, but allowed herself one spiteful thought, *You are always hungry.*

Marq motioned Jenny to follow her. "Let's leave them to do what is necessary. We'll go get a bite and talk."

Jenny sighed in resignation, swung her legs over the edge of the bed and put her shoes back on. Marq was out the door and she had to move quickly to catch up. Jenny stood by the car and pulled out her phone. "There's a Waffle House less than five miles from here."

"Waffle House? I see those by the highway exits. Never been to one." She checked the time. "You think they're open?"

"If a Waffle House closes, FEMA takes note. Most of my friends have at least one wild story that involves being in a Waffle House around this time of night." She studied her phone.

They drove in frustrated silence. The only speaking voice belonged to a digital map guiding them to the restaurant.

Marq broke the silence as they pulled into the parking lot. "You have questions?"

Jenny still felt emotionally drained. She wanted to feel what? Anger? Betrayal? Those feelings were not open to her, but neither was understanding or empathy. Accepting just took too much energy. "Okay, Christopher is a vampire and you are…?"

"Renfield," Marq replied. "You've read the book. Stoker knew some things. Vampires need helpers who are compatible, capable of becoming vampires. Those are very rare; I mean literally one in a million."

"So, you are going… to change?"

"It's is almost certain. Once we start to turn our metabolism goes weird. Very hungry, eventually craving raw, freshly killed meat. Or…" Marq grimaced. "Some of us crave live bugs and such."

"Ew, seriously?"

"Yeah, it grosses me out too. What you need to know, is—" Marq drew in a big breath, "—you are also compatible, that's what initially drew my attention."

Jenny went from numb to nuclear. "Woah. No, no, no. I don't want to be a vampire. I'm not compatible. You got something wrong." She paused and took a breath. "What makes someone compatible?"

"We think it is a series of specific genetic mutations. Incidents in life can cause the genes to express, basically rebuilding your body into another species."

"If you really mean one in a million, then there are about 300 could-be vampires in the US alone."

"Yes, I've met three of them. Christopher tells me he's met seven. Most are not suitable."

"What's not suitable about them?"

Marq touched her finger to her lips. "Character, values. We sense things. Sometimes we have to stress someone to get a good reading."

"Judge Fields? I still think that was a dick move."

Marq shrugged. "Anything else? Are we going in? I am hungry."

"How many vampires are out there?"

Marq sighed. "We know of six other vampyrs, seven if you include Magda."

"The previous housekeeper, is now a vampire?"

Marq nodded.

"And I—"

"You will have options."

"What if I don't want to be a vampire?"

"At this point, there is a treatment that will make it so you cannot change."

"And what about Magda? What were her options?"

Marq shrugged. "Things didn't go so well for her after the change and she needed to get away. Somewhere familiar. She went home to Hungary about ten years ago. We exchanged letters for a while and she got feeling better. She misses Chicago and says she'll be back one day. But she's on vampyr time. Nothing is rushed. Haven't heard from her in oh, four or five years." Marq shook her head. "It gets weird as you get so old. She is only ninety, but a decade can go by without her realizing it. I see Christopher fall into that from time to time."

"What is this vam-peer stuff?"

"A type of vampire, there is another, the nosferatu."

"I saw that movie."

"Think of them more as feral vampires. They feed on terror, it's like a drug. If their first feeding is full of terror they will kill and never regain rational thought."

Jenny shook her head. "How come we don't hear about this? Blood sucking lunatics would make the news."

"Oh, they make news. It is rare but every so often you will hear about cops killing some naked guy running out of control and trying to bite people. It is usually attributed to 'bath salts' or synthetic marijuana, or meth." Marq opened the car door. "Let's go, I am getting really hungry."

The two women ensconced themselves in a booth as far away from anyone else as possible. There were only two other patrons; a nicely dressed man reading a tablet, and a scruffy overweight man wearing a shirt that was two sizes too small, sporting drippings from his runny eggs.

The waitress took their order.

Jenny requested hash browns, "smothered and covered."

Marq chose "smothered, covered, chucked, topped and plastered in sausage gravy." She also asked for a generous helping of bacon and eggs, then topped that with an eight-ounce sirloin dragged from the freezer and fried on the griddle.

Marq leaned back. "I guess that sounds like a really large order."

"Meh." The waitress shrugged one shoulder. "We call that a number six."

The food arrived quick and they ate in silence. Jenny wanted to ask questions but Marq was shoveling food into her mouth at a rate that discouraged conversation.

"So," Jenny started once her friend came up for air. "What are the odds I'll be a..." she whispered the name, "nosferatu?"

"I'm not going to say it's impossible, but very unlikely without a previous vampire encounter. I mean you would have to worry if a vampyr fed on you multiple times and abandoned you. Christopher will not feed on you without your consent, and if he believes there is a chance you will turn, he will guard you and help you. Let me be blunt. Transitions can be difficult and the outcome is not guaranteed. If things go wrong, Christopher's help will be to cut off your head."

Jenny fell quiet. She still had a lot of questions; who were these other vampyrs? What was special about dirt? She went at a tangent. "What about werewolves?"

Marq looked taken aback. "What about them?"

"Do they exist?"

Marq shrugged. "Don't know, never met one. But I didn't know vampyrs existed until I met one."

"And all the witches, that's just names, nothing supernatural?"

"Christophe's Coven, yes. As far as supernatural abilities, there is Elaine, a Renfield for a book dealer in London. She says her subconscious mind has a savant talent for evaluating probabilities, but she's scary. She knows things, things happen around her."

"So, only vampires, no other undead group? Zombies?"

"Just the apostles."

"You mean like Jesus's..."

"They'd like you to think that. They're supposedly thirteen alchemists from 18th century France. Christopher only really knows one of them, Renard. Renard is convinced that there are immortal ancient Egyptians running around."

"Lovely."

Marq swallowed the rest of her food, including Jenny's toast, then looked at her phone for the time. "They should be done. We may as well go back and get a nap." She signaled the waitress and paid the bill, adding a generous tip.

They stepped out to the car.

"Jenny, you want to pull out those directions?"

"You don't remember?

"I was distracted. I just did what the voice told me to do."

"Okay, let me get the GPS back."

At "GPS" Marq froze. She stared at the car like *it* was nosferatu.

"What's up?"

Marq shook her head, as if observing something Jenny couldn't see. "I was just thinking we were parked at that guy's house for a while. They could have put a tracker on the car." She frowned. "Just being paranoid, I was with it the entire time. I would have sensed someone."

They got in the car. Jenny fumbled with her seatbelt, then let it go. "Now you got me paranoid. How would we know if there was a tracker?"

"I've got a wand—a technological one, not a magical one—in the trunk. But I don't think—"

"Look," Jenny sighed. "You put a bug in my brain and I won't be able to sleep like this. It'll only take a minute to check, right?"

"Okay." Marq got out and retrieved the wand from the trunk. She walked around the car absently waving it at the vehicle. As she passed over the passenger side rear the wand reacted and gave off an angry beep.

Marq stared at Jenny, eyes wide. "Holy shit."

Chapter Nineteen

"I thought he was supposed to be better after he, uh, fed," Jenny said as the motel disappeared behind them

"Should be," Marq snapped. Her earlier confidence in Christopher's recovery was gone. That loss coupled with the new urgent need to get her boss to safety was pushing Marq into a cold manic state. They'd attached the tracker to another car at the Waffle House and charged back to the hotel, afraid that the crossbow boys would already be there.

"You think he's comfortable in the trunk?" Jenny asked. She consulted Marq's tablet. She avoided looking outside because the poor visibility alarmed her as the car barreled up I-65 toward home. She understood that her friend's special nature let her see a great deal more in the sleet.

Marq gripped the steering wheel so tight her shoulders hunched as she leaned forward. The only sound was the rhythm of the windshield wipers as they swept the pouring rain sleet mix from the glass.

"The weather report says this will turn into snow by the time we get to Bowling Green."

Marq grunted.

"You want me to drive for a while?"

"No." The reply was unnecessarily sharp. She took a breath and continued in a slightly less severe tone. "Give Lilith a call."

Lilith and Hecate were following behind, watching for anyone tracking the grey sedan. Lilith drove fast and strategic. She varied the distance between them to see as much of the traffic as possible. And there was a lot of traffic for five in the morning.

"You know I just did. They dropped three miles behind us are expecting to catch up in a few minutes. Right now, and there is no evidence of pursuit."

"They don't have to pursue. They knew where we were, and they know where we are going. Once we get home there is special security, but until then…" She made a growling noise. "Looks like we may have to move again. He said our next home would be London, and I mean England, not Kentucky."

"You don't think they'd try to do something on the open road?"

"I don't know." Marq mimed hitting her skull against a wall. "This is my fault."

"How—"

"That fuckwhit Grant. I knew Leiter would tell him everything. Hell, this whole thing is likely a ruse to kill Christopher and I fell for it. I pushed him to get involved. When I get ahold of the good reverend…" Her voice petered out as her visceral anger left her too distracted to list the horrors she intended to release on that treacherous preacher. She punched the steering wheel and Jenny was afraid she'd break it.

Jenny frowned. "I don't think Leiter set us up, at least not intentionally."

"You don't?" Marq sounded incredulous.

"And how did my ex-husband get involved with this?"

Marq made no reply.

The wintry mixture tapered off and the wipers squealed, amplifying the silence.

"I think you can turn the wipers off," Jenny ventured.

Marq glared at the road, but Jenny knew that her friend was really glowering at her. After a short pause Jenny continued, "You want me to turn them off?"

When she did not get an answer, she reached over and raised the control lever. The squealing stopped.

"You know," Marq spoke up again, the anger in her voice morphing into suspicion, "there are some things that are just too coincidental."

"You can say that again." Jenny leaned back into her seat.

"You, for instance. You came into our lives at the same time Leiter was setting us up."

Jenny's eyes popped open. "Marq—"

"And it was your ex-husband trying to make like a guillotine."

"Marq, you know—"

"I don't know anything!" Marq yelled. "Who else had every opportunity to put a tracking device on the car? Who else could have told them our travel plans?"

"Marquessa, you are being unreasonably paranoid. You said you had a sense about me. You said you knew you could trust me. And why put a transmitter on your car? I could have just set up my phone for someone to track me."

Marq stared at the road ahead, but her shoulders softened. Tears welled in her eyes.

Huge, wet snowflakes hit the windshield. Marq waited until they stuck to the glass and threatened to obscure the road before she turned on the wipers back on.

Dawn broke outside the secluded cabin. Baden sat in a padded chair, kept awake by the thrill of watching his girl sleep, and a moderate dose of his lovely white pills. He used drugs with a purpose, thoughtfully. Not as some pleasure device like that pill sucking whore from the mall.

A shaded LED night cast a deep red glow over the small room. Tracey stirred in her sleep, mewling like a kitten. He suppressed a chuckle thinking about the headband with cat ears he found in her coat pocket. Tracey would be so cute wearing them as he played his games.

He felt unsettled. Usually he savored this part more, the anticipation. But since he had to get rid of the corrupt one, he felt impatient, driven, as if he had to correct an error.

The girl stirred again, this time gasping. She tried to sit up in the bed, her head craning around to get her bearings, her drugged mind abruptly comprehending she was restrained. She shook herself, struggling against the leather cuff that secured her to the bed frame, and grunted at the effort.

The sound melded into a low wail.

The wail died immediately when she noticed Baden. She took a deep breath to scream.

In that second Baden decided how he was going to start. There was a game he really loved, but only one of his girls actually fell for it. He jumped from the chair, frantically waving his hands. "Don't scream, he'll hear you." Baden talked through his nose, letting his jaw fall slack.

The girl choked back her scream.

"He's a bad man." Baden breathed through his mouth and looked over his shoulder as if expecting someone to sneak up on him. "You have to be good, or he will hurt you." His head bobbed. "I have to keep you secure, or he will hurt me. Again."

The girl glared at him. *Was she buying it?*

"Who are you?"

Baden bobbed his head again. "I'm Joey." He spoke slowly, his tone quiet, shy. "That's not like my real name, that's Joseph, like the Bible. But that's what my uncle calls me."

"Your uncle? What does he want?" The girl hissed.

He answered sluggishly, testing her desire to believe what he said. "Money. Your mother already agreed to pay fifty thousand. Now we just have to not get him angry and you will be home in another day or two."

Visible relief erased the terror in her eyes.

A warm thrill shot through him. She was buying it.

"Can you get me loose?"

Baden shook his head, bouncing it from side to side. "No, no, no. He will hurt you and your mother if he don't get his money."

The girl collapsed onto the thin mattress. She sat silent for a moment. Then spoke in a more controlled manner. "I have to go to the bathroom."

"There is one here. If you promise to behave, and let me secure you afterwards, I can ask if I can let you use it." He reached in his pocket and touched the send button on his flip phone. A phone in the other room sounded the special ring tone, a gruff voice calling "Joey?"

Baden spun around and clutched at his head with his left hand. "He's awake."

"Joey, get your ass out here!"

Hand still in his pocket, he broke the connection. "I'll be right back." He fled the room ensuring the girl saw the door was unlocked. That was for later.

Part of him wanted this game to go on for weeks, but he was too anxious to get to the climax. Two days. He would give her two days of false hope, maybe even have her think of him as a friend, a fellow victim.

Chapter Twenty

The Right Reverend Bobby Leiter stirred, irritated by the godawful ring from the landline phone in the next room. He sat up. The phone would go on as long as the caller persisted. No voicemail. It was his private number, and it would have to be important to call in the middle night or, judging by the red glow behind his curtains, early morning.

He slipped out from under the covers, his cotton pajamas swishing as they rubbed against the silky smooth 1500 hundred thread-count bedsheets as he tottered to his feet. He recalled an old sermon he once gave justifying his lavish lifestyle. He used multiple out-of-context Bible verses to confuse the issue and concluded by stating God wanted him to live in affluence. He winced at the arrogance of his younger self.

The familiar aches and pains in his legs and back called for attention but he merely grunted and moved to the phone, awkwardly dragging his left foot.

He answered with a simple, "Hello?"

"You need to get on the move."

Leiter barely recognized the demanding voice on the line. "Grant?"

"We nearly killed it," the militia leader sounded excited, almost manic. "I think he is pretty wounded. Even so, that Miss Koenig is packing a gun and I know she'll be out for revenge."

"Slow down," Leiter squeezed the receiver until his knuckles were white. "What the hell did you do?"

"What you should have done years ago!" Grant snapped. His excitement gave way to a sort of smugness. Leiter recognized Grant's tone, the condescending voice designed to belittle an opponent or rival. "Anyway, we put a stake through him."

Leiter clenched his eyes shut. "A stake?"

"Damn right! It was beautiful, but we were interrupted before we could finish the job."

Leiter felt gorge rise but he pushed the sensation away and demanded, "Why? Why did you do it?"

He could hear Grant's disgust through the wire. "Because it's a monster, a walking blasphemy. That thing is an insult to God."

The reverend took a deep breath trough his nose. "I've seen the work of a monster. I needed Christophe to help me find that true monster."

"Yeah? Well, good luck with that. A creature like that is more likely to kill you and join the serial killer. Like goes to like."

How many times had Leiter sang a similar litany? "Like goes to like." He had gone to Grant in the past, and now he went to Christophe. *What did that make him?*

Leiter fought to keep the fury out of his voice. His effort was not very effective. He clenched his eyes shut to keep from screaming. "I need him. We need to make this right."

"What we need to do is to plan our next assault, before he recovers and comes after us."

Leiter's rage converted to despair and self-loathing. "Thank you for calling." His voice now sounded thick with fatigue. "Don't call again."

"You are in danger. You need us."

"You've done enough already."

"Together we can accomplish great things!" Grant started to plead, then turned to threats. "You can join us, or you can die."

Leiter hung up the phone. There was nothing more he could say. Join or die? He briefly considered the guns in the next room and the option comforted him. But there were other ways to commit suicide. He took his cell phone from the table by the door. The number was still under "recent" and he tapped it with his thumb.

It was answered on the second ring.

"You have a great deal of nerve to call this number," Ms, King greeted him after the second ring. "You are a dead man."

"That's fair," Bobby Leiter admitted. "Please listen to me. If you need vengeance, you can have it. Tell me where to go and I will except your retribution on one condition. You must still find the man who butchered my granddaughter."

The other end of the line was silent.

"If I had any part in what happened, it was not intentional. I am sorry for Grant's actions. Tell me where."

"So, you can set another trap?" Ms. King replied warily.

"No traps." He waited as the woman took several slow breaths on the line.

"Why should I believe you?"

"Because I have nothing to lose or gain. I am going to die. Soon. By your hand or God's. I will have to answer for my sins. But if I know that monster, that human monster who kills the innocent, is stopped and justice served, then I go with peace."

The silence was back, so long he thought she'd hung up. "Are you there? Please, he's taken another girl, Tracey Weller."

"Lovely. Oh, I am here." She suddenly sounded preternaturally calm. "Send me the information. I'll be in touch."

The line went dead.

Marquessa put the phone in her pocket and closed her eyes so tight crow's feet appeared. She idly scratched at the bridge of her nose and tried to surreptitiously wipe away angry tears.

"What was that about?" Jenny asked, chewing a bit of toast and marmalade.

"Bobby Leiter saying he is sorry, but had no part in the attack, this is not like their previous relationship. And another girl is missing." |

"Damn," Jenny said, "Wait, Leiter and Christopher? Leiter tried to put a stake in him?"

Marq sighed. "It is more complicated but essentially that is correct."

"Why is Christopher helping him now?"

"I think it comes down to *noblesse oblige.*"

"What?"

"Christopher was born into nobility, the old kind. They are aware of the duty to serve and when someone requests aid, they should give it. Even an enemy. Leiter is very insistent he had nothing to do with the attack."

"I don't think he did." She nibbled at the toast. "So how old is Christopher?"

Marq frowned in thought. "He was born in Sofia, Bulgaria in 1832."

Jenny lips clenched as she did the math. "Vampires were fun to read about because they weren't real. I don't know what to make of any of this."

"I don't know what to make of Leiter's call."

"You need to eat."

"I'm not hungry," Marq replied irritably.

"We both know that's not possible. And you need to be at your best right now." She pushed a plate of scrambled eggs across the table.

Marq glared at her and spoke in a cold, clear voice. "I think, for the time being, you should go home. We will call you if we need anything."

Jenny munched at her toast much the way she ignored her mother as a teenager or tried to ignore Thad. Her stomach tightened as she held back an angry retort. She needed to be the calm one, to deescalate like when Thad went off accusing her of screwing around. The thought of his little "traps" like putting chalk marks to see if she moved the car without permission, or the time he produced a condom and demanded why she had it. *Deep breath.* "I don't think that is a good idea."

"You know, I don't care what you think. Get out," Marq demanded. "All this started with you. You didn't do anything when *your* husband attacked."

"Ex-husband."

"Whatever. I would have sent you away last night, but Christopher insisted I let you nap in this morning and have breakfast." She breathed quick, shallow breaths through her nose.

"You honestly think I am your enemy?" Jenny was embarrassed by the way her voice wavered. She meant to stay emotionless.

"Yes. No." Marq shook her head. "I don't know; and that is worse."

Jenny tapped on the plate of eggs. "You are hungry, hungry beyond human nature."

Marq's head snapped up.

"You need to think clearly and be ready to act. First is self-care." She tapped the plate again. "I can make more. And there is ham and bacon in the fridge."

Marq looked at the eggs. She sniffed at them. Then she salivated, damn near drooling. She sat down and ate the eggs.

Jenny made a trip to the other side of the kitchen and returned with the promised ham and bacon, as well as cheeses and bread.

"Eat. So you don't go ripping into me all day. You know you have to."

Marq took a few tentative bites and then shoveled food into her mouth. There was an animal ferocity to the way she tore through the breakfast.

Jenny stayed quiet until Marq paused and looked up at her. "It is the one thing I fear about my coming life, or un-life."

"Constant hunger?"

"The need. Vampyr are rational creatures but deprived of suitable food they fall into a stupor, or more like a coma. Then their mind slowly changes, and they devolve into bloodlust. It is a ferocious angry need to attack, to feed. Then it will take any blood it can get." Marq ate the ham as frustrated tears welled in her eyes. "It must be the stress that is escalating things. I can't really enjoy this, it all tastes like ashes."

"Are you going to be okay? You're being a little weird."

Marq chewed through more ham. "I don't know." She stopped eating and merely stared at the fully cooked meat in dismay. "It doesn't taste right."

Jenny reached across the table to touch her hand and Marq jerked it away.

"Sorry," Jenny said.

"No." Marq took a deep breath. "I'm sorry. You were right, hunger was, is, clouding my judgment."

"So, are we okay?"

"We will be sometime," Marq sighed.

"Go ahead, kiss and make up, dammit." Hecate spoke up from the kitchen door.

Jenny jumped. Marq just nodded.

"Hecate, how is Christopher?" Jenny asked.

Hecate shrugged. "We sort of force fed him. He's really out of it, but

155

the acid burns are healing. I think physically he is going to recover."

"Physically?" Jenny did not like the way that sentence was parsed.

Hecate shrugged. "He doesn't seem to be there." She tapped her temple. "He can wake up and go through the motions; but the fire, the passion, of an encounter is gone. We have to resort to drastic measures just to get him fed. I don't know when he'll be back."

Marq's phone beeped. She took it out and looked at it. "That's my ride."

"What?" Jenny said.

"To the airport. I'm flying to Chicago and getting a rental to go interview the incel guru up by Joliet. I should be back before Christopher is awake. But if not, make sure he reads the information Leiter sent about the new missing girl. Just have to be sure and account for Chicago Friday traffic.

"In this weather? Alone?"

"I have to do something. Something other than eat. This is all on me. I can take care of myself."

"What if he's like the others and won't talk to you?"

Her lips curled into a cruel smile. "I'm kinda in the mood to make him talk."

Chapter Twenty-One

Baden rehearsed his innocence as he arranged each item with care on the breakfast tray. A cheese omelet, biscuit with sawmill gravy, buttered toast and a spray of violets in a tiny vase. He would serve her the morning meal, promise the ransom had been paid and she would be home the next morning. *The look on her face when she realizes I'm lying…*

That's when the real fun would begin.

He hummed a bit of a forgotten 80's ballad as he picked up the platter, carried it to the door and balanced it on one hand to get the door open. He took one look at Tracey and the hum stuck in his throat.

The girl was bleeding; wet, dark red brown followed the center inseam of her jeans.

He slammed the tray down to the ground. Food, flowers and broken dishes scattered unheeded.

"Why did you do that?" he roared.

The girl whimpered and tried to bring her legs together, but the straps held them apart.

"You stupid bitch! Look what you made me do!" He turned his face away from her in disgust. Blood usually excited him, but not this kind. Only one of his guests had her period in his captivity, and that was during the final week. He rubbed his eyebrow. Tracey would just have to clean it up. He had some pads in the bathroom closet even though they were at least two years old. They didn't go bad, did they? How long did a girl bleed like that? Three days? Five?

He trudged to the bathroom and found the carton of hygienic pads, but there was only one left. He started to crumple the box but managed to take control of himself.

The phone rang, his most lucrative client's ringtone, Gordon Klein, a dealer in exorbitantly expensive antiques of questionable provenance. "God dammit!" He yelled. "I told the bastard I was on vacation."

He ignored the call and stomped back to his captive and threw the pad at her. "Clean that mess up." The pink plastic wrapped pad bounced off her forehead and landed on the bed out of her reach.

"Why in hell did you do that?" he sneered.

He knew, on some level she couldn't help it, but he needed to blame her to focus his anger.

The phone stopped ringing, then a second later started to ring again.

The girl cried on, hiccupping sobs that might be heard in the background of a phone call.

Baden closed his eyes and controlled his breathing. More composed, he moved to the bed to free the girl's arms. The phone stopped ringing, but before he could get the girl loose it started ringing again.

"What?" he screamed at the ceiling, barely aware of the frightened wail that echoed from the girl. He kicked the broken plates and tramped out the door to the phone.

He took a deep breath and accepted the call. "Baden." He took a step toward the other room and slammed the door shut.

"We have a situation—" the voice on the phone rushed out.

"Not my problem. I told you I was going on vacation this month and not to call me. You know that I do not like to be disturbed while I'm hunting."

"This is your problem if you ever want to work in this business again," the voice snapped.

Baden paused. Gordon Klein did not make idle threats. "What is the 'problem?'"

"You transported two vases from an estate sale in Mobile. The owner says you cracked one."

"Bullshit," Baden snorted. "He inspected and accepted the order."

"I know, but he's got his lawyers after me."

"I don't give a rat's ass about his lawyers, I have detailed photos of the vases when I picked them up, and another set when they were delivered. I'll email them."

"Good, but my lawyers want you to make a statement. I need to you to sign an affidavit."

Baden turned and looked at the door. "Not going to happen. I'll send you the pictures."

"I'll send someone to get you. I know where you are."

Baden froze. "What?"

"I had my people ping your GPS tracker."

Baden clenched his teeth. "You are only supposed to use that on my runs." He was sure he turned the GPS tracker off before he acquired Tracey.

"I mean the one in your phone. You have location services active."

Baden pulled the phone away and stared at the traitorous instrument.

"Listen," Klein bellowed, and Baden put the device back to his ear. "All I need from you is the pictures, and a signed statement. You don't have to come into town. My lawyer has an associate in Merrillville and another in Indianapolis."

He didn't relish the idea of going into Indianapolis. His van was clean, but he didn't want to drive I-65 while the Amber Alert was still active.

"Merrillville," Baden muttered. "That may be doable. Send me the address."

"Good. Can you be there before four?"

Baden grunted and looked at the door. He imagined the girl left alone for a day. "Not in this weather, say six?" He'd sedate her, leave her gagged. She'd already fouled the bed; she could make all the mess she wanted on the table. He'd take the back roads to Lafayette and grab 65 to Merrillville.

"I'm getting paid, right?" Baden muttered.

"Not for this. This is unfinished business."

Baden shook his head. "It's another run."

"Easy, Scott."

Baden flinched and his lips twisted into a snarl. He did not like when people used his given name.

"I promise to make it worth your while with your next run."

Baden mulled it over. He hated not getting paid. "Fine. Send me the address." He'd stop and get some pads for the bitch. He was tempted to just go ahead and slit her throat for more acceptable blood. Then start over, again.

He thought about how humiliated the girl must feel, bleeding in the bed. That train of thought soothed him. No point in playing innocent with her. She'd stop bleeding, and by then he would have played with her enough to soften her up. Then he'd be good and ready for some real fun.

Marq both dreaded and anticipated her eventual change. Her current metabolism was unreal, and she felt enhanced in many ways, but the Chicago wind still cut through her like a chainsaw. Part of her couldn't wait until the natural weather had little meaning—as long as she stayed out of the sun. She squinted at the leaden sky and pulled her heavy coat tighter as she made her way to the pick-up lane for her rental car.

In the vehicle and out of the wind she could think again. Her phone told her the weather was going to get worse. She figured her early evening flight would be delayed, or even canceled.

She programed the navigation system to direct her to the bladesmith and eased out into the hated Chicago traffic. When it wasn't stop and go for an hour at a time, people drove too fast and too reckless.

The GPS estimated about an hour south, a few miles west of Plainfield. That hour drive turned into two. Snow started to fall. The rural roads turned slick and treacherous as she drove them.

Her goal was a piece of private property surrounded by a wooden fence with signs warning the fence was electrified and plastered with hand-lettered NO TRESPASSING notices.

She stopped at the gate, spied an intercom and hit the button. The device a sounded a deep beep.

There was no reply for five minutes. She squinted at the rambling structure that was the main house. The fence was well tended and looked almost new, but the building beyond it had a rustic, weathered look. Smoke oozed from the chimney and she could see at least one light on. She pressed the button again.

"Go away!"

The sudden reply gave her a start. "I'm looking for Butch Dunn."

"Who's looking for him?"

"I was sent by Bo Morgan."

There was a long pause. "So, what is Bo up to these days?"

"Racist bullshit." She immediately regretted the words but she was hungry, and still angry.

There was a chuckle over the intercom. "Yeah, that's Bo."

The gate swung open as fat, wet snowflakes splatted on her windshield. She parked close to a flagstone path that lead to the porch.

The door swung open at her approach and she started to walk in, but stopped. A sudden fear clawed at her. No, not fear, dread? Disgust? She stood there in the doorway confused and unable to proceed, as if the other side of the door was crawling with ticks. She hated ticks.

"Don't just stand there lettin' in the cold. Come on in."

And just like that it was gone. She'd been invited in. *Oh my god, is that a real thing*? She regretted the number of times she made fun of Christopher dithering at doorways as she closed the door behind her.

Butch Dunn stood well over six feet tall, dressed in jeans with leather suspenders and a flannel shirt; sleeves rolled to display powerful corded forearms. His build was athletic except for a protruding belly that made him look pregnant.

He welcomed her with a warm smile, something she was not expecting from a craftsman that catered to misogynists. "Not a night to be outside."

"Yes," Marq replied, as Dunn studied her.

The man laughed. "I cain't imagine Bo had two words to say to you. What's your name?"

"Marquessa King."

"Come on, little Miss King, have a seat at the table." He led her into a large room with a kitchen area on the right and a living room/mancave set up to the left. She kept her coat on and walked to the indicated table. It had once been an elegant dining table with intricately carved legs, but was now weathered, with rings from innumerable drinks without coasters. Butch Dunn's furniture suffered from a lack of deliberate care. Or a deliberate lack of care. On close inspection she saw the table was artificially "distressed."

"I was just making tea; would you like a cup?"

"Yes, please." Marq watched her host as he pulled out a well-used tea service. The kettle on the stove was not yet boiling and she suspected he'd put it on before he let her up to the house.

Marq relied heavily on her ability to sense quite a bit about people. Christopher assumed it was a supernatural capability but Marq theorized it was simply a combination of superior sight, hearing and smell feeding information into her subconscious. Butch Dunn was not what she expected.

She *actually* liked him.

"So, what did Bo say that brought you to me?"

"That you cater to the incel community."

The kettle whistled.

"Milk? Sugar?"

Marq nodded, "Yes please." She noticed that the man used silver tongs (only slightly tarnished) to pick up a sugar cube. "Two lumps, please."

Butch fiddled with the set. "So, what do you want?" His tone was still light, conversational.

Marq went straight to the point. "Information. Looking into custom knifemakers in the area, and your clientele in particular."

He brought two cups to the table and offered one to Marq. "What do you want to know?"

"Pardon me for being rude, but you seem awfully friendly for a misogynist."

He waved that away. "The boys aren't here right now, the weather's keepin' 'em away. I don't hate women, hell most of them don't hate women, they just don't understand women—or, even make a real effort to."

"The rape jokes are just fun and games?"

"Yeah, mostly. Partly it's because they're frustrated and also each one is trying to more outrageous than the others."

"They're still joking about assaulting another person."

Dunn shrugged. "Boys will be boys."

"Bullshit."

Dunn chuckled and took a sip of tea. "I cain't believe you ever talked to Bo."

"I didn't. My boss did, but he is indisposed." Marq took another moment to size up the man. "There is someone killing teenaged women and leaving their bodies dumped along I-65. At least five known victims, almost certainly more. One of the few clues is a chip from a custom knife. Damascus steel."

The man nodded, his lower lip protruded. "Nasty business. So, you think one of my boys gotta grudge against women is using a knife I helped him make?"

Marq nodded. "In a nutshell."

"Who are you, again? You didn't say anything about being a cop or a fed."

"Private. My employer has been tasked to assist."

The man smiled. "That is a perdy vague way to put it." Then he frowned at his tea and his forehead wrinkled. "I see why you might have suspicions, but I can assure you my boys are all bark and no bite. Their reaction to seeing a woman is either they cain't speak, or they have to talk trash." He scratched the bridge of his nose. "I cain't see it, truly. Not from my boys."

Marq brought out a notebook from her inside pocket. "Can you give me a list of your boys?"

The man shook his head. "Nope, I don't think that'd be right. But, tell ya what I will do. I'll talk to them and if any one of them seems skittish about the conversation, I will give you a call, Miss King."

"Maybe you could get them together and I could talk to them?"

He shook his head again.

Marq took in a deep breath as her earlier anger seeped back and she smiled to hide her feelings. The well-rehearsed smile that her mother taught her. Butch wasn't hostile. In fact, he was honestly friendly, even a little charismatic, but also unhelpful enough to be exasperating.

She was getting frustrated and hungrier.

"Seriously, I'll make an inquiry." He paused; his forehead wrinkled tried to remember something. "There is one guy…"

"Yes?"

Dunn scratched at his sideburn with one finger. "He responded to a Facebook ad. Not like my usual. Tight-lipped, calculating instead of bragging."

"Where can I find him?"

Dunn's head wobbled indecisively. "Don't have no clue. I'm pretty sure the name he used was fake. But he had, well I wouldn't call it an argument, but it was something, with one of the boys. Kid made a joke about…" Dunn fidgeted. "Pretty sick really. But, this guy, he got offended—not by the subject, but by the guys description of a certain act." Dunn squirmed.

"I'm not easily shocked. What act and what happened?"

Dunn paused and looked her up and down. "The 'joke' ends with a discussion of raping someone dying a violent death."

Marq felt anger flashing in her eyes. The anger made her hungrier and for the first time the thought of biting into raw meat crossed her mind. "Just harmless talk?"

"The boy that told it was just hot air, but this other guy… Like I said, he got agitated. Told the boy 'that's not at all how it feels.' Then he laughed like it was a joke, but there was something in his voice. I believed him."

"And you reported it?"

"To who? And what, that some asshole gave me the willies? But there is one thing I can tell you, he mentioned he saw the ad reposted on the page for Freya's Forge."

"That's a start," Marq said. "What is Freya's forge?"

"It's a who. Some guy calls himself Rachel Starre."

"She's trans?"

"*He's* got a dick." He pursed his lips and actually looked a little apologetic. "He's a spirited one."

"Anything suspicious about her?"

"No, no, no. He's just a pervert. Makes a good blade, tho."

"Bo mentioned a knifemaker in Indiana and described the smith as a 'confused pervert.' And not the sort of person he'd associate with."

"That would definitely be Rachel. I'd call him by his real name iffin I knew it."

"You said she had a Facebook page? Freya's Forge?"

Chapter Twenty-Two

Baden stared ahead at a world that ended at the edge of his headlights. The road was dark, traffic so sparse Baden couldn't see taillights ahead of him. The only vehicles moving were the snowplows. This mess was expected to turn into an ice storm and a fat lot of good plowing would do. He had the steel studded tires on, and chains in the back.

He turned off the high beams as the snow fell thicker, the bright reflections confounding rather than illuminating. He'd prefer to drive with his fog lights only, but there was always a chance some snowplow driver would report him. He didn't fear being stopped, but he couldn't afford the wasted time.

He drove in silence. Driving took concentration and these conditions were extreme, but even so, his mind wandered back to the cabin, the games he was going to play with little Tracey, once she got rid of the red tide, of course. He kept his thoughts general to avoid getting aroused. He didn't see the car on the side of the road until he was right on it. There was no danger of collision, but the fact he only noticed the car at the last second frustrated him. He blinked a few times and put all his attention on the slick road. There was no room for extraneous thought.

He was less than ten miles from Merrillville when a red glow appeared on the horizon and Baden clenched his lips in a frown. *That better not be what I think it is*. He drew nearer and saw what he dreaded; the highway was blocked just at the exit by three police cruisers ringed with road flares. A lone state trooper dressed in an inadequate jacket and a knit cap waved a flare.

Baden put on his friendliest grin and rolled down his window. "Evening, officer. What's up?" He kept his words sociable and adopted the mannerism and facial expression of fellow law enforcement.

The young trooper walked to the window with tight controlled steps. A gust of wind hit, and he closed his eyes. He shrugged off the icy wet chill and addressed Baden. "We got a pileup about two miles past this exit, so we're waving everybody off here. I-65's closed all the way up to Gary."

"How bad? I need to get to Chicago. My mother's heat gave out and she doesn't have money. I'd like to get to her before this storm closes in."

The trooper shook his head. His exposed lips were chapped so bad they bled. "Not by 65. Two semis collided, then seven more cars hit them before they could be moved. You can't see for crap and the roads are a lot slicker than they look. Hell, the last two cars slammed into the pile-up after the warning flares were deployed. Drivers couldn't stop."

Baden pursed his lips; he was going to need the chains. The back roads would be completely snow covered, but that might be better than bare ice. He mentally calculated his route. "Hate to see you out here, you gonna be okay?"

The trooper shrugged. "It's the job."

"Got anything warm?"

The trooper cocked his head.

"I mean, I have a thermos of hot, hot coffee. Black no sugar. You're welcome to it."

"I couldn't but thank you."

Baden held the thermos out the window. "I have another. Go ahead, seriously. It is hot."

"Much obliged, but I couldn't," he said but his tone wavered.

Baden held the thermos further out. "Suit yourself, but if you don't take it, I'm just going to drop it right here." He forced an affable, sympathetic grin.

The trooper returned the grin sheepishly and took the offering. "Okay, thank you much."

"No, thank you. I know it's gotta be tough out here, doing what needs to be done."

The trooper squinted at him. "You on the job?"

"No, not now. Former MP," he lied.

The trooper nodded. "Best head up to the truckstop."

Baden kept the smile on his face. "You take care." He closed the window as the trooper walked away and waved his thanks. It always pays to be friendly with the cops. He found that mimicking their attitude and talking friendly won them over quick.

Before the backroads, he'd hit the truckstop to take a piss and put on the chains. It was one of the bigger places and was likely to have the damn pads for his guest.

Marq got the text that her return flight was cancelled just as she left Dunn's place. That was okay. She wanted to pursue the new lead about the transgender smith. The day was dark, cold and slick but Bloomington was only three hours away, she would change the car rental to one way and drive down there immediately. She snacked on some spiced meat sticks acquired at the airport and set out, intending to get back to 65 and drive south. She knew she should check in with Christopher, but he'd likely demand she wait until he could see the knifemaker with her, and that could mean sitting on her hands for a few days.

Nature did not cooperate, and the weather deteriorated. Marq had strength and endurance greater than an Olympic athlete but driving the iced-over roads exhausted her. It took almost two hours to get back to I-65. She'd devoured the sticks and her emergency jerky stash, and she was still hungry, and nothing tasted right.

New plan. She took the north entrance onto the highway, away from her planned destination. Tomorrow she would drive to Bloomington. Tonight, she'd get a hotel room in Merrillville, and a nice, very rare steak.

That plan also fell apart. She pulled up to the roadblock and heeded the trooper waving a flare and pointing to the exit.

Fine. The truckstop would have something to eat.

There were more cars than she thought would be out on a night like this. Every designated parking place was filled as far as she could tell. She cruised around and finally found a spot further down, away from the gas pumps and even further away from the entrance at an unmarked space.

Marq stepped out into the icy rain and her earlier encounter with the cold Chicago wind seemed like a tiny chill compared to the bitter bone freezing drizzle.

The truckstop was crowded with interstate refugees. She relaxed and went to the women's bathroom, which was in total disarray. There were half a dozen women in line, waiting to use the facility. One of the eight stalls was covered in foul-smelling bodily effluence. She resisted pinching her nose as her keen senses were overloaded. She looked around and noticed hair on the counter, and bloody spit in one of the sinks and she had an epiphany. A nice site for DNA collection.

Her overwhelmed senses made her nauseous and she could not linger waiting for a stall. She stepped back out to the slightly better smelling store area, and her hunger overtook her. Her bladder would have to wait, she needed fortification.

She headed for a rolling grill adorned with sausage like things and ancient tubular crispy tortilla taquitos. She gathered several of them onto a paper plate. The grill was surrounded by cheap looking tables and chairs, mostly filled with elderly women or young mothers trying to placate children. The area smelled much better, even the things on her plate smelled good and she felt her stomach lurch.

Food.

It wasn't going to be enough. She collected several sausages and hotdogs, picked up a bunch of high carb snack items and headed for the register.

Marq could generally ignore the avalanche of sensory input that assaulted her, but her subconscious did an excellent job of pointing out people and things of interest or threat.

The man was average height with a somewhat athletic build. A cute face with a John Travolta type cleft chin. He was dressed in sensible winter clothes, and he was confident. Not an affected swagger, he stood just right, moved just right, military or cop. He was clean-cut and well-built but had just enough of a bad-boy vibe to be very interesting.

She felt her breath deepening. She closed her eyes. Hungry and horny. *No, no, no.* She'd been warned there would be times when hunger and lust could become intertwined in her consciousness.

She was a very sexual woman and Christopher warned about an increase in her libido as her body adapted to the coming change. For example, getting aroused by too many things in inappropriate places. She'd fought, killed, and buried a desire for the new housekeeper. But this guy. She opened her eyes. They sort of stuck there. *Maybe he needs something to warm him up.* The thought was only half serious, but...

He turned and she saw he was carrying a package of pads. *He already has a wife or a girlfriend.* She sighed and watched him head toward the left check-out and she found it cute that he displayed no embarrassment about his purchase. She never understood why so many men get squeamish about anything that reminds them of a woman's physiology. That was also one thing she wasn't going to miss.

She purposely went to the left check-out counter and resisted the urge to shove half a dozen sausages in her mouth as she waited. And then gave up and swallowed three to take the edge off. And that led her to more inappropriate thoughts.

She pulled out her phone to call the house and share her epiphany. Now that she was going to spend the night in a hotel Christopher would not scold her, she could tell him about the lead she was working on and the new development about entering houses.

Jenny answered.

"Hey, Jen. I just got a weird thought."

"Where are you? Christopher is worried, the weather looks bad on the news."

"I'm safe. My return flight is canceled and I'm going to get a hotel room a soon as possible, maybe Merrillville if the road opens. Can I speak to Christopher?" She wanted to tell him about crossing the threshold.

Jenny sounded nervous. "He's down in the basement with three of his coven. I wouldn't like to disturb them."

Marq smiled. The way she felt she'd love to disturb them. "Okay, then listen. I have this idea. You know how the FBI thinks he is a long-haul trucker and he douses the bodies with DNA? DNA that comes from all over the country? Well I'm at a truckstop that is the perfect place to collect samples."

"Yeah," Jenny replied. "That's a thought. But the FBI tried to correlate the DNA with people traveling I-65, and they found too many variations to try and pin down his route."

Marq frowned. "Sorry, I wasn't paying as much attention to the disposal as I was the victims. Well, also, there is this knifemaker in Bloomington. She is a trans woman named Rachel Starre. Dunn gave me her address and I'm going to try and find her in the morning. I think she's the one Bo didn't associate with, and Dunn thinks she had contact with at least one sketchy dude."

"I'll tell Christopher. He's getting stronger. I think he'll want you to wait until tomorrow evening so he can go with you."

Marq sighed. If Christopher was up to it there was no use arguing. "Okay, I'll see about getting a flight back in the morning, we'll go up together."

"Call me when you get to the hotel. Christopher should be available then."

"Will do."

She hung up and looked for a place where she could inconspicuously devour her snacks. She settled at a table tiny table between two groups of tired people trying to doze and tore through the processed food. Her hunger was not completely satisfied but calmed enough she could be on her way. Surely there was someplace open serving red meat.

Her bladder ached and now, she really *needed* to pee. She headed back towards the bathroom.

Marq ducked into the nearest open stall without inspecting it. One thing about her nature that she truly loved was that microbes didn't like her. She couldn't get sick. A filthy bathroom might disgust her, but it didn't stop her.

She left the store, stepping out the automatic doors into numbing cold. The snow fell in tiny driven flakes rather than the gravid wet ones earlier. She drew her coat tight.

She wondered what other important detail she'd missed about the disposal. She tried to picture the files in her mind's eye as she used the fob to remote start the engine and unlock the door. She didn't have an ice scraper, but she could use the owner's manual to brush off the covering snow.

She had her hand on the door when someone grabbed her from behind.

She didn't panic. She heard her attacker a second before the assault. He was about to regret his choice of target.

If he'd startled her, she would have responded by reflex, but confidant in what was about to happen, she paused. Before she made her next move, pain shot through her body; red hot twitching pain. Her nature worked against her as her heighted senses echoed the jolt from the stun-gun on her neck. The gun activated again, her mind active, her body unresponsive; she couldn't even scream. Her assailant yanked her around and wrenched her head up to expose the front of her neck.

She didn't even feel the blade cut through her carotid artery, just wetness gushing down the front of her as the man shoved her into the car, the red liquid soaking the cloth seats. He used the stun gun once more, but she barely felt it. She watched through quickly growing fog as he reached over her and hit the power button to kill the motor. The last thing she heard in this life was the slam of the car door.

Baden looked around. There were a few running cars up by the entrance, but nothing back here. This was one of his usual prowling areas and he knew where all the exterior security cameras pointed.

It was good thing that bitch took her time in the ladies. Gave him a chance to get to the van and put on a disposable polyethylene jacket and hood. He was shaking. He'd killed this way before, a long time ago. Necessary, but not satisfying. She had watched him in the checkout lane with a stare he could still feel. A minute later he heard just enough of her phone call to hear about FBI, DNA samples and Rachel Starre. He had to neutralize her. *Now, who was on the other side of that call?* Damn, he should have grabbed her phone, but did not want to open the door again for fear of the interior light catching someone's attention.

He didn't risk a light but couldn't see any blood outside the car and the windows were blocked by ice and snow so with luck she wouldn't be found until morning. There were two sets of footprints leading to the car. He walked away, making a third set. Between the wind and the degree of snowfall there wouldn't be a trace of his movements in thirty minutes and by then he would be far away.

He moved quickly to the side door of his van, but not fast enough to draw attention. Inside he tore off the jacket, hood and black latex gloves. He bundled and wrapped them into a small plastic pouch. They would melt just fine.

He took out his cell phone as he scanned the parking lot to see if anyone had taken an interest in him, or the corpse inhabiting the car. He wished she'd had a reason to open the trunk. Well, done was done.

He made the call to his boss to let him know he'd be an hour late, cleared the windows and drove off. It was time he found a new route and hunting ground.

Chapter Twenty-Three

Christopher emerged from the basement, walking on his own. The vampyr looked weak but far better than the last time Jenny saw him. He wore slacks and a blue silk brocade robe that was probably a dressing gown, but Jenny wasn't sure about the difference, if there was one. Whatever it was, the blue color was perfect. She wondered how she could replicate that shade—in oil or acrylic, ink maybe?

A bandage artfully woven from gauze strips covered one side of his face, very Phantom of the Opera with an opening for his left eye. Jenny couldn't see any tape and wondered if the vampyr willed it to stay in place. "Do you still need to keep the burn covered?" More gauze covered his left hand and drew attention to his long, ragged, claw-like nails. His hair hung long and unkempt over the gauze.

"Not for healing, it is already much better. No, this is to hide how bad it looks so later I don't have to explain miracle healing." He blinked at Jenny sitting at the kitchen table, holding a book with a lurid cover. "Where is Marq?"

Jenny closed the book. "I thought Lilith told you." Even through bandage she could see his eyebrows raise. "She decided to follow up on the guy who makes knives for the incels."

Christopher scowled. "Right now, I would prefer we stay local."

"There is another girl missing."

"Yes, Tracey Weller, I did read the notes."

"She flew to Chicago and met with the guy, what's his name? Dunn? The plan was to fly back before you got up." *Woke up? Rose? Came back to life?* Was there a proper term for that?

"And?"

Christopher's sharp question interrupted her musing. "Her flight was canceled, huge ice storm in Chicago and sweeping down into Northern Indiana. But she's safe."

Christopher gave her a sidelong glance as he turned asway from her, produced a cell phone from his pocket and hit the speed dial for Marq. He listened to it ring for some time, then pursed his lips when it went to voicemail. "Call me," he said before pocketing the phone. He turned back to Jenny. "Why do you think she is safe?"

"Well, the highway was closed, some accident. She called and said she was going to find a hotel room."

Christopher's tone was even, dripping with feigned detachment. "And when was that?"

Jenny checked her cell phone. "Two hours ago. She said she'd call when she got to her room."

"I don't like this." He paced the length of the kitchen, and back again.

"The roads are really bad; she may have just stayed at the truckstop."

Christopher nodded. "Perhaps. And perhaps she is now driving on treacherous roads and does not want to split her concentration to answer the phone." He paused and cocked his head to one side. "Perhaps." He frowned in thought, then his demeanor changed. "Follow me." He went from recovering invalid to concerned… parent? She definitely got the worried dad vibe.

She followed him up the stairs to the business office. He turned the computer so she could see and brought up a browser.

"What are we doing?"

"Locator. Marq has an app on her phone so I can find her." He looked up at Jenny. "She is in a vulnerable state right now, whether she accepts it or not."

A red dot appeared on the screen and the gray area surrounding it resolved into a map.

"Still somewhere south of Merrillville," Jenny said.

He zoomed in closer and a truckstop appeared by the dot.

"So, she's still there." Jenny felt relieved; Christopher had made her worried.

"And that is more troubling. She should answer." He took out his phone and called her again. He let it ring six times. "Two hours," he mused. "Where are Lilith and Hecate?"

"They had to go; you wore them out. Elsbeth and Sabrina will be here in two hours. Hey, it looks like the dot is outside the store area. Maybe she's bundled up in the car and can't hear the phone ring."

Christopher turned to consider her. He sighed. "We don't think the same way. My kind stay alive by assuming the worst, developing a sense of threats." He frowned, "We don't have time to wait for the others. To quote one of Marquessa's favorite movies, 'I've got a bad feeling about this.'"

Tracey lay limp on the table, still drowsy from the drugs when Baden returned. He examined her, noting that she continued to bleed, overwhelming the single pad he gave her. But she hadn't soiled herself. Good, that left room for future humiliation.

He slapped her cheek with a satisfying thwack, then grabbed her chin to turn her face toward him. He wanted to see this up close. "I know you're awake. Don't think I'm stupid." He dug his fingers into her cheeks and her eyes opened. "I just wanted you to know that I lied to you. Your mother wouldn't pay your ransom. She doesn't love you and told me to do what I want with you."

Tears welled in her eyes. Good.

"I have tools and devices that will lay waste to every part of your body. You're a virgin?" He kept talking, not expecting an answer. "Bet you were waiting for the right man. Well, here I am."

The girl flinched then broke into sobs. Tears streamed down her face.

Baden kept his face frozen in a stoic expression even as he became aroused. He bent down and licked the tears off her cheek; reveling in the salty sweetness.

The girl squealed.

She was almost ready. He pulled a sheet covered cart to the table and whipped the material off with a flourish to display his cruel tools to his plaything.

She screamed.

He fought the impulse to take her right then by telling himself to harvest one more display of tears from her. They never cried in just that way after the physical fun began.

Baden ensured she could see the implements. He would leave the light on and give her the night to dwell on her fate.

Tomorrow. Evening. Play Time.

First, he was going to pay a visit to Rachel Starre. He respected her but now she was a dangerous loose end.

Christopher drove slow enough to maintain control over the treacherous route for almost eight hours. It was four a.m. and they hadn't seen a snowplow, let alone a car, since they passed Indianapolis. Jenny was tired but too wound up to doze. At the start of the drive she tried to ask questions, especially about the burgundy leather briefcase. When he put it in the trunk, he opened the case to check inside. Jenny caught a glimpse of slender silver spikes and a… weapon. It looked like a machete but with a heftier blade. The wooden grip looked well-worn and she saw a hint of a carving, but no idea what it might be. It also had a cross guard curved in an opened up "S" shape.

Snow swirled around the car like an ever-shifting curtain and the road was covered despite of the salt and plows. Only the car's headlights granted illuminations of the dark void. All Jenny could see was snowflakes impacting the windshield and melting just before the wiper cast them aside. Christopher must be seeing a lot more to keep the car on the road.

"Has her phone moved?"

Jenny jerked at the abrupt question then consulted the computer in her lap. "No, still in the same place." The interior of the car was warm, too warm, but she didn't want to say anything about it. Her heavy coat was open, her back damp with sweat. Heat had no more effect on Christopher than cold. He wore a heavy coat of fine black wool buttoned up with kid gloves and a white cashmere scarf around his neck, oblivious to the temperature. His hair was combed, but still too long. He still wore the bandage.

"How far ahead?"

"About ten miles. Am I allowed to talk now?"

Christopher nodded.

"I thought you couldn't drive."

He kept his eyes on the road. "I said it was distracting, irritating, but not outside my ability. Besides, the damn reflectors are covered in the snow. Call Marquessa again."

Christopher's use of Marq's proper name made him sound even more parental. She listened to the phone until it went to voice mail. The sound of Marq's cheery recording gave her goosebumps. Christopher's concern overwhelmed her previous optimism.

"Can I ask about the things you packed?"

He did not look at her. "What is the worst that could happen?"

Jenny did not want to imagine but spoke anyway. "She is injured, maybe seriously. Or abducted."

He shook his head. "Those are disturbing possibilities. But it could be a lot worse. She may have been killed in an accident and her body carried off to a morgue; and that would be a hell of a mess. She is too close to changing and she wouldn't survive an autopsy. But more to the point, any serious trauma could trigger her transformation."

The hair stood up on the back of Jenny's neck.

"Depending on the type of trauma we might have up to three days before she wakes. But if we don't find her and she can't feed, or the only thing she can locate are animals or a terrified victim, we won't be able to save her. She will be nosferatu." His voice turned so cold Jenny shivered in the hot car. "It would be my responsibility to kill her."

Jenny tried to reclaim her optimism. "I still think we are going to find her sitting out the storm in the truckstop." But she felt a hollowness in her words.

"I turned in one day. If you bleed to death, the metamorphosis is accelerated."

Christopher slowed the car as they approached the exit ramp. The combination service station, food court and general store was a bright cheery island in the cold, snow-swept scene. There was no roadblock left.

The lights were deceiving, there were no customers, just a bored clerk sitting behind the register, two guys stocking shelves and one sweeping the floor.

Jenny made a bee line for the bathroom. She'd been apprehensive, extremely apprehensive, about asking Christopher to pull over for a potty break.

She came out to find her boss waiting by the door, staring out at the night. "No one here has been on shift over four hours. None of them saw her." He gazed out from the glass door to the parking lot. There were maybe a dozen snow covered vehicles remaining. He turned to the cashier. "Where are the owners of those cars?"

"The county got a van to shuttle them to the high school. It's been designated a shelter."

Christopher nodded and studied the remaining vehicles. "The locator is not precise enough to tell us which car."

"What do we do now?"

He gestured with his chin. "She is out there. We need to find her."

"So, we go scraping off cars?"

Christopher shook his head. "I know the way Marquessa thinks. She wouldn't be concerned about deteriorating weather when she rented the car, so the jeep and the three SUV's are unlikely. We can rule out the pick-up truck and the mini-cooper."

He stared at an iced over four-door sedan near the door.

Jenny scrutinized the car.

Christopher shook his head. "She might not even be in a car. Definitely not that one."

"Did anyone ever tell you what a bright ray of sunshine you are? Why not that one?"

"I can see traces of rust; it is not new enough to be a rental." He surveyed the remaining vehicles and rested his gaze on the one farthest away from the front door. "The locator shows that the phone is definitely outside the building. If it was too close it might not be so unambiguous." He nodded toward the distant automobile. "That one."

Jenny followed him out into the cold, pulling her coat tighter as the wind drove tiny snowflakes into her face and stung her eyes. She had to trot to keep up with Christopher's broad steps.

"Do we have anything to uh, clean it off?" Her voice wavered, out of breath as they reached their goal.

"Pull on the driver's side door handle." Christopher said. "If the key fob is in there it will unlock." He held out his hand. "It won't react to my touch."

Jenny tugged and there was a double beep, but she couldn't budge the frozen door.

Christopher nudged her away, grabbed the handle and pulled. For a second she thought he was going to pull the handle right off, but there was a cracking, creaking sound as the door slowly released. Christopher blocked Jenny's line of sight. He stood there with his head bowed, his shoulders slumped.

"What, what, what?"

He leaned in. and then pulled back out and pressed his hand over his undamaged eye.

Could Christopher cry?

His voice cracked. "She's here. Her throat's been cut."

"Oh, my God." Jenny simultaneously believed him and knew he had to be wrong. She tried to push past him, but he barred her way.

"Go back to the car, get on the laptop find a motel near here. You know the kind of place I'm looking for."

"Parking close to the room door?"

"Exactly. Then, when I signal, you go there. I'll follow. Call Lilith, see if anyone from the coven are nearby."

Jenny nodded and stepped away, no longer concerned with the weather. No amount of ice could touch the frozen feeling in her chest.

Chapter Twenty-Four

Jenny sat in Christopher's car for twenty minutes while her boss cleared the ice off the rental. His movements were slow and deliberate as the rock-hard ice disintegrated under his scraper. He waved at Jenny before climbing into Marquessa's rental. Jenny followed him for almost half an hour to the hotel.

They made it to the parking lot. Christopher stopped across from the office and got out. Jenny pulled up to him.

He handed her a business credit card. "Ask for the furthest room, preferably in the back."

Jenny drove up to the office and carefully walked into the lobby, keenly aware of the ice-covered asphalt. The last thing she needed was to fall and hurt herself, as much as she wanted to run screaming. She came back with two key cards for room thirty-three.

The snow crunched as Jenny eased the sedan around the building. Christopher followed in the rental close behind. She located the room and pulled up short, leaving the closer parking spot for her boss.

She got out slowly and looked through the car window at the passenger seat as he parked. She gazed at her dead? Undead? friend for the first time. From outside the car Marq looked very natural propped up in the passenger seat, bundled in her heavy coat. To a casual observer she appeared asleep. Christopher's white scarf was wrapped around her neck, covering her wound and spread over the coat to hide the thickly crusted blood. She almost expected Marq to wake up and smile at her.

Jenny tore her gaze away and trudged to the motel room door to opened it.

Christopher pulled Marq's body from the car, cradling her against his chest as if the small form were a sleeping child. He swept past Jenny into the darkened room and lay his burden on the double bed, farthest from the window.

Jenny turned on the bedside lamp and examined her friend arranged on the bed. She moved closer and stood looking down at Marq.

She bent over and tugged at the coat buttons. Her stomach retched as the freeze-dried blood flecked away under her fingers. She was touching her friend's death blood.

"What are you doing?"

"I want this bloody thing off of her," Jenny snapped.

Christopher moved to help but left her to her task and sat inthe chair by a spindly desk.

Jenny opened the coat. She thought she'd steeled herself, but unexpected tears stung her eyes at the site of Marq's ashen body. She removed the scarf and struggled to roll the woman over, pointedly looking away from the disgusting gash across her friend's throat. She tugged away the long wool coat, the one Marq wore when they first met in that alley. The clothes underneath Marq's coat had been spared the bloody mess. As she maneuvered to get the coat away from the cleaner clothes, she felt something in one of the pockets, Marq's cellphone.

Christopher shook his head when she offered it. "No, you hold onto it. The code is 0666."

"Of course it is." Jenny crossed to her purse to tuck the device away. She turned back to survey the position of Marq's body, unsettled by the unnatural, and uncomfortable, position she left it in. She stooped down, prodded and pulled until Marq lay on her back in a more comfortable pose.

The cadaver's pallor was disturbing, as was the limp nature of her limbs. This was the first time Jenny saw a corpse; the dead body of her friend on a bed in a cheap motel room.

She rubbed a gentle hand across Marq's face and frowned. "Shouldn't she be cold?"

Christopher stood up. "She's not cold?"

Jenny grew anxious from Christopher's tone. "No, she's quite warm." Her hand cradled the still figure's cheek. "I don't know if it's my imagination, but she seems to be getting warmer. It's like she's burning up."

Christopher crossed to the bed as Jenny moved aside. He touched Marq's forehead and frowned. He pulled back her lips and examined her teeth. "Did you call Lilith?"

"Yes, she said that no one was nearby but she could get Elsbeth up here in about four hours."

"It's too late for that. She is changing."

"Now? You told me it took three days after…" She couldn't think of the right word. *Temporary death? The little death?*

"That is the lore, but there are many exceptions. Marq has been working since the nineties to acclimate to her nature." He touched the bloody gash on the cadaver's throat. "There was a possibility she may spontaneously turn, even without…" His lips drew back in distaste. "The heat indicates healing." He stood away from the bed. "Now we have a problem. She is going to wake up soon, very soon."

Jenny eyed Marq, suddenly afraid of her friend.

"You called. No one can be here until tomorrow. You understand what that means?"

Jenny shook her head, but she had an idea what he was getting at.

"She will need to feed. And it cannot taste of terror."

"So… I'm on the menu?"

"Don't make light of this," Christopher snapped.

"I'm not making light!" Jenny barked back. "I am trying to *cope*." She pressed her palms to her temples, trying to squeeze out her mounting panic. "This is really beyond me. I don't have a frame of reference, I'm not one of your coven girls." Jenny took a deep breath. "How much blood will she need?"

"Less than the Red Cross takes."

"I've donated before, as long as I can look away, I think I'll be okay."

"Jennifer, this initial feeding will not be—cannot be—clinical. You cannot be detached, or afraid. It must come directly from the source. I can't put an IV line in you and have you squeeze a rubber ball. She needs more than blood, she needs affection, tenderness, a focus for her desire. Your emotional state will determine the outcome of her change."

Jenny trembled. "I don't know that I can do this." She felt fear, she felt inadequate and she felt numb, disassociated as if watching the situation like a TV show.

"I will not ask you to. It has to be your choice."

"Okay." Jenny took a deep breath. "What are our real options? What happens if I don't feed her?"

"She will go into bloodlust and I will put her down, so she doesn't become dangerous."

"'Put her down.' Like an animal." Jenny's voice broke.

Christopher spoke quietly, his tone somber, "Without this feeding, she will be an animal."

"Could we tie her down and wait for someone more… experienced?"

"Even if we could find some way to secure her, she would be lost to the bloodlust long before anyone arrives."

"And if I am afraid, that's bad, right?" Jenny's voice passed beyond fear and became angry.

"I will have to put her down."

"No pressure," Jenny sneered.

"Jennifer, I will not ask this of you. I will not think any less of you if you do not offer."

Jenny stared daggers at Christopher. "Oh, I'm making the offer. If there is a chance to revive her, I'll do it. Just give me a minute to put on my happy face."

Christopher touched the wound on Marq's throat. "Minutes may be all you have. Let me get some things from the car."

Jenny sat on the opposite bed and stared at the carpet as Christopher made for the door. "You're getting the machete thing?"

His only answer was to close the door. He returned carrying his now familiar thick nylon case filled with dirt and the burgundy briefcase. He laid the bag on the floor and set the case on the other bed. He opened it and laid out the silver spikes as well as the wide bladed short sword.

Jenny stood and stared at the items.

Christopher did not wait for her to ask. "If she goes feral, I can use the spikes to get you away from her. They will paralyze her for a minute or so, longer if I can get one in her heart." He gave a sad nod to the other item. "Then I will use the falchion to remove her head."

"How the fuck can you stay so calm?"

Christopher shook his head slowly. "I have no choice," he said bitterly, "and neither do you."

Jenny closed her eyes, she wanted to cry.

"Think of Marquessa. Think about the friendship you were building. Think of light and life and bringing her back. She wants to come back."

Bring her back, what would I do to bring my friend back? What if it were Clio laying there? Suddenly Jenny realized she wasn't afraid of Marq, but of failing her. She shook all over, then stood still, straight, feigning calm. "I've got it under control. Happy thoughts. I'll be ready."

"One thing, before you offer yourself. May I give you a small bite?"

Jenny gave her employer a side-eye. "You're hungry, too?"

"No, but we secrete a venom. In a normal person it hides any pain from the bite, and has a mild sedative effect, like warm cup of chamomile tea. In the abnormal, it intensifies whatever you are feeling. I have to warn you; you are very abnormal."

"I got the one-in-a-million speech. So, the fact that I am about to be a juice pouch for the undead, that will mess with me, right? How much?"

"This one feeding will have no lasting effect on you, at least physically. If you are calm you will respond very well to the venom, making it easier for you to offer yourself. Also, if there is terror there, I will taste it, do you understand? Again, I will not do this without your expressed consent. It is important to Marquessa, so it is important to me that you know as much as you can about what is happening to you."

"All right," Jenny sighed. "In for a penny." She opened her blouse a few buttons and pulled the collar away from her neck.

Christopher bent his head toward her.

Jenny felt a warm rush, a tingling in her neck that slowly spread across her chest until Christopher stepped away.

The vampyr moved to the desk and sat back at the chair. "You are apprehensive, but you do not taste of terror."

"Well, I could have fooled me."

"When she wakes, she will be confused by her drive. She may mistake her hunger for lust, and that is good; it makes the transition easier. You need to be affectionate; you can start by—"

Jenny rolled her eyes. "I've been with a woman before, I don't need you to mansplain being affectionate."

"I was just saying you will want to arouse her."

"Christophe, Christopher, I get it. I am a girl, too." She held her hands up to indicate her breasts but was suddenly aware how hard her nipples were poking through her clothes, stimulated from the venom.

Christopher chuckled. The sound conveyed understanding, not mirth. "Warning. When her eyes open they will be red, don't be alarmed. Soon her fangs will extend for feeding."

Jenny fiddled with the buttons on Marq's silk blouse. She was acutely aware her friend was not wearing a bra. She stopped and turned her head toward Christopher. "Perv. You're seriously gonna watch?"

"I am only staying for your safety. Once Marquessa has successfully turned, I will close my eyes if you like. Or step outside."

Jenny made a sad chuckling noise.

She lay on the bed by her friend and stroked Marq's face, letting the back of her fingers trail along her cheek. The heat was beyond fever; Marq's skin nearly burned to the touch.

Marq twitched. Jenny swallowed a gasp. Marq's body spasmed randomly, then she lay still. But she was lifelike now, not the inanimate thing that lay there minutes before.

The first time she'd been with a woman, in college, the encounter involved several shots of tequila and a lot of awkward giggling. The warmth from Christopher's bite spreading through her body was an acceptable substitute for tequila. There was no giggling this time, only the awkwardness.

Marq twitched again. Jenny responded by sliding her hand over Marq's small, but very well shaped breast, surprised by how suddenly Marq's nipple became erect under her palm through the silk. Jenny eased her hand under the blouse and slipped it back over the nipple, teasing the flesh to greater arousal.

Marq squirmed.

Jenny moved her hand to Marq's other breast as she scooted up the bed to bring her face near Marq's.

Those luscious lips parted. She was no longer the limp object that Christopher laid out on the bed. Jenny took a quick breath, closed her eyes, and kissed her. Marq responded, their tongues entwined, then abruptly Jenny felt the hardness of the fangs extending in her friend's mouth. The same warmth as Christopher's bite spread through her mouth and down her neck. She was hungry for her friend and ravaged those plump lips with her own. She sought Marq's tongue with an intensity she could not control. Marq reacted frantically to the exchange of fevered kisses, her body rising, squirming to be closer to Jenny.

Jenny was lost to sensation as Marq awakened completely, her blood red eyes glowing. She let Marq's strong arms wrap around her, crushing their bodies together.

Marq seized Jenny and rolled on top of her, her knee between Jenny's thighs, as the new vampyr pressed herself against Jenny's core.

Marq pressed again, her knee now the center Jenny's rising arousal until her friend's hungry mouth pressed back against her lips.

Jenny realized that Marq was confused, she felt desire, but was channeling it the wrong way. Jenny grabbed the back of Marq's head and guided those rich, full lips to her throat.

She could not be prepared for what happened next.

The miniscule bites earlier were nothing compared the to the insane warmth that spread from her neck throughout her body. She shivered, shaking with pleasure. In addition to the venom, Marq's lips and tongue teased her nerve endings, arousing her beyond comprehension.

Then, Marq pushed away from her, settling on fours over Jenny's quivering body.

Jenny was barely aware of Christopher moving. "I am going to leave you now."

Jenny turned her eyes toward the man. Lust enveloped her, she wanted more. "You can join us."

Christopher shook his head. "That is the venom talking. Tomorrow is going to be awkward enough already."

Jenny looked back at Marq who hovered over her, studying her in the dim light, her red eyes shining.

Jenny shivered and tried to tamp down her arousal as Marq seemed finished.

Suddenly Marq was back on her, the vampyr's lips, tongue and fingers dancing across her body. Jenny's bra disintegrated under Marq's ardent assault. But before she could even form the thought to care about her clothing, Marq was on her again, using her new strength to rip Jenny's jeans away. The vampyr was a sensuous wild animal, just as out of control as Jenny, but with a different need, another hunger.

Jenny eagerly accepted as Marq put her head between her thighs. The warmth came again, like a mystical candle burning intensely, bringing light and warmth to the very core of her being. She gasped for air, the intensity overcoming her. The candle became fireworks. Pulsating waves of ecstasy thrummed through her body.

Jenny couldn't breathe. She rode each wave barely capable of groaning in response to Marq's movement. The waves changed from rapid explosive pulses to long rolling impressions, allowing Jenny to draw breath. Marq's tongue was still teasing her and she moaned as the last spasms rocked her body and she fell into a deep sleep.

Marq became aware of everything as Jenny touched her breast, caught by powerful forces. The blood tasted, conveyed, shared the pleasure. She had been unable to stop herself from trying to elicit even more pleasure to feed on.

It was only when Jenny passed out that she regained control. She crouched on all fours, with Jenny beneath her. A lassitude fell over her. One minute it was like she was on cocaine with limitless energy, then suddenly felt heavy. She lay down on top of her sleeping friend.

The door opened. She was aware that Christopher came in. He did not speak to her, but fiddled with the black plastic bag, getting the rods in place to form a box.

She did not want to move, even as he picked her up. She let him; not sure she could stop him. He placed her in the box, situating her comfortably. "This is your new bed, dearest Marquessa." He kissed her on the forehead, then closed the box.

Chapter Twenty-Five

Baden seethed at himself as he pulled the car onto the dirt road in front of the cabin. He had to kill that woman at the truckstop, but he didn't enjoy it, much. Somehow he screwed up, there was some kind of trail. They, whoever "they" might be, were after him. It would be difficult to set up a new route but could also be fun. That thought could not tamp his irritation. His headlights illumined a canine form slinking around the cabin. Fucking coyote. He thought about chasing it, killing it; but his rage was fixated on the girl bound up in the cabin. It was her fault he was buying the damn pads. She made him kill that woman.

Before leaving he'd stripped her down to her t-shirt and underwear, and her nearly naked body shivered under the thin sheet. Her bare hands and feet were fixed to the table with heavy iron manacles.

He turned his nose up at the smell; there was more blood, and she'd lost control of other bodily functions.

He slapped the girl soundly. "Wake up!"

Her eyes widened but that was her only response.

That would not do, he had to get her verbal again. You cannot enjoy degrading the degraded. This one needed to be convinced there was still hope. Hope/despair/hope/despair and on and on was the cycle he reveled in.

He took an allen-wrench from the table and released the clunky cuffs and chains that bound her to the table. "You filthy bitch." He didn't yell, but carefully kept his tone low, to let her know how enraged he was, but also to give her hope of forgiveness.

The girl, shivering much harder now, curled in a fetal position and clutched at the sheet.

"There is a scrub bucket, brushes and paper towels in the kitchen." He hauled the sheet off her.

She howled.

This one is shy. He preferred to keep them clothed until the first time he used them, but he enjoyed her reaction.

"You get this table cleaned up." He stuck his finger at her face and was rewarded as she flinched. "If you do a good job, you will get clothes and be allowed back to the bed. If not," he leered at her, "you will learn about all the special uses of this little piece of wood." He displayed a thin piece of bamboo, split on one side to make it razor sharp.

Tears streamed from her eyes and he longed to taste them but refrained. Get the little bitch cleaned up first.

Jenny woke slowly. The actions of the night before were fuzzy and sifted through her languorous dozing, causing her to smile. Not at the memory, which was still unformed, but from the raw sensuality and emotion that came with it. She snuggled into the warm bed, indulging in sleep.

Then she remembered. All the events tumbled through her thoughts, anxiety forcing her to sit up. She was aware of several things at once. Number one, she was naked. She pulled up the sheet and clasped it to her bare breasts. It wasn't the nudity that bothered her, but the vulnerability.

 She was still in the motel room, with Marq's travelling… coffin? Daybed? Bag? on the floor beside her. There was a feminine shape sleeping in the full bed across from her. *Lilith*? No, the sleeping woman was more full-figured.

It was well past sunup and even though the curtains were pulled tight using clips an ambiguous glow flowed through the center. Enough for her to see most of the room.

"I am glad to see you are up."

Jenny jerked at the voice, and located Christopher burrowed in the shadows of the passage that led to the bathroom.

She blinked, trying to see him. "What are you doing up? Sun's out." She shook her head. "You know, you guys have heard of sunblock, right?"

"Yes," Christopher's voice dripped forced patience. "I have experimented with many products. I have rated their usefulness by measuring the light frequencies that are not blocked. I found two formulas that block every wavelength of the sun's energy, at least as far as contemporary science can measure." He sighed. "And yet it burns."

"Ever just slather yourself in zinc oxide?"

"Believe me, I have been scrutinizing the science of photoprotection for decades." He paused and when he spoke again, he sounded like Jenny's eighth grade science teacher. "The most powerful light rays are ultraviolet A and B. A by itself does not affect our kind quickly. UVB burns after a few seconds. That is more like your traditional sunburn. It may blister if we linger. But direct sunlight, with all the components, x-rays, spectrum light, burns in minutes. And I mean the stereotypical skin-catching-fire sort of burning."

"That doesn't sound fun," Jenny muttered as she idly scratched her neck

"It's not that bad, it's actually painless."

Jenny was distracted as an incessant itching sensation exploded in several spots across her body. "Doesn't sound painless."

Christopher's voice was back to controlled patience. "No one knows how long our kind could live. There is a depression that sets in after a couple of centuries or so. We lose the desire to do anything, there just doesn't seem to be a point. Most vampyr die by suicide."

Jenny started to make a remark about psychiatrists but stopped. How could he get real help with depression secondary to vampyrism? Once he revealed that, they'd lock him up.

Christopher continued. "The most common act of suicide for our kind, is to chain oneself outside and watch the sunrise. Those first early morning rays are the most deadly. They burn the skin so fast that all nerve endings are singed away before the subject can feel any pain. One's eyes burn away, and then it is over." There was a sense of loss in his voice.

"You've seen this?"

"Too many times."

"But you are okay in the shadows there."

"No," he gave a rueful chuckle. "I am very uncomfortable, but I had to ensure that you were taken care of."

Jenny suddenly felt self-conscious being naked in front of the vampire. Also, she was forcing herself not to scratch her breasts where they itched around her nipples. Were there bedbugs in the room? She squirmed uncomfortably under the sheet.

"You itch?" Christopher asked.

"Yes."

"That is a remnant of Marq's feeding. The substance in our saliva causes the wound to heal incredibly fast, which is why our deepest bites look and feel like mosquito bites in the morning."

As he spoke, she became aware of more itching places. She forced herself to stay still. She was not going to start scratching between her thighs with Christopher there.

Christopher stood. "If you are all right, I will join Marq in the box."

He moved across the room. "Elsbeth will help you with the other considerations." He'd had his bandage replaced with one that covered a lot less of his face.

Jenny glanced at the sleeping woman. "What kind of considerations?"

"You don't have any clothes."

Jenny started at the pronouncement.

"They were collateral damage in Marq's feast. Elsbeth brought some clothes you can wear to go shopping. And it was a tough night, you and Elsbeth need to be sure to get some lunch."

"I don't think leaving you both here alone is a good idea."

"Sabrina will arrive shortly."

"Are you and Marq's feeding arrangements set? I can pitch in."

"That will not be necessary. Elsbeth and Sabrina can manage us. Also, I have to warn you that while one feeding is not likely to harm you, you will need to avoid multiple feedings. Unless you want to experiment with your own ways to tolerate sunlight."

Jenny stared at him.

"You are one of us. You are like Marq when I found her. I can sense your potential but will not force anything on you."

"Marq said there were only seven that you know about."

He tapped the bag with his toe. "Eight now. Lore says we were much more common before the fourteenth century."

"What happened then?"

"Plague."

Jenny blinked. "Plague can kill you?"

"No. But it killed so many, so fast, that many of our kind rose as nosferatu. The church was very effective at destroying most of our lines; along with a few hundred innocents. For centuries they kept hunting us in the Balkans, Germany and Austro-Hungaria. They produced many bodies, maybe one or two were actual nosferatu. On that note, I shall take my leave." He stooped down and unfastened the Velcro over the zipper.

"When are we going to look up that knifemaker Marq told us about, Rachel Star-ray?"

Christopher paused to consider. "We don't have time to follow up. Marq is going to need assistance for a few days, and I have to oversee it."

"Why don't I take the rental car—"

"The rental car is being detailed." Christopher's voice was firm. "By people who charge too much, but do not ask questions."

"Okay, but what harm could it do for me to find this Rachel person?"

Christopher looked up and fixed her eyes with a cold stare. Once their gaze locked, he led her vision down to Marq's container. "What harm was it for her?"

"We don't know what happened."

"All the more reason to be careful. Once Sabrina gets here, she will drive you to Chicago and you will take a flight back. I will bring Marq back tonight. Tomorrow night, or the night after, we can plan."

"But what about the kidnapped girl? The clock is ticking."

"We cannot help her until we are safe and stable." With that, Christopher closed the box and sealed it from the inside.

The discussion about Tracey Weller's fate was, for the moment, over.

Flights from O'Hare were stacked up and it was past midnight before Jenny reluctantly returned to the house on St. James Court alone. With Marq around, it seemed homey, even cozy for such a large residence, but by herself sounds echoed on the walls, and that was not as disturbing as the silence. The only way to keep calm was to pace the living room floor while she wrung her hands. She had so much to think about that she couldn't even grasp the enormity of information and questions she needed to process.

Everything made more sense as some sort of paranoid delusion, but she couldn't leave it there. The thought about her encounter with Marq; was it real? All the marks were gone, all she had was the memory. She'd done LSD once and her recent experience had more of the feel of drug reality, not objective reality; but...

The phone rang. A landline that terminated in a very old black Bakelite telephone.

"Christopher Stefanov's residence. This is Jenny, how may I help you?" The formal answer actually soothed her brain and brought her into the present.

"Hey Jenny, this is Nina. Sorry, Sabrina. I know the name thing is confusing."

"Not at all," Jenny politely lied.

"We are on the way, just finished, uh," Sabrina sighed. "Mealtime. Sorry, don't mean to be awkward but I'm not used to talking about this..."

"With an interloper?"

"No, I mean with anyone. I'm actually the newest to this group. Hecate brought me in right after they accepted her. Have you realized how absurd this is?"

Jenny felt a sense of relief as the other woman's words mirrored her thoughts. "Yes. I'm terrified that I'm crazy."

"Just checking. Late at night I get sort of like anxiety attacks, and I doubt my sanity."

"I fully understand," Jenny said, feeling a connection.

"Okay," Sabrina changed the topic. "We will be in by 6:00 a.m. We're grabbing food, people food, along the way, but Christopher wants us to have a proper breakfast at the house. There is a number on the fridge for a cook who can come in."

"You want me to call a cook in the middle of the night? No, I can make breakfast," she said, grateful for some task to concentrate on.

Sabrina sounded amused. "Works for me."

"What do you like?"

"Elsbeth is a pancake girl and I'm more of an eggs, ham, and bacon kind. Can you make omelets?"

Jenny felt a stab of panic. She could make an omelet but hadn't since Thad's meltdown because she didn't use enough cheese. He beat her with the steel turner spatula. She still had scars. "Yes," she said, her voice a little shaky. "I would love to make you an omelet. What kind of cheese do you like?"

She'd just hung up the phone when the doorbell rang.

Jenny frowned at the clock and walked to the door. She'd lit up every light in the front of the house to dispel an anxiety, her lizard brain afraid of all the things that lie in the dark.

She looked out and saw her ex-husband standing on the porch, no weapons evident. She thumbed her phone screen to bring up the speed-dial to security.

He knocked on the door with his fist. "Come on, Jen, I know you're in there."

She wanted to ignore him but that felt too much like cowardice. With a deep breath she channeled Marq's cool, confident, demeanor and engaged the sturdy chain bolt before opening the door. "Leave, Thad. I'm calling security."

Her ex-husband looked at her. He seemed... concerned? She'd seen him fake that so often she was certain it wasn't real.

"Look, Jen, I'm trying to save you."

"Save me?" She lowered her voice. "You tried to kill us, that's kinda the opposite."

"Not you, just them. You don't understand, you don't know what you're involved with."

"I assure you that I know perfectly well."

Thad looked over his shoulder as if someone might sneak up on him.

Jenny held up her phone. "I haven't called security." She paused for impact. "Yet."

"Where are they? Are they out hunting for me? You have to tell him not to kill me. C'mon, you *owe* me, Jen."

"They don't give a shit about you; they have other problems."

"Why would you cozy up to that bloodsucking freak?" He sneered, revealing his true nature. "Oh yeah, he keeps that veneer of being human, but let him loose..." He chomped his teeth at her. "I've seen one, once they go to their nature."

"You've seen what?"

194

He looked around again. "A fucking vampire, Jen. That thing's all teeth and claws, it'll rip the blood out of any living thing."

"Nosferatu," Jenny murmured. She traced her thumb over the phone. "Where did you see this?"

"That guy Grant, the one with the crossbow, he's had one locked up for years. He knows all about those things, Jen. You'd be smart to let us rescue you."

"Oh, my God, Thad. Who is the guy you have locked up?" She shook her head. "You know what?" She held up her hand, palm out. "There is nothing you can say that I want to hear. Tell it to security."

"Bitch, I'm trying to save you. Grant and the others, they don't know I came to warn you. I want to help you get away from those freaks before they fuck you up."

Jenny smirked as she saw the blinking lights approach. "You need to leave."

Thad stomped his foot and took off into the night.

~

A block away Thad slinked to the van and opened the passenger side door.

"So, find out anything?" Grant asked. The two men were alone.

"Not much. They're not there, but it looks like she's expecting someone. That bitch is all full of herself. The bloodsucker is still alive. Bitch did let on that the leeches have something more urgent to deal with than us."

Grant cocked his head. "Did you find out what?"

"Naw. She sicced security on me. Bitch is in bed with them now."

"We need to kill them all." Grant said. "'cept our little recruitment too."

"Yeah, I got me some special plans." Thad grinned.

Chapter Twenty-Six

Four members of Christophe's Coven carried in the folding box that held Marq's resting form into 1454 St, James court. Jenny watched, arms folded under her breast, then turned and hissed at Christopher. "I cannot believe we are having this conversation."

The other women ignored the argument and proceeded to the basement with their burden.

"Priorities," Christopher repeated emphatically. "We are not ignoring the girl. We will turn everything we have over to the FBI. At this point they will be more effective without having to deal with vampire hunters." Christopher sighed. "Once Marq gets better we will need to move."

"So, we're leaving an innocent little girl in the hands of a sadist with a blacksmith fetish? Look at the profile! This asshole rapes, murders and chops up little girls. He is no different than a nosferatu. You'd kill Marq, but leave him to the cops? I don't know how you un-live with yourself." She held her arms tighter as a rigid barrier and leaned against the kitchen counter. "The clock is still ticking for Tracey, whether it's convenient for you or not."

"Yes," Christopher said, his voice pitched low with forced patience. "But there is another ticking clock and the consequences of ignoring it are far more dangerous. The militia's attack on Marq is an escalation that cannot be left uncontested."

Jenny dropped her arms. "Wait, you think my husband and that little band of would-be vampire slayers went after Marq?"

Christopher cocked his head to one side and regarded his new housekeeper. "You were seriously thinking that some random murderer slit her throat? And just left her money?" He pointed at Jenny. "Marq started the escalation. She brought a gun and managed to wound at least one. That would make her a target."

Jenny shook her head. "She flew to Chicago, got a rental. How the hell would those guys know where to find her?"

"The, what do you call him, incel?"

"More of an incel enabler," Jenny muttered.

"The militia knew we were interested in him. They could have planned an ambush like they did before, but because they thought she was human followed her to a spot far away."

Jenny felt the hair on the back of her neck stand up and adrenaline-fueled heat rolled through her body. "That rat bastard. I am going to make him wish he'd never been fucking born."

Christopher held up a hand. "Easy. Our first concern has to be the nosferatu. That is the greater danger."

"To you?" Jenny retorted.

"To everyone." Christopher did not raise his voice but doubled the intensity. "If they have a feral nosferatu you cannot imagine the violence and destruction it could do if it escaped. Do you know how they've been feeding it?"

Jenny chafed at being talked down to but choked back a biting reply. Instead, she continued through clenched teeth. "I called security and chased him off before asking any questions. To be honest I don't believe him."

"I do." Christopher wrinkled his nose. "Your ex said Grant has had the thing for years. I misstated some things about nosferatu. I said they were unreasoning creatures and that is not entirely correct. When they first awaken, they are hungry and confused with no other thought than appeasing their hunger, but keep one alive for years…" He shook his head.

"What?"

"They will eventually regain much of their prior knowledge, only tainted by the desire to be cruel and to kill. Dealing with a reasoning nosferatu is fraught with dangers. And, possibly worse…"

"Worse?"

Christopher openly sneered. "What if Grant captured a vampyr and through deprivation caused the bloodlust to dominate? A completely self-aware killing machine?"

Jenny clenched her fists. "So, what are you going to do? What makes you think the FBI will find our evidence credible?"

"I'm working on the provenance of the information. As for the nosferatu, we have to kill it. Now."

"And you are going to do that how? March in and…what?"

Christopher frowned. "There is no marching in. The bunker is too well defended. Marq kept tabs on them for years until she was convinced they'd lost interest in us. We have a partial map and satellite images from Google, but no practical knowledge of the security measures inside. No, we will have to indulge in subterfuge."

"How?"

"Working on it," Christopher answered, his voice bitter as wormwood.

Jenny's voice mocked his tone. "So, while you are 'working on it' how about I follow up with the trans bladesmith?"

Christopher opened his mouth to speak

"I know, but Marq did not have her guard up. I checked Rachel Starre's Facebook page. Not only is she a blacksmith but she's also a performer. She does a burlesque show in Indianapolis two days a month. She posted her schedule and she will be at the theater all day. A public place where I can approach her and get information."

"You are not going alone, and that is final." Christopher no longer feigned patience.

"You can't order me," Jenny snapped back.

Christopher cocked his head and studied her. "Then you will leave this house."

Jenny sucked in a breath. She knew the words on the tip of her tongue would destroy this relationship, this job, this life. She felt the overwhelming desire to scream them at the vampyr, but one last reasonable part of her brain hesitated.

"She won't go alone," Lilith spoke up from behind.

Jenny had been too angry and focused on the conversation to hear the older woman approach from the basement stairs.

"Et tu?" Christopher said, his voice flat.

"You are both right," Lilith said with a tinge of anger. "We need to turn our information over to the FBI, but we need a complete picture to hand them. Your sources will not be forthcoming to federal agents. Anyone with a suit or a badge will have a much harder job getting answers, and that does not help that poor girl. Until we have a workable plan to deal with the nosferatu we should follow up as much as we can. We don't want to wait for tonight and be stuck in Indy, where we are vulnerable. We'll go, you get in your box."

"It is dangerous."

Lilith gave a rueful chuckle. "Yes, so is living, although you may have forgotten that. Besides, Marq isn't the only one who has a pistol and knows how to use it." She stepped toward Jenny. "Do you know how to shoot?"

"Long gun only. I can shoot a handgun but not accurately." Mentally she ticked off boxes, *Must learn to shoot and some fighting skills.*

"It is just a trip to Indy," Lilith said, placing a calming hand on Christopher's shoulder.

Christopher shrugged her away. "How will you even get out of the house without being followed? How will you get past the militia men watching this place?"

"How many men are we talking about?" Lilith asked. "There can't be more than one or two. If I can't lose them, then it is time for me to check into a retirement home."

Christopher sighed. "It's been two decades since you raced stock cars."

"I keep my hand in."

"Stock cars?" Jenny said with skepticism.

"Tried my hand at Indy car, couldn't make the cut."

Christopher raised his hands in surrender but lowered them slowly. "Yes Jenny, but you can't go today. I know you feel energized, but you will crash, soon. And Lilith, you will need to be your sharpest and how long have you gone without sleep? What does Facebook say about Rachel's day tomorrow?"

Lilith pulled back the curtain and surveyed the yard.

It was ten a.m. The air was crisp and cold. Snow lay thick on the ground and the sky was the color of lead. It hadn't snowed since the big storm and although St. James Court was still packed in snow and ice, she could see that Magnolia had been plowed and cars were moving. That was a good indication the main roads and highway would be just fine. She turned to Jenny, who was swathed in Marq's wool coat with a striped red and gold cable knit, scarf wrapped around her head, covering all of her hair and most of her face.

"You ready?"

Jenny nodded.

Lilith wrapped a deep purple scarf around her own head, obscuring her features. They both put on sunglasses.

Lilith's car was parked out front. Jenny tasted a light metallic tang in the frigid air as they attacked ice-covered windows with heavy-duty scrapers. The frozen doors were a greater challenge, but soon they were settled and pulled onto the snow-covered street.

Jenny kept a close watch for anyone following, but nothing stirred. No white van.

Lilith still took evasive maneuvers.

Jenny grabbed the "Jesus" bar above the window as the other woman made sharp skidding turns, running through alleys and side streets.

At Oak Street she pulled onto I-65 South, got off at University Boulevard and then back to Eastern Parkway to the ramp for I-65 northbound. There were more cars on the road than expected and Lilith slowed to speeds more suitable to the conditions. Jenny's heartbeat returned to almost normal.

The maneuvers had been so fast that the car heater hadn't time to warm the interior and Jenny could still see her breath.

They drove in silence as Lilith concentrated on the road. The highway appeared clear but Lilith was wary of black ice. Two hours later they made it to Indianapolis, got off on Prospect and made their way through streets better cleared than Louisville.

Lilith rolled to a stop before the last building at the end of a row of storefronts. The windows were tinted dark and only one very subtle sign indicated it was the cabaret. They got out of the car and approached the front door, oblivious to the maroon van parked a few spaces down. Jenny was afraid that no one would be there, or the place would be locked up. But the front door was unlocked. They entered and made it two steps.

"Hey!" A woman yelled from behind the bar. She wore a Pink Floyd t-shirt and brandished her polishing cloth at them. "We're closed."

"Sorry," Jenny said with what she hoped was a sincere smile. "We wanted to talk to one of your performers, her Facebook page said she'd be here all day, Rachel Starre?"

The woman took on a guarded look. "What do you want with Rachel?"

"It's personal. We have some questions about her blacksmith work."

The woman eyed both of them. "She's in dance rehearsal right now. You'll have to wait a few minutes. I'll tell her you're here."

The few minutes turned into an hour before a Red haired Amazon burst into the room. She was over six feet tall with a fit, curvy body and low blouse flaunting about an acre of cleavage. Jenny could believe this was a blacksmith, her shoulders were shapely enough to be feminine, but they looked powerful, like she was wearing 80's style shoulder pads.

"Can I help you?" she asked with a husky, seductive voice.

Jenny was taken aback but managed to blurt out, "Hi, my name is Jenny Torres, may we talk privately?"

Rachel looked around. "Small place, this is as private as it gets."

Jenny took in a breath to steel herself. "We are working on a private investigation into several murders."

Rachel cocked an eyebrow. "Private dicks, huh?"

Jenny felt like the woman was laughing at them. "Has the FBI or local police questioned you about the murder of Karen Quin?"

Rachel pulled her chin back and frowned. "I don't know who that is." Her manner became more serious. She looked at Lilith. "Who are you?"

"The driver," Lilith quipped with a neutral expression.

Rachel nodded and turned her attention back to Jenny. "I don't know anything about any murders. I avoid news, it gets me too worked up. But the feds have been by asking questions about my students, and some other knifemakers."

"They didn't tell you what it was about?"

"All they said was it was an ongoing investigation. I didn't tell them anything. Hell. I don't think I have anything to tell them."

"Did they ask you about a chipped knife tip?"

Rachel stared at Jenny. "What about it?"

"It was Damascus steel, broken in the cervical vertebrae of a young girl."

"I don't like the sound of that," she said, her voice flat.

"Butch Dunn recommended we talk to you, said you had at least one student that was a little shady. Made the icels nervous."

Rachel snorted. "Butch. He would know about sketchy clients." She chewed at her upper lip and then said, "Tab."

"Excuse me?"

"The guy said his name was Tab. Don't remember exactly when he took the group class, but he recently came to me because he chipped the tip off his knife. Pretty sure Tab's not his real name, too."

"The chip we're talking about wouldn't be recent. The piece was recovered over a year ago."

Rachel nodded. "He said he originally chipped it a while back gutting a deer but was able to do enough stock removal to make it work. Then he chipped it again. This time he paid for a private session." She grimaced. "He's a fetishist."

"What?"

"Most people who take my classes just want to know how to make knives. This guy wanted to make a specific knife." She scratched over her right eyebrow. "People like him think owning a special item grants them a certain quality. Usually it's white boys and katanas. They think owning one makes them a samurai."

"What did he look like? Do you remember?"

"Oh yeah. A little shorter than me, say five-ten. Medium build, athletic. Works out a lot. He had a cleft chin."

"Wait a minute, wait a minute, wait a minute." Jenny dug into her purse and brought out one of her sketchpads. "Do you mind if I try and draw what you describe?"

Lilith spoke up. "Can you do that?"

Jenny shrugged. She was good with caricatures and portraits but had never really applied herself to them.

"Well," Rachel said. "He had a cleft chin, like that guy in Pulp Fiction."

"John Travolta?"

"Yeah, if you say so. Angular face, strong cheekbones and…"

"And?" Jenny repeated.

"His eyes. Can you draw hunger? That's what they looked like, hungry, but not just like someone at dinnertime, but like well-trained dog with a full dinner dish waiting for the command to allow him to eat."

Jenny tried to draw hungry.

"And confident, he oozes confidence, but not cocky. He's polite." Rachel went on with details about his hair, lips and expression as he squinted at the forge.

Jenny showed her the picture. Rachel shook her head and made corrections. It was a tedious process but within another hour Jenny finally completed an acceptable likeness.

"We should to turn this over to the FBI. I think it would be good idea for you to contact them and tell them about this."

Rachel clenched her lips. "*You* can tell them he was driving a van. Very nice, looked expensive."

"License?"

"Sure, it had one, but I didn't really pay attention. I have a security cam but I only keep a week. Look, I want to help as much as the next girl, but if I don't get this choreo down tonight's show will suck balls." Rachel leaned closer. "And I make my money on the tips, you know?"

Jenny nodded. "Thank you for your time. I hope the show is great."

"I thought the FBI was keeping the existence of the chip a secret?" Lilith asked as they headed out the door.

"I think they'll forgive us for this sketch."

Baden observed the two women as they exited the cabaret. He checked his watch, nearly three hours since the pair went in. He'd dismissed them as being with the performers, but there was something about the way they spoke to each other as they were leaving, and the Kentucky license plate.

They didn't look like feds or police, but neither did that bitch he'd been forced to slit open.

An all-female detective agency? Probably a "Charlie's Angels" arrangement with some dude calling the shots. That made more sense.

He resisted the urge to follow them but took the plate number. He wasn't used to anxiety and did not like the idea of Rachel telling tales about him. He respected her, and she'd be hard to kill but it would be necessary. After that, he'd have to take care of that cute little wife of hers. She'd seen him at the forge too. From now on, no loose ends.

Chapter Twenty-Seven

Jenny sighed in relief. "Thank you for slowing down."

Lilith smirked. "Just giving you a break 'cause you are going to get a hellacious cramp holding onto that panic bar."

Jenny rubbed the strained muscles in her hand.

"Did you get a reply on the sketch yet?"

"No telling when anyone will check their inbox, but the sketch should be there when they do. I also texted a copy with a note to Hecate asking her to nudge them to look at it. I don't think Christopher does texts."

Lilith snorted and shook her head.

Jenny relaxed into the leather car seat and placed her hands in her lap, prepared to seize the grab bar at any moment. Not that she didn't take Lilith at her word about keeping it under seventy miles an hour.

A noise like an abrupt, muffled wail of the dammed came from her purse to shatter the silence, then was gone.

"What the?" Lilith said, eyes on the road. "Is that yours?"

She opened the bag and took out the foreign phone, holding it carefully as she stared at it.

"What is it?" Lilith asked.

"Marq's phone," Jenny said. "Christopher told me to keep it after we recovered Marq." Her voice choked at the memory. "Text message."

205

"What's it say?"

Jenny hesitated. She had the code to open the phone, but what if this was personal? Then she thought about the other night. She read the note and frowned. "It's from Bobby Leiter. Asking 'Ms. Koenig' to meet him." She deftly used her thumbs to type a response, explaining simply that "Ms. Koenig" was not available.

The next text demanded to know who she was. Jenny hesitated for second and texted back. "Jennifer Torres, personal assistant to..." She paused. "Christophe, right?"

"Correct," Lilith supplied.

"Right." Jenny added the name and sent.

Jenny stared at the frazzled replies, full of misspellings and spacing errors. Her eyes tried to follow the hasty messages. "He says he needs to meet with her. He is on the run, Grant and his boys have turned on him, called him a 'species traitor.'"

"Not our problem," Lilith muttered. After a second, she sighed, "Where is he?"

Jenny scrolled through the frantic messages. "He's in Louisville right now on a four-hour layover—doesn't mention final destination. He is trying to find protection."

"Well, tough."

"We could offer him to stay with Christopher."

Lilith gave her a side-eye. "Yeah. I'm sure Christopher would love a sleep over."

"Jesus, no need to get sarcastic," Jenny said.

Lilith shrugged.

"He still wants to know where Marq is." Jenny typed back, *Out of town for several days.*

There was a long pause.

Jenny closed her eyes and leaned back in the car seat. There was something she was trying to remember... she was interrupted by the alert of another text. She frowned at the smartphone screen. "He says it is urgent he meets her. He has a file from the FBI with urgent information on the missing girl." Jenny texted back. *It's not possible.*

"And?"

"He is in a bind. He planned the layover in Louisville hoping to meet Marq. He knew it would be too daylight to see Christopher. His flight departs at 7:20 tonight. He wants to turn over the papers before he goes. Still won't say where his flight is to."

Jenny typed. *She is not available; you can meet with me or leave town.* She frowned. "He still wants Marq." She glared at the phone. "Screw it," she muttered. Frustrated, Jenny typed *Ms. King is dead.*

They drove for fifteen more minutes before the next reply.

"He's agreed to meet me, but it has to be a public place near the airport. He says there is a bowling alley by the fairgrounds. I think I know the place."

"Me too." Lilith nodded and resumed her concentration on the road as the speedometer crept over ninety.

Jenny grabbed the Jesus bar and held on.

The bowling alley parking lot was about a quarter full as the sun cast long shadows over the frozen concrete. Lilith drove past glistening white piles left by snowplows to pull up to the entrance. Huge lighted letters proclaimed "Games," "Restaurant," and "Lounge".

Lilith eyed the place. "Ever been here?"

"Once. My friend Clio took me to Lebowskifest, and this is where we ended up."

"This must be where you go to abide."

Jenny ignored the movie reference. "He said to meet him at the restaurant. He's just going to pass me the papers. He wants me alone."

"That's not gonna to happen."

Jenny surveyed the lot as she climbed from the car. Not another soul in sight. The wind was evil and cut through them, but they walked slowly. Jenny tried to look casual but was determined to stay aware of her surroundings.

Even in these frigid temperatures, a lone woman in a miniskirt and black wool coat paced on the covered sidewalk outside the main door; a smoldering cigarette in one hand and a cellphone in the other. She was talking way too loud, and Jenny tried to ignore the drama.

"I don't care," the woman roared. "He'll just have to put up with it. Thinks he's such a big shit."

Lilith waved Jenny to go ahead so they did not enter together.

Jenny sighed with relief as the doors settled behind her, both from the sudden warmth and the absence of smoking woman's drama. To her right was the pro shop, a few patrons studying bowling balls, shoes and accessories. A dozen or so people were scattered along lanes.

She turned left toward the restaurant. The staff was busy behind the bar and a short-order cook was shoving sandwich baskets onto a shelf outside the interior window.

"Restaurant" was a generous term. The place was barely big enough for six four-person tables and one long table at the very back where Bobby Leiter sat, a full basket of cold greasy fries in front of him

Jenny scanned the room. There was only one other person present, seated to her right by the window. He had no order and to Jenny looked like a homeless man trying to get warm.

Jenny nodded to the preacher. His eyes widened and he shook his head. Undeterred, she entered the room. But the other man suddenly jumped up to block her way. He wore a hoodie, but she didn't need to see his whole head to recognize her ex-husband. She turned to run, ready to scream for Lilith, but Tommy blocked the older woman at the entrance.

His eyes gleamed at her before he yelled, "Help! Security! She's got a gun!"

Lilith looked confused and tried to push past the strange man.

Thaddeus Callun grabbed her sleeve. "You're coming with me."

Two men in black jackets labeled security pushed through toward Tommy, as did some curious looky-loos while sensible people ran away from someone yelling about guns.

Jenny couldn't believe her ex would be so brazen to create this sort of scene. Panic set in and her only thought was escape. She let her shoulders slump in surrender and felt Thad take the opportunity to readjust his grip. She jerked out of his hand and kicked him. She aimed for his balls, but he side-stepped and she only manage to hit his knee. That was enough for her to take flight out of the cramped room.

There was an exit sign about fifty feet down the left side of the alley, a ninety-degree angle from the main entrance. She ran for it as fast as she could and looked over her shoulder to see Thad struggling to catch her.

She could outrun him. He'd stopped smoking but never tried to build up any endurance. She had her phone and could get an Uber. Jenny barely broke stride as she crashed through the door. Something hit her in the face, hard, and she staggered back.

An older man in army clothes was rubbed his fist. "Goddam she's hard-headed."

Jenny's head spun. Her ex herded her to this spot, rounded up for slaughter.

The white van stood outside the door, motor running. The stranger hit her again and she collided with the front fender. The man grabbed her by the back of her coat collar and hauled her toward the open van door. She heard a weird whistling sound, barely aware of something making contact with her head, just behind her right ear. The world went black.

Baden drummed his fingers on the steering wheel and consulted the dashboard clock. He was confident no one could see him here away from the streetlights but as precaution he wore a balaclava.

9:09 p.m.; time to make a decision. The Burlesque did two shows on Sunday: a 4:00 p.m. and a 7:00 p.m., which let out an hour ago. He was parked just where he could see Rachel's van. How would she come out? Alone? Would other girls exit with her? Would they leave immediately or go to one of the nearby restaurants? His mind raced on amphetamine as he tried to plan for any situation.

Away from his van, streetlights flooded the sidewalk. Too much light. He had a knife, not Damascus steel, but an ordinary hunting knife which he'd honed sharp as a razor. He also had a subcompact nine-millimeter Barretta PX4 in a pancake holster in the small of his back. And, he had the van. Lots of options. Hit and run, drive-by, random street violence. He slouched in his seat, staying in the shadows.

He could predict the route she would take home. It was a good drive, but not so far that there was any guarantee he could get her when she'd stop for fuel or food. It was unlikely she carried a gun into town. She'd complained the cops paid too much attention to her. He didn't want to try and take her out at home. The woman made weapons, hunted. She likely had more firearms at her house. Too many risks.

A door in the ally opened and Rachel appeared with another woman, jointly pushing a bellman's cart with a bad wheel and hanging racks supporting four stuffed garment bags. A top hat and some feathered monstrosity of a showgirl headpiece sat on one of the two trunks on the flat bed. There was another bundle he could not identify, likely props.

Rachel seemed unhurried, dressed in thick skintight leggings and a short down jacket fastened up tight against the chill.

The second woman waved and walked off. Rachel forced the recalcitrant cart over the curb and around the back of her van. Easy target. Double tap and be gone. But no, the Indianapolis police had a very good response time. A report of shots fired and he might not get away clean. He'd keep that as second option.

He watched Rachel open the van's dual rear doors. She pulled one of the trunks off the cart, placed it in the back of the van, opened it and bent down. She rooted around, oblivious to her surroundings.

He was out of his van before he actually had a coherent plan. *Fortune favors the bold.* His prey was distracted, the street was empty. He could put the knife in her kidney, while reaching around to choke off any scream. He'd be gone before anyone realized what happened.

Two steps to go. Still no one on the street. He drew the knife, his target still reaching for something in the back of the van. Adrenaline mixed with the drugs in his body and he felt strong, super strong.

He reached to go around her throat to keep her quiet while he ended her life. She started and turned as he positioned the knife. She jerked to one side and the blade dug into the thick down coat.

Baden jerked the knife free of the material, leaving a rent that revealed tiny feathers of the insulation, tinged with red blood.

Most people would be stunned, unable to make the moves necessary to counterattack.

Rachel was not most people. She spun and viciously elbowed him in the nose.

Baden's eyes watered and he was aware of blood on his face but he pressed on and stabbed at her gut. Rachel turned again, and now had a stick in her hands, or maybe a cane from the pile of props. She stabbed at him, catching him full in the chest. The dull point staggered him back. Baden dropped the knife and reached for his gun.

Rachel timed out his movement, producing a collapsible baton from inside her coat and with a practiced move extended the baton as part of the strike on Baden's emerging hand.

He yelped as pain radiated from his right thumb, but even with the severely bruised digit he managed to hold onto the gun.

Rachel swung the baton again, aiming for the side of his head. He turned barely in time to take the savage blow on his thick deltoid muscle. But he had no time to bring the pistol to bear, she was hitting him again, blows glancing off the side of his head. Pain blasted across his face until his ears rang.

Badan covered his head with his hands to ward off the rain of pain assaulting him. He dashed away a few yards before he realized she'd stopped hitting him. He spun to get off a parting shot, but Rachel was nowhere to be seen. He shifted direction and gained his van. He turned the engine and threw the van into gear. Now he caught sight of Rachel where she'd taken cover in the alley doorway.

He had to get away. He knew he could beat her to her home. No, too many variables. He had his face covered, wore gloves. *She couldn't have recognized him. Even if she did…* He thought through his exposure risks. She did not know his real name or where to find him. Any previous doubts were gone, he had to move his hunting grounds.

She was still a loose end, but one that could be clipped later. Escape and evasion was now the order of the day. He'd have to get right to playtime with his guest.

Jenny stirred, her stomach roiling and her head throbbing. She tasted bile on her lips, and the smell of vomit seared her nostrils.

"You know you're going to clean that shit up, right?"

Jenny closed her eyes, trying to make sense of the situation.

"You're lucky. You slept through it, we had to smell that for hours. But don't you worry we're just about there. Then I'll show you."

Jenny slipped back to welcome unconsciousness.

When next she awoke, she was horribly cold, draped over her ex-husband in a fireman's carry, her hands bound in front of her and ankles secured together.

She stifled a moan and tried to stay a dead weight. He took her down a short flight of stairs and stepped into someplace warm. She saw Bobby Leiter following, limping, dragging his left foot. Tommy prodded him along with a pistol. Leiter's face had the visage of someone who lost everything, only to discover he could lose even more.

The room reeked of musty cooking odors; but compared to the van it was a bouquet of roses. They passed through another set of doors, Thad letting her head smack on the door jamb. The next room looked like a barracks, with steel-framed bunk beds lining the walls. Tommy shoved Leiter and he collapsed on one of the bunks, but Thad did not stop there.

The man in army fatigues followed and eyed her closely, he knew she was awake. "Hello, little lady. Mighty fine husband you got here. My name is Daryl Grant, pleased to meet you."

Jenny shivered as she realized where she was going.

Grant sped up and passed Thad, leading led them to a heavy steel door. Jenny heard three separate wheels turning, releasing the deadbolts, allowing it to open on creaking hinges.

"Put her down," Grant demanded. "Time to give her a show." Jenny was unceremoniously dumped on the floor of the dark room. This room smelled worse than the van and the previous room combined. Jenny gagged.

"Our new friend here, Grant, knows everything about these creatures."

Her oh-so-concerned ex-husband shoved her further in the room. "You know I'm doing you a favor, right?"

Jenny stared up at him with hate filled eyes.

"Those creatures got you fooled. They make you think they're some poor, misjudged, harmless people. They just need to have their special diet and go on all innocent. But that is not what they are."

A light came on. "This is what they are, Jen, wake up!"

Thad rolled Jenny over with his foot. She heard a guttural hissing sound and found her face within an inch of a demon, bars of a silver-plated iron cage the only thing separating them.

The demon hissed again and fangs hyperextended making it, *no, her*, look like a saber-toothed ghoul. Her eyes glowed read. The stench of blood and unwashed humanity roiled over Jenny.

"Just about time for dinner. Hey there, vampie, I have a special treat for you tonight."

Chapter Twenty-Eight

"No, it is one hundred per cent my fault," Lilith addressed her passengers in the back seat as the grey car hurtled down the country road. A sane person would be going no more than fifty miles an hour on the twisting lane but Lilith held the speedometer over seventy, the dried yellow cornstalks on either side of the track a blur as they flew by.

"I will not continue this argument," Christopher replied with the slightest resigned frustration in his voice.

Marquessa tuned out the conversation as soon as it started, but the change in Christopher's tone roused her from her creeping stupor. "Can we table the blame?" Her words were supposed to denote forbearance, but to her own ear they sounded petulant. Her super senses had jumped an order of magnitude and she needed to get adjusted. The world suddenly had hundreds of new colors, scents, sounds. She had to accept the fact: she was undead. *I can't even perceive the word coherently, let alone come to grips with what I am, what my limitations are, and what happens if I lose it and start killing people?* She considered herself a liability. Christopher had faith in her, god knew why.

"GPS says we will reach the coordinates in about ten minutes," Lilith said.

That got Marq's attention and she sat up straighter, brushing imaginary wrinkles from her black turtleneck sweater.

"How are you doing?" Christopher asked. He'd recommended the dark clothing and was similarly dressed in a black silk shirt covered by a formfitting, Kevlar-lined black vest.

"I'm hungry," Marq complained. She was at the point of transition where existence, so far, was a cycle of ravenous hunger and sleep. Not even really sleep but a cold, dark, dreamless state of unconsciousness. *Would it always be this way? So empty?*

Christopher patted her on the arm. "We need you to stay hungry. It will be an advantage if this comes to a fight."

"Besides," Lilith joined in, "I'll be available for a snack when we're done."

Marq glanced back at the woman, unsure how to reply. The hunger she felt was visceral, an aching sense of hollowness. But if she fed, she'd sleep, and be useless.

"I can't imagine a fight," Marq mumbled. "I have schematics of the external security and it would take a great deal of luck to get close, though I think we can likely approach the entrance. And we have no idea of the internal defenses." She paused. Her memory was very detailed. The only thing she could not remember were specifics of the attack that changed her.

"There is only the one way in," she continued, "but there are three exit-only tunnels."

"Exit only?"

"I was able to get pictures of the doors before they were installed. Thick steel with a mechanical locking device, a wheel that engages twenty different bolts keeping the door closed. The wheel is encased in a metal box with a combination number pad. I know there are three doors, but I only know where two of them are. The other one is labeled on a schematic as 'bolthole.' I never found the destination, but I suspect it goes over a quarter mile. The physical doors are impassible, even with our strength. Which doesn't leave us any good options."

Lilith slowed the car. Many of the cornfields they passed had been stubbled, offering little cover. An ivy-covered fence appeared in the headlights. Lilith pulled off the road and edged as close as she could, trying to pull the car under the cover of the thick vines.

The vehicle ground to a halt and everyone sat in silence. No one made any motion to get out.

"Marq?" Christopher asked with a tone that implied he already knew the answer. "Are you up to this?"

The young vampyr sighed, startling herself with the reflexive intake of breath. "What are we? Two miles out? I'm pretty sure I can run two miles. After that, I do not know what you expect us to do."

"Reconnoiter," Christopher said. "That is all we can do until we find a weakness."

"Grant's defense has no weakness."

Christopher snorted. "Humans are their own weakness. I just need for one person to come out…"

Marq felt her fangs reflexively extended. "Do you think Jenny will be all right until we can do something?"

Christopher stared out into the distant night, then back to Marq's. "No, Marq, I don't think she will be all right. Physically, she should be safe for a day or so, but mentally…" The vampyr grimaced. "Her ex is a sadist; he will engage in all forms of mental torture until he gets bored. Then there is the nosferatu."

The words sent a jolt of dread through Marq. "Do you think they will feed Jenny to it?"

"I don't know. That could go very badly, for both of them." Christopher opened the door. "Lilith, we may need to leave quickly, be ready."

Jenny winced as Thad's boot made contact with her ribs. The creature in the cage crouched and made no movement but watched intently, sniffing at the bound woman. Jenny felt the nosferatu's hunger in her core, an echo of what she sensed in Marq just before her friend's fangs found the right spot to feed on.

The naked creature barely resembled anything that had once been human. Jenny recognized it as female due to her shriveled, leathery breasts. All the creature's skin was shrunk in on itself. Gaunt, tight to the bones, resembling pictures of Auschwitz survivors. Her long hair was tangled into unkempt dreadlocks, like a bad wig.

It stared at Jenny with glowing red eyes consumed in hunger and rage. But her eyes did not frighten Jenny, not like those hyper-extended fangs.

Jenny stared back in those eyes, determined to show no fear.

Thad kicked her again. "You're too stupid to be afraid."

On one level, she *was* terrified, but maybe her experience with Marq helped her maintain her composure. She would not give her tormentors the satisfaction, though it took extraordinary effort to hold back tears.

"You know, Jen," Thad drawled in the lazy way Jenny once thought was charming, "we mostly feed it rats." He crossed the room to a lidded garbage can and kicked it over. The tortured corpses of mangled vermin spilled onto the ground. Drained of blood, they'd mummified in the dry air of the bunker.

Jenny lost it and tears flowed. She was afraid. But something more that enveloped her as she wept at the sight of the tiny desiccated rodents. More powerful than the mounting terror she experienced a wave of empathy for the poor creature bound in the cage. Blistering anger edged out fear. She knew that feeling, she was ready to do something stupid. Years ago, she felt that as she stood over Thad's drunk, passed-out form with a butcher knife. She did not know if she was relieved, or regretful, that she hadn't stabbed the bastard a hundred times in a hundred places. The next time she felt the stupids she used the same knife to slash all four of Thad's tires as she fled their home forever.

"That's more like it," Thad sniggered, completely misreading the emotions on display. "God, you can turn on the waterworks when you want to."

Jenny stifled a reply. It would only egg him on.

"Let's take this up a notch." Grant's eyes narrowed as if he suspected Jenny's true emotional state. He picked up a wooden club from the table of implements, an antique police truncheon; eighteen inches long and almost an inch around. Swinging the baton by a lanyard, Grant slowly made for the cage. "Maybe she needs to get better acquainted with our little friend." He fingered the lever by the door.

"What are you doing?" Thad screeched; his eyes wide. "We're not gonna feed her to it yet."

"Yeah, you said I get chance to use her first," Tommy whined, wringing his hands.

"Don't worry, everybody's going to get his turn." Grant placated the younger man with an airy wave. "We'll let this thing soften her up." He moved the lever a bit.

"Look," Thad said. "Is that a good idea?"

Grant turned his back on the creature and looked at Thad in disgust. "Don't be such a pussy. Look here, Thaddeus, we've dealt with this thing for years. Those manacles are half-inch forged steel. The chain is five-sixteenths grade eighty with a load limit over four-thousand pounds. Right now, there is no threat to us. Anyway, it can't think of anything but getting a few drops of blood from your wife. Look at the way its nose is twitching, it smells her blood and it's going crazy. No, the time to be careful is right after it's fed, when it's cunning."

Jenny stared at the heavy metal restraints wrapped around the emaciated nosferatu's wrists. The wrist manacles where held by chains fastened to cross bars above the creature's head. They afforded her just enough slack to kneel. The cage itself was made of silver-plated steel, tarnished where the nosferatu touched it.

As Jenny watched, the creature shifted her weight, gathering her feet under her.

Grant snarled, "Get that bitch out of the way!"

Thad grabbed Jenny's hair and dragged her away from the cage.

Grant dropped the lever and the front of the enclosure fell to the floor.

Thad jumped further back, taking Jenny with him.

The nosferatu howled with impotent rage.

Thad bent over and giggled as he shoved Jenny back toward the feral creature, leaving her inches beyond the creature's reach.

The nosferatu tried to leap free but was frustrated by the manacles. It howled again.

"That's right, time to get it revved up, makes the rest of the proceeding much more fun." Grant used the club to pound on the cage, eliciting a cry that originated from the depths of hell.

"See?" Grant boasted. "We feed it some street trash a couple of times a year. The damned thing makes a lot of noise, but we have it wrapped up tight."

The creature suddenly stopped shrieking, but stared hungrily at Jenny, her eyes glowing red, incisors hyper-extended. It hissed and Jenny flinched at its breath. Liquid venom dripped from the fangs.

"That thing is helping us…" Grant lips twisted into a smug grin. "Take a bite out of Chicago's homeless problem, a real 'murican hero." He handed the club over to Thad

Thad smacked Jenny on the thigh in an effort to force her to move closer to the dribbling teeth. Jenny took the blow, and then a second. She looked up at the glowing stare boring into her own eyes, looking through her, projecting hunger. The creature snapped its fangs at her, frustrated by the tiny space between them.

The nosferatu hissed again and Jenny felt her emotional resolve crumble. Tears rained down her face, tears of anger backed with tears of shame as the men laughed.

The nosferatu went quiet again, her eyes darting from the meal in front of her, to Jenny's ex-husband still brandishing the club, then fixing on her senior tormenter, Grant.

The undead being braced one foot against the right side of the cage, skin burning at the touch of the silver plate. It made a concerted effort to pull free from the manacle.

Breaking the restraint was outside the realm of possibility, even with the nosferatu's superior strength. Jenny watched in disbelief as the creature ripped its own flesh.

Oh crap, Jenny thought as she realized what was about to happen. The hardened steel did not give way, it didn't have to. She stared at the nosferatu and the creature stared back.

The nosferatu snarled and pulled with so much force that cords of muscle stood out on her entire body.

"Do it!" Jenny screamed.

The creature barely whimpered as it yanked its hand through the manacle. Pink, foamy ichor oozed from the place where her thumb and forefinger had been, and the nosferatu raised her disfigured hand in triumph.

Thad backpedaled. Grant shoved him aside and seized Jenny by her hair, with the intention of dragging her out of the way so he could close the cage.

Time to do the stupid thing, she thought. She rolled onto her stomach, dug her elbows into the bars beneath her and fought to keep the enclosure open.

Grant snatched the truncheon from Thad's dithering hands. He rained solid blows across Jenny's back. "Move, you stupid bitch!"

"I'll take my chances with her!" Jenny hissed through clenched teeth. "She smells better."

He hit her again, but she ignored the repeated blows and jammed herself harder against the bars of the door.

The creature ripped its other hand free with a triumphant snarl.

Jenny felt a wave of nausea sweep through her at the sight of the creature's mangled hands. In that moment Jenny wanted to reach out to the tortured soul, to give comfort. She thought the damaged creature smiled as it gathered to attack. The nosferatu reached for Jenny with mangled, talon-like hands and grabbed her shoulders, viciously shoving Jenny's face hard against the bars.

Chapter Twenty-Nine

It was late before Baden returned to the cabin. He'd just spent several hours prior severing ties with his current clients and getting his phones re-rerouted to new burner sets.

Tracey was still unconscious from the latest rounds of sedative and her state allowed him the opportunity run his hands over her body. He'd done this many times, of course, but now he was ready, she just needed to get prepared. He savagely pinched her nipples through her t-shirt. He imagined how much better it would be when she could react.

He smiled.

There was nothing like that first penetration. The sobbing, the screeching, the louder the better. And those tears. That salty nectar. It was the hottest thing imaginable.

He regained control of himself. He unfastened the girl's jeans and rummaged around, examining her. He jerked the used pad from her underwear and confirmed she was not bleeding anymore.

He smiled, tossed the pad into a trash can, then wiped his fingers on the coarse sheet before fastening the girl's clothing back into place. He calculated the dosages he'd administered. She needed to be fully aware, with no trace of the drugs in her to maximize playtime. He wanted Tracey, not the drugged-out ragdoll in front of him.

He calculated that around seven p.m. the next day she would be ripe.

Housekeeper

The day's failure drained from his body as anticipation quickened his pulse and he felt aroused. He was tempted to take some relief right then, but he knew that delayed gratification would make playtime that much more intense.

Jenny clenched her eyes and waited for the sharp bite, not knowing if the venom would bring her pleasure or pain. But there was no bite. Instead the nosferatu used her prone body as a springboard and the creature bounded over Jenny's head to land on her feet just in front of Grant. The militia leader swung his wooden club, catching the nosferatu on the side of the head, the blow landing with a sickening crunch that would have killed a human and pink rivulets of something trickled from the wound.

The creature was not deterred. She ignored the damage from the club and seized Grant. She used her ruined left hand to jam him by his throat into the wall. He rained a flurry of ineffectual blows rained down at the nosferatu.

Tommy screamed and went for weapons on the table, but Jenny's ex-husband ran. He shoved through the door and Jenny heard locks turning.

They were sealed in.

Tommy abandoned his scramble for a weapon and ran to the solid steel door, pounding and screaming. "Hey asshole! Let me out!"

The nosferatu brought her saber fangs closer to Grant's face

Grant windmilled his arms to break the creature's hold on him. The nosferatu licked his face. She drew back as if her prey was unsatisfactory and Jenny fought her own panic. *He's not scared enough.*

The nosferatu dragged Grant from the wall. What happened next made Jenny feel sick to her stomach, her mind trying to disassociate from the sight. The creature used the powerful talons of her mutilated right hand to seize Grant by the groin. The creature's eyes went wide with pent up rage that would not be denied. Her fingers dug through the clothing, her hand twisted and blood spurted as Grant squealed.

Jenny fought to keep her stomach under control, feeling as if she was connected to the agony screeching through Grant's veins. She could barely hear Grant's terrified screams over her own retching.

The nosferatu smiled and pulled in close to taste her prey again. Now she seemed satisfied and opened her mouth to fully display her wickedly sharp fangs.

Jenny waited for the feeding to begin, unable to look away. The creature did not use its teeth to puncture, but rather ripped a chunk out of Grant's throat, his screams progressing to a hideous bubbling screech. Nor did she suck at the wound. Instead, she let the blood burble out and slurped it up like drinking from an obscene fountain.

Something loud clattered to the floor and Jenny looked to see Tommy shakily wielding a hatchet and a vial of "Holy-water" acid. "The bitch is eating Grant! Come at me you blood cunt! C'mon!" he screeched, hopping up and down.

In a few seconds the blood ceased spouting and the nosferatu dropped Grant's corpse to the floor. The creature leaped at Tommy as he fumbled with the stopper on the acid vessel. Before he could open the vial the creature casually knocked the vial from his hand and seized him by the neck. Tommy swiped at her with the hatchet, lodging the blade deep into her ribs. Frothy pick ichor oozed down her side.

With a powerful, adrenaline fueled jerk Tommy managed to free the axe head and step outside the creature's grasp. The creature turned on him, the deep gash in her side already closing. The steel blade was less effective that the wooden club had been. Pink drops still seeped from Grant's earlier strike.

The nosferatu again used her left hand to seize her prey by the neck and shoved Tommy against the wall. Jenny stared in amazement as she realized the nosferatu had regrown much of her hand. In fact, the nosferatu's entire form filled out before her eyes.

Tommy tried to swing the hatchet at his attacker's head, but she knocked the weapon out of his grasp. He seized the hand strangling him, but nothing could break her iron grip.

"Oh my gawd, my gawd!" he screamed as he lost his ability to reason. Unlike Grant he'd already reached a crescendo of terror, twitching and gibbering. The terrified gibberish pouring from him was a signal to the nosferatu. She struck.

This assault was more surgical. The nosferatu's fangs drew back, giving her more precise control. Both teeth neatly punctured Tommy's carotid artery. She fastened her mouth like a lamprey over the wound.

He convulsed; his body wracked with violent seizures. The spasms subsided as his flaccid body had no more to give.

The room was silent except for a hideous sucking sound as the creature drew in the last swallow, not wasting a drop of Tommy's lifeblood.

After what seemed like minutes, the nosferatu raised her blood-stained mouth, gore literally dripping from her lips. The creature seemed to savor this feeding. Her fangs drew further back. Still evident, but not protruding from her mouth. She turned to Jenny, her eyes glowing brighter and she moved with quiet purposeful steps. Her body now that of a petite, sharp faced woman in her forties.

Jenny fought to contain her fear, but she was losing it. Her mind replayed what the woman had done to Grant to increase his terror. Now the creature was more in control and there was no telling what horrors she could visit on Jenny. Tears flooded her eyes and she pulled herself into a fetal position, hopeful the creature would spare her. The naked form stopped less than a foot away from where Jenny lay on the floor. The nosferatu knelt down. Jenny felt a compulsion to look up and found the monster's gaze fixed directly on her eyes.

"Help me," the blood smeared woman gasped and collapsed to the ground.

Thad had one thought: escape. He didn't really sign up to fight, he considered himself too shrewd to get into a battle where the other person had a non-zero chance of injuring him. He locked the room and scuttled down the hall. If Grant wanted to play dangerous games with the damned, let 'em. And double fuck Jenny for getting him into this mess in the first place. The image of the creature tearing his ex-wife apart was the only bit of satisfaction he felt.

He bounded through the bunk room and shouted at the old preacher sitting slouched on the bunk. "They're all dead, the damn thing is loose!"

The old man looked up with dead eyes.

Thad barreled through to doors he could not open. He was too impatient to try and figure out the locking mechanism, but he knew where the circuit breakers were. He pulled out his cellphone and activated the flashlight as he reached the switchbox and pulled down the main power control. The room went pitch black. Tommy swung his light around. Grant said he had twelve seconds before the backup generator switched on. He sprinted back the way he'd come, racing though the bunker; all his attention on getting as far away from the blood sucking mother fucker as possible. Los Angeles maybe? Australia? He had to go someplace where they spoke English.

He pushed on the slanted front door and it slapped into the wall beyond with a ferocious clang. He ran to the van, never looking back.

Christopher pulled something from the small nylon case hanging across his body by a quick release buckle.

"Binoculars?" Marq asked as Christopher studied the bunker.

The older vampyr gave Marq a sardonic glare. "Oh, did you acquire magnification of your vision?"

"You generally don't use devices. See anything?"

"No, it looks like an abandoned farmhouse, nothing to indicate it is occupied."

Marq's lips turned into an evil smile. "Oh, it's occupied."

Christopher tensed and even without binoculars, Marq could see the door open and someone run out, evidently in a panic. She couldn't identify the individual but hoped it was Jenny.

"Looks to be the ex-husband," Christopher said in a calm voice.

The darkened doorway was suddenly lit up, the entrance made more obvious by illumination.

The vampyrs looked at each other.

Marq spoke first. "A trap?"

"Don't care," Christopher called over his shoulder, moving with inhuman speed.

Marq followed and was surprised to find she could run faster than her boss, catching up to him before he gained the door.

He halted just short of the door like he ran into an invisible wall. Marq couldn't stop in time so she ran into him and bounced back. Christopher did not give an inch.

"What the fuck?" Marq snapped.

"Threshold," Christopher snarled.

"Get over it." Marq shoved past him but found that she could not go further. She closed her eyes, there was nothing physical stopping her, just an incredible sense of dread. She forced one foot forward.

"I guess you will have to learn the hard way." Christopher used all his enormous strength and shoved Marquessa through the door.

Marq crumpled to the ground and experienced a dizzying sensation as if she was dropping into an endless pit. She could not move. Couldn't think. She could only experience. When she was younger, the first few years she'd been with Christopher, she experienced panic attacks. Those were not even an echo of the power that enveloped her now. It was as if someone implanted a wire directly into the fear center of her brain and set it for maximum stimulation.

Marq spasmed on the ground and waited to die. The true death. Anything to release her from the unfathomable despair she felt.

"Please come in, both of you," Bobby Leiter slurred the invitation. He stood before them, propped up with a sturdy cane in his good hand, and held a whiskey bottle in the other. He looked a solid half-dead to the undead.

The words hadn't really registered in Marq's tormented brain, but the fear, the overwhelming avalanche of emotion, was gone. Instantly.

She pushed herself up to standing. Her relief was such that a part of her wanted to scream out in pure joy, but she remembered the feeling just seconds ago, and she turned to Christopher. "You bastard."

"You weren't going to listen."

"This is unacceptable. There are anti-anxiety medications, treatments, something. How do you live knowing you might feel that…that…"

"You are too late," Leiter interrupted. An alarm sounded, drowning out whatever Leiter said next. The doors closed behind the vampyrs with an ominous thud. Leiter took a swig from the bottle. "Look what I found. There's bottles hidden everywhere." He sighed as if it was his last breath. "They had a creature in a cage, something like the nosferatu you mentioned. It got loose. Everyone else here is dead, and I reckon I'm next. I don't know what it will do to you." He took another swig of whiskey.

Chapter Thirty

"In here." Leiter led the pair through the bunkroom to the solid steel door with three heavy bolts keeping it closed. "I heard the screaming until that one guy, I don't know who he was—"

"We do," Marq said.

"Well, once he closed the door, I didn't hear much screaming, just someone pounding trying to get out, and that stopped after a few seconds. There hasn't been any sound since then. That one guy said they were all dead, and I have no reason to doubt him."

Christopher pursed his lips. "If the nosferatu drank that much blood he—"

"She," Leiter said. "Doesn't look very human, but it was definitely female."

Christopher sneered, then his expression changed to something more wary, as if he anticipated tragedy. "What is that line from that movie you like so much?"

Marq closed her eyes, suddenly understanding her boss's dread. "I've got a bad feeling about this."

Christopher dug into the pack, but his manner was changed. He projected discipline before, a commitment to his duty. Now he was hesitant, but proceeded to go through the necessary motions. "She may be unconscious. One or more of her victims might not have bled out, we have to get to any survivors quickly." He pulled half a dozen silver spikes from the backpack and offered them to Marq.

She accepted them without enthusiasm. The metal blackened at her touch and they felt wrong in her hands. "You don't think…?"

"No, it is not likely." But his tone of voice did not sound convinced. "No, it is likely someone who turned spontaneously."

"They said," Leiter butted in. "She looked human when they took her."

The vampyrs glared at him.

Christopher extracted the heavy bladed falchion. "You," he addressed the preacher. "Go back to the entrance. That may be far enough she won't smell you. And I swear, in front of your god, if you attempt to lock this door behind us, I will end you. And it will not be quick."

Leiter shrugged and walked away.

"Is there a plan?" Marq asked.

"I am going to open the door. Stay out of its way. She may try to shove it open when she hears the locks disengage. Be ready for her to charge, get as many of those spikes in her as you can."

Marq nodded, moved out of the door's path, and steeled herself. She tucked four spikes in her belt and took one in each hand, ignoring the sense of disgust she felt holding them.

Christopher spun the wheels on the door and the bolts slid free. There was no sound from the other side.

Christopher heaved it open.

Marq charged in, ready to attack. The smell of recent death almost overwhelmed her, but she focused her attention to where she sensed a heartbeat. Two blood-splattered figures lay on the ground.

Marq sucked in an unnecessary breath. "Jenny!"

Jenny was curled beside the nosferatu, gently trying to wipe blood from the creature's face.

Christopher moved beside the other vampyr. They stared at the gore covered tableau.

"Magda," Marq whispered.

At the sound of her name the nosferatu looked up with sad, blood-filled eyes.

"Oh my god," Marq said and fell to her knees beside the woman.

Jenny looked up. "There are clothes on the table. I think they're hers. But I want to clean her up first."

"Jenny, Marquessa, move away from her."

"No. She asked for my help," Jenny countered.

"You should understand—"

"Save it. It can wait. First, I want her clean, dressed, comfortable."

The vampyrs exchanged glances.

Marq rose and spoke. "There's a shower off the bunk room. You'll need sheets or towels to wash her, she will not stand under the running water."

Jenny stood up and extended a hand to help Magda to her feet.

"Marquessa." Christopher stayed Marq with a hand.

The dark-skinned woman met his eyes. "There is nothing lost by giving Magda her dignity."

Marq picked up the musty clothes, guided the pair toward the shower then returned to Christopher. She found him rummaging through Magda's personal effects.

"There is a boarding pass here," he said, his voice flat. "She was flying to Louisville and had a sixteen-hour layover at O'Hare."

"How long ago?"

"Five years." There was pain and wrath in his voice.

"She didn't tell us she was coming."

"No, but she always ended her letters saying she would see us soon." Christopher's eyes flashed red. "I should have missed her. I should have checked on her. She was one of mine."

"But we have her back now."

Christopher gave an angry shake of his head. "Only to lose her forever. We still have to put her down."

Marq inclined her head. "She's calm, peaceful even. Do we know she is nosferatu?"

"She's not hungry. You feel your hunger? Hers will not be satisfied without killing."

"We can restrain her, find some way to treat her," Marq protested.

"Lock her in a cage and feed her rats?" Christopher snapped.

A dense silence hung in the air.

Marq joined Christopher at the table. He held up a wallet and showed old pictures Magda had kept with her; Marq at sixteen and another when she was in her twenties. Marq took the wallet and flipped through it until she found an older picture of her boss. "God, look at you with that 70's porn mustache." She tried to force cheerfulness, but it came out more as gallows humor.

"We all make poor fashion decisions at one time or another, I recall those huge overalls you were fond of."

They looked up as Jenny returned, leading a transformed Magda wearing clothes for the first time in years. Her hair was still in tangled dreads, but clean. All the blood was washed away. Her skin was pale, and she looked tired, but at least she no longer looked like a prisoner freed from a cage. She looked more like a woman who'd stayed out too late with friends.

"See," Jenny said. "She's going to be all right."

"No," Christopher replied, his voice somber. "She will not be all right. You've cleaned her. You have allowed her dignity, but that doesn't change what I have to do."

Marq looked like she was about to argue, but Christopher stifled her with a look.

Jenny stepped in front of Magda, protecting her from the other vampyr. "What do you think you have to do?"

"Magda is my progeny. I have a responsibility."

"No," Jenny snapped. "There has to be some other way."

"No," Magda spoke for the first time since Christopher opened the door, her lightly accented voice betraying an unnatural lethargy. "I want to live, but Christophe is right. For now, I am rational, but I already feel the urge to deceive you. I will swear that I am in control, knowing that I am lying." She took Jenny's face in her hands. "I like you. I am grateful to you, but if you are with me when the hunger returns, and I can feel it returning now, I will torture and kill you."

Jenny shook free from Magda's grasp. "No. I don't believe you."

Magda stepped close and regarded the young woman. "I was never comfortable with feeding; it was a necessity. Oh, I looked forward to the intimacy, but the actual drawing of blood was an inconvenience." She took a breath to make a deliberate sigh. "But I am not like that anymore, more like an addict who cannot stop thinking about how to make his next high better. Even looking at you I cannot stop thinking about how good killing those men made me feel. I've become obsessed with creating terror for my own satisfaction."

Jenny made an emphatic shake of her head. "No." She put her hands on Magda's shoulders. "There has to be some treatment. Something." Her voice broke.

Christopher picked up the falchion. "I will make it as quick as possible." His voice trembled.

The look in his eyes broke Jenny's heart. She blinked back tears. "No." She drew a composing breath. "What time is it?"

Christopher checked his phone. "Almost five a.m."

Jenny turned to Magda and touched her hair in a vain attempt to smooth away the snarls. "Christopher, there is something only I can do." Now the tears burned. "Magda, would you like to go with me to watch the sunrise?"

Magda gave a sad smile. "I would love to see the sunrise."

Christopher lowered his voice. "Marq, I think you should go get Lilith and bring her here."

Marq gave a terse nod and soon returned with Lilith in tow.

Lilith gasped upon seeing Magda and cried freely in front of the vampyr. She took a step toward her, hesitated and turned to Christopher.

"Patricia," Magda said. "Please come to me. It is safe, for now."

Christopher nodded.

Lilith ran sobbing into the vampyr's embrace. "Magda, my love, what have they done to you? How can…" The rest was lost in sobs. Lilith buried her face in her friend's shoulder.

Christopher addressed Jenny. "Lilith was Magda's first feeding."

Marq spoke, her voice cracking. "What a strange thing, Christopher, to feel so much and never cry. How do we live like this?"

Magda hugged Lilith with fierce affection, then suddenly pulled away. "Patricia, I need you to step away." She looked at Jenny and for an instant Jenny saw a flash of something… hungry. Violent.

Evil.

"It's time. I feel like I am drowning in the hunger."

Christopher spoke up. "It should be dawn in a few minutes."

Jenny took Magda by the hand.

"You may need chains," Marq said.

"No," Magda said in a soft, fatalistic voice. "Those will not be necessary. I have had enough of chains."

Lilith took the woman's other hand. "We will be with you."

"No." Magda patted her friend's hand. "I love you. I will be happy if you remember me like this. Free. Content." Magda hugged her old friend, and tenderly kissed her. First on the cheek, and then on the lips. Lilith cried even as their lips touched, tears streaming down her cheeks, clinging to Magda's flesh.

Magda broke the embrace, tugged on Jenny's hand and led her up the stairs.

They made their way out onto the concrete slab where the van had been parked. They sat in silence on the cold surface for a few minutes staring at the glow in the eastern sky.

"You know, when first they brought me here, I tried to escape. All my thought was bent on it and I tried to gather clues about where I was, what my surroundings might be when I got free." Her voice trailed off. "But then I found a freedom in the blood lust. The first time they brought me a person to feed on, I discovered ecstasy. I even felt elated at their mirth, they thought it was entertaining. But then it was rats again and I couldn't form thoughts for long periods of time. I just knew hunger. I am telling you, so you know, this is the best that can happen." She turned to Jenny and smiled. "Is that jacket enough for you, dear?"

"I'm fine," Jenny answered, trying to keep her teeth from chattering. Both from the cold and from the hungry look deep in Magda's eyes.

"You are a good person," Magda said calmly.

"I try."

"You will be good for them. I know how intimidating they look, how formidable Christophe thinks he is, but they are vulnerable. You have to protect them."

Jenny took the older woman's hand.

The sun emerged over the horizon. Jenny turned to Magda who stared at the light with sightless eyes. She smiled even as her skin started to smoke.

Jenny dropped Magda's hand as the heat seared her skin. "Are you in pain?"

"No," Magda's husky voice sounded content. "The cold hasn't bothered me since I turned, but this is the first time I felt warmth in so long." Magda laid down on the concrete, her pose a caricature of someone sunbathing. "Take care of them." She closed her eyes as her skin crumpled on itself like it was burning from within. Her skin blackened and her smoldering body collapsed.

And Magda Kovács was no more.

Chapter Thirty-One

Jenny wiped her tears away as she walked back through the open door to the bunker. She crossed to Magda's former cell and was stunned to find the two bodies were gone, the only clue to their existence being Lilith scrubbing up blood.

"What happened?"

"Christopher found a door to a pit of quick lime with at least two other skeletons. Once we seal this place it could be years before anyone finds them." She pulled something from her pocket. "Oh, here is your cellphone, it was on a table out front. I gave Marq's back to her."

"Where is Marq?"

"Here," the vampyr replied, coming in the room from behind her.

Christopher pushed past her. "Magda?"

Jenny tried to come up with a diplomatic answer. "She is at peace." The phrase sounded lame to her ear, but it seemed to reassure the vampyr.

"She didn't suffer?"

"No." Jenny turned her lips up into a wan smile. "She said it was the first time she felt warm in ages."

Christopher answered with a wry chuckle. "Feeling the heat from another's body... I mean, we can feel the heat, but it does not warm us."

Jenny frowned at the returned cellphone and opened it. There were two text messages from Clio and a missed call with voicemail. Jenny regarded the unfamiliar number and started to put the phone away.

"That was a funny look you gave the phone," Lilith said from the floor.

Jenny paused and studied the device. "Voicemail. Likely somebody wants to sell me a car warranty." She looked at the call list and saw that it came in after ten p.m. She reconsidered and activated the recording.

"Hey," the caller's tone was urgent.

Jenny turned her full attention to the familiar voice, but she couldn't quite place it.

"This is Rachel."

There was a good deal of background noise on the call and Jenny stuck her finger in her other ear to concentrate on the message.

"Give me a call. It doesn't matter what time. That bastard 'Tab' attacked me. I'm okay but give me a call."

Jenny hit the call back button.

Rachel answered on the first ring. "Hey, Jenny? Right?"

"Yeah, sorry to call so early."

"No problem. That weird guy I told you about, I think he attacked me yesterday." Rachel did not sound scared, but there were overtones of anger.

"Think?"

Rachel snorted. "Asshole was wearing a mask, but I'm sure I recognized the rest. Drove off in a dark red van, full size, nothing to distinguish it; just like 'Tab' drives."

"You okay?"

"Yeah, but I'm going away for a while. The wife and I go out to Vegas a couple times a year. We are going to make an extended stay. Did that drawing help at all?"

Jenny consulted Lilith. "We turned it over to the FBI. You may want to add that information to your own police report."

"Yeah, about that," Rachel drawled out. "There's no report. Ain't gonna happen. I have a history with Indiana police, and I am not going into that sewer again. You got everything I know, so leave me out of this. Anyone official reaches out to me, and I'll say I never heard of you. Just lettin' you know."

"That's okay, I tend to avoid the police as well." Jenny nodded as if the woman on the other end of the line could see her. "It's going to be difficult to associate that picture with our, what do they call it, a perp?"

"I think," Rachel said seriously, "serial killers are unsubs. Oh, wait that reminds me. I am pretty sure that bastard lives out of state, but when we were talking, he mentioned a hunting cabin. It sounds like it's here in Indiana."

"I don't suppose you can narrow that down."

"I think I can," Rachel continued. "I'm a trivia geek. It's fun to exchange useless facts when we are waiting for something to heat up or cool down. You never know what useless shit people know. For example, in the 1920's the government constructed 125 concrete arrows pointing west to help guide the new air mail system. Turns out 'Tab' thinks he knows all about those arrows and we got into a bit of an argument."

"Okay?"

"The internet is great, but there is a lot of bad info. There are three of them in Indiana, but there is one website, which has the best pictures and flashiest graphics, that says there's only one in the state, and he was adamant about it. From the way he talked, his cabin must be just east to the one listed on the flash website. Near Rushville."

"Never heard of it."

"Google it. You should be able to get GPS coordinates for the marker." Rachel terminated the call without a goodbye.

"Wait," Marq spoke up. "You have a picture of the guy?"

Lilith caught the tail end of the discussion on her return. "Jenny drew one from Rachel's description. We sent a copy to the FBI, but they weren't impressed. We don't have enough evidence to tie him to the murders. Want to see it?"

Marq shrugged.

"I have it on my phone." Lilith crooked a finger. She reached into her purse and pulled out a cell phone almost large enough to be a tablet. She accessed the camera roll and held it out.

Marq's eyes hardened. "That is a damn good resemblance."

"Huh?" Jenny and Lilith said in reflex.

Marq looked over to where Bobby Leiter sat listlessly on one of the bunks. "I've seen that bastard. I don't remember my murder, but I do recall being at that truck stop, talking to you about the killer. That man was there." Her voice sounded like she smelled something bad. "I thought the asshole was cute." Her eyes turned red.

"Marq," Christopher said, his tone stern but affectionate. "Enough of that. You need to feed and rest."

"One minute." Marq stepped closer to the preacher. "I owe you an apology. I thought you sold me out to the militia, somehow. I was certain you had something to do with my murder." She paused. "That doesn't mean I'm not going to kill you for helping to abduct Jenny."

"Marq," Christopher barked. He addressed the reverend. "She is hungry and not thinking straight."

"Yeah," Jenny chimed in. "He was just as much a prisoner as I was."

"I am the one who owes apologies." Bobby Leiter's voice had an aching quality. "I spent decades thinking you were the monsters. Instead I admired Grant for his fury."

"Lilith, take Marquessa into the next room and make sure she feeds."

"What about you?" Jenny asked.

"I am strong enough to go a few days without. Marq, however…"

"Yes," Lilith turned to Marq. "I just have to ask you not to feed too deeply. I'm almost tapped out." She glanced at Christopher. "He feeds heavily when injured."

"Hey," Jenny said tentatively. "I can help."

"No." Marq shook her head. "You are different, and I will not touch you again until you know all the risks. I had no control last time." She eyed Christopher. "I hope he gave you adequate information. There are dangers if a vampyr feeds off you too often. You need to know."

Reverend Bobby Leiter stood up and addressed Marq. "I don't know how my withered old blood would taste, but I'll give it to you."

"Thank you," Lilith replied with a toothy saccharine smile, "but I think we can handle it."

"I don't know." Marq considered Leiter the way one considers meat at a deli. "I'm hungry. I know I wouldn't take enough to kill someone, but I don't think I could stop soon enough to avoid weakening Lilith."

"If you want it, it's yours," Leiter offered.

Marq crossed to the preacher, bought her face close to his, and inhaled his scent. A human would have turned from the odor of the unwashed body flooded with stress toxins.

"I think I can work with this. He is sincere." Marq took the reverend's face in her hands and positioned her forehead against his. "Don't be afraid. I won't kill you."

"I am not afraid."

The female vampyr wrapped her arms around the much larger man. He enfolded her into a grandfatherly embrace.

"Everyone," Christopher commanded. "Let's leave them alone."

Jenny turned away from her friend to join the others at the table. She paused for a minute when she heard snuffling, crying sounds behind her.

"Grief, guilt are strong emotions." Christopher said. "But hard to swallow." He sat at the table while his voice took on a severe note. "Lilith, you and Jenny give the latest information to the FBI. When night falls, we will go home and regroup."

"Tick tock. Tracey is still out there," Jenny said.

"Right now, we've been feeding info to the FBI through the prosecutor in Indy. I don't know how seriously he takes us. We just don't have enough we can document. They are not going to commit manpower and resources without more."

"I have an idea," Jenny said as she took a seat at the table. "I've read the reports very thoroughly. The gouges in the body, the little bits ripped away and the burns…"

"You have a point?" Christopher snapped.

"Yes, I think he uses common tools, not dedicated torture implements. And he heats them up, likely to red hot. That would destroy the temper of the tools."

"He's been working with a blacksmith. He'd be able to fix that."

"Then why go crawling back to an expert bladesmith? There is a ritualistic aspect to this. The stalking, the abduction, and the elaborate torture. I think he enjoys each phase. Part of his anticipation is probably built by buying supplies."

Christopher drummed his spindly fingers on the table. "I can agree to a point, but he gets materials and samples from places hundreds of miles apart. There must be hundreds of hardware stores along his hunting route. Not to mention truckstops, and we know he frequents those."

"Yes." Jenny replied. "But the things the police found, he expected to be found. He doesn't expect anyone to track down his real tools. Lilith, can I borrow your phone?" Jenny took the oversized device, opened a browser, quickly located a website dedicated to the airplane markers and selected the one near Rushville. She zoomed out. "He is a control freak. I know, I married one and I really think Thaddeus would love to be like this guy. He made sure to keep a few items close at hand and headed right to the closest hardware store when he wanted to replace something. Our suspect would avoid a chain like Walmart. Too many security cameras." Jenny sighed at the map on the phone. "Lots and lots of farmland."

Jenny scrolled around the electronic charts. "We're not looking for a farmhouse. We want a hunting cabin located in hunting territory. Only a few miles east on W700S there is a forested area. I say we google hardware stores near Laurel or Brookville and show the picture around." She punched in the locations on the map. "It's just a three-hour drive."

"I can make it in two," Lilith muttered, looking over Jenny's shoulder.

Jenny checked the phone clock. Her sense of time was completely dissociated. It felt like Magda died days ago but it was barely two hours.

A loud snore came from Marq's direction. Christopher moved over and found Leiter asleep, and Marq unconscious. He picked up the young vampyr and laid her on a separate bed. "Lilith, can you get the travel boxes?"

"Lilith and I can go and survey the area and be back before dark," Jenny said as she followed Christopher.

"No," the vampyr sighed.

"It's our best—"

"*We* will go. Together. You and Lilith need some sleep. Sunset is roughly 5:25. We can get mobile around 3:00. Use the boxes to get us out to the car, and we will make reconnaissance in force."

Chapter Thirty-Two

Baden propped the door to the guest room open with his foot and eased his load inside. The girl was being docile which would not do, but that was hopefully due to the drugs. The first time he let her shower she was wary, obviously looking for a weakness, a way to escape. But this morning she'd meekly let him lead her into the windowless bathroom and cleaned herself. Afterwards, pretending it was a reward for behaving, he moved her back to the bed and its slightly better comfort. He fed her twice a day, ramen noodles with chicken broth. But today was going to be extraordinary and he carried a bed-tray heaped with scrambled eggs, fried potatoes, bacon and well-buttered toast. She'd need her strength for him to have his fun.

The girl raised her head and looked at the food dubiously, then settled back.

Baden set the tray down. "Special day today," he said brightly.

"Yeah, whatever."

Baden kept control of himself, that attitude was not going to work. "You shouldn't be like that. You're going home today."

Her eyes flicked up at him, displaying both hope and doubt.

"Seriously." He traced his fingers across his chest. "Scout's honor. Your mother paid the ransom. So, soon after dark I'm going to take you to a truckstop. You know your mother's phone number?"

"Yeah?"

"Good. I'll give you a disposable cell phone and you can call her to get you."

"Just like that?" She did not sound at all convinced.

"Are you concerned you've seen my face?"

"I won't tell anyone," she blurted without any attempt to convince him.

No, you won't, he thought and repressed a grin at the thought of setting her up for this next betrayal. "See, you remember what I looked like when we met? That was a disguise, just like this is." He was working hard to maintain a convincing tone.

She raised her head to look at him again.

He smiled. She turned away.

She may not believe it right away, but he would let her stew for a few hours. Hope can be insidious, and he would do everything to reinforce the idea she was going home.

He set the tray on the table and unlocked one wrist manacle to let her sit up in bed. He placed the tray before her. From his pocket he produced a plastic wrapped spork.

She fumbled with the utensil's cover.

Yeah, still the drugs

Once she had the plastic open, she used the spork to guardedly pick at the food, expecting him to take it away, or maybe she thought it was poisoned? He slipped back out of the room, returning with a bundle wrapped in brown paper and tied with twine.

"What's that?"

Baden scratched his head. "Your clothes are a little beyond saving." He nodded to the bundle. "That's something to wear when you leave."

The car hurtled down the country road.

I will never get used to this, Jenny thought. Her grip was no less white-knuckled than the first time Lilith let loose. The moon and stars overhead were cloaked in clouds. The twisting road kept the headlights from showing anything but a few meters ahead.

Marq and Christopher sat in the back, released from their travel boxes.

Marq squirmed.

"Is there a problem?" Christopher asked.

"Just testing muscles after a few hours locked in the trunk."

"You won't find any kinks or knots." Christopher said. "Cramped conditions do not bother us."

Marq shrugged, pulled out her phone and glanced at the GPS data. "We should be there in another forty-five minutes."

"I can do it in thirty-five," Lilith muttered.

Marq checked her browser search. "Not a lot of hardware stores near there."

"Not general hardware stores," Jenny replied, looking at her own search. "Most places out here are specialties; feed and seed, farm supplies, things like that. Not a big box store for thirty miles. But I still think he wants access to tools. There are three smaller 'mom and pop' shops. We should start with those."

The first store was maybe four hundred square feet. There was a night manager and a three-hundred pound cashier with a scraggly beard and unkempt hair, who had to still be in high school. Lilith stayed in the driver's seat and Christopher, concerned his presence would be more intimidating than two women alone, stayed with her.

Jenny showed the pair the sketch on the phone. "Have you seen this guy? He hit the front of my friend's car and ran off. He's driving a big red van. A guy outside said he might have seen him stop here."

"Naw," the manager shook his head. "That's a pretty good picture."

"Thanks. It's a little hurried, I just caught a quick glance at him."

The cashier scratched at his beard as he silently tried to look like he was studying the screen, but his eyes were locked on Jenny's chest.

The manager clasped his hands to indicate it was time to end the conversation. "Sorry your car got dinged."

"Us, too," Jenny replied, putting away her phone.

It was ten miles before they pulled up to the second store. The establishment sat slightly further out of town and was significantly larger than the last store, standing at the end of a mostly vacant stripmall. There was plenty of parking and more staff present. A young girl sat sulking at the cash register while three more industrious people were engaged in stocking shelves.

Jenny spotted a woman somewhere in her fifties, thin to the point of being angular, wearing a dark green apron with the store logo and a name badge that said "Anne." She had long black curly hair, crimson nail polish and wore faded jeans that looked like they were painted on. Likely the same style she'd been wearing in the '90's. Jenny nudged Marq and approached the woman.

"Hi, my name is Jenny. I know this seems strange, but have you seen this man?" She held up the phone.

The woman snorted. "What do you want with that creep?"

"So, you know him?" Jenny asked, working to keep eagerness out of her voice.

"Not by name, though Dorothy might. He's in here all the time. He likes to window shop, eyes everything in the place, and I mean everything. Then every so often he comes in and buys a bunch of stuff."

"Why did you call him a creep?"

The look on Anne's face wasn't a sneer, but it was damned close. "Dorothy, my niece, up front. He flirts with her. He's real keen to get flirty with girls that are far too young. And it's creepy because he knows exactly what to say to get them all flattered. I had to tell him his comments were inappropriate to make at underaged staff and he called me a jealous bitch and told me to mind my own business. I'd like to get him banned, but the owner doesn't think it's a big deal. Why're you looking for him?"

Jenny opened her mouth to tell the accident story, but Marq talked over her. "How old is your niece?"

"Eighteen," Anne replied.

"Well," Marq continued. "Jenny's sister is fourteen. This guy's been creeping on her."

"Lord have mercy."

"So, any information you have —"

"Dorothy?" The woman barked. "Get over here." She turned back to Marq. "Let me know if I can do anything to help you find him. Ain't no call to be acting that way. Dorothy! Now!"

The girl looked down at the cash drawer.

"Lock the register, girl. No one's going to be checking out for a few minutes."

The girl reluctantly did as she was told. "Yeah, what?" she said on her approach.

"These women are looking for your friend." Anne pointed to the picture.

Dorothy was suddenly defensive. "He's not my friend. He's just a dude that comes in here."

"Do you know his name?"

"Scott? Something like that."

"Last name?"

The girl shrugged. "I think it starts with a B. I only caught a glimpse of his debit card once, mostly he pays cash."

The older woman spoke sternly. "You need to stop being friendly with that man."

The girl tossed her head. "As if. Yeah, he's kinda cute, but he's ancient, like forty or something. He flirts and I flirt back, so what?"

Jenny recalled when she'd been so naive, and Thad had taken advantage. She wished she could transmit some female wisdom to the girl.

"Know where he lives?" Marq asked.

"Not really. He's got a cabin in the woods somewhere."

"How do you know that?" the older woman snapped.

"He offered to take me there last summer, said he knew a great hiking trail out toward the canal."

"Canal?" Jenny asked.

"Yeah, the canal? You know, the section that is still intact, kinda south, not the place they take all the school kids."

"She means the Whitewater Canal, state historic site," Anne elaborated.

"Geeze, I just said it's not the historic site, it's just the bit further south. Whatever."

The older woman took the girl by her arm. "Why didn't you tell me he was trying to lure you to woods? Alone."

"Jeez, he wasn't serious. He's practically an old man. It was like he was practicing on me."

Practicing being charming to young women. Jenny felt her stomach roil.

243

It was time. Baden sighed and stood up. Start slow, little indignities to lead up to massive betrayal and serious fun. He needed this.

He entered the room. She was much more alert, her narrowed eyes studying him. He moved out of her sight. He'd deliberately reduced her view by chaining her hands to the bed frame above her head. She struggled to look at him.

"Hold still, we're gonna get you ready to leave."

He didn't regularly chain his guest's feet when he let them use the bed, but there was a set of handmade leg irons that opened with a twist. No need for a lock, besides, it made rearranging her legs easier once the real fun began. He grabbed her left ankle and snapped the manacle in place. She kicked at him with the other leg. *Good.*

She squirmed, managed to roll onto one hip and land a kick right on his cleft chin.

"Oh, feisty," he muttered as he grabbed the offending leg and slammed it into the metal springs. She gasped and tried to break free again but was no match for his strength.

He brought out the knife in a leather sheath from a special pocket in his work pants. Forged, mostly, by his own hand, he felt intense satisfaction holding it in his fingers.

He held the knife up for Tracey to see. Her eyes widened and she redoubled her squirming.

This is going to be good. "I'm not going to hurt you." *Yet.*

He took the flat of the blade and slid it down one leg of her jeans. At the cuff he used the edge of the knife to slice through the denim.

"Hold still. I told you these clothes have to go. You ruined them with your blood and filth. We'll just get rid of these and start clean. I have other things for you to wear."

The blade parted the cloth easily. He sliced through the waistband, ignoring the zipper and button. It took only a moment to repeat the incision on the other leg. Once the material was free, he pulled it out from under her squirming body. The long sleeve t-shirt required no effort and he tossed the rags to the floor.

The girl lay shivering in her underwear; her eyes shut tight.

"Shower time."

He unfastened her hands first, and then her legs. The girl put her knees together and drew them up to cross her arms over them.

They're so cute when they try to cover themselves.

Still holding the blade, he grabbed her by the shoulder and forced her out of the bed to the bathroom.

"Go on, take a shower. You've got to go home presentable, don't you? You don't want them to think I mistreated you."

Her gaze was locked on the knife, as if she knew using the blade was an escalation. She backed into the bathroom and closed the door.

"Before you come out, you need to put your underwear back on, and wear a towel, understand?" He needed to keep up the charade just a few more minutes.

The water started to run. He waited as she spent a lot of time in the bathroom. She didn't know that prolonging the next phase increased his excitement. *Just a few more minutes.* He allowed himself to feel his growing arousal.

Forty minutes and the water shut off. The cabin had a limited supply of hot water from a propane-fed hot water tank, enough for ten minutes. He idly wondered if she ran the cold by itself for half an hour and then bathed. Or showered and let the hot water peter out before letting it run.

Either way, she would be cold and damp.

"Come on out," he ordered.

She complied, vainly trying to cover herself with a towel too short to actually go around her torso.

Little indignities.

He marched her back to the room and pointed to the brown paper wrapped bundle. "Go, on, see what you have to wear. I got it just for you."

The girl scrambled away from him and ran to the package. She paused before opening it, her fingers shaking. Those fingers finally untied the string and pulled open the package. Instead of clothing there was just more brown paper with a waxed back.

He could see her confusion. *Good.*

He grabbed her by the hair and jerked her back to the table. "You're not going home. Your mother doesn't want you; no one wants you, you're just a piece of meat."

Chapter Thirty-Three

Jenny ran back out to her car and slid into the back seat to discover Christopher on the phone and Lilith relaxed in the driver's seat, eyes closed, head canted to one side.

"We've got—" Jenny hissed.

Christopher held up a finger. "I do understand. The FBI has finite manpower. If I can get any more concrete information, I will let you know." He disconnected as Marq climbed in the front with Lilith.

"We have a first name and a possible location," Jenny blurted.

"Still not enough. I just got a call from Zien. He reports the FBI is not ready to commit resources based on the sketch." Christopher waved a decisive hand. "He tells me they wouldn't even make him a person of interest. They do not go on hunches or secondhand information from anonymous sources. They have their attention on Alabama right now."

"Alabama?"

"They created an algorithm based on time dates of abductions and body dumps. It predicts that he will dump the body within a week, south of Decatur."

"He's not a computer."

"But he may be predictable. To them it is more concrete."

Marq hovered over a laptop screen in the front seat, not listening.

"There," Marq reached over and shook Lilith's shoulder.

"I'm awake."

"Look at this." Marq held up the screen for Lilith to examine.

"I don't see…"

"Right there." She tapped the picture. "Zoom in."

Lilith did as requested. "Another cabin, that makes four."

"Yes," Marq agreed, "but, God bless Google satellite view, that's a flash of red. Looks to be a truck, or a van parked under that tree."

Lilith stared into the leafless tangle of branches and finally saw the tiny glint of metallic red. "It might be worth a look."

Marq pointed again. "Christopher. Look at this."

The vampyr pulled himself up by the seat and stared over her shoulder at the screen.

"Our most likely place," Marq announced

Christopher chewed his top lip and considered. "Let's be clear. The FBI has the resources to handle a rescue. We are just looking for the right detail to get them change their focus from the likely dump sites to this guy's lair."

"Like something to indicate the girl is, or was, there?" Marq said. "I mean, you and me, we can move quietly and see in the dark. We can get close enough to find something without alerting anybody."

Christopher made the effort to take in a deep breath and sighed. "I don't know. We have no idea what kind of security he has. Webcams? Alarms? Motion sensors?"

"He won't have motion sensors, except maybe at the doors," Jenny said. "I grew up in woods like these. There're too many animals moving around at night, too many false alarms. You would never get any rest."

Christopher nodded in thought.

"I doubt he'll have cameras covering the area," Marq continued with Jenny's argument. "If he has anything, it will be pointed at the road or the door. We can go around back."

Christopher spoke slowly. "If he sees us, he will likely kill the girl."

Marq smiled. "I know that tone of voice, so here's the clincher. He will definitely kill her if we can't get the FBI to act."

"Why don't you all just go get her?" Jenny asked. "I mean you're powerful, damn near immortal."

"Not that immortal," Christopher winced. "Still vulnerable to bullets. One to the brain and that is it." His tone sharpened. "I've commanded soldiers in battle. It doesn't matter if you have superior strength, or how good your plan is, the minute you make contact with the enemy, all hell breaks loose and the only way to maintain the advantage is by relying on your training. Marq and I haven't trained together. The FBI has hostage rescue teams. That is what they do."

"But we have to take a look," Marquessa said. "You know, for the effen FBI."

Tracey gave up screaming but continued to cry until the only sound she could make was a low whimper. It started so nice, her high pitch screeches as big salty tears ran down her face, pooling on the table by her head.

She was falling into despair, so he had to kindle some hope of respite. He hadn't even done any serious work yet. Baden put down the acid. His stepfather left a trail of cigarette burns down the back of his left arm when he was eight, and the resulting scars were beautiful. He liked giving a similar treatment to his guests, but he despised cigarettes. They caused cancer and stunk. He found one tiny drop of a mixture of hydrochloric acid and nitric acid made a burn nearly identical to his own. So he and his girls could be "matchy-match," to steal a phrase from Angela's Facebook.

"I think that's enough for tonight." He stepped away from the table to admire his handywork. He'd gotten a little excited and accidently broken the skin on her inner thigh, but the overall pattern of the other red welts on her pale skin pleased him. "Tomorrow, we will play a game, would you like that?"

She sniffled and moaned.

He produced a coin and held it in front of her eyes. "I'll flip this in the morning, and you call it. If you're right, I will leave you alone until the next day. Then we'll flip it again."

He dusted off his hands, then clapped them together. "Get some rest now." He walked to the door and called out over his shoulder, "Sweet dreams." That elicited a little sob.

He'd wait about an hour or so. Then he would take her for the first time.

He sat at the cheap Formica table in the combination living room and kitchen and absently ran his finger along the dented edge. How did he want to take this one? How to leave that first serious mark? There were streaks of rust on the chrome legs where the plating was worn. The blood-colored stains against the bright silver inspired him. He savored the thought of ending the night with an event he usually did after his guest was pretty far gone. He had the propane torch and a set of pliers he *could* use but...

He dug through his toolbox. It would be bloody, but it would set up the next day's fun. He frowned, the tool he imagined was not in the box. He checked the time on his wristwatch. The hardware store closed at nine, sometimes earlier. If he hurried, he could get the implement. Or not. He drummed his fingers on the distressed table.

Lilith parked the car in a copse of trees about a quarter mile from where a rutted dirt track led into the woods. It was cold and getting colder, clouds moved in, drawing a sheer curtain over a gibbous moon. The three passengers stepped out of the running sedan.

Somewhere in the distance something barked; a chilly, tight, high pitched scream.

"What was that?" Marq stared at the woods.

"Not wolves," Christopher muttered.

"That little yip?" Jenny said. "Coyote."

"Coyote?" Marq grimaced. "I thought they were only out west."

Jenny laughed. "I forget you are a city girl."

The lone coyote call was answered by more.

Jenny put on an outrageous Bela Lugosi Dracula accent to rival Lilith's. "The cheeldrin of da night, what muuusic they make."

Neither vampyr was amused.

"They're smaller than wolves, right?" Marq sounded worried.

"Yeah, basically scavengers. Pets or small children may be in danger, but coyotes are reluctant to attack anything that will give them a fight."

"Thank you, Jenny, for that moment of Wild Kingdom," Christopher remarked. "Come, let's make this quick."

Jenny watched the two figures evaporate into the trees and wanted to follow but settled for pacing. She stomped her feet and took a deep breath of the chilled air.

Headlights driving toward them captured her attention. She tapped on the car window and Lilith lowered halfway.

Jenny pointed at the moving light.

"I see it. We're far enough off the road he isn't likely to spot us."

Jenny's voice was quiet. "He's turning." She watched as the vehicle curved and ventured onto the rutted path.

She texted. "Car coming."

She wished she had vampyr night vision. All she'd seen were headlights. Could have been a car, truck, van, SUV. Probably some dark color.

"I'm going."

"Where?" Lilith hissed.

"I wanna see if that was a van. He might be coming up behind them."

"What if he sees you? What about cameras?"

"It's dark, doubt he has night vison cameras." She took off at a measured trot, but slowed before she reached the dirt road, cold air chilling her lungs until her entire chest hurt.

The track to the cabin was a mess of frozen lumps, ruts, and tire tracks. Jenny tread carefully, stumbling in the dark.

Five minutes later, she saw the cabin outlined in the dark. A light came on and she jumped.

It was just a light above the door. Jenny saw movement and a shadow passed into the cabin. The light went out.

A motion sensor.

Jenny crept closer. Now, she could make out the outline of the vehicle, a pickup truck with a bed cover.

Not a van.

She texted Marq. "There is a truck at the cabin. Not a van."

Marq texted back. "Where are you?"

"On the dirt driveway, about a hundred yards from the front door."

She frowned and waited for Marq to reply.

"Can I help you, miss?"

A flashlight shined into her face. She gasped and clutched her hand to her chest.

"Are you okay?" The person pointed the beam to the ground. A man in his sixties stood in a parka with a golden retriever at his side silently wagging his tail. "Didn't mean to scare you. What are you doing out here, anyway?"

"Oh, there you are." Christopher stepped out of the woods. "Sorry," he addressed the dog owner. "My niece gets a little confused."

The man stared at Christopher standing in the cold weather without a coat.

"We hit something—on the road," Christopher continued. "Bent the rim. I was changing the tire, and she, well, she wandered off."

"Good," Marquessa called, stepping into view. "You found her. Jenny, you know better than to wander off." She took brisk stride to stand by Jenny.

Christopher took the man by the arm and turned him away from the two women. "Sorry," he spoke in a low, confidential voice. "My niece had brain trauma as a little girl. She functions at about a fourth-grade level."

"Oh," the man said, turning sympathetic eyes to Jenny.

Jenny rankled at the remark but felt pretty stupid, anyway.

The door to the cabin opened and the light came back on. "Cliff?" A matronly lady in a parka that matched the old man's stood in the doorway with a quizzical expression

"Just some city types, Alice. Had an accident with their car."

He looked at Christopher's lack of a coat again, then turned his eyes to Marq's black silk blouse. "You better get back to your car, you'll catch your death."

Marq waved her hand. This time, when she spoke, she had an accent Jenny recognized from the movie "Fargo." "We're from Minnesota, don't cha know. We're used to it."

"Oh," the man said as if that was an explanation. He did not seem to know what to make of the dark-skinned woman.

"Sorry to disturb you." Christopher took Jenny by the arm to lead her back down the path.

"No problem at all. Y'all have a good night."

"You too." Christopher waved.

Marq took a moment before following. Still with the accent and sounding abnormally cheery, she asked, "You know anyone around here with a red van? That thing we hit fell from one speeding down the road." She threw in another, "Don't cha know."

251

"Can't rightly say I know of anyone hereabouts with a red van. Alice, you know anyone?"

"Can't say as I do."

Marq nodded thanks. "We'll be on our way." She turned to follow Christopher.

"The only one with a van around here," Alice continued, "is that navy boy; but I think his is rust brown. I mean in color, it looks new. He does drive fast, so I stay clear of him on the road."

Marq turned back. "Could it be a dark red, like a burgundy?"

"Could be," Cliff said. "The boy's got a cabin down the road a piece. At the end of the driveway go right, say three miles. Seen him in town just last week. Comes up here a couple times a year. I've talked to him a few times in town, the only thing he told me was that he was in the navy and he spent most of that time in Japan."

"Name?"

"Philip? I think." He scratched his head. "No, that's not right. Alice, you know that boy's name?"

The woman shrugged her shoulders.

"I'm not good with names." Cliff said.

"Or faces," Alice called out.

Marq wrapped her arms around herself, rubbing her biceps. "It's cold."

"Thank you for your time," Christopher said. He did not try to mimic the accent. "I'm afraid we need to get back to the car. Goodnight." He and Marq nodded at the man.

They trudged until they were out of sight of the elderly couple.

"That would have gone better if we just knocked on the door," Jenny said.

Christopher grunted.

"We going to check out the navy boy?"

"I don't know," Christopher muttered. "I'm going to have a moment with Lilith when we get back to the car. Marq? How are you holding out?"

"I'm not really cold."

"I mean are you hungry?" Christopher tried to convey his concern.

"Oh, no, I'm good. The reverend was surprisingly potent."

"Grief is strong, but it can burn."

"Yeah. But I didn't feed on his grief. I forgave him."

Christopher craned his neck to look at her.

"For what he did to us and on behalf of his daughter and granddaughter. I gave him a gentle bite as a feeling of relief rose and I reinforced it."

"You've learned well."

They trudged up the path and reached the car.

Lilith stood by the driver door, tapping her foot. "There's an Amber Alert in Columbus, Indiana. Blonde teenager forced into a van at a truck stop off I-65."

"Can't be our guy. He's been doing one at a time and he still has a captive."

"We don't know that," Jenny pointed out. "The FBI could have found a body and are keeping it quiet."

Christopher nodded. "You and Lilith use Google to see if you can spot Navy Boy's cabin."

The target cabin was the only one near their current location. Google satellite did not show any vehicles around the property,

"We should have a look," Jenny said.

"Or we can go back to Indy and find out about the missing girl," Lilith replied.

"I don't know about that," Christopher said. "Zien humored us because of Leiter, but he doesn't take us seriously. We need something rock solid." He sighed, "In addition to the navy boy, there are eight likely cabins?"

"Twenty," Lilith corrected. "I expanded a little further east. There's another secluded area there. They're close to another hardware store, but that's also farther east. If he habitually goes west…"

Christopher pinched the bridge of his nose. "Okay. Let's do this. There are too many to check out tonight. We need to get a hotel. Lilith, do you have anyone to call that can help with the meal plan? It would be best to get two. Tomorrow, when it is light, you two will check out the cabins, west to east. The idea is to eliminate targets. Families, couples, kids, not occupied. What is it, Jenny?"

Jenny cocked her head to one side and sucked in her right cheek. "I don't know. There's something bugging me."

Christopher continued thinking out loud. "Marq and I will set up a headquarters at a hotel and go over everything we actually know, everything we think we know, and try to identify which of our speculations have some validity."

"No," Jenny said with authority in her voice. "I remember now. We need to check out sailor boy first. That old couple said he spent his navy time in Japan; what if they meant Okinawa?"

Chapter Thirty-Four

"Okinawa?" Christopher asked.

"You really don't read the notes I leave you," Marq said peevishly, then continued with feigned patience. "There was a murder in Okinawa that was attributed to a U.S. serviceman. The details made the FBI speculate it could have been one of our target's early murders."

Christopher clenched his lips together and nodded. "All right, we will check out this one cabin tonight. Lilith?"

"Got the coordinates and ready to go."

It wasn't that simple. The instructions said to make a left turn but the road on the GPS wasn't there. Lilith swore under her breath as she turned the car around. She took in deep breaths through her nose and turned off the automated directions.

"Where do we go now?" Jenny asked.

"Sshh." Lilith gave Jenny a quick glare.

"Give her a minute," Christopher murmured. "What made her challenging in a race is her sense of direction. Spin her around and she still knows where she is trying to go. Even at a hundred miles an hour."

As if that was an order, Lilith took off at speed. She twisted, turned and worked her way through county lanes and poorly mapped roads for half an hour. She slowed and parked the car. "Here," she announced. "I passed the driveway to the cabin a quarter mile back."

Jenny dubiously looked out the windshield into a dark night with no sign of habitation.

"Let me get off the road." The woods were too thick to pull the car into the trees, but Lilith managed to avoid the deep rut on the side of the road and pull close to the very edge.

"Okay," Christopher said as he unbuckled his seat belt. "We will be back in a minute."

"No," Marq interrupted.

Christopher turned his head slowly and locked his gaze on her. "What?"

"The issue is the color of the van. Jenny and I should go."

"What?" Jenny asked, turning to Marq.

Marq gave her a side-eye. "Night vision."

"So?"

Marq took a breath to sigh. "Christopher and I can see perfectly in near total darkness, but in *black and white*." She turned to Christopher to make her case. "Jenny will be able to tell the color faster than you or me. She'll check out the color of the van and we'll go from there."

Jenny did not want to go. Her last reconnaissance had been *such* a success. "You could use a light; I mean I'll still need a light."

Christopher gave a long-suffering shake of his head. "The change from night vision to color vision is not instantaneous. It can take several minutes and would need more light than safety requires." He made an effort to manufacture a dramatic sigh. "Fine. Make it quick."

Marquessa moved through the woods with an unearthly grace while Jenny jogged to keep up. The bruises on her thighs hurt, but she ignored them and kept going. She felt like a clunking machine next to her friend. The pair came to a halt as a yipping cry echoed in the night, to be replied by a slightly deeper noise that was more similar to a dog's bark.

"Is that closer? You said scavengers?"

"There are very few reports of them attacking adult humans." Jenny paused and then was aware she was about to say something stupid. Her friend was human, *of course?* "Hear the echo? They're not close and their noise gives us cover."

Marq gave Jenny a searching look, then led on.

The night was clouded and the diffused moonlight provided Jenny with enough light to nearly match her friend's pace.

"Stop," Marq whispered as she held up a hand. "I see a van."

Jenny slipped up to whisper in her ear. "What color is it?"

Marq gave her a side-eye and slapped her arm. "Seriously?"

"Hey, I'm not used to you being undead!"

Marq progressed in a slow crouch. She looked back and gave an impatient wave for Jenny to catch up.

In contrast to the silent tread of the vampyr, Jenny was far too aware of her own progress. Her ears were filled by a cacophony of dry leaves rustling and unseen twigs snapping under each step. She imagined that Marq was some sleek jungle cat, followed by a wallowing hippopotamus crashing through the jungle.

Her heart raced and she could barely keep her breath by the time she reached the van. Jenny knew terror; but this was a new level and she couldn't say why. She was just there to look at the van.

Jenny got close to the vehicle and used her cellphone flashlight to check the paint. She frowned as mixed emotions hit her.

It was dark red, but hardly unmarked. A stick figure family paraded below the tinted rear window; a mom, dad, baby and puppy. In addition, half a dozen other stickers populated the bumper, including one for a popular Orlando theme park and a cartoon mouse.

"I think this is the wrong place," Jenny said. "Kids."

Marq growled, "There is a tricycle and a kid's ball up by the front porch."

"Wrong house?" Jenny hissed.

Marq examined one of the stickers on the van. She ran a tentative finger over it and pulled it right off. "They're magnetic."

"So?"

Marq's head jerked. "Did you hear that?"

Jenny listened. "No."

Marq closed her eyes and cupped her fingers by her ears. "I'm not used to this hearing. To me those coyotes sound a few feet away. I heard something, but I'm not sure…"

She jerked her head up. "That's a scream." She strained. "There again. This is the right house. Oh, God, she's screaming." Marq's eyes opened wide.

Jenny saw something feral in her friend's face that frightened her. She suddenly doubted Marq's hearing and her sanity. Should she take her companion's word? *Was Marq too hungry?*

Marq crept toward the house on all fours, seeming to go with an animal instinct.

Jenny scrambled to keep up with the vampyr. "We send a message to the FBI?"

"No time," Marq hissed. "I'm going in there." She leapt toward the porch and charged the door, only to stop abruptly, her hands clenching the sky in silent rage. Marq spun as though punching an invisible foe.

"What is it?" Jenny recognized the construction as a common reverse board and batten. The manufactured wooden sheets were not painted and resembled the cabin Thad's uncle Joe-Bob had in Tennessee.

Marq glared at her. "Try the door."

Jenny stood, confused.

"I have to be invited!" Mark pointed at the door with her fist.

"That's really a thing?" Jenny pulled out her phone.

"Yeah, it's a goddam thing. Look, he's doing something to her right now. He's not going to notice any noise. Get the damn door."

"I'm calling Christopher."

"Hurry up, I can smell what he's about to do to her, and, goddammit, I can smell her terror."

The phone rang once, and Jenny spoke in a rush. "Right cabin. Marq's going in and I can't stop her." She hung up the phone, stepped over an ancient, iron-framed boot brush, and examined the door. It did not budge, or even rattle.

Jenny felt a cold sinking feeling. Now she heard the sharp high end of a scream. A child's scream. A little girl was screaming her head off.

Marq pushed her aside and seized the boot brush, cocking her arms back to swing it into the single darkened window to the right of the door. She shook and lowered the instrument. "Dammit. Xanax, Diazapam. Molly, for god's sake, there has got to be something."

She whirled at Jenny and thrust the boot brush into her hands. "Smash."

Jenny grabbed the boot brush without thinking, caught up in Marq's urgency. The muffled scream sounded again, high, shrieking and desperate.

Jenny closed her eyes, turned her head, and swung the iron base at the window. The shatter sounded like an explosion to her ears.

"Get in there! Invite me!"

Fear twisted Jenny's guts, but she forced herself to move on, afraid that if she hesitated, she would bolt. She used the boot brush to sweep shards of glass from the window frame. She grabbed the sill with both hands and, despite her efforts, glass shards sliced and wedged into her palms. She clambered through the opening, feeling every bruise on her thighs. She heaved herself through until gravity made her tumble into a tiny mudroom onto a pile of broken glass. Pieces stuck in her heavy coat but did not pierce through.

"Come in, Marquessa!" she bellowed even as she hit the floor.

Marq elected to kick in the door, the frame splitting where a heavy bolt held it closed. She staggered in with the momentum of the kick.

The screaming stopped.

Chapter Thirty-Five

Baden was dressed for play. He wore a black, tight fitting T-shirt, a pair of fly-fronted drawstring pants and a very special leather tool belt to keep his favorite toys always within his reach. Tracey lay on the table, her legs free to kick as much as she wanted. Her hands were bound by the steel cuffs to the frame above her head.

She blinked at burning tears, and that inspired him. He took the steel encased glass vial of acid out of his belt. From the same belt he drew a glass dropper and used it to suck up a few drops of his special mixture, a type of *aqua regia*. Just one little drop on the inside of her left arm. Just a taste to teach her to fear the bottle. Tracey's skin smoked, bubbled and blistered as she screamed.

Time to get serious. Really serious.

Baden pinned Tracey's left leg in a bent straddle, meant to twist her knee as he got ready for the big game. Her right leg flopped around; she was too far gone with fright to kick at her tormentor. He held the bottle up for her to see. "Do you know what one drop of this would do to your pretty little eyes?"

She screamed again. He smiled and replaced the bottle in his belt.

A sound like a battering ram hitting the front door stopped his in his tracks. He shoved his hand over Tracey's mouth to silence her as he fumbled on the table for his Glock 21. He kept this particular make with him while he played in case he needed to put someone down hard and fast. His sudden grab knocked over the pliers he had been heating with a propane torch for his game of "Hot Tamale."

Baden knew every inch of his habitat. Including where likely interlopers were vulnerable. He used both hands, took aim and put two shots through the wall. Anyone standing in the front doorway would be hit. He heard a loud feminine screech and something drop as he changed his aim and sent another two rounds through the wall to the hallway outside his door.

Body dropping? Someone diving for cover? Something else?

The girl on the table made choking hiccup sounds as her screams transformed into heaving sobs, another sound he enjoyed but was too busy to appreciate.

He was torn between putting a bullet through Tracey's brain and bolting versus standing his ground. No, he was going to deal with this; he waited too long for playtime. It couldn't be a hostage rescue team; they would be swarming him.

He'd get ready to run but wouldn't end Tracey, yet. If it was a few local yokels he might be back for her. Whoever it was exhibited incompetence. Worst case scenario he could leave Tracey behind as a distraction to his pursuers

Keeping his pistol trained on the door, he shoved the bed aside and jerked the area rug away to reveal a trap door. He banged at one spot and a board lifted up, displaying the hidden release.

Someone could be crawling from the mudroom, so he took two shots through the wall. There was another feminine squeal.

He heaved the trapdoor open and glanced at the empty crawlspace, his way out. He hesitated, wanting to see who was coming for him. Clearly not professionals. Baden was a connoisseur of female pain and those shrieks were feminine. Could it be the truckstop lady's friends? Did that bitch put a tracker on his car? *Stupid fucking Charlies Angels.*

Whoever they were, they didn't seem to be heavily armed or very well trained.

He jumped into the opening. The space was deep enough that the floor came up to his chest. He rested his elbows on the floor and considered his next move. There was a thump by the door but this time he held off shooting. The Glock only had a fourteen round capacity. He'd wait to see who came in, then get at least one of his bug-out bags.

"Ow, ow, ow!" Marquessa groused, laying on the floor at the entrance. "That fucking hurts!"

"You okay?" Jenny hissed from where she was curled up in the far mudroom corner.

"Bullets. Metal. The wounds close up quick. No real damage," Marq stated through gritted teeth. "No one bothered to mention they hurt; I mean really goddam hurt." She tentatively pushed to her feet but stayed low. If the guy was lucky enough to land a head shot, that would be the end of it.

Two more shot rang out and a section just above Jenny head exploded. "We need to wait for Christopher," she screeched.

"No." Marq slipped down the hallway, moving vampyr fast. The shooter was in the first room. She tore the door off its hinges and dropped to the ground further down the hall; still holding the door for whatever protection it might provide.

The door disappeared. Baden intended to take a shot, but there was nothing to shoot at. He could put two rounds low on both sides of the door, but he didn't feel confident. "I can blow this place to hell," he yelled. "Come in, hands on head, or the whole place goes up!"

There was a scraping noise and then, like magic, an unarmed black woman stood in the doorway, her arms crossed in front of her. She was dressed in black with a black velvet choker around her neck, and she looked eerily familiar.

"Remember me?" she asked with a casual tone. She took a single step into the room and pulled the choker away to reveal a pale scar across her throat.

Baden stared in disbelief. He saw the arterial spray. Well, he'd make sure the bitch died now. He went up on tiptoes to get a clear shot over the bed. The hollow points would make her head literally explode. He squeezed the trigger, forgetting the girl on table.

Tracey kicked at Baden's elbow, grazing him just enough to send his shot wide of the black bitch's head.

With inhuman speed the black woman leapt over the bed and ripped the .45 from his hands like snatching a toy from an unruly child. She threw it across the room and the gun struck the wall with such force it imbedded in the wood panel.

She seized Baden's shoulders to haul him form the trapdoor and Baden fumbled for the stun gun in his belt. He shoved it in her face.

She didn't outright convulse but did let him go. He grabbed the trapdoor with all his might and closed it after him. The woman grabbed at the edge, but he had weight and momentum on his side. He took more than a small amount of satisfaction at the crunching noise her fingers made as he smashed them until the flesh kept him from engaging the latch. He heaved again and felt the lock click as the bitch screamed in agony overhead. Baden scrambled through the space and emerged behind the cabin.

The bitch was between him and one bug out bag. The second was out under the porch. The last of his gear was fifty yards down a trail around back. He ran through the night.

Jenny watched as Marq sped down the hall to rip the door off its hinges with unearthly speed and strength. She saw a roll of paper towels on the mudroom shelf and grabbed it. She tried to staunch the bleeding from dozens of nicks in her hands. Two more shots rang out and she dropped back to the floor. Jenny winced at the tiny gashes in her hands, sticky with paper towel residue caught in the blood.

She heard a man shout and one more gun shot.

Then a crash and she heard Marq howl in pain. She felt like a coward, staying behind. Her mind barely had time to warn her, *Going to do another stupid,* as she ran to her friend.

In the room she took in the sobbing girl, not more that fifteen, stripped to her bra and underwear. The hostage was bound with steel manacles to a rough, bloodstained plywood table.

"Take care of the girl," Marq commanded.

Jenny gaped at her friend's hands. Frothy pink clumps of flesh were all that remained of Marq's fingers.

The vampyr seemed oblivious to the damage. She moved, yelling something as she ran for the door.

There was no way to refer to her motion as running, it was far too fast. Her legs were a blur and it gave the impression she was gliding as if her entire body was in a different time dimension. All Jenny got was a feeling of pain, anger, and the impression the bastard was on the run. Then Marq was gone.

The girl let out a hoarse, desperate scream.

Jenny rushed to the bed. "Tracey? Is that your name? I'm here to help! I brought friends. It's going to be okay, I promise."

The girl did not respond but made mewling sounds as if too exhausted to sob anymore.

Jenny examined the manacles. They were bolted shut but mercifully appeared unlocked. She rifled through the tools spilled across the table. She would have preferred a crescent wrench but settled on a pair of piers.

She turned, holding the tool as she reached for the restraints.

The girl's eyes bugged out and she screamed harder. She jerked her body left and right, her wrists yanking at sickening angles in the steel manacles. Her free leg windmilled at Jenny's head.

"Please, Tracey, I'm here to help!"

Christopher entered the room.

The girl looked at him and let out a wail so pitiful it threatened to break Jenny's soul.

Christopher was at the girl's side. She fought him, but he effortlessly covered her eyes with his right hand.

Th girl stopped screaming and fell into quiet tears. "Jennifer, please bring me that blanket," he asked, still covering her eyes with one hand and pointing to a crumpled bedspread in the corner.

Jenny grabbed the sheet and covered the girl.

"I'm going to remove my hand. Please keep her eyes covered." He looked over the side table littered with tools and torches. There was a plastic box with three medical vials and a half dozen syringes.

He studied the vials, then opened a syringe and drew a very small amount.

"What—"

Christopher held his fingers to his lips.

Jenny did not know what to do so she followed orders and kept the girl's eyes covered.

Christopher stroked Tracey's right arm until it relaxed and he rubbed it with alcohol. He deftly administered the shot.

Of course he had no trouble finding a vein, Jenny thought.

The girl relaxed.

Christopher looked up at Jenny. "Where is Marq?"

"She went after the bastard."

Christopher glared at the girl and then back at Jenny. "I need to sit with her for a minute. Go find Marq."

Baden hurtled down the familiar path heading for the bug-out bag buried in a shallow pit covered by a rotted log. He shoved the log out of the way and swept aside some loose dirt to reveal black nylon straps attached to a triple waterproof ballistic duffle bag. He squatted, wrapped his fingers in the fastenings and bent to drag the bag out. Something crunched behind him and he froze. He looked up to see the black woman standing at arm's length away. She crossed her arms and silently scrutinized him.

Baden abandoned the bug out bag. The weapons weren't loaded and considering how easily she disarmed him, they were be a waste of time, anyway. He took several steps backwards along the path.

The woman did not move after him. It was as if she were carved in onyx. *Hell, she didn't even look like she was breathing.*

He turned and bolted down the trail, headed toward the state road. It was only two miles and he was confident he could make it in less than twenty minutes. Getting away without the supplies would be harder but he had credit cards under three names with him, so he had means to escape. He made it another fifty yards and risked a look behind him, seeing no sign of pursuit. *What was she doing? Could she be a fucking ghost?* He mentally sneered, only the gullible fell for that crap.

When he returned his glance to the trail, he skidded to a halt. The woman stood before him, blocking the path in that same silent, cold, motionless pose. A chorus of coyotes sounded off to his left and was answered by more in the darkness beyond.

He bolted off the track to his right. He could go cross country for a bit, and he would certainly hear if the weird bitch followed. He crashed through a clump of dry, thorny bushes only to find the woman standing in front of him again. He blundered back through the brush, intent on regaining the trail. The woman was there again.

He drew his knife, the Damascus knife, from his tool belt. The bitch may be fast, but he knew she'd bleed. He brandished the blade and pulled his only other weapon, the *aqua regia*.

"Come at me bitch, you can either bleed or burn!"

His bravado was rewarded by a flicker of fright in his adversary's eyes.

Then she smiled, revealing… *fangs*? He had just a moment to absorb what he saw before he heard a growl and something seized his hand holding the acid. The animal looked sort of like a coyote but was larger and its fur had a darker, bloody hue. He slashed at it, but the creature held tight, jerking him toward the ground, ruining his attack. He tried to pull against the animal to aim his next swing, but another red coyote leapt at him, knocking him off his feet.

That's when the smaller coyotes appeared. Regular coyotes, not red wolf hybrids like he was fighting. In seconds there was a whirling mass of animals gnawing at him. Not tearing at him, not going for his throat, just gnawing. Everywhere.

Baden screamed.

Jenny followed the shrieks and found Marq standing, her arms crossed and a grim smile on her face as she watched the pack of animals chomping at a mass of bloody flesh with flailing arms.

"My God! Should we help?"

Marq shrugged. "Eh? The coyotes seem to be doing just fine."

The man screamed again and Jenny turned away. Marq watched with inscrutable eyes.

Jenny felt sick to her stomach but did not judge her friend. "Are they going to kill him?"

"Soon."

Jenny stiffened. "You said Stoker had some facts right in Dracula. He said vampires could control wolves."

"He said all the 'mean' animals: wolves, rats, bats. But no, I can't control them." Marq cocked an eyebrow. "Just summon them. And honestly, I didn't know I was summoning anything until they showed up."

There was one more choking scream. Jenny steeled herself and turned to see one of larger animals tear out navy boy's throat. Her stomach heaved, but she kept from vomiting.

Marq turned to join Jenny, facing away as the smaller coyotes dug into what the bigger ones left behind. "There, it is done."

"Does revenge make you feel better?"

"No, worse. Vampyric empathy is a bastard. Except... I do feel cleaner now that he's dead."

Jenny looked at her friend's wounded hands. "Are your hands going to heal?"

"Damage by wood. It's going to take a while." Marq looked at Jenny's hands swathed in paper towels. "May lick your hands?"

Jenny reflexively pulled her hands closer to her body and was suddenly, acutely, aware that this was the first time the pair had been alone since... "Are you that hungry?"

"No, no." Marq shook her head. "The venom, it will prevent infection, speed healing."

"Oh, right. Then yes, thank you." She held them up and Marq adopted an air of clinical detachment as she went to work.

The touch of Marq's tongue and smooth feeling of her fangs sliding along Jenny's fingers spread warmth and she shivered in memory. Her cheeks grew hot and Jenny was glad for Marq's night color blindness.

The vampyr raised her head and spat out shards of glass. "That should be better." The dark woman touched Jenny's shoulder and together they trudged back to the cabin.

The abducted girl was asleep, but now dressed in oversized clothes from the cabin's closet.

Marq looked at the girl's slack features and turned to Christopher, "Did you?"

"I gave her something. Horse tranquilizer."

"You knocked her out to make manipulating her body easier," Marq said grimly. She turned to Jenny. "It's hard to teach an old vampire about consent."

Christopher ignored her. "It blocks short term memory. It will minimize her trauma."

"Forgetting is its own type of trauma."

Christopher frowned. "Marquessa. This child will never forget. She will never fully heal. Can you not feel that?"

The two vampyrs stared at each other for a long, silent moment until Marq's eyes drifted to Tracey's sleeping form.

Christopher held up a worn plastic grocery bag. "Please, you two, take her out to the car. This is what I found of her personal effects."

"What are you going to do?" Jenny asked.

"I found several cans of kerosene. I am going to erase this place."

Epilogue

Atlanta, Georgia

Senior detective Walter Sprigler stared across the interview room table. *This guy is batshit crazy*, he thought. When they first brought him in, Sprigler figured the man was trying to fake an insanity plea, but for the last hour the suspect spun out of control. He was the sort of disorganized that begged for an involuntary mental hold. His eyes were wild, and his hair stuck out all over. He was so agitated on arrest they were taking no chances. Leg irons and handcuffs were the only thing that made it safe to go within ten yards of this nut. "So, you were stealing the explosives to kill vampires." He tried to make it sound as if the logic was comprehensible.

"No! No! No! You're not listening." Thad banged his head against his cuffed hands with each exclamation. "The explosives and the guns were to keep the Chicago militia from killing me. They think I fed their leader to a rabid vampire!"

"Vampires carry rabies?" The detective worked to keep a straight face.

"You know what I mean. Fuckin' monster with big ass fangs and claws. Guns are useless against the vampires. That's why I got the acid."

"Stole the acid."

"Look, I know how this sounds…" Thad pleaded.

"How does it sound?"

A light went on in Thad's eyes and for a moment he seemed lucid. Then he banged his handcuffs into the table in a renewed frenzy. "You got to listen! Your people need to protect me. I'm a Callun, fer crissakes! You know what my family can do to you?" Thad sneered at the police officer. "I'm going to end up with a double tap in my skull or my throat torn out, and that will be on you, De-tec-a-tive Walter." His gaze darted around the room. "They're everywhere. My wife is one of them, fer crissakes."

"Your ex-wife?" The detective asked. "Would that be Regina or Jennifer?" He went to make a note.

"Jennifer, that stupid bitch. Get her to walk in sunlight, see what happens."

The officer looked down at the file containing Thaddeus T. Callun's arrest warrant for domestic battery. He'd called both of the exes and it was a reasonable assumption they'd want some payback. *They'll probably settle for coming in to testify against him. In court, during the day.*

Louisville, Kentucky

Clio raised her pierced eyebrow and leaned across the kitchen table. "Girl, what are you not telling me?"

Jenny returned a look of wide-eyed innocence. "I told you everything that is mine to tell."

Clio grinned. "We both know that's bullshit."

Jenny shrugged.

Clio placed both elbows on the table and laced her fingers together, her three diamond rings touching. "So, let me summarize, in case I get asked. The Atlanta police called you and said they have Thad in custody?"

"Yep."

"So, your boss—"

"And his assistant," Jenny remarked.

Clio grimaced. "So, you all shook up these incels and they told you where to find the missing girl. Then you go there, *boom!*" Clio spread her hands to mime an explosion. "Cabin on fire, bad man dead, girl miraculously unconscious out front."

"Essentially."

"And since your boss doesn't like his name in the papers, he had his 'friend' from the party drive the girl to a spot on I-65 south and call the cops claiming she found the girl there."

Jenny nodded.

Clio nodded back with a sardonic frown. "Of course. It all makes so much sense. But, just for my personal enrichment, how can you be sure that the body at the cabin was the bad guy?"

"We're very sure."

"And the bruises, those are from your ex?"

"He is the cause of my bruises, yes."

"There you go, again. You know a half-truth can be considered a whole lie, Jenny."

"I made a promise to protect Christopher's privacy." Jenny smiled. "Also, I signed an NDA."

"Are we gonna see you down at the coffee house?" Clio crossed her arms and cocked her head to the side.

"Oh yeah, I made an agreement with Roger to be a silent partner. Also, I'm sending Sabrina, Nina, as my shift replacement. She needs a day job while she works on her art. You'll like her, she's a lot like me."

Clio snorted, "Another painter?"

"Bronze sculptor. Her art supplies cost a shit ton more than mine." Jenny glanced at her phone on the table. "Boss will be home soon."

Clio stood and took her coat from the back of her chair. "You don't have to kick me out the door, I have a date."

"With who?"

"You know Dominic?"

"Oh, is he your new gay BFF? I thought you meant a romantic date."

Clio smiled. "He's not gay."

"The hairdresser with a side hustle as a wedding planner and florist? He sings showtunes at karaoke for chissakes."

Clio put her hands on the table and leaned toward Jenny. Her smile morphed into a cat-who-ate-the-canary grin. "He ain't gay."

"Oh?" Jenny took in her friend's expression. "Oh!"

"The boy's got skills, just saying. Anyway, gotta go."

Jenny accompanied her to the door, they hugged, and Jenny found herself alone. She checked the time again, five thirty. Christopher would be up soon and would want to know about the business meeting she'd attended for him, so she headed up the stairs to her tiny office. She was lost in meeting notes when there was a knock at the door. Jenny started and looked up to see Marq. "Marquessa, I love you, but you have to stop that silent vampire lurking shit."

Marq looked dressed to go out; tight, expensive jeans and maroon silk blouse open to show just a hint of cleavage. She also wore black leather gloves to hide her healing fingers.

Jenny sighed. "I was just entering notes about the meeting with the rental agent for Christopher's new commercial building. I think the boss is not going to be happy."

"Yeah," Marq replied. "The boss and I were wondering if you got a minute?"

"Of course," Jenny said, puzzled. "You pay for my time."

Marq crooked a finger and led the housekeeper back to the first floor where her employer waited by his own portrait, the only image from his breathing days. His left cheek and hand were uncovered, allowing Jenny's first glimpse at the burns; now just angry red blotches with minimal visible scars.

"Look at this." Marq tugged at the painting and it swung away on hidden hinges to reveal a blank wall.

"Okay," Jenny said. "Is this the secret passage to the batcave?"

Christopher stepped up to the wall and placed his outstretched hand against the surface. He paused for a moment and his brow furrowed. He grimaced as he pushed, his jaw tight with the effort. A large section of the barrier depressed two inches and locked in place with a steady click.

With the panel in the proper position, the vampyr easily slid it aside to reveal a steel door with a glowing white square.

"Palm reader," Marq said. "Know anything about them?"

"Just what I've seen in movies."

"So you know the Hollywood version." Marq smiled. "In movies people will use some dead guy's hand on a reader and it works, but that's not correct, at least not for the high-end ones. There are sensors on the glass that detect temperature, pulse and oxidization level on the scanned appendage. A dead hand won't register." She ran a finger over the plate.

"This one has the same sensors, but it's programmed differently. Christopher and I don't breathe at detectable levels but the fluid in our veins does contain oxygen, just much less than other people." She looked at her hand. "To open the safe, the hand that touches the screen must have a skin temperature below ninety degrees, no pulse, and vampyric oxidization, about twenty to thirty percent." She stepped out of the way.

Christopher placed his hand on the screen.

A line of super bright light trailed across the screen, then from top to bottom. There was a palpable click and the three-inch thick steel door swung open.

"So, this is where you keep the family jewels?" Jenny asked.

"No," Christopher replied. "Those are in a Swiss safe deposit box."

"Ah."

"This is far more valuable." He took a pair of cotton gloves from his pocket and handed them to Jenny. "You should wear these."

She complied as he pulled a large, old, leather-bound book from the safe and carried it to the next room. He gently lowered the book onto a plastic mat on the kitchen table. He stepped aside and motioned for Jenny to open it.

She examined the comically massive tome. There was no title. It looked like a professionally made vintage book. She opened the cover and saw that it was actually handwritten by a very careful scribe. The Cyrillic letters were completely incomprehensible. She turned a questioning eye to her boss.

He nodded at the book. "This is the Lore. The first responsibility of very candidate for vampyr in my line is to make their own copy. I made that in 1873."

Jenny flipped through the pages. Anatomical sketches and symbols that looked like family crests cluttered the text, but she couldn't read any of it.

"Okay," Marq said as she picked up a tablet. "Here's mine. I scanned the whole thing, worked with multiple translators and made a digital copy. This tablet contains the original, the translation and notes from the two vampyrs Christopher has actually talked to." She took a flash drive from her pocket and handed it to Jenny. "Here is a copy for you. The drive is encrypted, and I will give you the key."

Christopher sniffed. "Marq took a different meaning from the word 'copy.' Reproducing the information by hand sets it into the brain."

"Modern research shows there are more efficient ways of learning." Marq pointed at the physical book. "That is history, but this," she tapped the tablet, "is knowledge. Indexed, searchable, cross referenced."

"Yeah, but is it a good idea to give me this knowledge?" Jenny said, still tracing her fingers on the pages. "I don't know if actually becoming a vampire, or vampyr is what I want. There is a lot baggage being one of you guys."

"I understand," Marq put her hand on Jenny's shoulder. "It is a lot. But you have years to decide. And a fresh pair of eyes on the material can help me start my research."

"But how can you go to medical school now?" Jenny asked.

"Don't have to. You only need money to fund research. The med school was to ensure I understand the research we'll be funding. And guess what? Several universities have all their medical classes available online. You can't get a degree that way, but you can get the necessary education."

"Oh."

"The biggest question now is where to set up my lab. I'll be travelling a lot in the next few months as I interview candidate institutions.

"You're leaving?" Jenny asked.

"Yes, you will understand when you read the Lore. Each vampyr is an apex predator, and any other vampyr, related or not, soon becomes competition and things get tense. We can't live too close together, just like we can't live with the living."

"Why not?" Jenny looked at the book.

"It's not right. If breathers spend too much time with us, they lose themselves, becoming an extension of us."

Jenny clasped her hands in front of her chest. "I'll miss you."

Marq gave an awkward smile. "You could come with me, be my housekeeper."

"I thought I had dibs?" Christopher mumbled.

Jenny stared, dumbfounded.

Marq stared back with a questioning gaze.

Jenny felt a knot of regret forming in her stomach. "I can't. Moving in with you would be very difficult."

"I wouldn't feed on you without your consent." Marq's gaze trailed to the Lore.

"I know. But being that close to you… I don't think I could sustain that type of relationship. Being professional and intimate at once."

Marq smiled. "You know what is best for you." She gave a side-eye to Christopher. "So, you're saying I'm more tempting than him?"

"Leave me out of this," Christopher muttered.

"I just…"

"Well, you don't have to decide now, Jenny. On anything. Read the Lore. Become informed." Marq took Jenny's clenched hands in her own.

Jenny couldn't help but think, *They don't seem that cold.*

Marq let go of Jenny. "Anyways, I have a dinner date tonight."

"Anyone I know?" Christopher asked.

"Yes, as a matter of fact, I'm going to spend the evening with Robert Leiter. The former reverend has a surprisingly powerful energy and tastes really good."

"TMI!" Jenny said, covering her eyes. "I can't unsee that mental image."

Marq smiled at her friend's dismay. "He's writing another book. *Losing Faith to Find God.*"

"He still believes?" Christopher asked.

"He believes differently. On that note, I bid you all a good night."

Connect With Me Online.
I am eager to see your thoughts.

Email me at:
gmandragora@gmail.com

Like my page on Facebook:
http://www.facebook.com/GeoffreyMandragora

www.ingramcontent.com/pod-product-compliance
Lightning Source LLC
Chambersburg PA
CBHW020245180626
46810CB00006B/2374

* 9 7 8 0 9 9 7 0 5 6 9 2 1 *